Ship of Dreams

MARTINA DEVLIN

POOLBEG

Also by Martina Devlin

Three Wise Men
Be Careful What You Wish For
Venus Reborn
Temptation
The Hollow Heart (non-fiction)

Published 2007
by Poolbeg Press Ltd
123 Grange Hill, Baldoyle
Dublin 13, Ireland
E-mail: poolbeg@poolbeg.com
www.poolbeg.com

3 5 7 9 10 8 6 4 2

A catalogue record for this book is available from the British Library.

ISBN 978 1 84223 301 6

Typeset by Type Design in Bembo 11.75/15
Printed by Litografia Roses, S.A. Spain

www.poolbeg.com

Acknowledgements

I owe an enormous debt of gratitude to Senan Molony, *Titanic* expert, author and *Irish Independent* political correspondent – he's a man who wears many hats. Senan generously took the trouble to read my novel and correct my mistakes. Any that may have crept in subsequently are down to my own landlubber stupidity. Senan is author of a number of works including three non-fiction books about the *Titanic*: *The Irish Aboard Titanic*, *Titanic and the Mystery Ship*, and the forthcoming *Titanic Villainy*. His comprehensive and compelling *The Irish Aboard Titanic* is a book I found particularly useful while preparing to write this novel.

Thanks also are due to Poolbeg's wonderful editor Gaye Shortland, whose tactful editing helped me knock the book into shape. I don't know how she does it – but I'm glad she does. She's a very fine writer in her own right, too.

Thanks to Poolbeg's publisher Paula Campbell for her support, and to David Prendergast from Poolbeg for finding the jacket photograph – we know we're a little out with the period but the mood captures the novel perfectly.

On a personal note, thanks to David Murphy for putting up with having a *Titanic* obsessive on his hands – it hits you that way – and to Sarah Webb for dragging me away from the laptop for walks on Dun Laoghaire pier. Even if the sight of all those boats started me obsessing all over again.

Finally, thanks to my uncle, Bernard English of Barna, County Limerick for being endlessly willing to talk to me about Tom O'Brien. And to a cousin – I haven't yet worked out how many times removed – Mona O'Brien of Templemore, County Tipperary for giving permission for the use of Tom's photograph and Hannah's letter.

This novel is dedicated to the memory of my grandmother's uncle, Tom O'Brien of Bonavie, County Limerick, who was lost on the Titanic.
She always referred to him as "poor Uncle Tom" because of the tragic way he died, but to me "nothing in his life became him like the leaving of it".

I was inspired to write this novel when I was doing some research on the Internet for a different book, and stumbled across the passenger list for the *Titanic*. Idly running my eye down it, a name and address leapt out at me: Thomas O'Brien of Bonavie, County Limerick. My grandmother, Josie English née O'Brien, came from Bonavie. It's such a small townland that I assumed there had to be a connection between the two and, sure enough, further investigation revealed Tom O'Brien was her uncle. Then I learned how he had eloped with a local girl, Hannah Godfrey, taking passage on the *Titanic*. His family in Ireland only knew that he was emigrating to his sisters in Chicago. No-one knew he was bringing a wife with him.

An iceberg intervened and Tom went down with the ship, while Hannah survived – and had a baby girl five months later in New York. However there was a question-mark over whether the couple had married and a dispute broke out when both Hannah, who insisted she was his wife, and the dead man's mother in Ireland claimed compensation for him.

This was as much as I was able to discover, because it wasn't spoken of freely in the family – I suspect there was a sense of shame about it all – until I heard about Senan Molony's book *The Irish Aboard Titanic*. I got my hands on a copy, looked up Tom O'Brien – and lo and behold, there was his photograph. I'll never forget how moved I felt, looking at this small, grainy image of a relative caught up in such a momentous event. I fancied I could detect a resemblance to uncles and cousins on my mother's side of the family, and had the strongest sense of blood calling to blood.

The book contained a second photograph, one of Hannah and their daughter. There was also a copy of a letter from Hannah to Tom's sister Mary O'Brien Hunt in Chicago. I was told that subsequently Mary (my great-grand aunt) had offered her a home but she declined.

I wanted to reclaim Hannah and her daughter for the family, but above all I wanted to recover Tom O'Brien – this great grand-uncle of mine who never lived to see the US or his child. Inspired by the little I knew of their story, I started writing *Ship of Dreams*. I should stress that the book is fictionalised – the version of events my imagination suggested – because we don't really know what happened beyond a pregnancy, an elopement and a death from drowning aboard the world's most famous ship.

* * *

This is the letter which ended all contact between Tom O'Brien's family and Hannah Godfrey O'Brien. It was sent by Hannah to Mary O'Brien Hunt, her sister-in-law in Chicago, and caused so much consternation it was forwarded by Mary to the family in Ireland to shake their heads over:

My dear Mrs Hunt
I have just received your letter this morning, you need not bother yourself about that law suit. I have all that fixed long ago. I settled with them, you need'nt worry about me. My Baby and myself will be alright. I knew ye were all trying to get some money. I produced my marriage certificate, and I had the nearest claim, so you nor the lawyer needn't bother.
with love from Baby and myself, your fond Sister
Hannah O'Brien

"The *Titanic* lies in 13,000 feet of water on a gently sloping Alpine-like countryside overlooking a small canyon below. Its bow faces north and the ship sits upright on the bottom. It is a quiet and peaceful and fitting place for the remains of this greatest of sea tragedies to rest."
Dr Robert D Ballard, who found the wreck of the *Titanic*, announcing his discovery September 9th 1985

"I cannot imagine any condition which would cause a ship to founder. Modern shipbuilding has gone beyond all that."
The *Titanic's* Captain EJ Smith, speaking in 1906

"We place absolute confidence in the *Titanic*. We believe that the boat is unsinkable."
PAS Franklin, vice-president, White Star Line New York, on April 15th 1912, as the first reports of disaster began to filter in.

"Sentimental idiots, with a break in the voice, tell me that 'he went down to the depths': I tell them, with the impatient contempt they deserve, that so did the cat."
GB Shaw, about Captain Smith.

"I still think about the 'might-have-beens' of the *Titanic* . . ."
Walter Lord, author of the *Titanic* book *A Night To Remember*

1

New York April 14th 1913

A curious stillness settled on Nancy Armstrong. Time seemed suspended as she stared at the open doorway, where Louis Stubel balanced on the saddle-board. Neither spoke as they gazed at one another.

Violet Markova glanced up from admiring the ruffles at the elbows of her sleeves and noticed the intensity of her daughter's concentration. She followed her eye-line and her voice shattered the spell.

"Mr Stubel, we'd given you up. Our little commemoration party is over – the others left hours ago."

"My apologies." He bowed. "I'm late, forgive me, but I suspect I had the furthest to travel. I come directly from Vienna. Unfortunately I had to stop off on Wall Street to conduct some business, which delayed me longer than I expected."

Nancy rose and took a few steps in his direction. "You've moved to Vienna? You aren't in New York any more?" There was distress in her tone.

"I had business in Vienna – I still do. I'm not sure where I live any more."

Their eyes locked.

Violet came forward and placed a hand on Nancy's arm, urging discretion. "Do come in and join us, Mr Stubel. I'll ring for refreshments."

"Please don't trouble yourself. It is refreshment enough seeing you beautiful ladies." The habit of flattering women was engrained in the Frenchman.

Violet had to remind herself not to succumb. "A glass of champagne? In honour of the day?"

He hesitated. "Perhaps later. If there is something to celebrate . . ."

"We were marking the day, Mr Stubel, not celebrating it." Reproof narrowed Violet's eyes but Louis was intent only on Nancy.

He moved further into the room, and as he did Sam grizzled on a rug near his mother. Noticing him for the first time, Louis looked from the child to Nancy and back again.

She scooped up her baby, claiming him. "This is my son." She extended him at arms' length, Sam kicking his legs in furious choreography.

He nodded. "I haven't forgotten you're a mother now. So much has happened in the year since we met. Too much, perhaps." He sagged then, pressing the heels of his palms into each eye.

Violet sank onto a brocade sofa, trying to regain a sense of normality. "Do let's all sit down."

Nancy complied but Louis seemed not to hear. He took his hands away from his face and his travel-weary eyes lingered on Nancy in a way that made Violet shift in her seat. Why did he never look at her like that? The jealousy she'd believed was crushed spiked through her again.

Louis spoke to Nancy as though there was no-one else in the room but the two of them. "Can it really only be a year to the day since we met? Is it possible there was ever a time I didn't know you existed?"

Nancy nestled her son against the side of her neck. "Sam's five months old already."

"We were in the lifeboat together. You lent me a cloak to keep me warm."

"It was a velvet evening cloak, ashes of roses. The salt marks never did wash out." She laid her cheek on her baby's downy scalp and the ghost of a smile played across her features. "A night on the open seas will do that, I guess."

"Some marks never come out. Just as some connections can never be broken. I believe in the *coup de foudre*. Do you believe in it? Do you believe in love at first sight?"

She lifted her head, searching his face, and nodded once.

It was enough. "Come away with me, my Nancy."

Violet gave a gasp, like material ripped by a violent tug. Involuntarily Nancy glanced at her mother. Then she looked at her baby, wriggling in her arms, and propped him in a corner of the armchair, wedging him in place with a cushion. She stood, trying to find the words to give Louis his answer, but there was a blockage in her throat.

He closed the gap between them, so close he could scent rosewater on her skin. And something else: the whiff of panic, perhaps. His voice was urgent. "The *Olympic* sails for England tomorrow night, *chérie*. From there we could travel on to Vienna. Don't worry about packing, we can buy whatever is needed. All you have to do to make it happen is say yes."

Nancy's eyes fastened on the man's, hypnotised by his conviction.

"Yes, Louis," he prompted.

Her lips were parched, making a rustling noise as they rubbed against one another.

He seized her hands between his own, pulling her so close it was almost an embrace. "Did what happened a year ago teach you nothing? Don't you know happiness is fragile? That you must reach for it, guard it, prize it, if you're to have any chance of keeping it?"

Her fingers curled around his, clinging to his hands, and her face betrayed the helter-skelter of her thoughts. But still she did not respond.

Exasperated, a harsh note entered his voice. "I've come into money, if that's what bothers you. I can keep you in comfort."

His change of tone fractured the spell which had paralysed Violet and she glided up, moving between the pair and forcing Louis to fall back. "How dare you come into this house and seek to kidnap my daughter, Mr Stubel! And on the anniversary of her husband's death, too. Have you no shame?"

"Shame?" He tasted the word. "No, I have no shame where love is concerned."

"Do you dare to tell me you love my daughter?"

3

"Certainly I love Nancy. What else but love would bring me back to her?" His response had dignity and Violet was silenced.

Suddenly Nancy threw a hunted look at her baby. "I don't know what to do. What should I do? I wish somebody would tell me – I'm in torment!"

The appeal crackled around the room.

"If you go with this man, it'll all end in tears. Your husband's family will never forgive you. We rely on the Armstrongs for the roof over our heads. For our place in society. Think of everything you stand to lose, you silly creature!"

Louis stepped in front of Violet. "If you don't come with me you'll live to regret it. I love you, Nancy, and I know you love me. My heart tells me it's so."

Nancy's eyes on Louis's were scalded. "I do love you. I don't want to, but I do. The trouble is I love my son too."

"Bring the child. I'll care for him for your sake."

"I can't, it's all too uncertain. In Vienna he'll be nobody. With the Armstrongs behind him he *is* somebody – he has family, a name, a place in life. I can't steal that away from him."

A muscle clenched in Louis's cheek. "The future is always uncertain. Even love is uncertain. Please, put your trust in me. Let me spare you this stifling death by slow degrees. You weren't made for widowhood – you were made for the world, Nancy. I can show it to you."

The air in the room seemed to thicken as Louis and Violet waited for her answer. Even Sam was saucer-eyed. The suspense was broken by the footman walking in and bowing to Nancy.

"Excuse me, madam, there's some newspaper people at the door. They want to take a photograph of you and Master Samuel, on account of the anniversary. What with you being saved from the *Titanic*, they say. He cleared his throat. "Shall I send them away, madam?"

North Atlantic April 14-15th 1912

It was the wails of the drowning that the survivors remembered afterwards.

"Help! Over here! For the love of God!"

The cries seemed simultaneously to swoop down from the heavens and up from the bowels of the ocean.

"Save me! Come back! Help!"

The *Titanic* survivors crouched in their lifeboats – some with palms pressed against their ears to block out the clamour, some listening, horrified; others, fewer in number, begging their fellows to row back.

The entrails of the great liner floated on the Atlantic, and clinging to the flotsam were insects with human voices who batted their despair into the indifference of the night. Many held grimly on to debris, while others thrashed in the water, but its freezing touch quickly impeded movement.

The survivors shivered, waiting. Waiting for rescue, yes, but also for escape from those howls.

Finally, long after there was no sound but that of water lapping against keels, one of the lifeboats broke ranks and rowed back. It negotiated a cautious path through the debris – a lady's parasol here, a piece of wreck-wood there – zigzagging past deckchairs hurled overboard as makeshift rafts. It was too late. Flesh, turned blue within minutes by the icy North Atlantic waters, was already stiffening. Lifebelts bobbed in the gentle swell, but the bodies inside them were dead, while those without anything to prop them up had lost their grip on jetsam to sink silently, lungs inflating with salt water. Just a handful of people remained alive to be plucked from the water.

As for the *Titanic*, this triumph of marine engineering had split in two, both halves lying two and a half miles below on the ocean floor. Her captain, her designer, her senior officers, her bandsmen, her lift attendants, her engineers, more than two-thirds of those who sailed on her – millionaire and emigrant alike – went to their deaths with her.

And more than 700 survivors simply watched as it happened.

Among them was American bride Nancy Armstrong, who buried her face in her lap to blot out the shrieks that carried across the water to her lifeboat. She felt no sense of relief at having a place in a lifeboat – no sense of entitlement either. Instead, nauseous, she concentrated on not retching. Behind Nancy sat an Irish girl. Bridie Ryan was staring ahead, eyes flat. She wondered if her three room-mates' cries were among those slashing the air. Light-hearted girls, they were; she'd danced the Siege of Ennis with them earlier that evening. Or was Charlie Chadband's voice part of the din – the Cockney steward who winked at her as she boarded at Queenstown?

Bridie rested her arm along her friend Hannah Godfrey's broad back. Hannah was rocking back and forth, tears streaming down her face. Hannah wished she'd never left home. She wished the American dollars had never arrived. She wished it had been a pre-paid ticket sent from Chicago, like so many others, that she wouldn't have been able to travel on with Tom. She wished she'd never heard the name *Titanic*. Sweet suffering Jesus, she just wished!

At the oar nearest the two Irishwomen was Major Richmond Hudson. He held himself erect, and in his mind he was a man of twenty-nine again, a United States Cavalry officer at Wounded Knee. He had watched as Chief Big Foot, clearly on the verge of death, was carried from his wagon to a powwow between Sioux braves and the officers sent to arrest the elderly warrior. In the ensuing battle – if you could call it that – some three hundred and fifty Indians, mainly women and children, were slaughtered. The Army lost twenty-five men. He counted back: that was just over twenty-one years ago. Major Hudson resigned his commission soon after. At Wounded Knee, he thought he was witnessing all there was to see of man's inhumanity to man; he believed it, too, for twenty-one years. Until this night. He pressed his lips together until his jaw ached and waited. *This too will pass.*

Louis Stubel stared into the pitch darkness that masked the swimmers gasping for life. He knew they were there, although he couldn't see them – their voices called out from the obscurity. If they could hang on to debris for long enough, maybe a ship would arrive and save them. The Frenchman was not able to see the torpor that overcame marbled faces in the water, nor how fingers were losing their grip, bodies sinking with a silent capitulation that barely parted the waves. But he could hear the voices weaken, their cries petering out. Louis was a pragmatist, accustomed to the idea that survival was an unequal battle, but he turned away from this human driftwood.

The death throes of fifteen hundred souls pursued the living – pouring from throats which gasped for help, then gasped for breath, and finally stilled. In a time that was neither long nor short but occupied its own savage space, the cries evaporated – sucked into the void where night met sky and sea. But these despairing sounds would pursue Nancy, Louis, Major Hudson, Bridie and Hannah. Just as they were to haunt all those who heard them for a lifetime afterwards.

* * *

A hand snaked over the side of the lifeboat near where Hannah crouched, followed by a second one. They clutched the rim, their owner too weak to do any more. Nobody else noticed, distracted by an argument in the middle of the boat involving a woman in a pair of bed socks and a sailor.

"I don't see how you can sit there and calmly say, 'Most of those coves in the water are only a lot of stiffs now'. My nephew is one of them and I won't tolerate your referring to him as a 'stiff'!"

"Callin' 'em stiffs or not won't help your nephew now, lady."

"It's just improper. And insolent. I am a personal friend of J Bruce

7

Ismay of the White Star Line. When we reach land I shall make it my business to report you to him. You will never work for White Star again!"

"No odds to me, lady. Me wages stopped as soon as the ship sank. I'm on me own time now."

Hannah nudged Bridie, nodding towards the eight bony fingers clinging to their side of the boat. Bridie hesitated. The ship's crew were saying they would be swamped if they started taking in swimmers. The boat was lying low in the water already. Perhaps the fingers would slide off. Hannah threw an impatient look at Bridie, even as she reached for one of the hands. Each girl took hold of a wrist, followed by an elbow, and heaved.

A tousled wet head appeared but their combined strength could make no further progress: this was a dead weight. Hannah leaned right over, almost toppling into the water. Her coronet of plaits was soaked by spray as she groped and found a belt at the newcomer's waist. She strained at that, Bridie helping, and they hauled, panting, until a pair of shoulders covered by a sopping pyjama jacket appeared.

"'Ere, what are you two at? You'll ruin it for all of us," protested a sailor, as they rocked the boat in their efforts to land the swimmer. "Let go of 'im! You let one in and the floodgates open."

A knee scrabbled for traction and Bridie grabbed it, guiding it over the side.

"Watch what you're doing there, you'll up-end us!" shouted Peter McLeod, the officer in charge of the lifeboat.

With a final heave, the girls tumbled the man in. He spluttered, bleeding from the nose, and curled into a foetal crouch.

"We're dangerously overcrowded as it is – this is ridiculous!" said McLeod, a junior officer who found himself elevated to captain.

The women ignored him.

"Has anyone a sup of whiskey at all before this fellow dies on us?" panted Bridie.

"I have some Scotch." Major Hudson passed along a hip flask.

Hannah crouched to cradle the newcomer's head, trickling a little into his throat. He coughed, regurgitating some of the spirit, but a healthier colour crept into his cheeks.

Bridie wrapped him in the steamer rug lent to her by a passenger ten minutes earlier, while Hannah coaxed in a few more drops of spirit.

"I absolutely forbid you to allow this person on board," said McLeod.

"He's here already. Now away and play with your toy boats!" Bridie disliked any show of authority on principle.

McLeod's cheeks pinked up and he turned aside, pretending to study the horizon. There had been no advice in the training manual on giving orders to contrary women who refused to obey them.

With the help of Major Hudson, the two women managed to clear enough space to prop the man against the side of the boat. The major chafed his hands, while Bridie and Hannah each took one of his bare feet and rubbed briskly. The half-drowned man opened his eyes and squinted.

Hannah hoped that on another boat, someone was as merciful to her Tom.

By and by, the man scuffled through a trouser pocket for something, failed to locate it, blinked and tried to focus. But the effort shattered him. Edmund Newton wheezed, then his eyes closed and he let his chin drop back onto his chest.

"Well done!" said the major, his American tones sounding exotic to the women. "I believe you young ladies have saved this fellow." He would have liked to reach out and pat their hands but thought better of the gesture in case they were Suffragettes. He had a healthy terror of women who banged on about equality and votes.

"*Do unto others as you would have then do unto you,*" quoted Hannah, shy of this gentleman with the booming voice and bushy moustache – yet hopeful, if there was such a thing as natural justice, that Tom O'Brien would benefit from her act of charity.

Bridie shivered in the night air, glancing around once more to see whether there was anyone she might recognize on board. The only person she could identify was a young woman with a sheaf of rich brown wavy hair. Young Mrs Armstrong was elegant in a shell-pink evening gown, even with a jersey over the top. A string of opals alternating milk and fire nestled along the neckline. The previous morning Bridie had noticed her clicking her parasol against the timbers, promenading on the first-class deck, and inquired her name from her pet steward, Charlie

9

Chadband. Nancy Armstrong was a bride, she learned, only eighteen years of age, and much admired by the gentlemen. Her husband was a millionaire hotelier who divorced his first wife to marry her.

"High jinks in high places and no mistake," Charlie Chadband had winked.

He was always winking, that fellow. Bridie wondered if he'd be able to wink any more after this night.

McLeod suddenly remembered that all lifeboats were equipped with biscuits, water, a compass, a light and oil to burn for eight hours, according to the manual. He commanded the passengers to feel about in the bottom of the boat for supplies but they could find nothing, provoking a ripple of frustration.

McLeod was needled by the women's questions.

"I think the best thing is for you ladies to take a nap," he announced, with twenty-two-year-old gravitas.

"Will you make us walk the plank if we refuse?" taunted Bridie. Large features crammed into a tiny face emphasised her elfin appearance, and she was accustomed to latitude when it came to her pert remarks.

The rasp of matches being struck disturbed the taut air.

"Stop wasting matches, my man, we may need those," a railroad magnate's wife scolded a cook.

"I'm not your man and I don't take no orders from you."

Match after match spluttered as he tried to light his pipe.

"Imagine lighting up at a time like this! You have no respect. Anyway you shouldn't be on this boat, when gentlemen were left behind."

"An officer told me to get in." He managed to light his pipe at last, jacket gleaming white in the flare.

"Don't you go giving my mistress your lip," warned her maid.

"Tell your mistress not to go givin' me none of hers."

"Let me remind you that you're addressing a lady," rebuked the major. He retained the habit of authority, and it quashed the cook.

"Sorry, guv'nor. But she 'as no right to claim I oughtn't a-be on this lifeboat."

* * *

10

Lifeboat Number 16 had been launched from the *Titanic*'s port side – odd numbers from starboard, even from port. Thirty feet long by just over nine feet wide, it was designed for sixty-five occupants – instead it was only two-thirds full, mainly with women. Most of the boats had space for more passengers – officers felt it would be unsafe to lower them full.

Hannah Godfrey's teeth were shaking with the cold but, overwhelmed by the shipwreck, she was too numb to wish for her warm green shawl left behind in her cabin. She still couldn't quite believe the cabin was at the bottom of the ocean. What a palace it had been! Everyone in steerage had been amazed by the *Titanic*'s luxury, even in third class: electric lights, planking floors, three designated meal times included with the price of the ticket. "We've landed on our feet, Hannah." Tom O'Brien's face had creased into his ready grin. Was it really only the early hours of Monday morning, less than four days since setting off from Queenstown? Hannah leaned against Bridie, needing the reassurance of her presence. Bridie felt like someone she had known all her life, instead of a girl met for the first time in Queenstown a few days before boarding the *Titanic*.

Nearby, Nancy Armstrong was drained by the relentless bleating of her lady's maid. Roberge babbled a list, grief-stricken by the loss of all her possessions. Nancy regretted paying attention during French classes; she'd prefer to be unable to translate Roberge's inventory. When they landed she'd find a solid, reliable English girl to act as her lady's maid – it was impossible to hire an American as they insisted they were freeborn and were too proud to submit to service. There were Bridgets to be had off the boat, of course, but she was dubious about the Irish. They might be useful to mind children, they were an affectionate race, but they weren't sophisticated enough to minister to a lady's requirements – certainly not one of her social standing. That was what Nancy's mother said, and there was little about social standing which escaped Violet Markova's attention.

Major Richmond Hudson kept an eye on the man fished from the water by those pretty Irish girls. Plucky little creatures. The newcomer wore tweed trousers and a striped pyjama top, as though he had dressed in a hurry. Life appeared to be stirring in the fellow's body – look, his leg was twitching and there was a trace of colour on his face. Probably counting his lucky stars to be saved, thought the major.

The stimulation chasing the blue tinge from Edmund Newton's cheeks was not gratitude but vexation. He had just realized he had lost his spectacles in the water. He could get by without them, but reading and writing was difficult. His irritation was overtaken by a wave of frustration at having been so unprepared for the sinking. The ship's officers had gone about reassuring passengers the vessel was unsinkable. "This ship is as solid as the Rock of Gibraltar," said one. Now here he was, humiliatingly half-dressed, instead of having had a chance to get fully clothed and take anything of sentimental value from his luggage. Good job he'd had the foresight to slip his wallet in its watertight pouch into his trousers. He patted his pocket, where its bulk comforted him. It was all very well for those millionaires and Trust-Fund Johnnies, but he only had what he could earn by the sweat of his brow. When he reached America he'd invest in a course of tonics or his health would never be the same again after that soaking.

* * *

The night wore on and, for even those inclined to optimism, hope ebbed.

Hannah began keening. "Tom!" she wept. "We must go back for Tom. I don't even know if he can swim!"

"Hush now, Tom will be sound as a pound on another boat, never you fear." Bridie did not believe Tom O'Brien was alive but the lie tripped fluently from her tongue.

A fireman noticed Hannah's tremors. "There's a good chance your man is on another lifeboat like your pal says. Never say die."

She nodded. Never say die, while there's life there's hope, no news is good news – it all applied to Tom. "Would you like this seat, miss?" Those were the first words he spoke to her, standing to offer his place on the train into Limerick. That was only a matter of months ago – she could not believe their time together could be so brief.

Hannah dug her nails into Bridie's forearm. "Do you really think he's on another lifeboat?"

"There were still a couple waiting to be launched when we left."

Hannah squeezed shut her eyes, conscious of the unfamiliar weight of the band on her wedding-ring finger. It was only cheap brass, not gold, although it had the sheen of it. Please God, keep him safe. How had he looked when she last saw him? Brave. Yes, brave. But brave and resigned or brave and bent on survival? She frowned, but her memory would not supply the detail she needed. She had not observed Tom's hand edge into the pocket where his rosary beads lay coiled nor the glitter of alarm dilate his pupils. All she could call to mind was his determination to get her into a lifeboat.

* * *

Louis had been accompanying his employer's baggage to New York on the *Titanic* when the liner struck ice. Monsieur Pires was to follow and rendezvous with him in the United States. With no employer to dance attendance on, Louis had been enjoying the crossing until the shipwreck. He had just turned in for the night when he felt a judder as ice and liner made contact. Dressing quickly, he made his way on deck where passengers milled about smoking and chatting. Most were saying they would prefer to take their chances on the ship rather than step into one of those insubstantial little boats. But a boiler-room man with bleeding stumps on his right hand where his fingers used to be bumped into Louis.

"Get off this bloomin' girl if you know what's good for you – she's a goner!" he wailed, before staggering away.

The Frenchman saw at once that loading the lifeboats was a priority and worked alongside the sailors, Captain Smith issuing orders through a megaphone nearby. Despite the injured crewman's warning, Louis was struck by the curious absence of panic. The ship's officers showed no signs of alarm and people behaved as though the evacuation was no more than a precaution. Men bowed and smiled, saying "after you" and tucking the women into boats before stepping back. While he laboured, it occurred to Louis that his own chances of a place on a lifeboat were slight. Initially, men had been allowed into boats to help fill them and to set an example, since the women passengers were reluctant to disembark from the *Titanic*. People had trouble believing the vessel might actually sink. But as she tilted and the water levels rose, it became clear the maiden voyage was doomed. Now the officers were insisting on women and children only.

As Lifeboat Number 16 began to be lowered down the flank of the *Titanic*, an infant's wail sliced the air and a woman's voice cried out, "My baby!" She struggled to climb out of the lifeboat, bucking it, and several passengers screamed.

"Someone control that woman!" shouted a voice.

"I won't leave without my little boy! I thought my husband was right behind me with him!" howled the mother.

A man was holding an infant in his arms. "They won't let me on board, Ruby," he called to his wife. "They say the boat's full."

"Then I'm getting out." She struggled against restraining arms and the craft tilted dangerously, almost tipping passengers into the sea.

"Make that woman sit down," snapped the officer. "She'll kill the lot of them."

"How about if we lower the baby on a rope, sir?" suggested a sailor.

"Out of the question. It could be dashed against the side of the ship. You there, the father, climb down that rope with your baby and get into the boat."

The man gulped. "I couldn't do that, don't ask me. I've no head for heights. Besides, how could I hold the baby and climb down a rope? I'd be afraid of dropping the little fellow or falling overboard. It's beyond my strength, sir."

The officer raised his eyes to heaven. He looked around and his glance landed on Louis. "You, my man, could you climb down that rope without dropping the baby?"

"I think I could."

Louis threw off his jacket and waistcoat and the baby was passed to him. Ignoring its indignant howls, he took off his belt, tucked the child inside his shirt and tied the leather strap tightly around both of them. Then he remembered something. He could never explain afterwards why he did it, when time was so pressing, but acting on instinct he ignored the officer's impatience and reached for his jacket again. He removed a leather case about four inches square and pushed it into his trouser pocket, tearing the material. It was far from ideal but he couldn't bring himself to leave it behind. If he fell overboard – it went with him. Finally he stepped off the rail, dangling from the rope and trying not to look at the oily black Atlantic so far below. His descent was more of a slide than a calculated shimmy, and the rope's friction burned his hands. Unable to bear the pain any longer, he let go, jumping the last few feet. The mother screamed, the father let out a yell, and Louis landed awkwardly on his knees in the rocking boat. The leather case fell out of his pocket and dropped to the floor with a thud but he held tight to the baby. The mother snatched her infant from him, smothering it in kisses, and he fumbled for the box he valued so highly before turning to gaze up at the ship, uncertain whether the officer intended him to climb back on board.

A sailor pushed him into a seat. "Don't be a damn fool, man! Besides, we could use another pair of hands to row."

The pale blob of the officer's face appeared over the *Titanic*'s rail far above them. "Get going! Now!"

The boat started its jerky descent again, ropes creaking. As it bobbed on the ocean near the *Titanic*'s waterline, Louis shivered in his shirtsleeves, sorry that he had left his coat on deck. A woman pulled a velvet cloak from her head and shoulders to expose shining coils of hair, untied the ribbon at her throat and threw the cloak around him. He opened his mouth to protest but she laid a forefinger against her lips.

"Take it, I'm warmly dressed. Do you want to freeze to death?"

Louis looked into eyes with summer sky in them, for all it was night, and was too dazed to speak.

* * *

Towards morning the sea grew rougher and the air was stiff with the smack of brine. The men's hands became too cold to hold their oars and they had to stop rowing while they beat life back into them.

Bridie mopped at her stinging face and thought she would never be warm again.

When I get to America I'm going to the moving pictures, she promised herself, remembering one of her brother's letters home in which he described the latest craze. I'll eat pies the size of cartwheels and wear clothes so grand I'll be taken for a lady.

As Bridie fantasised about a dress that swished as she walked, Hannah was rigid with shock. Waves wrinkled against the rim of the lifeboat and whispered to her, *Tom's gone, Tom's gone.* Some valve in her heart was choking up, its congestion telling her that Tom O'Brien survived on no other boat. She knew she'd never again see his narrow face with that hank of dark hair forever falling in his eyes.

Hannah Godfrey had been eloping to America with Tom O'Brien, who came from the parish next to hers in County Limerick. They were the same age, twenty-six, but she was uncomfortably aware she'd be considered old for an elopement. Her father wouldn't have withheld consent – he was forever teasing her about how she'd wind up an old maid. There was a song about being left on the shelf – *"For it's oh dear me, how would it be, if I die an old maid in the garret?"* – her father used to sing it to her when he had drink on him, and Hannah always winced. She was not choosy, just unchosen, until Tom O'Brien from Bonavie took her by the hand. There was no reason for her and Tom to elope, except the daredevil thrill of it. "It's an exciting way to start our new life together," Tom coaxed her. Nothing as mundane as waiting for banns would do for Tom O'Brien. "We'll elope to America and write and tell our families about it from Chicago. Won't that set the village tongues clacking? It'll keep the gossips in fodder until it comes time to lift the hay."

Nancy Armstrong used the pretext of bending to adjust her shoe to steal a peek at the man wearing her cloak. He should have looked ridiculous but he didn't. McLeod's voice intruded.

"Watch for a single light on the horizon, the masthead light," he instructed the passengers. "There'll be a second light vertically below it, lower down. That's how we'll know the ship that's coming to rescue us."

McLeod gaped at Nancy when he imagined she was unaware of him – as if she'd condescend to notice a junior ship's officer! She was Mrs Samuel Armstrong, on the verge of taking her rightful place in the vanguard of East Coast society. Except to the untrained eye she looked like an anxious girl staring until she was cross-eyed, seeing lights everywhere but none in the correct alignment.

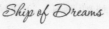

* * *

A drab facsimile of dawn breached the night at last, bringing with it a wind that snapped at frozen noses and ears. But when dawn came, darkness seemed preferable.

Bridie gasped, nudging Hannah. "Icebergs," said Bridie.

They reared on every side: a continent of shimmering ice. Some prisms towered up to 200 feet, others were smaller but had spiked or double-toothed pinnacles. The lapping they had heard all night was the sea washing against the bergs, but they only became visible at daybreak. Glistening pink, each berg was more improbably chiselled than the last, and the passengers stared in awe until ice and sky converged.

Nancy imagined she could pick out the one that had punctured the *Titanic*, not realizing their boat was miles from the wreck scene and the iceberg long gone. The berg she looked at appeared – her mind struggled to define it – indifferent. Not sinister, just neutral. She shivered. Louis noticed Nancy was troubled and reached out to chafe her hands. It was a minute or so before she reacted. Gasping at his boldness, she pulled away and sat on her hands, crushing her oval diamond engagement ring against flesh. She had hankered after a sapphire but her mother had told her to ask for diamonds. "Much more becoming, Nancy."

The girl's skin smarted. The human contact felt reassuring, but it was presumptuous. Didn't this person know who she was? She hesitated. Just who was she without Samuel? He must have found a way off the *Titanic*. She needed him too much for him to die. The Armstrongs would never accept her without him by her side. New York society would shun her, with the Armstrongs leading the charge. Her mother had impressed on Nancy that the Armstrongs were sixth-generation Americans. That practically made them Founding Fathers. She refused to surrender her husband to the ocean. He must be on another lifeboat!

Nancy thought of her last hours with her husband. Samuel had kissed her shoulder and fastened on the opals she was wearing, then they had attended a dinner in the captain's honour. Jiminy, wouldn't Captain Smith have shown some anxiety if they were in danger of hitting an iceberg? But he had been first-rate company, amusing them with stories.

Nancy shook her head. Nothing seemed definite any more. She must trust to Samuel as her only certainty.

At his oar, the major listened to the crew discuss wireless communications between the *Titanic* and other liners. They seemed to expect a sister ship called the *Olympic*, calculating it would be 2 p.m. before she arrived, at which Major Hudson pursed his lips. That would amount to twelve hours drifting among the ice floes – he wasn't certain the ladies would be able for it. A number of females from steerage had scrambled on without shawls or coats – he should see about organizing a discreet redistribution of blankets. The major glared at the young officer in charge – McLeod, if he wasn't mistaken. He would have expected more leadership from someone with a Scottish name. Major Hudson was convinced the Scots were a superior race, due to his regard for his Edinburgh-born wife. He might need to have a word in his ear.

Hopefully some other ship would reach them before the *Olympic*. His glance drifted to the horizon. A distant gleam rewarded him.

"Look!"

A faint boom sounded, like lightning at first, followed by thunder. People quivered with excitement, training their eyes towards the horizon and slowly, over the edge of the sea, a single light approached. Presently a second glowed below.

"We're saved!" yelled McLeod. "Anyone got paper to light?"

The railway magnate's wife tore off her straw bonnet and he set fire to it, signalling to the steamer.

As she drew nearer, her red funnel visible now, Hannah's eyes welled up and Bridie squeezed her hand. But fear, not relief, was at work in Hannah. Rescue was all very well, but what was to become of her afterwards? She was in trouble and had nowhere to turn.

3

Deliverance operated to a different time frame than their expectations and the *Carpathia* made slow progress. Impeded by an iceberg, the rescue ship hunted for a way past as watchers waited impatiently. A number of the rowing boats crept together, huddling in a pack. Some were taking in water and passengers bailed with their caps.

Major Hudson leaned towards Hannah. "We'll soon have you safe and sound on board, little lady." He noticed her hands and face didn't match: the knuckles were reddened and swollen from labour, but her complexion was the texture of one of the sundaes he used to buy his boy after his wife died, trying to temper his son's incomprehension with ice cream.

Louis Stubel burrowed into his borrowed cloak, a scent of roses floating up from it. He felt like a fool in this lady's finery but in his shirtsleeves the cold would finish him off if he returned it to its owner. He tried counting the boats that were waiting but visibility was still poor – everything seemed to merge into the ice. There seemed to be terrifyingly few.

The *Carpathia* sounded her whistle to let the nearest boatload in the ragged line know she was ready to take on passengers. Then the ship stopped altogether.

"She can't come any closer, she's afraid of sinking us," interpreted McLeod. "We'll have to row to her. Men, put your backs into it. Full ahead."

"Aye aye, sir." They set to with a will.

Nancy's eyes alighted on a sodden mattress floating with the current, a tiny shape spread-eagled on it. It resembled a rag-doll. With a jolt, the American girl recognized it as the frozen corpse of a baby. She recoiled, concentrating on the frill of foam left behind by a wave on the side of the boat. It was her first close-up of a dead body, made all the more poignant by its diminutive frame. Against her will, she was drawn back towards the baby's pale perfection, her gaze brushing against one of the Irish steerage passengers, a strapping woman with tawny hair. The woman had also spotted the infant and her face puckered with an emotion which shocked Nancy. 'I'm alive and it's dead,' that expression seemed to read, 'and God knows which of us is better off.' Astonished, she stared at Hannah until their eyes met and Nancy dropped hers.

The crew of the rescue vessel had been busy during her dash through the night sea. (*Notes 1*) All hands were roused, her officers given their instructions and the ship's three doctors – English in first-class, Italian in second and Hungarian in third – were ready with restoratives. Chair-slings were in position at each gangway to winch the sick and injured aboard, with canvas bags for hoisting the babies. Blankets were stacked for distribution and hot coffee, tea and sandwiches prepared.

Lines were thrown and minutes later the first survivor clambered aboard from Lifeboat Number 2. Others soon followed, among them a woman sailors thought was carrying a baby, so tenderly did she nurse it in a shawl – they were amazed to see a small dog set down on all fours, wag its tail and bark. Passengers from the *Carpathia* crowded the railings, awakened by the unusual activity, ignoring the stewards posted in corridors who tried to persuade them to stay inside.

The delay seemed interminable until the party in Number 16 were close enough for boarding. By now the waves were increasingly brutal. As well as frozen stiff, the passengers were drenched – spray caking their faces with salt. The *Carpathia*'s crew had poured oil down the forward lavatories to make the water calm for boarding, but their little boat kept being dashed against the side and bouncing off. Water slopped over the sides and some of the children started crying.

Bridie's attention was drawn to a lifeboat behind them lying dangerously low in the water and wallowing in swells and troughs. The officer in charge seemed convinced it would not be noticed, or worse, might be run down by the vessel towering above it, and blew repeatedly on his whistle. Some mannerism in the way he pursed his lips reminded her of Freddie Bowe-Spencer eating chocolates. Sometimes when they met he would produce a handkerchief knotted around chocolates pilfered from his mother. They were violet creams sent all the way from Harrods in London, and he would pop ovals into her mouth, calling her his baby bird. But afterwards she would feel nauseous, unaccustomed to such rich fare.

"Ma, I'm going to be sick!" yelped a small boy.

People crushed together to make room as he was hustled to the side. Watching him heave, Nancy could restrain herself no longer. She staggered to a space beside him. When she raised her head, face waxen from morning sickness and shame, the russet-haired woman reached her a scrap of cloth.

"It's only natural," said the woman in a thick brogue Nancy struggled to follow.

Nancy wiped her face, the material coarse against her skin. She hadn't seen Hannah tear it from the hem of her petticoat, lacking a handkerchief.

It was around 7 a.m. before their turn for rescue came, and by now water was lapping in and feet squelched. Several first-class women stood automatically, expecting preference. Bridie took the initiative, dragging Hannah upright: "First come, first served," she said. Overboard went her cumbersome lifebelt, and she gestured to Hannah to do likewise before stepping into a swing fashioned from a rope.

"Careful, we have a tiddler here." The voices of her saviours rang in her ears. "Steady, fellows, not so fast. Easy does it."

"Oh no!" One of Bridie's boots fell off and splashed into the ocean. It had barely sunk before she found herself opposite a hatchway, hands helping her down. On deck she staggered, but more hands caught her under the elbow to set her right, and someone wrapped her in a blanket. It felt wonderful to have a solid surface underfoot instead of the uncertain swells of the wooden boat.

An officer spoke to her. "Are you all right, miss?"

"I lost one of my boots."

"We'll fix you up with another pair."

Another bosun's chair lowered Hannah in behind Bridie.

"Don't you feel like falling to your knees and kissing the deck in gratitude, Hannah?" Bridie hugged her.

"Yes, of course." Hannah was distracted. "But I don't have time for that, I must find Tom." She stretched out a hand to the purser assigned to meet passengers at their gangway. "Have you seen my husband? His name is Tom O'Brien – he works in a creamery. He's a skinny little spidogue of a fellow, Irish, from County Limerick. Dark hair, he has, and green eyes. You must have seen him!" The bare bones of Hannah's description reproached her. Yet how could she explain that Tom had eyes to remind you of light filtered through a hedgerow, and a schoolboy's fringe flopping across his face?

The officer shook his head. "It doesn't ring any bells, I'm afraid. But we're chaotic here, as you can see. Why not go below deck to the dining saloon for a hot drink, and I'm sure you'll find your husband when the fuss dies down."

"I can't. I have to find him now – there's something I never told him."

"Time enough for that later. Go below and have some hot soup. You've been through the wars, you know, you need to rest."

There was a glitter in Hannah's eyes which unnerved Bridie. All night long she had been moaning that Tom was gone, ripped from her, and now she was hysterical to find him. Did she think him resurrected – or was she unbalanced by grief?

"Come along, *alanna*, let's find you somewhere warm to sit. That soup sounds like manna from heaven to me, even if you're not hungry." She slipped her hand around her friend's waist.

The *Carpathia*'s crew hardly dared question the stupefied survivors shambling past. They could tell by eyes fled into their sockets that these people had been through a terrible ordeal. Most of the seamen had heard about the transmission picked up by Harold Cottam, their wireless operator, just before turning in shortly after midnight. They knew the

Titanic had hit an iceberg and whispered together about her last message to the *Carpathia*: "Come as quickly as possible. Engine room filling up to the boilers." The messages had grown fainter as the set's power had drained away. But they couldn't understand how she had sunk so quickly. A liner of her strength should have been able to stay afloat for many hours. They were puzzled not to see the *Titanic* on the horizon, only this rag-tag flotilla.

The resilient Bridie was eager for breakfast. She sniffed at being offered coffee, having tasted it on the *Titanic* and dismissed it as foreign muck. But there was tea ready in giant pots, and she stirred spoonful after spoonful of sugar into a cup.

"If this ship wasn't so quick off the mark, Hannah, there's no telling how many of us might not have lasted the night, between the shock and the cold." Bridie filled her mouth with bread and ham. "Not us, of course, sure we're tough as old boots, but some of the other ladies and their babies." Hannah was staring into middle distance. "Don't you want that soup? Pass it here."

While Bridie ate ravenously, Nancy was greeted by the reception committee. She was among the last of the women from their lifeboat to board, lagging behind. It was a reserve she was never able to explain afterwards to her mother, who believed Captain Arthur Rostron of the *Carpathia* should have sprinted down the companionway from the bridge to welcome her in personally. Much later Nancy grasped, finally, why she had prevaricated: she was still wife to Samuel Armstrong on the lifeboat. On the *Carpathia* she might learn she was widow to him.

Fourth Officer Geoffrey Barnish steadied the young woman as she set first one and then the other satin high-heeled pump on deck. Even in a tousled state, rips in her gauzy evening gown, it was apparent she was someone of distinction. "Allow me, miss. I'll have you escorted below deck for some refreshments. We have a medical officer who might be permitted to check you over?"

"It's madam, not miss. My name is Mrs Armstrong. My husband, Mr Samuel Armstrong, may be on board already. Would you tell him I've arrived? He'll be anxious about me."

Her confidence was contagious. Barnish made a note of the name to cross-reference with the purser, who was compiling a list of survivors. He didn't like to see such a charming young lady caused any further distress. They must do everything in their power to reunite her with her husband. As he ushered her towards the saloon, she paused by the surgeon and murmured a few words.

The doctor nodded. "I'll escort Mrs Armstrong to the captain's cabin, Mr Barnish. He told me he'd vacate it for any lady whose need was pressing."

The officer turned his attention to the next arrivals. Major Hudson had an arm around Edmund Newton, still weakened by his soaking. Edmund had tried to climb a ladder to the *Carpathia* but his legs buckled and he suffered the indignity of a bosun's chair, as if he were one of the women. Meanwhile, Major Hudson sprang up some netting thrown over the side of the ship, to speed up the rescue operation for those able to make their own way on board. He caught Newton by the shoulders on deck.

"Can you stand up? Not to worry, nothing to be ashamed of – not many could survive as long as you did in those waters. Treacherous element, the sea. Cavalry man myself, third regiment. Hudson, Major Richmond Hudson. Like the river. What's your name? Let's get you below, Newton, and one of these doctor fellows might take a look at you. That cough of yours doesn't sound too promising."

Edmund allowed himself to be herded below deck by the major, who relished the opportunity to take control. Besides, the major liked the cut of the fellow's jib – he reminded him of his wife Jean's brother, Hamish. Died in the Boer War. He must remember to ask young Newton if he had any Scottish blood.

In the saloon, Louis Stubel accepted a tot of brandy and added the spirit to his coffee. He reflected on the unusual silence. Nobody was speaking, apart from the crew directing survivors in hushed tones. Not a single question about the shipwreck had been put to him – or to anyone in his vicinity. He revived as the coffee and brandy infiltrated his bloodstream. Why, people are hesitant to use the name *Titanic*, he thought. It's almost as though the word is cursed.

The *Carpathia*'s passengers whispered together about these newcomers suddenly among them. The *Titanic* survivors struck an incongruous note: they had the outer shell of party-goers, some in evening gowns – yet how muted they were. Mainly female, they crowded the rails on topside scanning each lifeboat as it emptied. As yet another boat proved bare of the face they were looking for, a wisp of sobs floated through the air. It was not showy weeping, but it sent the *Carpathia*'s passengers tiptoeing away and deadened the eyes of the crew.

Hannah tugged the sleeve of a woman in a Persian lamb jacket who was watching the lifeboats' arrival. "Excuse me, have you seen my husband, Tom O'Brien? A small man, he is, but you'd notice him all the same. He's wearing a cap and a navy gansey with a dark coat over it."

"I'm sorry." The woman backed away from the reek of her desperation.

"Hush now," Bridie soothed. "Don't be upsetting yourself. Let Tom find you." Bridie racked her brain for something to distract her. "I know what it is saved me from drowning." She reached inside her clothes and produced a small cloth bag on a drawstring. "See? Clay from St Mogue's grave – it protects from death by fire or drowning. My mother comes from Leitrim, where he's buried. She said I was never to leave it off until I reached my brother's house in New York." She kissed the lip of the bag and dropped it back inside her blouse. "Not that I believe in those peasant superstitions, I'm a modern girl."

"I wish you'd given it to Tom when we left him behind. Maybe he'd be here with us now."

"Sure wasn't I nearly left behind myself? It was only by the skin of my teeth they let me on that lifeboat after you. If I hadn't said I was your sister, and 'Surely you wouldn't split up sisters, sir' to that uppity officer, I wouldn't be here at all."

"I can't stand about, I have to find him."

Bridie held on to her, for Hannah had a frenetic air. "Isn't this the best place to find Tom? Nobody can board without you seeing them. Just look hard at all the faces. Do the same as that captain fellow below us – see how he takes everything in?"

Captain Arthur Rostron was watching his men help to embark the last of the *Titanic*'s passengers. It was disheartening to see so many young women who could only be widows. In the captain's pocket lay a scrap of paper which read CQD CQD SOS SOS CQD DE MGY MGY. It was the final Morse code message rapped out on the *Titanic*'s spark transmitter – MGY was the *Titanic*'s call sign. His wireless man Cottam had translated it for him. *Emergency-Emergency-Emergency-Emergency-Emergency-from-Titanic-Titanic.* SOS was the new distress call, replacing CQD. Desperate, her wireless boys had signalled with both calls. CQD. Come Quickly Danger. SOS. Save Our Souls.

When the captain had received it, he had checked twice with his radio operator that he was absolutely certain it was a distress signal, before hastily calculating a dead reckoning position for the *Carpathia*. At 12.35 a.m. he directed his ship to be turned towards the Grand Banks, scene of many shipwrecks. "Full steam ahead, mister, and all hands on stations."

As he threw on his uniform, he dictated a message to the *Titanic*.

"Coming immediately to your assistance. Expect to arrive in four hours." Then he doubled his lookouts, knowing he'd be driving at top speed through the night towards ice.

It was now 8 a.m. and the *Titanic*'s senior surviving officer, Second Officer Charles Lightoller, was last to board. He had gone down with the ship, but had managed to swim to one of the lifeboats. "I didn't leave the ship the ship left me," he would later snap at people.

Captain Rostron spoke to him. "One of your officers told me the *Titanic* is at the bottom of the sea. How could she have sunk so quickly?"

Lightoller shrugged, his voice hoarse. "We thought she could float for eight hours and help would surely have arrived by then. She was gone in not much more than two and a half hours. She was an empress among ships, but she's lying on the ocean floor. Absolutely intact." He barked out the final two words, for already debate swirled about whether the *Titanic* had snapped in two. Lightoller refused to believe there was a design flaw in the cream of British shipbuilding (he did not regard her as Irish, even if she was constructed in Belfast).

Just then another ship answering the SOS arrived, the *Californian*, and its master signalled he wished to communicate with Captain Rostron. There was little to say, however, and less left to do. The sea was rising and Captain Rostron was keen to be on his way. They agreed the *Californian* would continue the hunt, with one boat still unaccounted for among the twenty the *Titanic* had carried. It was one of two collapsibles which had not been launched in time and had floated away, but they were anxious in case it was overlooked.

"No bodies, I see. Must be a fair scattering of them somewhere else." Captain Rostron scanned the sea with his binoculars as he addressed his First Officer. "Anyhow, that's a job for another ship and another day."

Some empty lifeboats bobbed on the water – others had already been winched aboard in the gaps between lifeboat arrivals.

"Shall we bring these on board too, captain?"

"May as well, mister. They're all that remains of the *Titanic*."

Of the liner's nineteen lifeboats, those that could be salvaged were hauled in, although several judged not worth retrieving were left. While his orders were carried out, Rostron ordered a final turn about the rescue site. Odds and ends of detritus floated there: a barber's pole, a picnic hamper, a glove.

The captain consulted with his senior officers on a more pressing matter: he had a shipful of exhausted survivors and must decide what to do with them. Pacing the chartroom with rapid strides, a cup and saucer between his hands, he debated where to carry his unconventional cargo. The *Carpathia*, specifically designed for the Adriatic migrant service, was Gibraltar-bound. He could continue on his voyage, landing the survivors in the Azores, but he would need more linen, clothing and provisions before then. His supplies were already being depleted, intended for 700-odd passengers as opposed to double that figure. One of his officers suggested transferring them to the *Olympic* but the captain discounted it at once. The *Olympic* was 550 miles away when the *Titanic* began sending her increasingly urgent series of SOS messages – and despite responding at once, it was estimated she was still at least six hours away. "How can we expect them to sail in the sister ship of a vessel that's just sunk beneath them? It would be cruel, mister."

Alternatively, Halifax in Canada was the nearest point, but it meant steaming through ice to reach it. "Ice is the last thing these passengers want to see," he said.

It would also mean a long overland journey after docking. "These poor souls should be brought to their destination as quickly as possible, they've suffered enough," said the captain.

He made up his mind to head back to New York. This was easier said than done: they were skirting along the edge of a huge ice-field, sheets of ice speckled with bergs and their calves or growlers – large chunks of ice – stretching as far as the horizon. But he gave orders to search for open water.

Next, Captain Rostron decided a brief religious service should be held. He checked with the purser which of the officers' cabins had been allocated to Bruce Ismay, chairman and managing director of the White Star Line, and left the bridge to call on him. Many were surprised that Ismay, who was on the maiden voyage, should have occupied a lifeboat place when passengers were left to drown. Although Ismay spent almost two hours helping with loading, he seized his chance and entered a starboard lifeboat before it was lowered away – one of the Engelhardt collapsibles.

On the way to Ismay's cabin, the captain overheard a couple of *Titanic* officers discuss the expanse of ice: the winter of 1912 had been unusually mild and exceptional quantities had broken free from the Greenland glacier sheet. Preoccupied, the officers did not notice the captain.

"The ice looks solid. Do you suppose we could have landed our lifeboat passengers on it and gone back for some of the swimmers?"

"But we were exhausted from rowing. And we didn't know the ice was there in the dark."

"No, we didn't know. But I can't help wondering . . ."

"Wondering will leave you with a sore head, old man."

"Hang it all, McLeod, I can't help asking myself if we could've done more to save people. They're all dead now, poor beggars."

The captain was sombre. At least he'd see to it that nobody in his care died.

He knocked on a cabin door and a hushed voice said "Enter". Captain Rostron had met Ismay once before, and his memory was of a spruce man with an air of aplomb. This did not fit the description of the figure at the cabin porthole. He had never seen eyes to match those turned towards him – as though what they had witnessed was burned on the optic nerve.

"I believe a few prayers are in order," said Rostron. "I thought we should hold a service."

"Yes. Of course."

"Would you like to address it?"

"No!" Ismay had not been able to look at the *Titanic* as she sank, and he could not now face those who had sailed on her. "I leave everything entirely to you, captain."

"Very well."

"I only got in to help row the lifeboat. They needed men for that," croaked Ismay. "There were a few places left and we called for women, but there was no answer. I'd never have dreamed of taking a place otherwise."

* * *

As they cruised over the scene, the *Carpathia*'s engines were stopped and her flag lowered to half-mast. Brief though it was, the service pulsed with emotion. Men and women stood with tears streaming down their faces, not troubling to wipe them away, while children played in ignorance.

Bridie studied Captain Rostron in his peaked cap. At forty-two he was clean-shaven, wiry and younger than the *Titanic*'s Captain Smith, his presence less imposing initially. In her few glimpses of Captain Smith, she had thought him a distinguished old sea dog with his silver whiskers. Yet this new captain had an understated confidence. Her gaze strayed from Captain Rostron to the other officers, admiring the show their gold braid and buttons made against the dark cloth of their uniform jackets. She liked looking at men: there was something compact and crisply self-sufficient about them. A jag of bitterness brought her back to earth – she should have learned her lesson by now.

A few rows behind Bridie, Edmund wondered if he could afford his tour of the United States, now that all his luggage was lost. His cash was intact, thank heavens – he hadn't been panicked into leaving it after him in the cabin when the alarm sounded. Funds would be tight all the same. Edmund realized he should count himself fortunate to have his life. But he brooded on those clots from the White Star Line who took his passage money and left him stranded a thousand miles from his destination. Imagine if he had to call the whole thing off and retreat to Dulwich College with his tail between his legs, after swanking to the other masters! How they'd torment him! As for those little toads he taught, they'd snigger into their blazers every time he met them in the corridor. Edmund had not yet grasped the magnitude of the disaster, nor how it would impact on the world at large. Instead he simmered during the service, imagining himself persecuted.

Money and status preoccupied Edmund Newton, who had little of either. This had been the case most of his life, although he had been particularly conscious of it at Cambridge, where there were fellows with cash to burn. "Rolling in it," he muttered fiercely, and a woman from his lifeboat shot him a sympathetic glance, thinking he was thrashing about in the sea again.

Life as a classics master was not lavish, but it was better than the existence he had eked out as an undergraduate. Some weeks he couldn't afford a stamp to write to his younger sister, Minerva, who looked forward to his letters and scolded him for neglect. Edmund had felt humiliated by the pinched life he led, by the lack of coins in his pocket which affected him in petty ways – he couldn't allow a porter to carry his trunk because he had no tip money, he refused invitations because he couldn't reciprocate. Every treat had to be eked out.

He had admired men at college who were extravagantly wicked but, inherently conservative, he could not copy them – whether in accumulating bills they knew they were unable to pay or in ruining girls' reputations. Despite the Exhibition he won to take him to King's College, he was gripped by a sense of unworthiness because funds were a perpetual problem. He watched the bright young men, many of them titled, but could never be close to them. He saw them strolling arm in arm in the cloisters at night, on their way to hear the nightingale sing or chant sonnets while they drank champagne by moonlight, and envied their carefree natures. Money seemed an irrelevance to them, but Edmund Newton had too little cash to feel indifferent to it.

His eye caught a flutter of movement in front of him, but he didn't recognize Hannah as the woman who'd saved him.

She swayed for a moment and steadied herself. She closed her eyes, wishing with all her might that Tom was safe on a raft or lifeboat that some other ship would find. Instinctively she knew she was fooling herself, but Tom didn't deserve to be surrendered easily. "The heart doesn't think, it feels." He had said those words to her once, in that poetic way of his.

"Who said that, Tom?"

"Why no-one, only myself."

She repeated them now, hoping for reassurance. *The heart doesn't think, it feels.* And then hope refused to uncurl any further. I've lost Tom forever, she thought. A fierce joy snapped open her eyes and fused her spine upright. Maybe I'll lose Tom's baby too.

4

As the service closed, the captain withdrew to the bridge and ordered the engines to be started up. People dispersed, some to cabins vacated by the *Carpathia*'s passengers, although there weren't cabins enough on this teeming ship. Bridie and Hannah were sharing a straw mattress in the library, which had been converted into women's dormitories along with the saloon, while the men colonised the smoking room. Some chose to sleep on deck, however.

Aghast at her capacity for evil in wanting her baby dead, Hannah told Bridie she needed to lie down. She trudged off, hair feathering in the rising squall. Bridie lingered by the rails despite the cold, noticing reddish-yellow cork on the surface of the ocean where the *Titanic* had struggled to stay afloat. It looked a little like seaweed to her – she had no idea it came from the shipwrecked liner's refrigeration plant. The sea's shifting surface fascinated her: even on a calm day it would suddenly dimple and ripple, twisting from grey to pale green. There were no flowers at the service, Bridie thought suddenly. On her blouse she wore a red silk bloom she had paid thruppence for at Queenstown. It was bedraggled but better than nothing. She tossed it overboard. She had bought it on the morning she had boarded the *Titanic*, reminded of the crimson rosebud Freddie wore in his buttonhole. Charming, faithless

Freddie Bowe-Spencer.

A shadow touched her and she looked up. Louis Stubel leaned beside Bridie.

"You were in my lifeboat." His breath fogged in front of him, tiny clouds expanding when he spoke.

Bridie didn't recognize him. "Was I?"

"Yes, Number 16. I saw your friend talking to the beautiful young American lady. Do you know her?"

Bridie's glance skittered away. Who did he think he was, quizzing her without so much as a by-your-leave? People were never done asking you questions. This fellow didn't even have the grace to introduce himself. He sounded foreign, Italian or something. They were supposed to have manners, too many of them if you asked some, but your man here was altogether lacking in that department.

Louis must have sensed her reaction because he swivelled towards her, giving her a melancholic, sweet smile which showed his arc of white teeth to effect. "Forgive me, *mademoiselle*, you must think me bold. I believe the lady may be a relative of mine, but I don't like to approach her unless I'm certain. She has endured so much already. I thought perhaps you might know her name? That would allow me to establish whether we are related."

Bridie's eyes engaged his. Could he be connected to such a fine lady? He had that aristocratic reserve which she could not define but recognized readily. His fingernails were clean, too. He smiled again and she was loath to believe such a face could lie.

"Where are you from?"

"Paris. And you?"

"Ireland, twenty miles from Limerick city. We don't really know the lady but I heard she was married to a Yankee millionaire. He owns hotels, one of the stewards said."

"And her name?"

"Mrs Samuel Armstrong."

"I wonder if she . . ." He turned away and gazed out to sea.

"If she what?"

Louis couldn't bring himself to finish the sentence. I wonder if she loved her husband? The wind teased his hair, fluffing it across his forehead, Roman-emperor fashion, and he seemed to forget Bridie was there.

She was piqued. This foreigner with the air of entitlement had neither volunteered his name nor inquired hers. She wasn't accustomed to men taking such minimal interest in her.

"She's expecting a little stranger."

Louis looked puzzled.

"A baba. Whether or not she still has a husband, she'll have her hands full with a wee one. That girl's going to be a mother before the year is out." Bridie was gratified to see she had captured Louis's attention again – even if he looked winded by her news.

* * *

The *Carpathia* had left New York the previous Thursday, the day after the *Titanic* set sail from Southampton. Each kept to agreed shipping lanes and neither carried a full load. But the *Carpathia* was a much smaller vessel, with 735 passengers compared with the *Titanic*'s 1,300 odd, plus crew. *(Notes 2)* The newcomers lay on deckchairs in the metallic sunlight, too exhausted to move, as the *Carpathia* steamed towards the United States of America. One Good Samaritan en route to a family reunion in Naples circulated with a box of toothbrushes bought from the barber's shop. "*Prego,*" he smiled, offering the box.

Neither Hannah nor Bridie had ever possessed a toothbrush, depending on the edge of a towel to clean their teeth. They each chose one but neither liked to use it. Perhaps before going to Mass, thought Hannah, investing hers with a Sunday glaze. Except how could she face a priest after what she and Tom had done? Hannah knew she should go to confession, repent of her sins with him and get absolution – but she was not yet ready to renounce Tom.

Lists of surviving passengers and crew were compiled and taken to Harold Cottam, the *Carpathia*'s wireless operator. Since his equipment was not powerful enough to reach land – night range was more powerful – he set to work transmitting names to the *Olympic*, the *Titanic*'s sister ship, which relayed them to Cape Race. The operator thought it natural he should begin with the names of first-class survivors.

Shortly after lunch a steward approached all passengers with bundles of Marconigram forms and said they might transmit for free. People perked up and set about composing messages.

"My mother has never received a Marconigram in her life – this will give her the head-staggers!" Bridie was jubilant.

At twelve shillings and sixpence for the first ten words, and ninepence for each subsequent word, they were out of their budget under normal circumstances.

"Should you leave it so?" asked Hannah.

"Are you mad? She'd be raging to think she could have had a message from a fine big ship on the Atlantic and me not bothering my head to send it. The neighbours will be calling from miles around to inspect it."

They examined the slips of paper, marked *The Marconi International Marine Communication Company Ltd*, with boxes showing charges to pay and time of sending.

From Miss Bridie Ryan to Mrs Denis Ryan

Monday April 15th, 1912

SAVED FROM TITANIC ON ANOTHER SHIP BUT MANY BOYS AND GIRLS FROM HOME LOST IT WAS A CLOSE CALL BRIDIE

The wireless operator edited it down to a rather more succinct: SAVED FROM TITANIC MANY FROM HOME LOST BRIDIE

"Now you do one for your mother, Hannah."

"Sure I hardly know what to say – there's still no word of Tom. I should wait until I hear something definite about him."

"The woman is entitled to a Marconigram. Weren't you spared? Isn't that worth telling her?"

From Mrs Thomas O'Brien to Mr and Mrs Michael Godfrey

WE WERE ON TITANIC I GOT A LIFEBOAT PLACE BUT NO NEWS OF TOM HANNAH

"Didn't your parents know you were on the *Titanic*?" Bridie was curious.

"We eloped, you see." Hannah blushed. "I left Mama a note on the kitchen table saying we were getting married and going to America, but she wouldn't know we were on the *Titanic*. We bought a ticket for another ship, and then it didn't sail because of the coal strike in

England. Poor Tom was delighted when he heard we had a transfer to the *Titanic*."

"*Imagine, Hannah, we're part of history, you and me – sailing on the maiden voyage of the greatest ship ever built. What better start to our new life? It's an omen, that's what it is. We're going to make it big in America!*"

He grabbed her around the waist, pulling her against his chest, and she tasted tobacco on his tongue.

"You eloped! You never told me that. Was your father against the marriage? Did Tom's family insist on a dowry?"

"Nothing like that, it was just one of Tom's notions. It's a sorry day I went along with it. I should have made him marry me in my parish church, in front of Father Byrne and all the family. But there wasn't time. He was due to leave for Queenstown, and when he asked me to go with him I said I would."

The passengers felt a sense of accomplishment after the Marconigrams were collected. Connections with the outside world had been re-established. It was only later, in New York, they learned nobody had received their messages – there was only one operator on the *Carpathia* and he couldn't cope with the volume of traffic. Harold Cottam fell asleep over his work the following night, still wearing his headphones, after being continuously on duty since hearing the SOS. He heard it everywhere now, even in his sleep: dit-dit-dit-dah-dah-dah-dit-dit-dit.

* * *

That first night on the *Carpathia* thunder and lightning terrified the passengers, especially the children, who mistook it for the rocket distress signals set off as the *Titanic* foundered. Nancy was disturbed by the shatter of crockery as the ship was buffeted, and sat up all night in her cabin, knees hooked under her chin. "I want Momma," she whimpered, longing for the perfumed comfort of her mother's presence for the first time since marrying Samuel.

When Nancy was a child her mother would come into her room during storms, pull the chenille bedspread over their heads and tell stories to distract her from the elemental hurly-burly.

In his borrowed cabin, Captain Rostron cocked his head to count the seconds between thunder rolls. Good, it was coming no closer. He pulled out a sheet of writing paper and began to compose a letter to his wife, Ethel.

"One thing stands out in my mind about it all – the quietness. There was no noise or hurry. When our passengers at length came on deck it was some time before they realized the stupendous nature of the tragedy; it was too big to assimilate at once."

Captain Rostron let the fountain pen slip from his fingers. It seemed too much for him to absorb, too. The *Titanic's* sinking exploded the myth of Britain's shipbuilding supremacy: if the vessel had been properly designed she would not have sunk, at least not so quickly. Well-designed ships were crucial to Britain's seafaring dominance. As for the lifeboats they had taken on board – there were so few of them. Captain Rostron foresaw questions in the newspapers and in Parliament about lifeboat provision.

Tap-tap on his door. "You asked me to check in with you, sir, when I was going off watch."

"Yes, Mr Barnish. All quiet?"

"All quiet, sir. The *Titanic* people seem to have settled down for the night."

"How many have we taken on board?"

"Seven hundred and five, sir."

"So few? Her crew alone would have been more than that." Captain Arthur Rostron sighed. "It strikes me the world has fallen into the habit of believing large liners are floating lifeboats. This has proved a rude awakening."

Barnish waited. The captain seemed introspective tonight.

"Carry on, mister."

"Very good, sir."

Captain Rostron retrieved his fountain pen to continue his letter to his wife. He saw so little of her and their children; every time he returned home they seemed to have grown, not incrementally, but in surges. *"We know not the hour,"* Captain Rostron quoted, before shaking himself. He could not afford to let morbid notions take hold – there were busy days ahead.

* * *

Hannah went through the motions of asking everyone she met if they had news of Tom O'Brien. She owed him that much. There was a language barrier with some she approached, a class division with others, for first-class remained a race apart despite their common misfortune. The answer from everyone was no. Sometimes it was couched in cautious language – "There's always a chance" – sometimes it was accompanied by a sympathetic glance. But nobody could place him anywhere except on one of the *Titanic*'s decks. Hannah accepted each negative with dull submission.

She had no hope of finding Tom yet she dared not surrender him, so she criss-crossed the *Carpathia* with her question. She relied on Bridie increasingly. Hannah wondered that the shock of the shipwreck didn't cause her to miscarry, but her strong body seemed impervious.

By comparison Nancy Armstrong allowed time to wash over her, docile as she waited for her husband, while Roberge attended in a desultory fashion to her needs. Roberge was one of thirty-one personal maids and valets on board the *Titanic*, in case the regiment of stewards and stewardesses employed by the White Star Line proved insufficient to the requirements of the moneyed class.

Samuel would find her, thought Nancy, as Roberge positioned a cushion under her head. She was never able to forget she was at sea on the *Carpathia* – she could smell its salt tang, feel its bounce underfoot. Designers had created the illusion she was still on dry land on the *Titanic*. No comfort had been overlooked, right down to a fifty-line telephone exchange which allowed communication between cabins. Their stateroom on B Deck had been equipped with ceiling fans, dimmer lights and an individually controlled electric heater to boost the ship's warm air system.

Nancy traced a petal on the pashmina shawl lent to her by a lady from St Louis and recalled how, during her last meal with Samuel, she had touched the trumpet of a daffodil arrangement, delighting in its just-picked freshness. All of a sudden she swung her legs off the edge of the bed, sitting up so quickly her head spun. "I wonder what happened to my Irish lace?" Samuel had bought it for her, for collars and cuffs, as the ship idled by Queenstown and linen, lace and curio dealers were permitted on deck. "They'll have greased the Chief Officer's hand, it's one of his privileges," Samuel had remarked, unpeeling the money for the lace from a wad of notes. The hawker with brown stumps for teeth was wishing the blessings of heaven on the gentleman and his fine young lady, may she bear him a dozen sons, when the call came to raise anchor. She had to scramble back to her little boat as the *Titanic* prepared to sail away.

A knock sounded on the door. "Yes?" A smile budded on Nancy's lips, anticipating her husband. But it was only the surgeon checking in on her.

*   *   *

People claimed it happened because the *Titanic* was built on a Sunday. Because gambling was permitted on board. Because no prayers were said at her launch. Because her number, 3909 04, spelled out No Pope in mirror writing, if you made the 4 an open digit. Because the body of a murdered Catholic was hidden among the planks of the hull by Protestant shipbuilders – tribal hostilities surfacing, amid the theories. A cock was heard crowing at daybreak in Queenstown on the day she set sail, forecasting disaster. Survivors hypothesised freely, sprawled on deck, the sun failing to heat their chilled flesh.

Four burials had taken place early that morning while they slept: three of the *Titanic's* seamen who died on the *Carpathia* and a third-class passenger taken off dead from one of the collapsible boats. Captain Rostron ordered the burials at dawn to disturb as few people as possible.

Hearing it described – how the crew bowed their heads as the bodies were returned to the sea – Edmund felt as though he had been present at his own funeral. Then a passenger piped up with yet another theory about why the *Titanic* foundered and he could listen to the doomsayers no longer. He staggered to his feet, buttoned up the Harris tweed jacket donated to him by a passenger, and shambled around the deck for a constitutional. Still weak, he needed to hold the railings for support.

As he walked, he pondered the irony of attainment. Before joining

40

the *Titanic*, Edmund had never attended so much as a first night at the theatre. He had scarcely been able to believe his luck at securing a place on such a palatial vessel.

His sister, Minerva, had clapped her hands with gratifying excitement. "Imagine, Edmund, you'll travel on the Wonder Ship!" Then her face clouded. "I do hope you won't suffer from seasickness. I must check my book of remedies. I seem to remember chewing root ginger is a way of avoiding it."

"Silly goose," he said, affectionate. "Sailing on the *Titanic* will be as smooth as walking down Regent Street."

A classics teacher should, perhaps, have looked to the ancient world for his first overseas trip, but Edmund had surfeited on ancient civilizations and fancied observing a defiantly modern one.

Major Hudson rattled his coffee cup against its saucer in the first-class dining saloon. He was dressed exactly as he had been in the lifeboat because everything, right down to his shoes, had been taken and placed in ovens to dry the previous day. A team of ladies – stewardesses and volunteers from among the *Carpathia*'s passengers – had relieved the survivors of their wet gear, offering blankets as replacements until trousers and jackets were dry. The major had approved the operation, carried out with military thoroughness.

Yet he felt lacklustre this morning. "I shouldn't be bowled over by this, I fought during the Apache Wars," he tried to rouse himself, forgetting he had been in his twenties then, rugged from military discipline. Now he was closing in on fifty-two and had been leading a relatively sedentary life. Major Hudson rose to his feet, determined not to submit to fatigue. Tramping around this ship would be child's play compared with the *Titanic*'s two miles of deck.

On Edmund's second circuit they ran into one another, the major inhaling extravagantly and thumping his chest with his arms. "Sea air, nothing like it for cleansing the lungs!" he hollered. He turned and matched his steps to the younger man's. "How are you, Newton? Manage any shut-eye?"

"Feeling a bit dicky, to tell you the truth."

"Only to be expected. You'll be right as rain in a day or two, fit young fellow like you. How did you manage to get off the ship, anyway? I saw those Irish girls pull you into our lifeboat. You owe them your life, you know. Others tried to shout them down but they wouldn't hear of it."

All Edmund heard was the question. Unconsciously, he had been waiting for it. In common with most people who escape a disaster he had the urge to relive the penultimate moments – perhaps to make sense of the miracle of his escape. Too exhausted to walk further, he indicated a cast-iron deck bench with slotted wooden seating. "Shall we?"

Huddled under a steamer rug, Edmund began his story. He had a nervous way of rushing his words, as though not expecting to retain his listener's attention – even for a story as momentous as this. "It was shortly after quarter to midnight when I came up on deck, a matter of minutes after we struck the iceberg. I was kitted out rather inappropriately, as you may remember, in my pyjamas – thank God I'd pulled on some trousers and a jacket, at least. I thought about going back to my cabin for my Ulster. That's a goner now, of course." Briefly, he regretted the buff and black overcoat. "A couple of men were standing about talking politics, as though nothing much was happening. It was some humbug about Home Rule for Ireland. Ungrateful bunch, the Irish. They should be thankful to be part of the British Empire, not agitating against it. By and by it struck me my life was in danger – I don't know why I didn't realize it sooner. I looked for a lifeboat but the last one had just been launched, port side, and it was every man for himself. The crew had linked arms and formed a line to block male passengers approaching that last boat.

When the ship stood on its snout, I knew I hadn't much time. I saw the forward funnel topple and crush two officers and a passenger I played bridge with earlier. That's when I knew I had to get off the ship, so I climbed on the railings, took a deep breath and jumped into the water. The shock was electric, like dozens of blades piercing my skin. I fell through the water, down so far it seemed I might never stop, and when finally I surfaced my lungs were on fire. It felt as if I couldn't possibly have held my breath a second longer. I bobbed around until I spotted a length of wood and made a grab for it. But I didn't want to hang about, I was petrified of scalding water from the boilers underwater. I'd overheard some crewmen on deck talk of swimmers being burned alive. So I pulled off my tweed jacket – I couldn't swim properly in it – and struck out. As I swam there was a slight gulp behind me and the waters just closed over the *Titanic*. Easy as a knife cutting butter." He shook his head, mystified by the effortlessness of the liner's disappearance.

"Then?" The major nudged him when it appeared as though his narrative had limped to a close.

"My limbs felt leaden, I could barely slice through the water. But I knew I had to keep moving – I refused to submit to fear, it has a paralysing effect, you know. Once you give in to fear you're a dead duck. I reached our lifeboat and, miraculously, helping hands pulled me in. I'll never forget the sensation of relief that swamped me once I was on board. I allowed myself to believe I might survive, after all. I thought the cold would finish me off. It seeps into your bones like the very devil."

"You must be some swimmer." The major was impressed, approving of physical fitness.

"Used to swim every day when I was at the varsity – I'm a Cambridge man. I'm a little out of the habit now but it stood me in good stead when I needed it. I intended taking a dip in the *Titanic*'s saltwater bath before we docked. Never got the chance."

They fell silent for a time until the major roused himself. "I've heard talk of a thin grey vapour that hovered like a kind of ectoplasm over the spot where the *Titanic* sank. Did you see it?" His fingers were balled into fists.

"No, it was pitch dark," Edmund replied, "and I had other things on my mind."

"I can't help wondering what that vapour signified."

"I presume if there was a vapour, there's a scientific explanation for it."

"Aha!" The major blew air through his moustache. "Ours is a scientific age, but not everything has a scientific explanation. Some things have a psychic resonance." He was hoping for a reaction from Edmund but the Englishman seemed not to have heard, shivering in his borrowed clothes.

"I think perhaps I need some elevenses. Will you join me in a pot of tea, major?" He thought longingly of hot buttered crumpets. The *Titanic*'s bakers had been masters of their craft – he somehow doubted the *Carpathia*'s kitchens would scale similar heights.

"No, I should cut along and see if I can get my shoes properly dried out. Some charming little ladies popped them in the oven for me yesterday, but they didn't quite bake them long enough. Still a bit damp. Another blast should do the trick. Resourceful creatures, the fair sex." He bent to tighten a lace. "I send to London for my footwear. Firm called Peels, only footwear to trust." An Anglophile to the hilt, the major was returning to the United States from his first visit to Britain, but he behaved as though he was raised there. Even his accent was a curious hybrid of English country house and privileged East Coast class. "I have my suits sent over too, darned good tailor on the Strand – he has my measurements. Hell's bells!" He broke off, vexed.

"What's the matter?"

"I bought two new pairs of stout walking brogues when I was in London. They were in my baggage."

"The fish are dining on them now."

"I'll have to write and re-order them."

"I suppose the insurance will cover your shoes, major."

It was the first time insurance had occurred to Major Hudson. He was financially snug, his Army pension supplementing already comfortable private means, and he rarely worried about economies the way Edmund did as a matter of routine.

"Yes, I expect so. Still, it can take forever before they pay up. And sometimes they only offer so many cents in the dollar."

"Not with a case like the *Titanic*. It's open and shut: we struck an iceberg, act of God."

"Do you suppose so, Newton? Insurers tend not to regard facts the same way you or I might."

"I can't see, in all conscience, how they could make people wait. The steerage passengers are probably destitute, and I'm not exactly well-heeled. I have the contents of my wallet – fortunately, I made sure to bring it with me before I left the cabin. My sister sewed a nifty little watertight pouch for my papers as a bon voyage present. But I've lost all my luggage. White Star will have to speed this through, major – it'll look frightfully bad for them if they don't."

Walking toward the saloon, they paused to study the icebergs. Later they heard the sea of ice stretched for forty miles.

"Believe I may have seen the berg that did for us yesterday. It was a monster," said Edmund.

"They all look grotesque. Somebody drew my attention to one that stood a good hundred and eighty feet out of the water."

"It probably stretched a thousand feet below water. There's a ratio you can use, isn't there? Seven-eights of the length is hidden. I should think any number of these bergs could ruin a ship, no bother."

The major was not a man easily unnerved, but he felt something akin to fear as he looked on. "Nature at her most insensitive is a magnificent sight, but a haunting one."

"The ancient Greeks spoke of beauty and terror in the same breath, you know."

"They knew a thing or two, those fellows."

*   *   *

Nancy Armstrong strolled on deck with Roberge, taking the air on doctor's orders. "Fifteen minutes of daily exercise will be good for you and Baby," he had said.

Louis had been watching out for Nancy and now caught up with her.

"Allow me to introduce myself: Louis Stubel. I place myself at your service, *Madame*."

Nancy paused. He radiated self-confidence, this Frenchman with the beguiling accent. She remembered him scrambling down a rope from the *Titanic* with an infant. He had bowed to the mother, returning the child, but the woman had been too distraught to thank him. He was bowing to her now, holding something out. She met his gaze and noticed gold flecks deep in his irises. An expression in his eyes which she could not define – did not want to define – caused Nancy to drop her glance abruptly. It fell onto her velvet cloak lying folded over his arm. That was what he was holding out. The fingertips of his other hand caressed the nap, admiring its texture, and for a moment she had the heady sensation he was touching her rather than the cloak. Her breathing quickened and she reached for the ship's rail for support.

"*Merci bien* for the loan, *Madame*. I fear I did not do it as much justice as you. But I was grateful for its warmth. However, I regret the salt water

45

may have damaged it."

His hand brushed against hers as he passed the cloak to her and she turned her head aside. He was too forward – she was a married woman. She bundled the garment at Roberge.

"Forgive my directness – these are unusual circumstances," he said. "May I ask, what is your name?"

"Mrs Armstrong." She began walking away.

"I meant your own name."

Involuntarily, she paused and skimmed a glance back over her shoulder at him. There it was again, that expression in his eyes that made her catch her breath. Nancy's lips parted. Almost against her will, she smiled. "Nancy."

The smile surged through him.

Roberge coughed, disapproving, and the young bride remembered her position.

"You must excuse me, my husband is waiting." She did not admit she hardly knew where he might be waiting. So long as she clung to the conviction he was alive, it must be so.

Louis pitied her, watching her walk away. He did not believe her husband could have survived, for he had seen how few men were allowed on the boats. The light tan skin on his forehead pleated. He regretted her unhappiness but he did not want Nancy Armstrong to be reunited with her husband either. He could not imagine her as another man's wife.

*   *   *

The assistant purser was checking names. "Hannah O'Brien (Mrs)," he wrote. "And you? Bridie Ryan? Is that the name you were christened with? We have to get it right for the records. Bridget, that's more like it."

Bridie admired the way he held his pen. She always gripped hers with suspicion, as though it would buck and rear in her hand. Distracted by her dark eyes, tired and hungry because he had missed lunch with all this extra work, the assistant purser wrote down Ryan Bdget and forgot the "Miss". Later he would transcribe the name as Ryan Bert.

The assistant purser moved on, nodding at Major Hudson as he passed him. Prowling the ship, the major found himself among steerage, and now he recognized the girls from the lifeboat. The redhead with a countrywoman's capable arms seemed to be looking for someone, her eyes flitted everywhere. Of course, she'd left a husband behind on the *Titanic*. He approached the women.

"Major Hudson. Like the river." He clicked his heels together. "Any news of your husband?"

"No. No news is supposed to be good news but I'm not so sure about that. Not knowing is hardest of all. Some say the men could have been picked up by another steamer. They think they might even reach port ahead of us if it's a faster ship." Her voice thickened. "But something tells me I'll never see Tom again."

The major hoped she wasn't going to weep; tears flustered him. Emotions were better reined in, you never knew how far out of control they might spiral otherwise. He cast around for something to say. "Forgive my impertinence. Are you ladies adequately provided for – financially, I mean?"

"We've lost everything," said Bridie, who had money in the hem of her dress. "We're completely destitute – God knows what'll become of us."

"Upon my word, we must – we should think about – yes, something will have to be done."

"You're a gentleman." Bridie flashed him a blinding smile that panicked him almost as much as the prospect of tears.

Something should certainly be done for these young women and others like them. Perhaps he might establish a relief fund. An idea struck Major Hudson. Edmund Newton might like to offer a reward – he owed this pair his life, after all. Without their intervention he would be just another corpse, like those poor bloated wretches floating on the sea.

"If you'll forgive me, ladies, there's someone I must find."

"That's the last we'll see of him," sniffed Bridie. "One hint about a helping hand and he shows us a clean pair of heels. Sure they're all the same, the gentry, never mind if they're American or English. Only out for what they can get." She lumped him in with Freddie Bowe-Spencer of Mount Regius and sniffed again.

Bridie's humours changed like running water, however. She flexed her toes inside the leather shoes given to her by a lady with a sing-song voice, and was mollified. Never having worn anything but hobnailed boots, she was astonished by how soft they were. On fine days in her home village of Oola she'd gone without footwear, luxuriating in the feel of grass and earth beneath her soles, and these shoes almost replicated the barefoot experience. But Freddie had laughed at her dirty feet. "They're as hard as a rhino's hide!" he had hooted.

Afterwards she'd no longer liked the feel of soil underfoot.

"I've taken to the American gentleman," said Hannah loyally. The major's moustache was stern, but his eyes were as round and friendly as boiled sweets.

*　*　*

Major Hudson found Edmund in the smoking room, examining cuts and bruises that bloomed all over his body.

"You wouldn't have a cigarette on you, major? Thanks, old man. I'm covered in scrapes, must have been hit by debris in the water. Didn't feel it at the time but I do now, by jingo."

They smoked companionably.

"We emptied a flask of my best grog into you after you were fished out of the water – if that doesn't set you on the road to recovery, nothing will, Newton. Feisty little ladies, that pair who saved you."

Edmund clapped the heel of his hand to his forehead. "I knew there was something. So it was a couple of women who pulled me in? Would you recognize them? I'd like to thank them."

"They're on deck with the rest of steerage, I was talking to them earlier. Irish from the sound of it. One of the pair is quite a looker, a little dark creature with flashing eyes. Bit of a handful, I shouldn't be surprised. Her friend has a gentle way about her. I'll go along and point them out, if you like. They might be glad of a few dollars – they don't seem too well set up."

*　*　*

"You again?" Bridie made a breastplate of her arms and flitted an arch glance at the major. "Looks like you can't keep away. What's the big attraction?"

Her familiarity left Major Hudson uneasy, shifting from foot to foot. Edmund waited for his introduction, as formal as a maiden aunt, wincing as he parted his legs for a firmer footing on deck. He seemed to have strained a few muscles during that swim.

"Allow me to introduce Mr Edmund Newton of London, England. Mr Newton is a classics master at Dulwich College. This is the fish you ladies caught."

Hannah and Bridie looked him up and down. They could easily have passed him by, now that he was no longer in his blue and white striped pjyama jacket. Mr Edmund Newton of London, England, had the mother and father of all bruises on his forehead. Tall and gangly, his hair was thick and swept back from his forehead without a parting; it would have been blond as a child and was light brown now. He had a stuffy manner from fourteen years of lecturing schoolboys, but there was a cleft in his chin and his eyebrows were dark and delicately arched.

Edmund felt tongue-tied under their scrutiny. Women at close quarters panicked him – even the common sort of female such as these milkmaids or farm girls, or whatever they were. He cleared his throat. "How do you do? It seems I'm indebted to you, miss. And also" – he nodded at Hannah – "to you, miss."

"She's a missus," said Bridie. "And she's the one who saw you first."

"Forgive me." Edmund's eyes watered in the wind, vulnerable without their glass barricade, and he rummaged in his trouser pocket. He produced a handkerchief embroidered with *From Your Sister*, and blew his nose. "Major Richmond Hudson – this gentleman beside me – tells me–"

"Sure we're old friends with the major already. It's Hudson, like the river, isn't that so?" Bridie's grin towards the major was infectious.

He returned it, noticed the tip of a sherbet tongue, and swallowed.

"I was hoping I might be able to offer you some service, to repay you for saving my life," said Edmund.

Hannah burst in, her natural reserve forgotten. "Please, sir, if you could find out if anyone has seen my husband. His name is Tom O'Brien from Bonavie, County Limerick. The last I saw of him he was standing beside Mr Armstrong, sir, the American gentleman that owns the hotels. His wife was in our lifeboat."

"I'll do my best. Tom O'Brien of County Limerick, I have that. Is that all?"

"Well, we could use –" began Bridie.

Hannah cut her off. "No, we couldn't. We want nothing else, Mr Newton. What we did for you was no more than one human being ought to do for another. A reward wouldn't be fitting."

Major Hudson coughed. "I was planning to call on Mrs Armstrong and offer her my protection. She may have had news of her husband by now. I can ask about yours while I'm there, Mrs O'Brien."

"God bless and keep you, major!"

Her fervour embarrassed him. "Of course it may not be convenient for her to receive me. I understand she's, ahem, in the family way. I make no promises."

"You'll let me know the minute you hear anything, sir?"

"You can rely on it."

After they left, Bridie turned to Hannah. "I'd say that Newton fellow never did an honest day's work in his life. Did you see the hands on him? They were whiter than yours or mine. At least the major looks like he knows one end of a shovel from another."

Hannah frowned. "I don't want a child of mine to grow up to dig ditches. Where's the use in that? If they can have a bit of learning in them like that schoolmaster, so much the better."

For the first time she saw a life shaping for the baby inside her, a life that could be better than hers and Tom's. Then she recoiled: she had revealed her pregnancy to Bridie.

Bridie did not notice. She was drawn to a crowd clustered around the *Titanic*'s lookout, Frederick Fleet, who was talking about the iceberg which "murdered" the *Titanic*, as he phrased it.

"What's going on over there? Come on, Hannah, let's find out."

They hovered on the perimeter as Fleet described spotting the danger from his perch in the crow's nest. "It were just after seven bells had been struck. A great black mass, I saw, nothing white at all, and we approached it through a haze."

An officer from the *Carpathia* interrupted. "Weren't you using binoculars?"

50

"No, sir, there weren't none supplied, sir. They was lost after the sea trials was done earlier in the month. But there's nothin' wrong with my eyesight." He jutted his chin, truculent under the perceived attack. "Soon as ever I sees it I reports it. I strikes three bells, then I goes straight to the telephone in the nest and rings 'em up on the bridge. 'Iceberg right ahead,' I says, and the officer, he says, 'Thank you'. Nothin' else. My mate tells me later they swings the wheel hard over to starboard – turns the rudder, see – so we goes to port. That puts the berg on the starboard side. And that's where we strikes the blighter. There was hardly a sound, just the smash of ice hittin' the fo'c'sl and the weather deck and a bit of a grindin' noise. Meself and Reg – he's the other lookout, Reginald Lee – thought we'd only just scratched agin it. 'That was a narrow shave,' I says to Reg. We don't know there's a spur sticking out from the berg as rips into our girl's underbelly, going through metal easy as sand. She hasn't a prayer after that. Mr Andrews, that's the bloke what designed her, he looked like he see'd a ghost after he inspected the ship."

"Why was it so hard to see thees iceberg?" A voice spoke in heavily accented English.

"It were black, see, black as night. A berg only looks white when the sun's shinin' on it. Sometimes you get a' inkling from the waves beating agin the side of it, and there's white foam at the base, but the sea was like a sheet of glass the other night. We done our best, Reg and me." He trudged away, muttering to himself.

"Sailors do develop night vision from long practice," offered a man.

"Never mind the blinking night vision, what about supplying them with binoculars?" snorted his companion. "If Captain Smith were a soldier under my command I'd have him court-martialled! Remember, we're the lucky ones. What of the poor devils still floating out to sea?"

*   *   *

Samuel Armstrong was one of those bodies. Nancy's husband was face down, salt water lapping through his mouth, coat tails twisted into knots. He drifted with the current in a fashion that might almost be described as leisurely, his body intact save for a gash on his temple which had scarcely bled. The only incongruous note was struck by his feet, gleaming palely in the daylight. He had kicked off his patent pumps and socks trying to swim for his life.

In his pockets were a silver cigarette-case with the monogram SFA, a gold hunter watch, a wallet containing more cash than Tom O'Brien earned in his lifetime and a dog-eared rectangle of paper inclined to tear along the fold, as it was entitled to, after being carried around by Samuel for nine years. It was a drawing of a train, steam billowing from the engine. Underneath the wheels was written in uneven lettering: *"Happy birthday Papa from Adam."*

5

Initially the world heard a muted version of the catastrophe, believing it to be a stroke of misfortune rather than a tragedy.

Ill-Fated Maiden Voyage. Collision With An Iceberg. Women Taken Off By Lifeboats. All Passengers Saved. Titanic On Her Way To Halifax.

Those were the first headlines in New York.

At White Star's New York offices on Monday, company officials were only aware the *Titanic* had collided with an iceberg, not that she had sunk. Calamity was unthinkable. Special trains with Pullmans for first-class passengers, day coaches for second and third, were dispatched to Canada, where the *Titanic's* passengers were expected to be safely landed and awaiting transport home from Halifax, Nova Scotia. By Tuesday evening, almost two days after the sinking, the scale of the disaster was becoming apparent and 4,000 New Yorkers stood transfixed in Times Square as notices were chalked up on blackboards around the *New York Times* building.

Titanic sunk – all lost except women and children.

For Danny Ryan, Bridie's brother, it was a day of lists – and incomplete lists at that. When he heard the news about the *Titanic*, he walked off the building site without a word. The foreman let it pass, for Danny Ryan was his most reliable worker. He never turned up his nose at any job he was asked to do. In his first week in the United States, a priest had advised Danny, "If you want to succeed, you must turn your hand to everything poor American labourers do, coloured and white, no matter how degrading or backbreaking or just plain dirty, and do it for less money than them." Danny Ryan had adopted it as his credo.

Sombre under the peak of his cloth cap, he waited in Times Square for news, convincing himself that Bridie was not in harm's way. Wasn't she gathered up safe and sound, none the worse for wear, when she fell out of the loft? Didn't she escape with only a few scratches when she borrowed the postman's High Nellie, without so much as a by-you-leave, and the brakes failed? "The sun shines on that lass," his father always said.

As dark as his sister but a sturdier version, he queued to scrutinise the roll-call of survivors posted up. Regan Bernard. Ripley William (Mrs). Rourke Alice (Miss). Sanderson Henry. Nobody called Ryan at all. It had to be a mistake. Rooted, he re-read the names which did not include his sister, until he realized he was looking at a second-class list. There didn't appear to be one for steerage survivors. A grumble from behind persuaded him to step aside.

Danny made his way to the White Star offices in Bowling Green at the end of Broadway, in time to see a youngster of fourteen or fifteen ask the clerk to name his price so long as he confirmed his father's survival.

"That's Samuel Armstrong's son. He stands to inherit nearly fifty million bucks if his father's gone down with the ship," mumbled a man ahead of Danny.

"Guess the money's his," said his companion.

"His name, please?" asked the clerk.

"Samuel Frost Armstrong."

"We have no record of Mr Armstrong. I can tell you both Mrs Armstrong and her maid were saved."

"But what of my father?"

"No information has been received as to the fate of Mr Armstrong."

"There must be some mistake. Will you check again?"

The man turned a page and traced his index finger down the names. "I don't see your father's name here. I'm sorry."

A man with a central hair-parting so precise as to suggest he took a slide-rule to it touched the boy on the shoulder. "We should wait with your grandmother, Master Adam. Further inquiries can be made later."

"I don't know what to tell her, Powell."

The butler guided him to where a chauffeur-driven automobile wheezed on the street, startling a passing horse despite its blinkers.

Just then Mrs Benjamin Guggenheim swept to the head of the queue, taking Danny's place. She named her smelting millionaire husband, the second-richest man on board the *Titanic*, the clerk shook his head and she erupted into uncontrollable weeping. She did not, at that stage, know he was travelling with a lady companion.

"This would never have happened if White Star hadn't wanted to set a record for speed on her maiden voyage," complained the gentleman with her.

Danny dodged around Mrs Guggenheim. "Bridget Ryan, a third-class passenger. She joined the ship at Queenstown."

"The list of steerage survivors hasn't been transmitted yet. We have a record of first and second-class only."

"They sent the names of first and second but not third-class survivors?"

"That's right."

Danny caught the clerk by the wrist. "That's inhuman!"

"It's policy. Let go of my hand."

"I came to America to escape this sort of class distinction!"

"Let me go. The information will be made available as soon as we have it. You must understand communication with the *Carpathia* is extremely limited – its wireless doesn't reach to shore."

It was evening time before Danny Ryan could garner any information about his sister. He learned there was no record of a Bridget Ryan among the survivors.

"We have a Bert Ryan. Perhaps he's some relation?" The clerk lifted his head from the ledger.

"No relation." Danny's feet were leaden, turning for home.

* * *

Danny talked it over with his wife in their one-room apartment in

Manhattan. "It's all my fault," he insisted. "She'd never be coming to America at all but for me. All those letters I sent home about the opportunities here gave her notions. Pigs in America feed better than Hyde Park duchesses, I wrote. Every man is as good as the next one here. Sure it's no wonder she had her head turned. How will I face Mama and Dada again?"

It was an academic point, for he had not met his parents since emigrating a decade earlier and would never be united with them again.

Kathleen Ryan, a second-generation Irish-American, poured him a glass of foaming porter from the jug. This is some howdy-do and no mistake, she thought. She went back to nursing their son, Daniel Junior. "Look, Danny, they didn't tell you for sure she's dead. They just said they got no record of her. Another ship might have survivors on board – there's more ships besides the *Carpathia*."

Danny seized on it. "Do you think she's still alive?"

"There's a good chance, honey. Didn't they let the women and children off first?" Kathleen couldn't honestly rate her sister-in-law's survival chances, but she never objected to lying if it kept her husband happy.

Danny's face relaxed and he swallowed a long draught of beer. "Here, let me take Dan off your hands. He must be heavy for you, our big bruiser of a boy."

"Daniel Junior," she corrected automatically as she held out their nine-month-old baby.

* * *

Adam Armstrong was not having anywhere near as reassuring a time with his grandmother, Rebecca. He had moved in with her temporarily, following his parents' divorce the previous year, but lived in hope of his father reclaiming him after his wedding tour. His mother made it clear she didn't want the responsibility of a growing boy. Rebecca Armstrong, on the other hand, took kinship seriously and spent most of Adam's life usurping responsibility for him.

Despite her wealth and privileges, Rebecca believed life was unpleasant at best and tragic at worst. Her only son's death was precisely the type of blow she was, while not quite prepared for, certainly not unprepared for. "Tell me the news exactly as you heard it, make no attempt to shield me," she ordered in clipped, patrician vowels.

Adam had no intention of shielding her. "The White Star folks said Muh-Mrs Armstrong and her mmm-maid were saved but there's no news of muh-muh-muh-my pater."

Rebecca Armstrong's mouth thinned. There were only two Mrs Armstrongs as far as she was concerned: she herself, who took precedence, naturally, and her son's first wife. That baggage he sneaked off to Europe with didn't deserve the title Mrs Armstrong. "Anything else?"

"They said the list of survivors was still being trans-mmm-mitted. It was possible muh-my father's muh-might have been left off by by mm-mistake, but it would've been natural to list him with Muh-Muh-Mrs Armstrong."

She frowned. That boy's speech impediment was exasperating. Wasn't there some operation to cure it? Still, this was neither the time nor the place. "There is no body?"

The boy hesitated, a child again despite the exclusive education which was rapidly lending him the deportment of a man. Generally it was only in his grandmother's presence he stuttered.

"Speak up, Adam, is there or is there not a body?"

He made a glottal sound as he swallowed. "I didn't think to ask, Grandmuh-mother."

She reflected. "Very well. It is premature to order the household servants into mourning, but I shall certainly adopt it and you must do the same. Kindly convey my request to your mother to don mourning too. We must present a united front. It will be expected of us."

"She's in Muh-Muh-Acapulco, grandmother. We don't know for certain that my father is dead. It may be too soon for muh-mourning."

"Cora must leave Mexico to its own devices and return to New York at once. As for the question of how soon to adopt mourning," she paused, impressed that the boy had challenged her, "perhaps black armbands might be sufficient in the interim. I shall ring for Powell and instruct him to purchase crepe. He must also send a message to your tailor – you seem to have sprouted since your grand-uncle's funeral. A suit should be made up. We must be prepared for all eventualities."

"Even my father's survival!" In his passion, the boy managed to contain his stutter.

"Quite."

With a disapproving glance at her grandson's lanky legs, which had recently graduated from knickerbockers and were indeed stretching at an accelerated rate, Rebecca swept out, the train of her dress rustling like dry leaves. In her boudoir she unfastened a triple string of pearls. She could not wear jewellery while her son's survival was uncertain. Then she crossed to her dressing room to cast an appreciative eye over her extensive selection of black dresses. Rebecca Armstrong was always equipped for mourning.

*　*　*

In England it was Tuesday April 16th before a newspaper ran the headline that stopped Minerva Newton in her tracks as she walked through West Bridgford in Nottingham. Edmund's governess sister had not heard the news, closeted in her schoolroom bubble of children and lessons. Now she gazed at the banner headlines in *The Times*, slack-jawed.

Titanic Disaster. Sunk After Collision With An Iceberg. Loss Of Life. Wireless Calls For Aid.

"How could the *Titanic* have sunk? Edmund was on board!" she cried.

She adored him – he occupied a role midway between brother and father for Minerva and was always there for her. He had even remembered to send her a postcard from the *Titanic* shortly before setting sail, just as she asked. It was hooked into her dressing-table mirror. She was word-perfect on it.

Dear Minerva, progress is wonderful. It took Christopher Columbus 90 days to cross the Atlantic. But we can leave Southampton on a Wednesday and dine in New York the following Wednesday. Tell that to your classroom charges. Ever yours, Edmund.

She'd go home and find the postcard, read it again to check there was no misunderstanding and her brother had definitely sailed on the *Titanic*. Perhaps she'd mistaken the name of the ship. Minerva pelted back to Musters Road, spectacles bouncing on the bridge of her nose, the newspaper she forgot to pay for crushed against her chest.

* * *

Special editions of newspapers were printed to report on the tragedy which transfixed people around the world. The names of millionaire passengers were listed, including Samuel's, and newspapers dismissed by Rebecca Armstrong as muckrakers added titillating details about his divorce from the woman they described as "popular society hostess Cora Armstrong, daughter of sportsman Black Jack Van Doren". They included the age difference between Nancy and Samuel – at thirty-six he was twice his eighteen-year-old bride's age.

How tawdry, it makes him seem so seedy, thought Rebecca Armstrong, nettled.

How tawdry, it makes him seem so seedy, thought Cora Armstrong, vindicated.

How odd to have a stepmother only four years older than me, thought Adam. He was neither nettled nor vindicated, simply curious.

Kathleen Ryan, Bridie's sister-in-law, read every detail voraciously. There was something curly about her, with her globular little frame, tightly frizzed hair and button eyes. They gleamed as they digested the names of celebrities on board. "*Dorothy Gibson, the moving pictures star, was travelling on the* Titanic *with her mother after being recalled from a holiday in Europe by Éclair Studio,*" she read aloud. How glamorous! She turned to columns which detailed the sumptuous appointments of the vessel and the cost of each item. "It's a crying shame Bridie's dead," she sighed. "I'd love to hear about revolving doors in the first-class lounge to keep out sea breezes. About Turkish baths with gilded beams and a mosaic floor. About beds of roses, real roses, growing on board, and a Palm Court with trees, real trees, where the ladies and gentlemen took their coffee after dinner."

White Star had promoted the *Titanic* as an exercise in superlatives, a floating palace with 10,000 lights to gild life on board and 1,500 bells to summon a steward, and its splendours were meat and drink to Kathleen Ryan.

She set aside the newspaper reluctantly. It was time to prepare Danny's dinner. She never knew a man so fond of his potatoes – she'd happily alternate with vegetables occasionally, but Danny didn't consider himself fed without potatoes lining his stomach. It was one of the differences between the Irish straight off the boats and the Irish born in America; the narrowbacks, as the boat-Irish called the second-generation, because they were unaccustomed to physical labour. As she peeled potatoes, Kathleen revelled in opulence that was already disintegrating beneath the ocean. Meanwhile the headlines grew more gruesome as each day passed. *Her Side Ripped As By Giant Can Opener* screamed one. The emerging story of what had happened to White Star's pride and joy was as spellbinding as any penny dreadful serialisation.

* * *

The *Carpathia* continued westwards, the sea pounding against her hull with a sullen roar, her occupants impervious to the world's microscopic interest. On board they were sheltered from the shockwaves caused by the *Titanic*'s sinking, stunned into meekness by the realization of how narrowly death was cheated. Doctors inspected everyone and reported a clean bill of health, apart from frostbite and nerves.

Hannah touched the sleeve of the Hungarian doctor as he concluded her inspection. "Would it have hurt? Would dying have hurt my Tom?"

"It's likely he died of hypothermia." He saw her blank look. "That's the harmful effect of cold on the human body. Eventually, muscle control is lost and the victim slips into a coma-like state prior to death." He added kindly, "It doesn't hurt." He knew the water temperature had been extremely cold at 28 degrees Fahrenheit, so survival times would have been short. "No-one could have survived more than forty-five minutes to an hour at that temperature – but I suspect most were dead much sooner. In any case, unconsciousness would have set in within fifteen minutes of entering the water."

Hannah felt comforted. She did not care to think of Tom's death as prolonged, even if Father Byrne at home said pain in this lifetime meant time off from Purgatory. *Quid pro quo*, he called it, to near-blanket incomprehension among his congregation.

As she walked away from the doctor she saw young Mrs Armstrong with her fancy maid. Mrs Armstrong appeared changed by her ordeal. Not older, exactly, but less carefree. Welcome to the real world, thought Hannah. The American girl was still immaculate, however, with those opals at her throat. Hannah gathered her shawl around her. It was a flimsy donated piece, not the warm green one knitted by her mother whose dexterity with needles was known across two counties. Misfortune didn't hit everyone the same.

I bet that fine lady's not worried where she'll go or who she'll turn to when we reach New York, she thought.

She noticed a child nursing a doll with a neck that moved, blonde ringlets of real hair topped off by a hat with a feather. Rouged cheeks and contoured eyebrows made its face almost human. Hannah found it strange a doll should be saved from the shipwreck but not her Tom.

* * *

While Hannah was wandering about, Edmund Newton visited steerage. He wanted to discover who the genuinely indigent passengers were, so that help could be offered courtesy of a fund the major intended to establish in his wife's name. There seemed to be quite a few Swedish and Irish girls among the survivors.

"Such a difference between the races," he reported back to the major. "The Irish girls have nothing but the clothes they stand up in, while the Swedes have saved most of their money, including railway tickets through to inland destinations. Are some races more feckless than others?"

"Maybe the Irish had less worth saving," said Major Hudson.

Bridie had resented being quizzed on her resources by Edmund (naturally she told him she had nothing) and had changed the subject. "What does this name, the *Carpathia*, mean? It's such a funny word."

"The *Carpathia*ns are a huge mountain-range, 900 miles long, located principally in Hungary and the Ukraine, if I'm not mistaken. I'd need to check my atlas." He had a notion they might stretch as far as Romania; hadn't that Irish fellow, Stoker, set a lurid novel about a bloodsucking vampire in the Carpathians? He wouldn't mention it – the subject matter was too scandalous. Such a sensationalist book was probably out of print now anyway.

"Mountains, is it? It's a rare thing to be calling a ship after mountains."

"No stranger than the *Titanic*, named for a mythical race which waged war on Zeus, to its ruin. The Titans defied the gods and were thrown into the sea."

"Well, that's hardly a lucky name for a ship, then, is it?"

Edmund was stopped in his tracks.

*   *   *

When Hannah returned from her walk, Bridie was impatient to tell her about the questions Edmund Newton had put to her. "A cheeky divil, he was, asking all sorts about how much money we have and whether we're destitute. I don't see him putting his hand in his pocket – he never even offered us a couple of shillings for hooshing him into the lifeboat."

Hannah shrugged, indifferent. She hadn't a brass farthing to her name – it made no difference how many knew it. She shaded her eyes with her hand and gazed upwards, seeking the source of a clacking noise. Something had come loose on the mast, perhaps. There was a flap and then a report as an object struck wood. She would never become accustomed to shipboard life.

"A right pup," fumed Bridie. "He'll be asking us if we're wearing bloomers next!"

"Bridie," Hannah interrupted her, "I'm expecting a baby."

Bridie softened immediately. "Are you sure, *alanna*?"

"I'm regular as church bells, never late."

"When's it due?"

"Not 'til the heel end of the year. Late November, maybe."

Bridie was uncertain how Hannah felt about her pregnancy – after all, she'd just lost her husband. It could be the best news in the world, or the worst. She searched her face. Something seemed to be troubling Hannah. "It is Tom's baba?" She felt her way cautiously forward.

"Yes."

There was none of the reproof Bridie might have expected. But some nook of Hannah's face betrayed uneasiness.

"What is it, Hannah? What's troubling you?"

"Promise you won't despise me."

"I'm nobody to go about despising other folk."

Hannah averted her eyes as she poured out her confession. "We were never married, Bridie. Tom was going to ask a priest if he could do it on the *Titanic* – he thought it would be something to tell our grandchilder. But we ran out of time. It's a child with no name I'm carrying. I wanted Tom to be saved for his own sake, but I wanted it even more for mine." Hannah's frame was racked by a shudder. "Without him to stand by me, I'm ruined."

* * *

Edmund lingered over lunch, wondering if Bridie Ryan might have been making fun of him. She left him uneasy – but there was something about her. She reminded him of a peach of a girl he had taken punting on the Cam, back in his undergraduate days. A girl called Daphne who trailed her fingers in the river as he tried not to stare at her. For three months he churned at the thought of her. That day on the river he was desperate to yield to a burst of gallantry and fill her lap with long-stemmed white roses, uttering reckless words of passion. But he hadn't a bean. The bursary that took Edmund Newton to Cambridge didn't stretch far; not nearly far enough to shower flowers on a girl with liquid sunlight melting in pools at her feet. Daphne married a vicar the year after Edmund's graduation.

He banished thoughts of Daphne and Bridie and made light work of the *Carpathia*'s turbot, rounding it off with a wedge of Gruyère. Food always improved his mood. Then he adjourned to the library to compose a letter to *The Times*. It would probably strain his eyes, without his spectacles, but he had to do something; the more he pieced together about what had happened on the *Titanic*, the more outraged he felt by the cavalier manner in which passengers were treated. Ice-warnings ignored, speed levels kept high, false assurances given by officers – and

63

as for allowing so many crew-members to survive when fee-paying passengers were left to drown, it was downright immoral! Borrowing a fountain pen from a gentleman who had just finished a long letter home, he helped himself to some notepaper, screwed up his eyes and started writing.

From Mr Edmund Newton to the Editor, The Times, London
Wednesday April 17th, 1912
The North Atlantic

Sir,

As one of that endangered species, an Englishman who has survived the tragic sinking of RMS Titanic, I should like to lay some facts before your readers in the hope that action may be taken to improve safety at sea.

It was known to those in charge of the steamship that we were in the iceberg region. A number of wireless messages were received by Captain Smith, alerting him to the presence of icebergs during the day on which the disaster occurred, with latitude and longitude given. The Titanic appears not to have slackened speed in accordance with the information received. I understand from some of the ship's officers that this is a common practice and I condemn it unreservedly.

After the collision it was apparent that lifeboat provision was wholly inadequate. Furthermore their loading was not carried out in a professional manner. My calculations tell me there was a one-in-three chance of being saved in the event of an accident, due to the derisory nature of lifeboat allocation. I was fortunate enough to be among the elect, when I was pulled from the sea by passengers in a lifeboat. Had I been relying on the White Star Line's employees I would be a dead man.

Ergo I propose that the following four steps should be implemented to minimise the possibility of any repetition of this tragedy:

I Lifeboat seats provided for all passengers and crew

II Boat drill mandatory as soon as practical after leaving port

III A separate crew dedicated to lifeboats and trained in rapid loading

IV Ships obliged to slow to crawling pace in the iceberg region.

It is surely an irony that a special chef was engaged for the crossing but there was no boatman responsible for provisioning and lowering the lifeboats.

Luxury was given more consideration than safety and the fruits of this deplorable policy were catastrophe on an unprecedented scale.

I remain your faithful servant,

Edmund Newton BA (Hons) Cantab

Yes, that should do the trick. Shame his handwriting wasn't up to its usual standard. He'd been wearing spectacles since his undergraduate days – he was dependent on them.

Major Hudson dropped by and he showed him the letter.

"Impressive, Newton. Excellent point about the chef. I heard there was some talk of more lifeboats when the ship was built, but the White Star people thought they cluttered up the deck. It's scandalous! Boats would have served better than a lot of useless decoration."

Edmund pondered re-drafting his letter to include the point.

"Of course," continued the major, "we shouldn't lose sight of the bravery of the *Titanic*'s officers who went down with the ship. At least the *Titanic* upheld the Anglo-Saxon ideal."

Edmund decided to leave his letter well alone. The major could send his own missive to one of the New York newspapers if he felt strongly enough about it.

"Speaking of cowards" – the major hesitated – "a lady taxed me with saving my own skin on the lifeboat. I've been thinking about asking for a testimonial from Lightoller, as senior surviving *Titanic* officer. To prove I came by my place fair and square, don't you see? I was asked to board our lifeboat because they had a shortage of people who could row. Might do no harm for you to get a testimonial too, Newton. We know we did nothing underhand, but there are stories circulating about cads tricking their way into boats."

"I heard there were even some coves trying to sneak on by passing themselves off as women."

"I see you catch my drift. I'll push off and have a word with Lightoller. Hope for the best, expect the worst, eh? Always my motto in the Third Cavalry Regiment."

* * *

Nancy Armstrong lay with her feet up on the captain's bed, surrounded by charts and nautical instruments whose function she could not begin to fathom. It was all so male. Surrounded by a masculine presence, Nancy felt abandoned by the one man for whom she longed. Why hadn't her husband tracked her down yet? "I'll see you at breakfast, little girl," he had said.

She scolded him now, in his absence. "You should never have given up your place in the lifeboat. You were safe with me. And I needed you, you knew that. Much good it was saying Roberge would look after me, she's had one attack of the vapours after another since we left the *Titanic*. Jiminy, that woman's as useless as a paper parasol in a downpour!" At a loss what to do with herself, she rang for tea. She preferred coffee but Samuel said tea was more ladylike, except after dinner. Nancy couldn't tell the difference between Indian and China tea, but if Samuel wanted her to acquire a taste for it she'd oblige him. He asked so little of her and gave so much.

What would become of her? There could be no mistaking the Armstrongs' hostility to her marriage. The shockwaves of their match were still eddying around New York society. His father was dead, but Samuel's mother Rebecca had refused to meet Nancy, let alone attend the wedding.

"The prominent families must maintain standards or the social fabric will disintegrate," she stormed at him the day before his wedding to Nancy. "One is obliged to one's ancestors. There is a debt to be paid in consolidating the position they have built up for you. It is not all about assets and trust funds."

"It can't all be about duty either, mother. Remember the Constitution? Every man is entitled to life, liberty and the pursuit of happiness. I intend to pursue my happiness through Nancy Markova, bless her pretty blue eyes."

It was the first time he defied her. But on their honeymoon trip, eager to make amends, Samuel bought his mother a superb set of Whitby jet jewellery – choker, dangling earrings and a pair of bracelets – from

Asprey's in London. It cost an astronomical sum but he did not hesitate. Nancy was still unaccustomed to the wealth she had married into; but riches, she was discovering, acted as a passport. They allowed you to mix with extraordinary people irrespective of your own gifts, which might be slight. Hers, she knew, were grounded on her looks.

She had ended an arrangement – nothing as formal as an engagement – with her sweetheart next-door to accept Samuel's advances. Her mother ordered it, and at eighteen Nancy was still in the habit of obeying her mother. She assumed she loved Samuel because he was so insistent about loving her: he said he fell in love at first sight when they met in the lobby of his flagship hotel, the Adelphi. He was also overwhelmingly generous with his tokens of affection. Nancy's mother persuaded her she was smitten by him, even as she directed her to discourage Teddy next-door.

Nancy tried to remember exactly when she fell in love with Samuel, but it was impossible to pinpoint because everything happened with dizzying speed. "I'll spoil you, little girl," Samuel said, and he lived up to his promise. He gave her everything she wanted, things she didn't know she wanted. Still, she wished bridges could be built with Mrs Armstrong Senior. She had never met her mother-in-law and that couldn't be right. She and Samuel must make it a priority to pay her a visit with the Whitby jet after they docked. It would help smooth everything over.

"Oh jiminy, the jewellery must have sunk with the *Titanic*!" she wailed.

That meant her scarabs from Egypt and her haute couture gowns from Paris were also lost. How was she to make her début in New York society without her high-waisted tubular Paul Poiret gowns? Poiret was spearheading an Oriental craze in Paris. She had visited his salon at 5 rue Auber and bought a dozen gowns in exotic fabrics: brocades flecked with gold and silver, fluid, shaded velvets and diaphanous silks that almost turned liquid on the body. It was so easy to make a selection with her own personal *vendeuse* assigned to her. Samuel accompanied her, showing no hint of impatience while she clapped her hands together at such bounty. The only time he put his foot down was over Poiret's harem pantaloons, much in demand with the Parisian fashion plates. "Little girl, they're vulgar."

Nancy's slim frame was racked by a series of shudders and she sank back on the bed. Where was Samuel? Why wasn't he calling her his little girl and making everything better? He had to be on another ship, she couldn't possibly manage without him, especially with a baby on the way.

A knock on the door stalled her tears. It was probably that good-for-nothing Roberge, with her tea. She'd dismiss her the instant they reached New York. Roberge could turn right around and go back to Berne. Imagine passing herself off as French when she was really Swiss! Nancy had never dismissed anyone but realized she would be expected to control servants as Samuel's wife. "Treat them pleasantly and servants will do anything for you," her mother frequently advised. "But at all costs avoid letting them think they have the upper hand." Unlike Nancy, Violet Markova had been raised with servants. Violet had never forgiven her bankrupt merchant husband for reducing her to a servantless existence. Even his death at the age of forty-one from a pickled liver did not appease her.

The knock rapped again.

"Enter."

The door opened to reveal Major Hudson, who radiated horror at finding her in the vicinity of a bed, even though she was quite decent, fully clothed and resting on top of it. Silly old bird.

"Major Hudson, how kind of you to call." Nancy was accustomed to men's homage and never disconcerted to receive it. They had been introduced on her first night on board the *Titanic*, after the bugle call to dress for dinner.

"Forgive the intrusion, ma'am. Least I could do was to call and check on your health. I trust I find you as well as can be expected, under the circumstances?" He executed a quaint, heel-clicking bow.

"Under the circumstances," she agreed. She stared mistily at him, near-sighted but too vain to wear spectacles. It lent her the impression of intensity.

He left the door ajar to signal the utmost propriety. "I simply wanted, ma'am, to make you aware of my willingness to perform any little service you may find useful."

Nancy was touched, in spite of his pompous manner. "Major, you're so thoughtful. I can't think of anything right now . . . it's all been so . . ." Her voice petered out.

"Naturally, Mrs Armstrong, this has been an ordeal for you. May I say I think you're being wonderfully brave? It occurs to me there might be someone I could wire on your behalf. Your family, perhaps?" He touched the tips of his moustache, first one, then the other, delicate in his movements. "Mr Armstrong's?"

Nancy sat up, dislodging a pillow, which the major rushed to pick up. Mrs Armstrong Senior might expect to hear from her, especially now she was carrying her grandchild.

"Could I dictate a Marconigram, major? I've already been in touch with my mother, but my husband's people mightn't have heard from him yet. He may not be in a position to make contact. He's probably on another ship but there's no guarantee it has wireless."

Major Hudson started, before recovering himself. He suspected everyone except those picked up by the *Carpathia* had perished, but it wasn't his place to shatter her illusions. Reality would intrude soon enough. He produced a notebook from his inner breast pocket and she dictated Rebecca Armstrong's name and address.

Nancy pursed her lips, trying to compose an appropriate message for a mother-in-law she had never met but whose reputation preceded her.

To Mrs Rebecca Armstrong from Mrs Samuel Armstrong
Wednesday, April 17th, 1912
REGRET INFORM YOU SAMUEL STAYED WITH SHIP PRESUME PICKED UP ANOTHER VESSEL ARRIVING NEW YORK ON CARPATHIA MRS SAMUEL ARMSTRONG

As he made his way to the wireless operator's cabin, Major Hudson remembered he'd forgotten to ask about the O'Brien fellow. Tarnation! Oh well, if Mrs Armstrong had received no news of her husband, she'd have heard nothing of some steerage chap standing beside him. He probably hadn't even noticed the man.

* * *

Tom O'Brien of Bonavie, County Limerick, a remote little townland near Pallas Green, was still going unnoticed. He lay spread-eagled on the ocean floor where a shoal of fish, winnowing through gaps in the Grand Staircase, approached his body. But they flickered past him, more interested in the subdued lustre of a chandelier. Tom was not trapped by some collapsed limb of *Titanic* infrastructure, as others were, but his remains would never be found. Bodies sink once lungs fill with water, and in cold, deep expanses gas cannot form and lift a corpse to the surface. A lifebelt would have kept him buoyant, but he had unstrapped his and given it to a girl without one. When the ship turned on her nose and dived, she took him with her. In time, Tom's flesh and bones would be devoured by bottom-feeding fish and crustaceans, while any bones missed would be dissolved by salt water, along with his clothes. The rosary beads which his mother pressed into his fist leaving home had floated out of his grasp and were twined around a rock, waving in the currents. But his workingman's boots would rest there intact, long after his body crumbled, indicating where his legs once lay. The *Titanic's* deathbed was also his.

6

Louis Stubel stood at the ship's rail, wondering how his employer would react to the loss of his baggage. In justice, he couldn't be blamed – the sinking had been out of his control. Still, it had been in his care and gentlemen didn't always deal fair by their employees. He didn't know Monsieur Pires well enough to second-guess his response, having been engaged only the previous month. At least he was still en route to America, even if he lost his position. The prospect of life in this young, vital country where anyone could succeed had persuaded Louis to throw up an agreeable job with a gentleman banker and accept Jean-Claude Pires's offer. Monsieur Pires's family had a flourishing import-export business and he was relocating to the Boston office.

Louis craned his eyes toward the horizon, as though he could pierce the fog for a glimpse of the Promised Land, but instead Nancy Armstrong's face swam before his eyes. She could be medieval, he thought, with that smooth, high forehead and white skin. He wished he could discount what Bridie had told him about Nancy's pregnancy – he wanted nothing and no-one else to have a claim on her. But Louis had made inquiries among the *Carpathia*'s stewards and it was whispered that the young lady occupying Captain Rostron's cabin was indeed *enceinte*.

Louis knew he had nothing to offer Nancy: he had neither wealth

71

nor position nor a distinguished family lineage to recommend his suit. He was an orphan and did not know who his parents were, although it seemed impossible to him that he could be the offspring of common folk. Louis had a sense of destiny, even if destiny had no sense of him. He had made a series of attempts to trace his connections, but knew no more than that his grandmother had brought him to a Paris apartment block as a baby and hinted to the concierge that his father was a royal duke. The grandmother died when he was three and Louis was taken on by the concierge, in return for a bag of francs from the dying woman.

Early on, the boy learned to become self-sufficient. The concierge put Louis into service but it quickly became clear he was out of the ordinary. Coached by a well-disposed employer, he progressed to the position of secretary. Louis always suspected he came of better stock than those he served, but the only proof lay in a solid gold christening mug with his initials picked out in it, a ruby embedded in each letter – LSS, Louis Salvator Stubel. Tempted to sell the christening mug many times over, to his credit the concierge kept it from harm – apart from one ruby, which fell out, was therefore an act of God and was pawned by him. He had passed on the heirloom to Louis, virtually intact. Still in its original leather presentation box, it was the item Louis retrieved from his jacket before scaling down the side of the *Titanic* with a baby.

"That fog's a real pea-souper." Edmund spoke to Louis at the ship's rails.

"Pea-souper?" He tested the word, doubtful.

"Thick, you can't see through it," Edmund realized he was dealing with a foreigner. Blast! He was sorry he'd troubled himself to exchange civilities. He had noticed Louis in the second-class smoking lounge but the fellow hadn't looked foreign. Perhaps his complexion was a little darker than an Englishman's, now he saw him up close.

"Ah yes, foggy." Louis turned and faced Edmund, one of his elbows resting on the rail. His grace of manner both attracted the onlooker and forced a certain distance.

"Lose much?"

"Almost everything." Louis's lips parted in a smile. He was thinking that at least he'd salvaged his christening mug. All his life he regarded it as a talisman, believing it would lead him to his parents, or to wealth, or to some fortunate conclusion. Fish could so easily have been making exploratory nibbles on the mug's rim and there would have been nothing to mark him out from the herd.

Edmund wondered why the foreign Johnny was grinning if he was impoverished. "Me too." It didn't do to tell strangers you were liquid, even if they could pass for gentlemen.

"So we're in the same boat." Louis gave his austere smile again, arresting Edmund as he was about to move away.

"What will you do in New York?"

Louis shrugged. "I await instructions from my employer. He was to have sailed to New York on the *Titanic*. But he telegraphed to me at Cherbourg on the morning of our departure, saying he would travel by another boat. For three nights in a row he dreamed that the ship was doomed, and his wife persuaded him to take the premonition seriously. He cancelled his crossing after his luggage was already checked on. Unfortunately his anxiety did not extend to my safety. I was told to travel to New York with his suitcases, convey them to the Waldorf-Astoria Hotel and wait for him at a more modest establishment."

Edmund's interest was piqued. Rotten luck for the poor blighter. "You have excellent English, where did you learn it?"

"In Paris, with my previous gentleman. He was a banker from a place in England called Brighton. Have you heard of it? I'm told it's close to London and people bathe in the sea there. When I was with him he insisted I always speak English, for which I'm grateful. It will make my life easier in America. Americans also speak English, I understand."

"A brand of English." Edmund's expression was forbidding.

"I've seen you with a gentleman who looks like a soldier," said Louis.

"Ah yes, Major Hudson, interesting chap."

"There's also an American lady the major is acquainted with – a beautiful young lady called Mrs Armstrong. Does she live in New York?" Louis couldn't help himself talking about Nancy.

Edmund narrowed his eyes. Hang it all, it wasn't gentlemanly to bandy a lady's name about. "No idea." He left, with a curt jerk of the head.

Louis stayed at the railings watching the fidgety swell of the sea. He could feel its restlessness as it defied gravity to claw up the ship before falling back. A sense of restlessness twitched within him too. Instinct told him he was saved from the *Titanic* for a reason, and that reason was bound up in Nancy Armstrong.

*   *   *

The major was in a state of barely suppressed excitement when he met Edmund for a brandy after dinner, away from the roar of wind and sea that was deafening on deck. "I keep hearing about passengers who had omens about the sinking. I'm inclined to start making inquiries. It's a fascinating subject, Newton – we know so little about the other dimension."

"The other dimension?"

"The psychic world. *There are more things in heaven and earth*, my boy."

Edmund was silent. The old fellow seemed sincere and he'd no wish to offend him, but really, he expected more commonsense from a military man. One of the stewards had mentioned something about Major Hudson being present at Geronimo's surrender, which was practically prehistoric by American standards. A country without castles or ancient ruins could hardly lay claim to much in the way of history.

"I must speak to some of the sailors," said the major.

"They tend to be a superstitious lot."

"For good reason. When a man risks his life regularly, he develops a healthy regard for the unknown." Major Hudson thought about confiding his theory that his Jean had pierced the veil dividing those in the after-life from the living, waking him in time to escape from the *Titanic*. But he decided against it. There was something of the doubting Thomas about this chap, for all he had a likeable, manly air.

Edmund Newton had few close friends, and had been starting to think – cautiously, because he was not a man to count his chickens – of Major Hudson as one. Bally shame if he turned out batty. He thought about mentioning Louis's employer's presentiment of doom, but decided it would only get the major even more stirred up.

"I know you're a sceptic, Newton. But think how many sailors deserted before she sailed – my steward spoke to me about it on Sunday afternoon, before the *Titanic* was lost. He said in all his years at sea he'd never known so many fellows bunk off before we left Southampton."

The major spent the rest of his time on the *Carpathia* logging examples of forebodings. A steward called Lewis told how the White Star insignia his wife was sewing onto his cap fell to pieces under her needle. "My old girl was in a right state." Some passengers referred to an incident as they boarded, in which they were frightened by a stoker's head – face black with soot – sticking out of the fourth funnel, the dummy one for ventilation. Another lady mentioned an Egyptian soothsayer reading her palm in Cairo and warning of danger from the sea.

The major scribbled and smoked, his brain whirring. There was so much here, perhaps he should consider publishing a book highlighting the stream of coincidences. A consideration struck him, re-reading his notes. Perhaps it was all more than coincidence. The body of evidence was mounting.

"What if the *Titanic* was a hoodoo ship from the start?"

* * *

The survivors may have been sheltered in their sanctuary on the *Carpathia* but a maelstrom raged outside. The world marvelled, accused, mourned, speculated. Above all, it anticipated their arrival. The public needed answers – indeed, it was clamouring for them. This was the modern age and maritime disasters were not part of the equation. Figures that reflected unfavourably on the White Star Line were bandied about. However you dressed up the numbers, there was only lifeboat space for half of those carried by the liner. Initially "ill-fated" or "ill-starred" became interchangeable with the name *Titanic* – but soon people wondered if the accident had been avoidable.

"Who is responsible for this tragedy? How was it allowed to happen?" thundered newspaper editorials.

In Washington, an energetic senator by the name of William Alden Smith decided action should be taken and set in motion the wheels of a Senate inquiry. If the public was roaring for answers, he was the man to see they were supplied. Everybody – families of the dead, newspaper editors, preachers, politicians – demanded a reckoning. Someone must be held to blame for this senseless tragedy. Almost immediately, White Star's managing director was cast as the villain. "J Brute Ismay," he was dubbed by one newspaper, which suggested the White Star emblem be changed to a yellow liver. Ismay's crime was to have been indiscreet enough to survive, whereas at least Captain Smith and his senior officers remained at their posts and perished with the ship.

The *Carpathia* passengers saw nothing of Bruce Ismay. Some said he was half-demented with grief, others that he was consumed by guilt, and it was generally agreed he was pumped full of opiates.

At least they could cling to stories of heroism. Survivors reminded one another how Colonel Astor stepped back from the lifeboat his wife was boarding, yet space was found for her maid. Samuel Armstrong's name was invoked, and what about the US President's aide-de-camp, Major Archibald Butt? He went to his death without any attempt to pull rank.

In steerage, questions batted back and forth about locked doors and blocked companionways – they didn't mind preference being given to their betters, such was the nature of things, but it rankled they had been penned up for so long while the boats were lowered. Some noted how there were quite a few first-class male survivors, despite all the trumpeting about women and children first. It later became clear that the loss rate for first-class men was lower than that for third-class children.

Questions crackled over the *Carpathia*'s airwaves but were either ignored on captain's orders – he felt everyone on board had enough to deal with already – or couldn't be handled by the limitations of the ship's 200-mile wireless range. The ship's silence fuelled conjecture as rumour and counter-rumour inflated and became engorged. Some accused the *Carpathia* of a censorship policy, others suspected that Bruce Ismay intended to sneak back to Britain without cooperating with the US authorities.

The questions of how and why remained unanswered. But they continued to ferment, for the *Titanic*'s fate had shaken the western world's conviction in its own omnipotence.

* * *

Another thunderstorm on Wednesday night ploughed up nerves already strained.

"We'll all be killed," moaned Hannah, as the ship bucked. "I wish to God I'd never left Doon!"

"Go back, if you like, ships sail both ways across the Atlantic," Bridie snapped.

"I never want to set foot in another ship so long as I live. If I survive this crossing I'm staying put, wherever I land."

Bridie felt impatient with Hannah's leaping, scalded, at every lightning flash. Just because you felt scared didn't mean you showed it; that was no use. Bridie believed in putting on a brave face. "Be thankful it wasn't like this the night the *Titanic* went down. We'd have known all about it then. Chances are neither you nor I'd be sitting here if the sea was as stormy as it is now."

"Perhaps I'd be as well off at the bottom of the sea, along with poor Tom. At least our child would have its father by its side."

Bridie couldn't seem to persuade Hannah there was no reason for her secret to come out. The only person who could give her away was dead, after all. "Why don't you just carry on passing yourself off as Mrs O'Brien when you get to America, sure who's to know different?" she whispered.

"There's bound to be an inquiry. I heard that schoolmaster say so. Once people in charge start asking questions, they never know when to stop. What if they want to see my marriage paper? I don't have it to show them. Maybe they won't let me into America if I'm expecting, and me with no husband to support us. They'll say I could be a public charge. Tom's sister Winifred put that in one of her letters, she said the Yanks are in mortal terror of immigrants becoming a public burden. I'll be sent home to Doon and the shame of it will kill Mama."

"Hush!" Bridie laid her forefinger to Hannah's lips. "Your imagination is running away with you. Tell them your marriage paper went the same way as your husband."

* * *

Nantucket Lightship was sighted the following morning, to general relief: it was the first US landmark, 200 miles offshore. Not long now. On deck, Hannah and Bridie craned for a first glimpse of the American shoreline, wondering what lay in store for them in this new land they had put their faith in. Bridie was hoping for work in a factory – her brother said the money was mighty and she'd be sure to get a start. Hannah had less idea about what she might do.

"Where will you go?" Bridie squeezed her hand, relieved she seemed calm after the hysteria of the previous night.

"I can't very well go to Tom's four sisters in Chicago now – sure I don't know them from Adam. I suppose I may as well stay in New York. Maybe you and I might meet up from time to time, Bridie. I hate to say goodbye to you." Her glance at Bridie was hopeful. She was a great girl for raising your spirits.

Her friend, however, was smiling at the assistant purser as he tipped his cap to her.

* * *

That afternoon the *Carpathia* ran into dense fog. "Reduce speed to half, mister," ordered Captain Rostron. The fog-whistle's mournful blast at one-minute intervals set everyone's teeth on edge as the ship groped its way towards port.

"It hoots like a lost soul," murmured Hannah,

An officer offered some cheer. "Steerage survivors are being spared the usual Ellis Island inspection. The immigration authorities are sending people to board us and deal with the formalities."

"That's a mercy. I've heard it's an ordeal. You'd be queuing for weeks in that place they call the Great Hall," said Bridie.

"First and second-class have customs clearance suspended altogether. The Land of the Free seems to be a whole lot freer for some," muttered a Clare man, who'd bucked the odds to survive. He would die in France in the World War I meat-grinder within five years, however, a charred hole the size of a fist in the breast of his American infantryman's uniform. Not impregnable after all, despite surviving the *Titanic*. Still, he would use his extra years to the full: gaining a tattoo in his first year in New York and a wife in his second, impregnating both her and a prostitute in his third year and contracting gonorrhoea in his fourth.

Bridie nodded at the speaker and he nodded back.

"What are you going to America for anyhow, a lovely girl like yourself? Don't you have a young man at home? It's breaking his heart you must be, haring off halfway across the world."

Bridie leaned over the railings and clicked her fingers into the breeze. "I don't give that for him any more."

No sentimental memories of Freddie Bowe-Spencer would anchor her to Ireland – she'd have a clean slate in America.

Hannah paid no attention to the Clare man. She was grateful for small mercies, even if larger ones were extended to her betters. Mind you, they'd been checked and triple-checked already in Queenstown, never mind America. Passages were only allowed for the young and fit.

The questions they're expected to answer amaze Hannah. The ship's log is filled out at Queenstown with their answers to twenty-nine different queries, some of them downright disrespectful.

Tom is stoical when Hannah complains. "What odds, once we get what we want? They can ask me to sing Yankee Doodle Dandy *standing on me head and I will, if that's what it takes to reach Chicago."*

Anyone who can bail out of Ireland is leaving. The steamships are filled with boys and girls in steerage. There is a sense, as Tom and Hannah buy their ticket, that emigration will never end and the Irish are destined to wander the earth forever.

"I have a sod of earth from Bonavie in my pocket," says Tom, after they clear customs. "We're bringing something of Ireland to America."

America has the best of our boys and girls already, it hardly needs our soil as well, thinks Hannah.

A murmur went around as passengers were informed the US Secretary of the Treasury was also suspending customs regulations regarding baggage inspection.

"Baggage inspection! Sure what bags have we to inspect? They must think it's a *céilí* we had and not a shipwreck!" Bridie was indignant.

"Didn't that Cockney fellow who had an eye for you say something about a party when you were boarding?"

Bridie grinned. "He said I looked like a girl who was fond of a party. Poor Charlie Chadband, I don't think he made it. I'll light a candle for him in New York."

She saw the steward as she had the first time, boarding shortly after noon the previous Thursday. The great Atlantic rollers had rushed in to chivvy the cliffs while seagulls wheeled overhead, swooping for fish disturbed by the liner. A couple of stewards watched the transfer of Irish passengers from two tenders that sailed out from Deepwater Quay. The *Titanic* had not docked in Queenstown but remained in the harbour mouth for a quick departure.

"At least this lot speak English," remarked one as they were counted in, their possessions in bundles.

"Better than you from the sounds of it!" Bridie flashed.

He grinned. "We've a sparky one here. What's your name, young lady?"

She patted the thick black hair springing in curls from either side of her hat, glossy as bunches of grapes. "That's for me to know and you to guess."

"I'll tell you mine if you tell me yours."

"You first."

"Charlie Chadband. Your turn." He winked.

She winked back and kept walking.

Charlie had planned to kiss her before they docked in New York. He had meant to slip off to Chinatown and buy some silk for his old mum. He had intended to propose to a girl three doors away from him on the Bethnal Green Road when the *Titanic* made her return trip. Instead Charlie Chadband was wearing a lifebelt and drifting with the current, the eye that had winked at Bridie gazing sightlessly ahead.

* * *

The *Carpathia* remained uncommunicative as she approached New York, despite the incessant interrogation that crackled across the airwaves. Her silence fuelled speculation, waxing ever more melodramatic as frustration mounted. "*The Death Ship*," the newspapers dubbed her, conjuring up scenes of brooding widows maddened by grief. A reporter turned up the figure that there were eleven bride-widows on board, and the pathos ratcheted up another couple of notches.

Danny Ryan decided to meet the *Carpathia*, even though Bridget's name was not among the survivors. Nobody seemed to have a definitive list so he refused to give up hope. Besides, what if his sister had made it and nobody was there to greet her? "Sure she'd be in flitters," he told Kathleen, "not knowing where to turn." His fantasy of a helpless girl would be shattered within a week of meeting her, and the family back in Ireland were astounded it lasted so long.

Adam Armstrong also suggested meeting the *Carpathia* as a gesture of respect to his father's widow, but his grandmother vetoed it.

"It will delude her into believing she has some claim on us," pronounced Rebecca.

"Surely she does, Grandmuh-mother?

"Do not stand with your hands in your pockets like a corner-boy, Adam. Of course she has no claim on us. I cannot accept responsibility for all the strumpets your father was imprudent enough to take up with."

"Don't say such things about my papa!"

"If your father had not left your mother and slunk off to Europe, we would not be in this pickle. I will not hear another word about this woman who styles herself Mrs Samuel Armstrong."

Rebecca, in full mourning regalia by this stage, consulted the gold watch which dangled from a brooch on her firmly corseted bosom – she believed punctuality to be one of the cardinal virtues. "I am due to meet Powell in the morning room for a consultation about dinner menus in seven minutes. I wish there to be no further discussion about this person. She will never be an Armstrong. Never." She went off to take a laxative powder. These tussles with Adam played havoc with her digestive system.

Adam thought Nancy was entitled to some consideration, if only for his father's sake. His grandmother never listened to him. "One day I'll make her sorry," muttered Adam.

But being fourteen seemed to last forever.

* * *

It was evening time on Thursday night when the *Carpathia* sailed into New York. As she rounded Sandy Hook Light Vessel, nine miles from docking, she was met by an armada of small craft. Ostensibly they carried officials and the pilot who was to guide them, but a posse of over-excited reporters was also on board, questions zigzagging through the air.

"Is it true officers shot steerage passengers?"

"Did any officer commit suicide?"

"Did passengers shoot each other for lifeboat seats?"

The questions were hollered through loudhailers. One reporter tried to entice crew-members to abandon ship and give him an exclusive. He shouted a figure at some sailors within hailing distance, which incited a fellow reporter to compete with a higher sum, and as the numbers were bandied about it sounded to the Irish girls as though they were at a cattle market.

"Any minute now they'll be spitting on their hands to seal the deal," Bridie nudged Hannah.

They stared down from the railings, magnesium flares and flash powder igniting the scene. Shouting could be heard as reporters who had bribed their way aboard the pilot vessel leapt from it, trying to climb the Jacob's ladder to the *Carpathia*, but were rebuffed. Bridie giggled, watching the melee. But Hannah had no heart for laughter. Tom's face was before her constantly. She loved him, God knows she did, but she was in this mess for love of him. And love was no use to her now, she had to be practical. He had held all their money – she hadn't a penny to her name. Wherever Tom lay, their precious dollars and pounds were with him. Hannah had heard about the ladies and gentlemen of first-class organizing a collection, raising nearly £900 in pledges to distribute among the *Carpathia's* crew in thanks. She didn't begrudge them the money but it seemed a fortune to her, who was without so much as a change of clothes. She had pelted out without even her Irish linen tablecloth, which she'd been bringing to the New World to start life as a married woman. Her Uncle Kevin bought it for her bottom drawer when she was twenty-one, giving him the right to crack the same joke every time he saw her. "Never judge a woman or linen by candlelight," he always said, slapping his thigh.

"Maybe we should go below," suggested Bridie. They were drenched with spray as the *Carpathia* steered through the Narrows between Staten Island and Brooklyn.

"Maybe."

Still they lingered on deck for their first glimpse of New York. The Statue of Liberty came into view at last on Bedloe's Island in the Upper Bay, colossal in her dimensions. Beyond her were the skyscrapers of Manhattan – Jersey City to port and Brooklyn to starboard. The women twisted their necks to see this symbol of their new home, with her torch and tablet.

"*Send these, the homeless, the tempest-toss'd to me,*" quoted the Clare man destined to be cannon fodder in the trenches. "I'd say that fits our description."

Bridie gazed, dumbfounded, at the statue. It's the Virgin Mary all over again, she thought. The gargantuan effigy wore an expression as mild and unfathomable as Our Lady's. Imagine travelling halfway around the world to leave all that Catholic mumbo-jumbo behind, and meeting something that'd remind you of it before docking!

Edmund Newton, watching nearby, thought of his sister Minerva who had begged for a postcard of the Statue of Liberty. Minerva collected postcards. Edmund was more impressed than he had expected by the vista: she was a goddess and no mistake. One of the wonders of the ancient world had been a statue at another harbour, the Colossus of Rhodes, erected to the sun-god Helios. He wiped the stinging rain from his face, riveted by this wonder of the modern world, and said, "I do believe it was worth crossing the Atlantic to see her."

The major, who had a hazy boy's memory of Liberty being erected nearly forty years earlier, felt an impulse to salute the old girl.

Louis was stirred by a flash of pride that she had been given to the American people by the French.

Nancy was too busy having Roberge arrange her hair to look at the statue. "Imagine if Samuel reached New York by a faster ship and is waiting for me there!"

"Yes, madam," agreed Roberge, and wondered how long before her mistress took another husband.

All hands and officers were on deck now as they entered port, lightning spotlighting the cityscape. It looked immense, larger by far than anything Hannah could have envisaged. She had never visited Dublin, let alone a city of this scale. She shivered; how would she survive in such an intimidating place? She had relied on Tom to be by her side.

Bridie was externally impassive as she finally arrived in America, only a day or two later than scheduled, but inside she was a-whirl. For the first time she allowed herself to remember why she was emigrating. It was not only due to the man who had disappointed her, but what she had done because of him. For love of him – and then for hatred of him. Or maybe just to survive.

The love came first. There was so much about Freddie to love: his clear, carrying English accent which always sounded confident, his Anglo-Irish sense of entitlement. She was a seamstress, like her mother, in the village near his parents' estate. Bridie could have married the head groom but held out for the son and heir to Mount Regius. "Reaching for the moon again," her mother had taxed her, sour, but helping to clean up the mess Freddie Bowe-Spencer left in his wake. Bridie's sense was that the greatest hazard in life was to risk nothing. Freddie Bowe-Spencer had been worth the risk.

"At Eton the chaps called me Paddy," he says.

That puzzles her, for he sounds like an Englishman through and through, this lover of hers who boasts his family has been in Ireland since 1652.

"And at Oxford, what did they call you there?" she asks.

Freddie laughs, his sharp jaw-line with its cluster of moles quivering in the candlelight. "At Oxford they ragged me about not having a title. They said all the Paddies have the most outrageous monikers, Lord Ballygohere and Baron Ballygothere."

"But you will have a title one day. Didn't you tell them you're to be a baronet when Sir Frederick dies?"

"Certainly not, my sweet. Why should I justify myself? I was as foreign to the Oxford chaps as I am to you and your family. I belong in both countries and in neither of them. I'm neither fish nor fowl."

His mouth turns down and she presses her own against it to lift his mood.

Freddie Bowe-Spencer is always questioning Bridie, when he isn't touching her; quizzing her about the legends she heard at her grandfather's knee. He wants to know about the lovers, Diarmuid and Gráinne, and Diarmuid's love spot that he hides under a hat. "Is it true a woman had only to look at it to fall unconditionally in love with Diarmuid? I say, that would be a handy old mole-thingy."

He can't pronounce his name properly. "Deah-mid", he calls him, stumbling over the word.

"Tell me about the washerwoman, daughter of that frightful old goddess of war, who loitered about at the stream washing the clothes of warriors fated to die in battle that day. Such a fag for the daughter of a goddess!" Sometimes he even pretends to yawn.

While he affects flippancy, Bridie knows he treats the stories seriously. He makes her feel important because he listens to her. For his sake she tries to remember the legends repeated by her grandfather around the fireside. It's only nonsense, but if that's what Freddie Bowe-Spencer wants he can have it and welcome.

He's mesmerised by Cúchulainn and his Gae Bolga, a barbed spear thrown from the foot that could pierce any armour.

"He chose deliberately to take up the arms of a warrior on the day the druids foretold would make him the greatest hero in all Ireland, his deeds on the tongues of all – but his life would be a fleeting one. His wife Emer, who possessed the six gifts of womanhood, keened over his grave and then fell dead on it." Bridie offers him her treasures. The only ones she has – her stories.

"A chap rather like Achilles," murmurs Freddie, but she doesn't understand the reference.

When her store of legends is depleted she badgers the seanchaí for more to retain his interest. Sometimes she suspects Freddie might be wearying of her – his kisses are offhand compared with a few months previously. She knows it's because she won't give in to him. He's sulky, calling her a tease. So, hoping to please him with her gift, she recounts the tale of the young warrior, Naoise, loved by Deirdre for the three colours that define him: the colour of the raven in his hair, of blood on his cheek and snow on his skin. "His is one of the three sorrows of Irish storytelling."

Naturally he demands the other two.

He hears about the Milesians who invaded Ireland in the years before time was counted, driving underground the godlike De Danaan, people of the goddess Dana. "They divided the country into two," she explains. "The Milesians – that's who we're descended from – had the upper half, and the people of Dana, the fairy folk, had the underground half. This lower part was Tír na nÓg, the Land of Eternal Youth. Sometimes the fairy folk see a beautiful mortal and lure them away from their families to Tír na nÓg. And sometimes they steal a baby and leave an ugly changeling in its place – May Eve is when they get their chance to steal human babies. You, now, Freddie Bowe-Spencer, I bet they'd have loved to get their hands on you."

Freddie laughs along with her and rains a series of kisses on her ear and neck, calling her his Scheherazade, and tells her a story of his own. It's about a band of robbers in a place called Sherwood Forest, and the spirited woman called Maid Marian loved by their leader. Bridie is captivated by it – and especially by its happy ending.

But there are tales she doesn't share with him. Her grandfather was a lad during the Hunger years.

"God sent the potato blight but the British sent the famine," he'd spit, grinding the globule underfoot.

Freddie never wants to talk about the Famine. His grandfather was master of the estate and used the opportunity to clear his lands of his forever-breeding, unprofitable tenants. Sir Roger Bowe-Spencer was never forgiven. "Sir Rot In Hell," the locals call him.

Bridie fancies Freddie might wed her because he's always spouting about how the gentry are doomed without intermarriage. "The future lies in mating with healthy native stock," he'd say, before proceeding to mate with some healthy native stock.

She has submitted to him by now, fearing his loss of interest otherwise. Her stories alone are insufficient by this stage, he's heard them all and the seanchaí has moved to another parish in his circuit.

Freddie would speculate about the sort of heir to the Bowe-Spencer name and property they could produce. "Come live with me, and be my love, And we will some new pleasures prove," he quotes, and Bridie takes him seriously.

The fantasy ends abruptly when she tells him she's carrying his child. He doesn't want it – it is no more than a game to him.

Bridie aborts Freddie Bowe-Spencer's baby. She pays his money to a woman with a fondness for drink in the village, who keeps her clay pipe clamped in her mouth as she gives Bridie a bitter draught that gouges her body and jack-knifes her into spasms of pain. The abortionist will not dispose of what is ejected from between Bridie's legs as she lies on her kitchen table, so the young woman does it herself. She buries the girl-baby which carried the genes for her father's facility with languages and her mother's Spanish eyes on the Hill of Oola after dark.

She is barely able to walk – willpower alone keeps her legs moving. At the Fiddler's Stone she rests, with a sixteen-week-old foetus in her arms and a shovel strapped to her back. Then she tackles the ascent, laying her baby on the grass with an oddly tender gesture while she scrabbles a grave. Bridie thinks her child might like a high elevation with a view of the townland. It's her way of making amends.

Afterwards she drags herself home and spends a week in bed with fever, while her mother mops her sweat during the nightmares, feeding her nettle soup when she's conscious. Josie Ryan knows what her daughter has done and keeps it from her husband. Least said soonest mended.

She doesn't discuss the abortion with Bridie. But she doesn't try to dissuade her, as she would once, when Bridie goes to the shipping subagent's in Tipperary town on the first day she can get out of bed. Nor does she ask where the passage money comes from.

Bridie buys a ticket on a steamship called the Cymric, due to depart Easter Sunday – resurrection undertones she doesn't fail to notice. The coal-strike across the water keeps it from sailing, however, and her passage is transferred to the Titanic. She hopes the change of ship means a change of luck.

Freddie pays for the ticket, just as he pays for the abortion.

His trademark air of assurance is absent when he produces his wallet, hands palsied as they extract all the paper notes from its calfskin interior. Bridie reads and re-reads the entwined initials on the rectangle of leather while he counts out twenty-four pounds, crumpling them into her hand, avoiding her eyes. FRCBS is etched on the wallet. Frederick Roger Conyngham Bowe-Spencer. Heir to a baronetcy. No husband for a tenant farmer's daughter. He has five names, she has two, no need to look further for proof of their disparity in station. She realizes, with a wrench that begins as pity and ends in scorn, that he's terrified.

Twenty-four pounds is more money than she has seen in her life. She still has £19 left over, after accounting for the village woman's services.

"It's rearing children for the export trade we are," complains Bridie's father, when she tells him her plans. He doesn't stand in her way, however.

She takes two of Freddie's £5 notes to the sub-agent's and leaves the rest of the money under her mattress. Bridie Ryan is learning caution at last.

"Some folk like to bring a souvenir from home with them," the shop-hand suggests, indicating a shelf of holy statues. He holds her change from the ticket, waiting for the girl to make a selection. There is an array of Our Lady statues for sale, some holding the Infant Jesus, others crushing a serpent underfoot. It is March 17th, the feast of their patron saint, Patrick. The day, as her grandfather used to tell her, when the warm side of the stone turns up: spring is on its way. But there is no spring in Bridie's heart. She casts a contemptuous eye over the Blessed Virgins and extends her hand for what's due to her. The clerk thinks her a hard one as he reaches her two pounds, five shillings in change.

The money was in the hem of her skirt now, part of the nest-egg that would help her make her way in America. She thought of her aborted baby – a mortal sin for which she would roast in hell for all eternity. Bridie gritted her jaw until her teeth ground against each other. She was leaving guilt and regret behind in Ireland, along with that pitiful mound on the Hill of Oola.

"The rules are always pitched against women." Her mother said it to her on the day she left home. "Perhaps where you're going, things will be different." It was the only hint Josie Ryan gave of knowing what Bridie had done.

Marian. She would have called her daughter Marian. The day when Freddie told her the Maid Marian story was the day her baby was conceived.

But that was in another life.

Bridie stood on deck on the *Carpathia*, entering the portal to the United States. Unblinking, she watched New York, and New York watched her back.

7

The *Carpathia* was expected around 9 p.m. at Cunard's Pier 54, at the foot of West 14th Street. Only close relatives were allowed passes to admit them to the pier, two per survivor, but onlookers congregated from late afternoon onwards – rubberneckers, in the new slang of the day – avid to see the survivors of this shipwreck which had captured the popular imagination.

As dusk gathered, police officers set up a series of ropes with green lanterns on either side of the pier's main entrance. Mounted police, patrolmen and detectives manned the barricades, under orders to prevent pickpockets operating amid the 30,000-strong throng.

Stuart Hudson still managed to have his wallet pinched waiting for the major. Fortunately he had spent most of his quarterly allowance and was hoping to touch his father for an advance.

"You suppose they'll be able to raise the *Titanic*?" a reporter asked his colleague from a rival newspaper.

"Not likely. Her grave's a coupla miles down."

"I hear there may be airtight compartments. Some poor devils could be trapped – buried alive."

"Nah, there's nobody alive at that depth."

"You never know. Might look into it for a page lead."

Meanwhile the *Carpathia* glided slowly up the Hudson River and along Eleventh Avenue parallel to the docks. Ten thousand people stood along the Battery Gardens in the driving rain, many men with their heads bared as a mark of respect. The vessel paused opposite the White Star piers, 59 and 60, and onlookers gasped to see the *Titanic*'s lifeboats unloaded.

Even Nancy was on deck now, lured by the prospect of home. She shivered, re-looping the image of her husband stepping from their lifeboat, giving way to that nobody from steerage. Gentlemen were supposed to display gallantry but Samuel's gesture had been excessive. She would scold him about it when they were reunited, and make him promise never to be so rash again.

Stately, the *Carpathia* proceeded to Cunard's Pier 54. At 9.30 p.m. the gangways were lowered, while outside on the misty streets the silent throng strained against the police cordon. Doctors and nurses boarded with stretchers, with wheelchairs left ready on the quay. Survivors – first-class, naturally – began disembarking.

The survivors were bewildered by the throng and some hesitated at the foot of the gangways. Then familiar faces detached themselves from the mass and they heard their names called. Pandemonium erupted as they moved towards the exit, reporters clamouring questions and flash explosions popping in pursuit. On the street a fleet of cars waited to convey people home or to hotels, courtesy of White Star. Those who needed medical attention were assisted into ambulances and taken to hospital. Just beyond police lines, a Salvation Army band played rousing hymns.

Mrs John Jacob Astor, four months pregnant, was greeted by her twenty-year-old stepson Vincent, accompanied by two doctors and a nurse. They hurried her to the family's mansion a block away from the one Samuel had bought to set up home with Nancy. The Astor family wanted to use their yacht to approach the *Carpathia* and spirit the young widow away before docking but were dissuaded by White Star officials – conscious such overtly preferential treatment might rankle.

Nancy wished the Armstrongs had despatched a team to whisk her off. As though reading her thoughts, Major Hudson whispered in her ear, "It's said old Astor made his money when one of his ship's captains found Captain Kidd's treasure." In other words, they were common to the core, for all their posturing. Nancy smiled, tickled.

She was supported down the gangplank by the major, her head swivelling above the ashes of roses cloak which she had lent to Louis, as she searched for Samuel. It would be so like him to emerge from the gathering, a bouquet the size of a cartwheel in his arms. She peered, but her short sight blurred everything. For the first time, it occurred to Nancy to wonder where she should go, just supposing her husband was not waiting and she had to fend for herself. She and Samuel didn't have a home, exactly. Samuel had occupied a penthouse suite in the Adelphi, part of his family's hotel chain, during his separation from his first wife. Shortly before the wedding he had bought a mansion in one of New York's most select addresses for them to move into on their return from honeymoon, but they had never lived there. Her mother had been flitting in and out for the past three months, chivvying the decorators. Indeed, Violet Markova had scarcely left the magnificent house and progress reports followed them to Cairo, Paris and London trilling of the pleasures awaiting them on their return and hinting at her efforts on their behalf. Violet intended to shake off the dust of New Jersey and set up house with the couple in Fifth Avenue. She was uncertain how exactly to broach this with her son-in-law, but remained convinced she could manage him. Hadn't she managed him well enough to prompt a marriage proposal for her daughter?

Nancy's hands grew clammy inside their silver elbow-length evening gloves. Where was Samuel? And where was her mother – surely she had come to meet her? There she was! "Momma," she cried, waving a little more frantically than was ladylike. Nancy was swept by a surge of nostalgia for her childhood home in Avalon. She longed to be snug in her bedroom with its cherry-blossom wallpaper, listening to the apple-tree rustle against her windowpanes. She wanted her mother to swish in with a glass of warm milk, tweak her quilt and kiss her on the forehead, as though she were a little girl again instead of a married woman.

For someone of short stature, Violet Markova cut an imposing figure in a chinchilla fur presented to her by her son-in-law. The weather was on the warm side for the coat and fur should not be exposed to rain, but she knew the press would be out in force tonight. Her ash-blonde hair was piled high at the top of her head. Yet she forgot all about presenting a sophisticated image and caught her breath when she saw her daughter supported off the ship, looking so wan. Nancy leaned on a gentleman's arm, with a ship's officer on her other side in case further assistance was necessary.

"Darling!" Violet stretched out her arms and Nancy collapsed into them.

"Momma! I heard a noise and thought it was some mishap in the kitchen, I never dreamed we'd struck an iceberg!" She burst into tears.

Violet's hand caressed the small of Nancy's back. "I've been out of my mind with worry." She appraised Major Hudson discreetly over her daughter's head. He held himself erect, sympathetic but slightly embarrassed by the display. Violet extended her gloved hand to the major. "Sir, I am grateful to you for taking care of my daughter. My name is Violet Markova."

"Major Hudson, ma'am, at your service. That's Hudson, like the river."

He accepted the tips of her fingers and bent his mouth to them, lips just failing to make contact with cloth. While the mother was not as beautiful as the daughter, she had a burnished elegance which drew the eye.

Violet was charmed. "Major Hudson, you've been through a nightmare. It must have been dreadful for you."

"Takes more than a shipwreck to finish off an old warhorse like me, madam. But I'm conscious others were less fortunate."

"Of course," Violet fluttered. "We mustn't detain you any longer, major, I'm sure your family are anxiously awaiting your arrival."

"I believe I see my son. May I organize a carriage for you? Ah, you have one waiting. Then if there's really no way I can be of service, I'll take my leave. Mrs Armstrong, perhaps you'll permit me to call on you in a day or two when you're feeling stronger?"

"Thank you." Nancy dabbed at her eyes with a scrap of cambric.

Violet puffed out her lower lip, determined to cultivate such a distinguished gentleman – those Armstrongs needn't imagine the Markovas knew nobody of consequence.

"Have you heard from Samuel?" asked Nancy, as they turned towards the exit.

"Why no, darling."

Nancy sighed. So he hadn't reached New York ahead of her.

Her mother stared at her. All the reports suggested Samuel was dead.

The women were intercepted by a compact, clean-shaven man, hair parted scrupulously down the middle, who raised a hand to halt them. Gerald Powell was the Armstrongs' family butler, so grand even the unassailable Rebecca Armstrong was in awe of him. He had previously been butler to a minor member of the British royal family, accompanying his lordship to Balmoral on three occasions when the old Queen was still alive. Once, Powell had even been permitted to fold some towels used by Victoria. She had condescended to notice him during the last visit.

"Where do you come from?" the Queen-Empress had asked.

"Penarth, Your Majesty."

"I see, one of our Welsh subjects. Carry on."

The conversation had concluded there, but Powell never wearied of narrating this momentous encounter and Rebecca Armstrong never wearied of encouraging him to do so. She felt it reflected appropriate merit on a family in whom a dozen bloodlines converged dating back to the Mayflower.

"Mrs Armstrong, Mrs Markova. I am Powell, butler to Mrs Rebecca Armstrong. She has sent me to ensure you reach home safely. She also wishes me to say she will call on you tomorrow, Mrs Armstrong."

"Tell your mistress my daughter will be delighted to receive her. I absolutely insist she rests in the morning, and I've arranged for a physician to give her a thorough health check after luncheon. But late afternoon would be perfectly convenient."

"Very good, ma'am. Mrs Rebecca Armstrong has sent a car to convey Mrs Armstrong home. She wants to be reassured that Mrs Armstrong is taken home as quickly as possible. There are members of the press about, as you can see. The vehicle is parked by the police cordon. If I may, I'll lead the way." His manner was a curious combination of deferential and insistent.

Nancy raised her eyebrows at her mother. "I thought you said we had a carriage waiting for us?"

Violet put a finger to her mouth. "If the Armstrongs are kind enough to send their automobile, it would be unmannerly to refuse. Come along, we'll soon have you settled.

"Can we go home to New Jersey, Momma?"

"New Jersey? Mercy! Fifth Avenue is your home now."

The young woman trailed along, too exhausted to argue.

* * *

Major Hudson started talking about his wife as soon as he and his son were in the hackney cab. "I smelled her scent, Stuart. There was a distinct perfume of gardenias in the cabin when I woke up after we struck the iceberg." His wish for this to be true supplied the detail. "It was as though your dear mother leaned over my bed and shook me awake."

Stuart Hudson wondered how soon he could ask his father for a loan. There was a humdinger of a girl he wanted to present a trinket to, and he'd hosted a couple of sherry parties in his rooms, running up a steep drinks bill. Not that he worried about settling his bills, but the store refused to send any more bottles on credit until he paid what was due. Tradesmen were so materialistic.

The major closed his eyes, the roar of the ocean pounding in his eardrums, remembering how he was startled awake. Yet no jolt had been discernible in his first-class cabin as the *Titanic* scraped along the underwater spur of an iceberg. It was obvious he had been alerted by his wife. "Jean lifted the veil between the quick and the dead to reach me," he would insist afterwards, and people hesitated to scoff in the face of his sincerity. It was certainly true that just before disaster struck, the major was dreaming of his wife, dead for twelve years from tuberculosis, but she flitted through his dreams most nights.

"So you cheated death again, sir? The Apaches couldn't get you and neither could the ocean. I should think you're indestructible."

The major leaned towards his son, eyes lambent. "Stuart, your mother saved me. Saved me for your sake, I shouldn't wonder – she didn't want you to be an orphan."

Stuart Hudson, a dandified young man with his father's treacle eyes and a smudge of hair on his upper lip, was glad his pa was safe and well. He'd always behaved decently to him, and the *Titanic's* sinking had been alarming. Nevertheless, he was uncomfortable with the old man rambling on about his mother. He hoped it was just the shock and his father wasn't going to start seeing her in every nook and cranny.

Stuart was only eight when they buried her. He remembered white hands and a cameo brooch at her throat. His father was right, Mamma had smelled of gardenias, and she used to sing a Scottish lullaby in the nursery. But Stuart was no longer clear about what he remembered and what was woven from stories recounted by his father. The summer holiday in Oyster Bay, Long Island, for example, when he was six: did he really recall throwing a pebble to scare away the seagull that swooped on Mamma's sandwich, or had he heard about it so often he thought he remembered it?

He did remember her growing thinner and frailer by the week, how even talking became an ordeal, and yet she used what little breath she could muster to sing that lullaby to him. Something about a bonnie bairn and a distant glen. He'd give anything to hear it again.

Sometimes Stuart had felt overlooked during Mamma's last year, as his father consulted specialist after specialist, trying to save her by taking her to Yosemite in California, where the air was clean and crisp. Her treatment involved lying on her back on the balcony of their hotel, rugs heaped over her, breathing the air. Stuart visited her during his school holidays and one afternoon kept watch beside her, tucking the rugs around her feet and blowing on his mittened hands to stay warm. She died two days later. He remembered the sound the earth made thudding against her coffin lid.

And now his father was babbling beside him in the carriage about veils being lifted. It was hogwash!

His father squeezed his boy's shoulder and Stuart Hudson sighed, contrite. He'd undergone a near-death experience, he was entitled to blather. Now where had that word sprung from? It was one of Mamma's. Perhaps she was intervening to ask him to be a little more tolerant. He smiled with Jean Hudson's lopsided mouth. "I'm so glad to have you here with me, safe and sound, sir."

The hackney cab stopped outside the Waldorf-Astoria on Fifth

Avenue and a uniformed attendant darted to open the door.

"Say, what are we doing here?"

"Your apartment in Washington Square hasn't been occupied in two months. I thought you might be more comfortable here until we get Mrs Burdich in to have it aired." Stuart was already half-out of the cab and speaking over his shoulder. "Didn't you hear me give the hotel's name to the cabbie?"

"My mind was elsewhere. But I wrote Mrs Burdich from London, instructing her to prepare the apartment. Everything should be ready, I'm only a day or two late."

"Naturally, sir, we can go to Washington Square if you prefer. But I was acting for the best. I thought we might have a bite of supper here and you could grab a decent night's kip. Then in the morning we could assess the situation."

The boy thinks of nothing but pleasure – time enough for him to grow up and realize life isn't all nickelodeons and vaudeville shows, thought the major. He dragged his hand down the side of his face. "You're right, Stuart. Supper for two sounds just the ticket."

His son helped him to the ground, noticing how creaky he was getting.

"How about I ask them to send up some lobster and champagne to our suite?"

The major would have preferred a Scotch and soda and a slice of roast beef, but he remembered what it was like to be twenty. Not that there had been much champagne drunk in the Third Cavalry Regiment during tours of duty in Arizona. "Perfect, Stuart. You're spoiling your old father."

* * *

The Hudsons were enjoying a bottle of Jouet in one of the Waldorf-Astoria's gold-brocaded private sitting rooms as the *Titanic*'s second-class survivors finished disembarking. Louis Stubel was immediately ahead of Edmund Newton and the Englishman noticed Louis was carrying a large package wrapped in sailcloth. How the dickens did he manage to save some of his possessions? thought Edmund.

The previous night, Louis had unscrewed the *RMS Titanic* nameplate from Lifeboat 16 when nobody was looking – it was opportunistic, he knew, but he felt it might be lucky to have a *Titanic* memento. Besides, White Star owed him.

At the meeting area, a White Star representative addressed Louis and Edmund, thinking they were travelling together, and told them rooms were reserved in a hotel on Seventh Avenue with the first night's accommodation complimentary. Louis and Edmund were driven there, each assimilating snatches of New York as they rattled along. A shaggy porter greeted them at the street door to the Excelsior Hotel, close to Pennsylvania Station, and tried to wrestle Louis's bulky package from him. But the Frenchman held on grimly. He and Edmund separated at the registration desk, both too weary to suggest a nightcap.

* * *

It was 11 p.m., an hour and a half after the first-class passengers had begun disembarking, before the 174 steerage survivors trudged down the gangplanks. They tended to be women, thinly clad and shivering. Those who were met were the lucky ones. The huddled masses were headed, in the main, for Manhattan's Lower East Side, a densely packed tapestry of tenements, factories and docklands. Into it were jammed more than 700 people an acre, making it the most crowded neighbourhood on the planet. Many of these *Titanic* survivors would live in rooming houses, some owned by the multi-millionaires who had also sailed – and died – on the ship, among them John Jacob Astor. Luxurious skyscrapers surrounded these slums, rich and poor America separated by a sliver.

"Danny! You came, Danny! I wasn't sure you'd still be here. They wouldn't let us off! I was nearly going to make a jump for it."

"Bridie! Is that little Bridie? Sure you're all grown up and pretty as a spring morning. They told me you were dead, but thanks be to God they were wrong!" Danny Ryan snatched off his cap and smothered her in a hug.

"They kept us waiting while the other passengers were getting off. I was afraid you'd have given up on me."

"Oh, Bridie, I'd have waited all night long. I didn't know if you were on the ship at all but I had to come. There was no record of you among the survivors."

"Cheek of them!"

Simultaneously laughing and crying, they clutched at one another. Hannah felt desolate. She waited to say goodbye to Bridie, conscious of relief workers moving among the survivors offering assistance. It would mean accepting charity, something she'd been warned against all her life by her parents, but at least she'd be sure of lodgings for the night. She watched a knot of people focus on everyone who came off the ship.

"The best we can ask for now is a body to bury," muttered one.

Hannah started. Would she have a chance to bury Tom? Or was he doomed to lie somewhere anonymous, without so much as a flower on his grave?

"Where are your folks?" A tall woman from the Red Cross, mouth crowded with teeth, stopped in front of Hannah.

"Chicago," answered Hannah, although in truth Tom's four sisters were not her people and she didn't know how they'd receive her if she went to them. He hadn't told them about her, he was keeping it as a surprise. "But I thought I might stay in New York."

"Let's find you a bed for the night and see about making arrangements to take you to the train station tomorrow." The woman caught Hannah by the arm.

She quaked: this was it, then, she'd never see Bridie again.

Bridie spoke up. "That won't be necessary, thank you. My friend has made other arrangements."

The volunteer shrugged and moved on to an Armenian woman with a huddle of children clutching her skirts.

Bridie looked beseechingly at her brother. "Danny, Hannah has nowhere to go. Can we take her in for a night or two, just until she finds her feet? It doesn't seem right to let her disappear with strangers after all we've been through together. Please let her come home with us!"

"I wouldn't hear tell of it," said Hannah, although her heart leapt at the thought of staying with Bridie.

Danny Ryan held up his work-roughened hand. He had started as a labourer, worked his way up to hod-carrier and hoped to make bricklayer before he retired – or if not him, then his baby son for sure. "You're more than welcome. I wouldn't be able to live with meself if we left you to fend for yourself."

They were driven by horse and cart by a neighbour of Danny's who refused payment, and arrived at a lodging house at 33rd Street and Third Avenue. Sandwiched between the Shamrock Saloon and the Fat Man's Pawn Shop was a lanky brownstone building. A ladder of concrete led to a front door that must once have been impressive but was now rotting to a puffball. Danny Ryan paused in the entrance, where the air had an exhausted quality as though too many lungs were breathing it, and extended his right arm with a flourish of the wrist. "Welcome to America."

8

A succession of unfamiliar sounds awoke Bridie on the fourth floor of the six-storey tenement block which was now home. She listened, charmed: it seemed to be a street vendor plying his wares. Was he selling peaches? She'd never tasted one. And what was that grinding noise? Was that the thing they called a streetcar? Even the way light entered the room was different. In Ireland sunlight crept inside in tentative shards – here it streaked in brazenly. She stretched, a feeling of contentment washing over her. It was as though this fractured voyage from one world to another had sanitised her. Oola and Freddie Bowe-Spencer were washed away and she was ready to embrace her new life. Bridie Ryan was going to be an American success story.

She became aware of Hannah's cushiony flank alongside hers. Bridie wondered if she ought to mention how there were ways to avoid having a baby, if the prospect of motherhood was truly repugnant. An innocent quality in Hannah made her hesitate to suggest it. Bridie knew she had lost something of herself when she buried her baby, and she was made of sterner stuff than Hannah.

Her nephew chirruped on the other side of the curtain dividing Danny and Kathleen's room into sleeping and living areas. Kathleen had rigged up a second partition for Bridie, which condensed their living space still further. She had bought a ticking mattress, intending to add the bed to go with it when Bridie started earning and contributing to the household. It was far from ideal – there was no privacy for any of them – but Bridie was family and needed a hand to get started, and the extra income would be useful. Danny had promised it to Kathleen as pin money since she'd have most of the trouble.

Daniel Junior drummed his tiny heels on the pillow, and the sound of Kathleen shushing him made Hannah yawn and open unfocused eyes. Disorientated, she thought she was with Tom under their red and white coverlet on board the *Titanic*, and joy rushed through her body. The shipwreck had been a nightmare! Tom was safe and sound beside her, she could feel his warmth reach across the bed to her. They had slept in twin bunks on the *Titanic* but Tom used to slip in beside her as soon as the lights dimmed, spooning his body around hers, even though they were obliged to share their cabin with two strangers. Hannah had never heard of bunk beds and had burst out laughing to see them stacked like shelves, one on top of the other, to save space.

Hannah closed her eyes because something was wrong with the light coming into the room.

"Will we go to the service today?" Bridie yawned, jaw clicking. "Out of respect?"

Hannah opened her eyes again, surrendering her fantasy that the *Titanic* had never been wrecked. "All right," she agreed.

Memorial services were being held simultaneously in London and New York, and Hannah felt it would be right to attend one. She generally liked to do what was proper. She was nervous about stepping inside a church after lying in Tom's arms. Not just once but again and again. Oh God, and revelling in it! But this was only a service, not Mass with Holy Communion – which she couldn't take anyway because she wasn't in a state of grace. There were stains on her soul. She knew the marks could be wiped clean if she went to Confession, but she was not yet ready to renounce Tom. It felt disloyal to his memory to call what they had done together a sin, and ask forgiveness for it.

As for Bridie, although she intended to have nothing more to do with religion in this new life across the water, she felt a superstitious need to offer thanks to someone for surviving. Pagan or Christian, any god would do.

A thundering rumble which peaked at a roar, setting their mattress juddering, passed overhead.

"Saints preserve us, what's that?" gasped Hannah.

"A train. We're right under the elevated train tracks. This is the life, Hannah, we're in the thick of things."

At breakfast, Bridie nudged Hannah and indicated the window, through which a fire escape's metal skeleton was visible. Luxuries were in short supply in the tenements but at least they had fire escapes. New York was fire-conscious, if nothing else.

"How would you like to go skipping up and down that thing?" Bridie's eyes sparkled.

Hannah shuddered. She disliked being so high up, afraid her head would split from the pressure.

There was only Kathleen and the baby to keep them company during the meal, for Danny had already left for work. He had crept out in his stocking soles, boots under his arm and a wedge of bread and a cold sausage in his pocket, to avoid disturbing the women, although his splattering bladder evacuation into the chamber pot caused them to turn over and grumble before sinking back into unconsciousness.

Kathleen was agog for a gossip. "You should hear some of the stories about the survivors, it would make your hair curl."

Already Bridie loathed her confidential manner. "Stories?"

Kathleen nodded. "About dozens of them panicked and screaming on that rescue ship, the what-do-you-call-it. Like wolves howling at the moon, they were. They couldn't settle at all. Dementia, some of them had."

Bridie flicked her eyes over her nephew, digging his fist into the sugar-bowl, and looked away. Babies reminded her of what she had done.

"Tell us what it was like." Kathleen smacked her lips.

"I never came down with so much as a sneeze let alone an attack of the heeby-jeebies, and neither did Hannah."

"I guess some of those blue bloods lost their minds, though. Bet they had to be pinned down for their own safety."

"Your imagination is working overtime. Is the baby meant to be putting his toes in the sugar?"

"It would have made the stones weep to hear the cries of the swimmers in the water," said Hannah, and something in her manner deterred Kathleen from further questions.

As the women prepared for the service in clothes lent by Kathleen and her neighbours, other arrangements were in train. The search for bodies was under way by a Canadian cable ship chartered by White Star. The *MacKay-Bennett* set out that same morning for the area where the *Titanic* had foundered. More than 100 plain wooden coffins were on board, tons of ice in its hold and embalmers' supplies securely stowed, because only preserved bodies could be brought to port. All the crew were volunteers, promised double pay. The ship's master had little appetite for his work as he pored over maps, making calculations. The *Titanic* struck the berg hundreds of miles from Cape Race, the last finger of Newfoundland, at a point where the sea was 13,000 deep. The accident happened 1,070 miles from New York and 2,020 from Southampton; two-thirds of the way to safe haven. He sucked in the flesh of his cheeks and pondered. Even if he steered for the *Titanic*'s last recorded location, 41° 46' N, 50° 14' W, bodies could have floated for miles – he might be hunting for weeks. He folded away his charts. Somebody had to find them and give them a decent burial.

"Send out a request for communication with ships sighting wreckage and bodies," the captain ordered his wireless operator. "We need all the help we can get."

* * *

Kathleen Ryan was unwilling to let Bridie or Hannah out of her sight. These *Titanic* survivors lent her kudos in the neighbourhood – three neighbours had already stopped by to gawp at them. She insisted on leaving Daniel Junior with a neighbour and shepherding them to the church service. When Hannah and Bridie stepped out of their tenement they were awestruck by the tumult of noise, colour and movement in the street. But there was no time to linger. They caught a streetcar, and again Hannah and Bridie were dazed: so many permutations of public transport in this clanging, clanking city. There was the subway for those daring enough to go below ground (the girls were relieved Kathleen didn't suggest it), while electric streetcars whirred along the avenues at ground level and elevated trains ran overhead. Horse-drawn vehicles thronged the avenues, as did spluttering motorcars – automobiles, as Kathleen called them, with that American twang Bridie itched to copy. Horns beeped constantly, louder than the bugle old Commander Browne from Cullen used to warn people off when he cycled. Everyone in this city continually rang bells or tooted horns or, if nothing else was to hand, roared their heads off. The noise never stopped and nobody was fazed by it.

Hannah was disorientated by the cacophony of noise and speed – nothing in her Doon experience had prepared her for this – and she inched closer to her friend. She distrusted the skyscrapers' towering height, secretly convinced sooner or later they would collapse on her. Even years later, she always sidled quickly past them. But Bridie was exhilarated, invigorated by anything new. New York's skyscrapers reminded her of giant pins jammed in a pincushion.

"Why build so high?" Bridie asked Danny that evening.

"Too many people, not enough space."

"The country's enormous – wouldn't people just go somewhere else?"

"Sure everyone wants to live in New York. There's nobody to have a laugh with on the prairies."

At St Patrick's, they were confronted by a sombre black multitude which seemed to share their grief. No seats were reserved, although ambassadors, government ministers and titled folk were among the congregation, and rich and poor sat alongside each other.

My, aren't things done differently in America, thought Hannah, scrutinizing the swarm for that lovely Mrs Armstrong. She was nowhere to be seen.

"Let us bow our head and remember our *Titanic* dead," intoned the clergyman. "Let us pray, too, for the living, that God will give them strength to endure their great loss. The Lord moves in mysterious ways."

Bridie dug her elbow into Hannah's ribs, jerking her head towards Kathleen. She was quivering, eyes squeezed shut and a fat tear trembling on each lash. People darted sympathetic glances in her direction.

"You'd think it was your one who'd just come through shipwreck!" hissed Bridie.

105

"Maybe she's soft-hearted."

Bridie's expression curdled.

Now Kathleen was leaping to her feet as sacred music ballooned from the organ and the congregation raised its communal voice.

Nearer, my God, to Thee,
Nearer to Thee!
E'en tho' it be a cross
That raiseth me,
Still all my songs shall be,
Nearer, my God, to Thee!
Nearer, my God, to Thee!
Nearer to Thee!

Already people were claiming *Titanic*'s orchestra had played the hymn shortly before the finish, but Hannah didn't remember it.

The band plays without pause during the evacuation, Alexander's Ragtime Band keeping spirits up as the passengers wait in line for places on a lifeboat. Hannah sees Tom's right boot twitch. It has an insistence on response, this syncopated rhythm, although it's yet another novelty for them.

"It grows on you," Tom says. "It's more alive than any music I've heard, even a jig." Later when she's in the lifeboat, looking up at the mammoth liner with all of her lights blazing, the music slows its tempo. "Ah, a waltz. Much better than all that ragtime they've been blasting out," Major Hudson remarks. Hannah has never danced a waltz but it looks so elegant, as though the dancers are floating. "How does the orchestra keep playing?" she marvels under her breath. She pictures the bandsmen in their green uniforms plucking at strings and blowing into mouthpieces, and thinks of Tom listening to them too, back on the Titanic.

Bridie tugged at her sleeve and Hannah realized she was still standing, while everyone else was seated. Face burning, Hannah folded herself down beside her and Kathleen. "A *Titanic* widow," someone mumbled, and she gnawed her lower lip. She was no widow, but she had to become one to protect her unborn baby. It was entitled to Tom's name and he'd want the mite to have it. God knows, he had nothing else to give his child. The disadvantages of widowhood, without the benefit of ever having been married, pressed on her. There was no Tom to help her cope with life in this strange new country. No Tom to help her plan for the future. No Tom to help her raise their baby. At least she was in America now – they hadn't turned her away, as she had feared.

"The man with a hundred million dollars stood aside for his wife's serving maid," chanted the clergyman. "The man who swayed continents with his pen remained on the sinking ship that a babe in arms might have his place in a lifeboat!" The congregation was kindled by his oratory but Hannah's mind raced in decreasing circles, fingers tangling in her lap – one of them wearing the brass wedding band Tom gave her for the sake of appearances, rather than the gold ring he promised her. What use was sparing her life if she and her baby had to live in shame and poverty? There was talk of compensation but she wasn't legally entitled to it – Tom's mother was his next of kin.

Her brain searched and discarded. She could take a job and save up for later on, when she was heavily pregnant. But who would look after the child once it was born and she went out to work again? She had no family here to rely on. Bridie Ryan was her only friend in America. Could she even earn enough to support both herself and the child? Keeping body and soul together would be hard enough in this strange new land, without complications.

Then Hannah realized she was lumping in her baby among the complications. She knew she should be grateful for this legacy from Tom but she didn't feel thankful. Just trapped. If only she'd made him wait until they were legally man and wife. She was too eager to climb into his arms, grateful for this chance of a new life in America. The day he showed her the ticket with Mr and Mrs Thomas O'Brien written on it, she joined her fate irreversibly to his. It was the white card with its magical lettering that persuaded her. Mrs Thomas O'Brien, it proclaimed her. Not Miss Hannah Godfrey. She knew what it said off by heart. *Ticket number 37065. Paid £15 10s. Boarding at Queenstown. Third-class.*

Bridie and Kathleen were respectful on the journey home, allowing her space, imagining her brooding was due to heartache. Hannah was engaged in an internal diatribe in which she flailed at Tom for making her pregnant.

You promised you'd be careful! she raged at a dead man. You promised you'd make me your wife. You promised we'd have a life together. You kept none of your promises to me. It was all talk where you were concerned. Talk was cheap with you, Tom O'Brien!

And still her baby thrived inside her.

* * *

Louis Stubel breakfasted in a diner adjoining the Excelsior Hotel on toast, which was adequate, and weak coffee which affronted his taste buds. He was offered pancakes, bulky globes which bore no resemblance to the crêpes of his own country, and declined. Likewise the eggs, "Sunnyside up, over easy, any way you like, buddy": he preferred his eggs whisked into a feather-light omelette but doubted the ability of this establishment to execute it. He would have to investigate New York for a decent French patisserie.

Back in his hotel room, it struck Louis how anonymous furniture became when it occupied a room not owned by the inhabitant. The pieces floated in space like islands. He could not exist without beauty in his life, any more than he could survive without decent coffee, freshly ground. He must locate a florist and buy a buttonhole. A bud of the precise shade of blushing pink worn by Nancy on Lifeboat 16 would lift the parochialism of this city, in which they tried to foist chunky pancakes on a man and stained inferior wood to resemble rosewood. There was still no word from Monsieur Pires about travelling onwards to Boston, as intended. Still, he would use this holiday opportunity, gloomy though the circumstances were, to explore New York.

"*Mon dieu!*" Louis was struck by a thought that weakened his legs beneath him. He sat on the bed. "If I go to Boston I may never see her again."

By and by he rallied. This could not be allowed to happen. He had been saved for a purpose, and that purpose was to love Nancy Armstrong. She was an American, and he would need to understand the American way if he was to win her. Returning from breakfast, Louis had spied a copy of the *New York Times* outside the room next to his. He stepped into the corridor and listened for sounds of his neighbour stirring. All quiet. In that case he saw no reason why he shouldn't borrow the newspaper – his English might need some Americanizing.

He flicked past advertisements for Mrs Adair's Toilet Preparations and La Goute-A-Goute Hair Coloring, to an item that read *Thrilling Story By Titanic's Surviving Wireless Man*. Louis glanced at it, then turning the page, saw another *Titanic* article – the newspaper seemed to contain no other news. This one interested him more, although there was no clear reason why. On the face of it, it was all mumbo-jumbo. Still, concentration knitted his brows.

It has come to this newspaper's attention that an unusual item of freight was carried by the Titanic. *Alongside the millionaires' automobiles, the Parisian couture, the casks of silverware for Tiffany & Co, was a singular and infinitely more ancient passenger. Readers, an Egyptian mummy lay in the hold! This mummy was en route from London's British Museum to a private collector in the US – we are not at liberty to name the party, although his identity is known to the editor. The mummy was that of a priestess called Hetare, a daughter of the Egyptian royal family. She was said to have excited the enmity of the ancient gods because she deserted the religion she was born to serve, that of the god Amen-Ra, and followed her brother the Pharaoh's new religion instead. Hetare was cursed for her heresy – as are all those who come into contact with her. The British Museum sold her to escape this curse but the wrath of Egypt's ancient gods could not be turned aside. It extended even to the ship in which this mummified priestess sailed; and so the accursed one lies at the bottom of the ocean – along with the* Titanic. *Egyptian hocus-pocus, some may say. Others believe the iceberg was pushed into place in the* Titanic's *path by a force more malevolent than our minds can readily encompass, and that those 1,500 souls who lost their lives in its wreck were the unwitting victims of ancient gods whose vengeance could be assuaged only by a blood sacrifice.*

Louis was not superstitious, he believed neither in ancient curses nor retribution from beyond the grave. Yet something made him tear out the article and slide it into his pocket.

* * *

Nancy received a visit from a society doctor engaged by her mother, replacing the family medic who had treated her as a child in Avalon, New Jersey. The newcomer pronounced her a healthy young woman and

109

prescribed light exercise, regular meals, early nights and a glass of milk morning and night.

"We'll take a spin every afternoon in Central Park in an automobile," said her mother. She crossed to the window to admire the view of the park. Automobiles were the playthings of the rich and she intended to be taken for a woman of means.

"Excellent," agreed the doctor, hasping his black leather bag. "Everything is as it should be with regard to your happy event," he added to Nancy.

"Thank you, doctor. That's a relief."

A screech of brakes outside meant Violet missed their exchange.

"Momma, we have no auto to take a spin in every afternoon," Nancy protested when they were alone.

"Automobile. Don't be common, Nancy. It's high time we purchased one – all the best people are driving around in automobiles now."

"I rode in one last Christmas. We had to yell at each other to make ourselves heard – the noise was deafening."

"I'm sure you're exaggerating, Nancy. I really think we ought to consider ordering one, we have a position to maintain."

"Jiminy, I wouldn't know how to choose between autos. Leave it to Samuel when he comes home."

Violet Markova funnelled her gaze onto her daughter. Nancy's blank refusal to accept her widowhood struck her as wilful. She had let it pass the previous evening, attributing it to shock, but it was high time she addressed this. She sat on the edge of the chaise longue where Nancy lay, wavy hair loose on her shoulders and held back from her forehead by a velvet ribbon.

"Darling . . ." She paused while the words took shape in her mind. "You must prepare yourself to accept the fact that Samuel may never come home."

"Fiddlesticks, Momma! I won't listen to such insinuations."

Violet laid a hand on her daughter's. "Nancy, if I could make it different I would. But White Star has precious little hope of finding anyone else."

"What about the ships commissioned to search?"

"They're hoping to find bodies, Nancy, not survivors. Too many days have passed – nobody could possibly be left alive on a raft. There are icebergs out there, you know that better than me. The temperature is simply too cold for survival."

The girl took her head between her hands and shook it from side to side, as though dislodging a buzzing sound. "No," she cried, "no, no, no!"

Violet caught her daughter's wrists and tried to pull her hands away from her head but Nancy struggled against her, still wailing that single-note protest.

Violet rang the bell for Roberge. "Your mistress needs a sedative. Bring me the plaid toilette case in my bathroom."

Roberge took one look at her mistress and flew.

On her return, Violet rooted out a brown phial and measured a dollop the size of a silver dollar into a glass beaker, diluting it with water. With Roberge holding her, Violet managed to force most of the draught between Nancy's lips. Soon she was unconscious.

When Rebecca Armstrong arrived later that afternoon to inspect her son's widow, she met Violet but not Nancy, who was still sleeping. Violet received her in the drawing room and apologised for her daughter's indisposition.

"It's the strain," explained Violet, thrilled to be on speaking terms with one of the 400 of New York society at last. "My daughter is very young and has suffered a great loss."

Rebecca Armstrong was ramrod straight in her chair, the result of a childhood spent walking with a cane across the small of her back and crooked through each elbow to teach her posture. She directed a withering look at this plump woman of forty or thereabouts – at an age she should know better, in any event – wearing scarlet lipstick like a creature of ill-repute. Her hair looked an unnatural shade too. Frivolity eats into the character like acid, thought Rebecca; it was obvious the creature had no moral fibre. How dare she remind her of how juvenile that chit of a girl was! It was the mother's way of advertising her own role in the affair, no doubt. The daughter would have been too inexperienced to snare her son – she must have directed the entire, sordid enterprise.

"I am well aware of the loss your daughter has suffered. My own, I venture to suggest, is no less grievous."

"Naturally." Violet was conciliatory. "But you're a woman who seems capable of enduring much, whereas Nancy" – her hands fluttered, dismissive – "is a mere child." She watched the woman to gauge her reaction. It was essential to have Samuel's mother on side. She had control of the purse strings.

"I have endured," Rebecca conceded, although it was unclear what precisely a woman born into wealth and privilege, who married equal wealth and privilege, might have had to bear. Even widowhood had been a blessing in disguise, for she discovered a live husband was an occasional encumbrance whereas a dead one had his uses. He could be reinvented endlessly as and how it suited.

She stood, signifying her visit was at an end. She had not loosened her furs, removed her gloves or signalled any intention of staying. These upstarts did not deserve that mark of respect from her.

Violet stood too, absorbing the unrelieved black of their visitor's ensemble – a three-quarter length coat, cut away at the front to display the matching dress. It was expensive material, there must be fifteen yards in the train, but the old dear might have managed a brooch at least. She must have barrel-loads of jewels.

"Please don't leave so soon, Mrs Armstrong. Won't you stay to tea?"

"Certainly not. I never take tea out. I only care for it the way my man Powell makes it." Her gaze encompassed the room, rested on a Japanned tray which she could not fault, and moved on to something she could. The frescoes on the ceiling were uncouth. Mistaking her gaze for interest, the Markova woman said they were allegorical, depicting scenes representing virtues and vices in marriage. Really, these people were the height of pretentiousness. Imagine such upstarts reaching close to the upper echelons of society, thanks to her misguided son. Proper social behaviour was a question of tone – these people would never grasp that.

"Perhaps you might call tomorrow? My daughter would be charmed to receive you then," suggested Violet. The matriarch made her nervous, with that frosty stare, but she intended pressing their claims for kinship.

"I think not. I have engagements." The girl's grandfather, her inquiries had revealed, had been an immigrant shopkeeper. Regardless of money, to belong to the best society a person needed at least three

American generations. Rebecca smoothed out an imaginary wrinkle in her glove. "My son's burial will require my attention, apart from anything else."

"Surely it's for me to bury my husband – assuming he needs burial."

Mother and mother-in-law pivoted, to see Nancy just inside the door.

"Darling! I thought you were sleeping."

"Of course he needs burial. You don't honestly imagine he can still be alive. Today is Friday, the *Titanic* sank in the early hours of Monday morning." Rebecca inspected Nancy and thought Samuel a dolt, even if he was dead. She had an appealing face, no-one could deny that, but imagine appearing in public with her hair strewn about so wantonly. Rebecca's lips clamped together as she reviewed this opulence – even in her youthful heyday she had relied on a hairpiece to boost her own limp strands.

Nancy looked at this woman who held herself with an air of entitlement and opened her mouth intending to say "How do you do?" Instead an accusation tumbled out. "You refused to see Samuel before he sailed!"

"That is hardly any of your concern. Good day."

"Nancy, show some respect," scolded her mother. "You're addressing your husband's mother."

"And my son's grandmother."

Rebecca's eyes glittered.

Violet flopped onto a chair, fanning herself with her hand. She was close to swooning, between her emotion and the tightness of her stays. This was perfect, a spare heir for the Armstrongs. She couldn't have planned it better. Her daughter's position was unassailable now.

Rebecca advanced towards Nancy, her face contorted. "You appalling creature! You baggage! How could you be heartless enough to practise this deception? And at such a time!"

Nancy and her mother exchanged mystified looks.

The older woman inhaled sharply. "There is no way you could be carrying my son's child. He had the mumps shortly after Adam was born. His physician confided in me as he lay recuperating. The mumps left him sterile."

9

Edmund Newton availed of the complimentary accommodation at the Excelsior Hotel for a night. The next morning he went out and bought some new horn-rimmed spectacles, after which he transferred from the Excelsior to a more economical establishment. He was on a budget, after all. The Excelsior's shaggy porter recommended the Station House, half a block closer to the railway station and correspondingly noisier, where his brother was night clerk.

The clerk in the new hotel looked Edmund over leisurely. "You one of those *Titanic* survivors? You must be one lucky dog. How come you managed to get in a lifeboat? I heared it was women and children first."

Louis realized how astute the major had been to arrange their testimonials from Lightoller. He did not yet know the overall survival rate for men was just one in five, but understood he was in a minority. It had been obvious on the *Carpathia*. "I swam like the dickens and was picked up by a boat."

"I heared fellows dressed up as women to escape."

"One or two may have, I really couldn't say – I was too busy fighting for my life. I did hear a number of men on the *Carpathia* explain they were obliged to climb into lifeboats to show the ladies they were safe. The ladies were nervous, naturally."

115

The clerk chortled. "Sure, that's why the guys got in the boats!"

A pulse ticked at Edmund's jaw-line. The impertinence of these Americans was beyond belief – they had no concept of their place. If this hotel weren't so keenly priced he'd check out immediately.

"How long you plan on staying?" The clerk took aim and sent a wad of chewing tobacco flying towards a spittoon.

"Not long."

Edmund retired to his room, which was half the size of last night's, with the crushing sense that other people's eggs had two yolks. Still exhausted after his drenching in the Atlantic, he lay on the bed cracking his knuckles, and brooded about the setback to his adventure. Somehow he hadn't the heart to start applying himself to the itinerary devised so assiduously in Dulwich College's staff-room. "Hang it all, I'm only thirty-eight, I should be able to survive a bit of a soaking!" he exclaimed, forgetting the water had been punishingly cold.

After a time the mosaic of his thoughts shifted and realigned, and the Irish girls who saved him preyed on his mind. His conscience pricked for not forcing a few pounds on them before disembarking. The little dark one looked well able to fend for herself, but she had a way of catching her lower lip between her teeth that gave the lie to her feistiness. Perhaps her bravado was just an act and she was as apprehensive about the future as he was. He should nudge the major to find work for the girls. He was bound to know someone who needed a maid – his type was always well connected. Major Hudson had given Edmund his address before disembarking, and he wondered if it would be appropriate to call on him. He realized the major was wealthier than he, but was he so far above him in station that he'd resent Edmund pressing on his attention? Had he supplied his address as a polite gesture with no substance behind it? Maybe their common bond as *Titanic* survivors overcame any ticklishness about social niceties. Edmund fretted over it, in his cramped hotel room near Penn, as the locals referred to Pennsylvania Station.

He had intended to spend two weeks in New York sightseeing, back when he drew up a schedule for his trip. But he found himself uncharacteristically lethargic. Physically he was still at a low ebb after his lengthy immersion, lacking the energy for the tourist trail. His blood was coursing sluggishly in his veins and he wanted no more than to eat and sleep. Yet he felt marooned without company: there had been a sense of camaraderie among the survivors on the *Carpathia* and now that community was lost to him. He cracked his knuckles again and decided to drop a line to Major Hudson. Edmund was dubious about how many daily postal deliveries New York was served by – not as many as London, surely – but there must be at least a morning and an evening post. With luck, he might hear back from Major Hudson that night.

Armed with a sense of achievement and a letter to post, he ventured outdoors in search of food. He fortified himself at something the natives referred to as a lunch counter, on a delicacy new to him called liverwurst sandwich. He had to admit the food was tasty here. Afterwards he sat in the hotel's communal sitting room, where commercial travellers lounged with their sample cases passing time. But all they wanted to do was pump him about the shipwreck, and Edmund had enough of being a peepshow. He retreated to his stuffy room, banging the heel of his hand against the wall in frustration when he tried to open the window and found it painted shut.

By Sunday morning, when his letter had brought no response, he assumed the major was tacitly declining his invitation. "America's not half as exciting as I expected," Edmund told the washstand. Normally scrupulous about religious observances, he did not attend a service. Instead he stayed in bed, shivering with cold although the room was warm, until hunger drove him to get up in the late afternoon. He slouched to the window, where a railway bridge obscured his view. A set of church bells started pealing, persuading him fresh air would be therapeutic, and he decided to go for a walk. He could find a cheap chophouse for dinner afterwards.

Edmund's feet led him towards the Waldorf-Astoria and he gazed at its facade, making comparisons that were far from favourable to the Station House Hotel. Chap needs plenty of the readies to stay in a place like that, he thought. Turning away, he bumped into a young man dressed with exhaustive attention to detail. "Excuse me," he muttered.

A hand on his elbow detained him: it was the major, who fell on Edmund like the prodigal son. He was missing his fellow *Titanic* survivors.

"Nearly missed you there, Newton. You look different with your spectacles on."

Edmund adjusted them on the bridge of his nose, self-conscious. "I dropped you a line." He was studiously casual.

"Did you, Newton? To my apartment in Washington Square? But I'm staying here at the Waldorf-Astoria – my mail hasn't been forwarded to me. I meant to return home today, but somehow I still seem to be . . . at the moment I find it . . ."

He trailed off, at a loss to explain why he was living in a hotel when he had a perfectly comfortable, indeed, sumptuous set of rooms at his disposal. It was almost as though he dreaded the resumption of daily life.

"Convenient," interjected Stuart. "We find it convenient right now."

Edmund contracted an instant dislike for this fop in his high-buttoned suit of a particularly garish check – and was that a horseshoe tie-pin? He looked like a turf accountant. But the major was gazing at him as though perfection glistened from his every crevice.

"I see. Of course." Edmund's tone was shot through with severity.

Stuart fondled his walking stick with a silver key on top – a reference to his college club – and matched Edmund slight for slight. As his father chatted, he made no effort to mask his boredom. He might have to return to college if things didn't liven up around here, although he'd planned to bunk off for the rest of term, citing compassionate grounds. Heck, Pa seemed to be issuing an invitation to this Britisher who looked a thundering bore. The fellow had just asked him what he was studying, as if it mattered which subjects a Yale man took. He was there to make contacts, not worry about a degree.

"Have you dined, Newton? Do come and tuck in with Stuart and me."

Stuart stifled a yawn and adjusted his tiepin.

* * *

Major Hudson forced himself to wait until after the Filet Mignon had been eaten and the cheeseboard was in front of them before he posed the question that flailed at him. "Why did she sink?"

"We sailed too northerly a course and hit an iceberg."

"Yes, that's the physical reason. But what's the true reason? Have we grown too egotistical in this machine age of ours? Do we believe man has mastered all before him? Could this have been a reminder that we're inherently puny, despite our accomplishments?"

From under his eyelids, Edmund peeked at Stuart. The major's son crumbled a cracker and maintained a bland exterior, although he was assessing whether he could slip out to a playhouse near Times Square – he'd heard the chorus girls there were peaches. It was becoming tedious, this constant banging on about the *Titanic*. He wondered what the chaps at Yale were doing that night – playing a hand of poker, perhaps. He'd be better off in Connecticut than in New York with Pa in his current state of rampant morbidity.

No help there, thought Edmund. He loaded a cracker with a wedge of Stilton and injected a note of brisk commonsense into his voice, as though dealing with a mopey first-former. "We sank because we were going full-tilt with a poor look-out in an ice region. A great gash along the side made the watertight doors useless. They were supposed to seal off within twenty-five or thirty seconds of being activated, and make her unsinkable as long as any rip was confined to a couple of compartments. (*Notes 3*) If there was presumption, it lay in the ice warnings being ignored. It did not arise from man using his God-given ingenuity to construct the *Titanic* in the first instance."

A grandfather clock chimed in a room beyond theirs.

"That's balderdash!" Major Hudson exploded. "There must be a message in it – there has to be more to the sinking that that!" He dropped his napkin and excused himself. "Bit tense, I'm afraid. Think I need some tobacco to calm down. I'll shoot up to the suite for my pipe."

In his absence, Stuart tapped his forehead significantly. It was, Edmund noticed, rather a high forehead, soon to become higher when Stuart's cinnamon-coloured hair would begin receding from it shortly after his twenty-first birthday. "Old man hasn't been the same since this *Titanic* business. Nerves are shot to pieces. He isn't getting any younger, I guess."

"It was a most trying experience, I assure you. Your father's entitled to feel agitated."

"Still, I'm surprised he's so upset. He saw some sights in his Cavalry days, after all. He's not exactly a greenhorn."

Edmund struggled to contain his aversion to the major's son. This whippersnapper had no right to judge: he hadn't been in a lifeboat surrounded by icebergs, unsure if help would come. He'd been at his Ivy League college, drinking and playing cards with his Scroll and Key chums, spending his allowance with the abandon of one who knows he only has to hold out his hand for more. He'd made a point of letting Edmund know the name of his frat club. As if a Cambridge man cared tuppence for the Scroll and Key club or the Grill Room Grizzlies, or any of those ridiculous affectations. Edmund looked at him with all the pent-up inferiority which had dogged his college years.

Stuart recoiled. He didn't know what was bothering this irredeemably pompous Britisher. Perhaps he was born with a poker up his butt – the fellows said all Englishmen were. He wanted this snooty Newton to wipe that supercilious smirk off his face. And then to agree to keep his father company, so he could cut along and admire some chorus girls' calves. He was twenty years of age and the weekend was nearly over. It was unnatural to be closeted with a pair of dry old sticks when there was a city throbbing with energy outside these four walls. There was something about the camber of a chorus girl's legs as they curved down to the ankles that made Stuart feel intoxicated with life.

When the major returned, a pipe clamped between his teeth, they adjourned to the library for coffee and liqueurs. Stuart excused himself, claiming he'd promised to look in on some fellows for a game of pool.

"Newton will keep you company, Pa," he volunteered on Edmund's behalf.

"Delighted," said Edmund, who was. He had no desire to rush back to his hotel room, where the window-panes rattled every time a train passed.

"Good idea." The major, humour restored, sent out a cloud of tobacco smoke. "You should get out and meet some young blood. I've had you cooped up here most of the weekend." He turned to Edmund as Stuart departed. "What are your plans, Newton? Seen much of New York?"

"I was thinking of moving on, to be honest. Don't seem able for the hustle and bustle right now. Thought I might push on through the state, just hop a train and see where your railroad brings me."

"Say, perhaps you could go to Washington and look in on the Senate hearings. They were being relocated to DC today."

The investigation had opened on Friday morning in a room of the hotel Edmund was dining in. "I suppose they must be public. Did you drop in on any of the sessions?"

"Matter of fact, I did. I called into the East Room for Ismay's testimony. He was first up. They gave him a bit of a grilling. Bear in mind he was pooped after everything that's happened, but he handled himself well." The major sucked on his pipe. "Dashed thing, though. Ismay said if the *Titanic* had hit the iceberg head-on she'd be here today. Senator Smith checked it with him and he repeated it. The newsmen are lapping it up. I'd have liked to stay longer but Stuart was a little bored by it all." The major meditated on his son, regretful he had only one. His father had impressed on him the need for members of the Anglo-Saxon race to reproduce as copiously as possible. "We owe it to the future of the United States to spread around our superior blood strain," he had explained. Jean, however, had been unable for the burden of repeated childbearing.

Edmund recalled him to the present. "Is Ismay finished?"

"Absolutely. Oh, they'll pretty it up, delay it for a time and then say he has to retire for the sake of his health, but I give him a year until he's out. Business is cutthroat, Newton. The Indians scalped a man more humanely."

"Actually," Edmund gave an apologetic cough, "I meant was his testimony finished?"

"Oh, I see. He asked leave to go home to England but Smith refused, said further questions might be necessary. Think he's showing who's boss."

"What did you make of the chairman, Senator Smith?"

"Ambitious. But he may well be the man for the job. He does most of the questioning, the other senators tend to observe. He was pushing for an acknowledgement of negligence but Ismay held him at bay. I imagine Smith will take the same tack in his questions to the crew."

"Important, eh?"

"I should say so. It allows passengers or kin to sue the owners of the White Star Line, if negligence can be established." The major removed his pipe and held it by the bowl. "These hearings are causing quite a stir – on both sides of what you call the herring pond, I shouldn't wonder – and they'll continue to raise hackles one way or another. The Hearst rags are screaming never mind all that talk of chivalry and Captain Smith telling his men to be British – there'd have been no need of that gentleman's code of conduct they're so proud of if he'd slowed down in ice, or stopped the engines and floated until morning."

Edmund nodded. "They have a point, but I can hear axes being ground over this one." He swirled his brandy in its glass bowl and inhaled. This was the life! If only he could afford to check into the Waldorf-Astoria. "I say, I heard this Senate investigation has powers of subpoena over British citizens. I call that a bally outrage – it's a provincial display of authority."

"Provincial? We're not part of your empire any more, Newton. Besides, White Star is owned by Pierpont Morgan. Once you pierce the corporate shell it's essentially American. As for subpoenas, the *Titanic* was serving American ports and soliciting passengers in the United States. The American people have a right to answers about the ship's approach to safety."

The major's tone was mild, but it reminded Edmund he was a US citizen for all his Anglophilia. Edmund recalled, in addition, whose brandy he was drinking. "Of course. We all want answers."

They settled into a comfortable silence, firelight winking off the crystal edges of the brandy decanter left on their table by the waiter. The major found Edmund a restful companion. By and by Edmund had a sneezing attack.

"If you don't mind my saying so, you seem a little under the weather, Newton. Perhaps you should see a quack?"

He snuffled into a handkerchief. "Been feeling jaded since that soaking I took in the Atlantic. A good rest will cure it."

"Nothing like activity for taking a man's mind off his ailments," said the major, who did not believe in men mollycoddling themselves. "You ought to get yourself off and have a listen at the Senate inquiry."

"You could have a point. *Quis custodiet ipsos custodes?*"

"Hrmph. Seem to have forgotten most of my schoolboy Latin."

"Who will guard the guardians?" Suddenly, Edmund had a vision of

himself as a monitor for fair play. His letter to *The Times* had given him a taste for newspaper correspondence, and he wondered if he could be engaged to write a number of reports from the hearings. After all, he was virtually on the spot, give or take a train journey. Perhaps he could offer a series of letters from Washington: *Our correspondent's view from the bridge*. By Jove, he'd do it! First thing tomorrow morning he'd telegraph to the editor volunteering his services.

"I do believe America really is the land of opportunity. Just being here seems to make me want to give things a try."

* * *

Astor, Guggenheim, Widener, Straus and Butt were the names that took precedence in American obituary columns – in which Tom O'Brien could not figure at any level. Samuel Armstrong did rate a mention, however. His mother had his appreciation notice framed in black and hung on her dressing-room wall, studying it daily while she was laced into her whalebone corset. Phrases such as "prominent family" comforted Rebecca Armstrong. All her hopes rested on Adam now. She would personally oversee his education: he would not be allowed to become a dandy or an idler. His father's divorce of Cora and marriage to Nancy had to be due to some slackness in Samuel's upbringing. Rebecca was determined Adam would be protected from similar neglect. Sometimes Adam sneaked in and read the testimonial to his father. It represented a death sentence of sorts for him too, because it meant he was condemned to live with his grandmother until he reached his majority.

Hannah tore a photograph from the newspaper and pinned it above the mattress she shared with Bridie. It showed the *Titanic* sinking in a blaze of lights with the legend *Nearer My God To Thee*. Hannah liked the idea of Tom being held in God's hand as death loomed. She worried that his refusal to go to Confession at Queenstown might tell against him when he went before the Judgement Seat. Most of the Irish passengers had queued for absolution before boarding, herself included. Please let Tom have recited an Act of Contrition before he drowned, she thought. There would have been plenty of time.

Nancy's newspaper copy of Samuel's obituary was too wet to frame because she wept over the words, seeing her dream fragment. Yet she remained reluctant to admit her husband was dead. Simply because they wrote it in the newspaper didn't make it true. She wouldn't don mourning – not yet.

Violet was too busy spewing retribution against Rebecca Armstrong and her wicked insinuations to think about ordering mourning clothes. "It's slander, appalling slander!" she spluttered.

"But Samuel did have the mumps, you know, not long after Adam was born."

"You don't understand, child. Rebecca Armstrong is implying your baby isn't Samuel's. It's a monstrous allegation. Not only is it a slur on your reputation, it will affect your financial position. I believe the old witch is bent on having his will revoked. Do you know its provisions?"

"I never asked him – it never occurred to me. I naturally assumed Samuel would care for me always."

"We need to arrange a meeting with his lawyers, darling. Your position is far from guaranteed and I, for one, won't sleep easy until it's clarified."

"Jiminy, Momma, I can't possibly consider money at a time like this."

"Oh course not, darling – leave everything to me."

Violet couldn't believe the idiocy of the man, surrendering his seat on a lifeboat to some peasant woman. Imagine exposing his wife to this unpleasantness! She had specifically raised Nancy to be cherished by a wealthy man, not thrown to the wolves by one. If she had it to do over again she would never encourage Samuel Armstrong's courtship. She would have shown him the door and yielded the field to that mannerly factory owner from Maine. Still, those Armstrongs couldn't be left to ride roughshod over the Markovas, for all their wealth and status.

Violet had an inspiration. Instead of dealing with lawyers, she'd pay a visit to Rebecca Armstrong and settle this nonsense about their grandchild's paternity woman to woman. She'd threaten publicity – that should take the wind out of the old lady's sails. Such a pompous family would never tolerate its name used as tittle-tattle in the public arena. They needn't think they could get away with some hole-in-the-corner deal, either. Violet Markova intended to drive a tough bargain on her daughter's behalf – the grandchild too, of course. Violet had mixed feelings about being a grandmother.

"I'm too vivacious to be a grandmomma," she told the cheval glass in her room.

By which she meant too young. Still, Nancy's pregnancy would help secure her daughter's future. Violet's too, naturally.

*   *   *

The Lower East Side was foreign to the point of outlandish to Bridie and Hannah. Nothing prepared them for this squawking, vibrant world which was their new neighbourhood. It wasn't just the congestion, the racial mix – it was the sheer otherness of it. Everywhere their eyes landed they were met by the unfamiliar. The tapering houses seemed to jostle the skyline, so that only patches of blue could be glimpsed. Every back stoop was occupied by women until long after sundown. Sometimes they worked, shelling peas or darning clothes, and sometimes they folded their arms and surrendered themselves to the pleasure of gossip. Children pitched balls at each other in the street, traders wheeled handcarts, horses clattered past as did the occasional car, horn tooting impatiently and clouds of dust raised. Some of the smaller children didn't know to move out of the path of these shiny black monsters and stood, mesmerised, causing the driver in his goggles and dust-coat to swerve, or an older sibling to dash out and snatch them to safety.

Into this miscellany were lobbed snatches of the recognizable: Irish accents, although there were also American, Italian, German, Yiddish and the vowel-caressing speech of the black population; Irish food including boiling bacon, although there was also chop suey, pizza and sauerkraut; Irish laments spilling from the saloon on the ground floor of the apartment block next to them, although there were also arias from German operas, French torch songs, plantation spirituals and gondola songs.

Bridie and Hannah were bemused by the hotchpotch. But Bridie, a city girl by instinct, quickly grew to revel in it. She admired the clothes the women wore, of a cheaper cloth but closely modelled on society ladies' wardrobes. The young women worked hard but they had money in their pockets, and in the evenings they tripped out in their finery, hair fluffed at the front or built up in a pompadour. Some of them wore the daring new pneumonia blouses made from diaphanous material, with collarless square or V-shaped neck-lines. "Downright immodest – those girls will get what they deserve," Kathleen denounced them. But Bridie longed for one.

She noticed how American girls deliberately set out to catch a fellow's eye, teasing and flirting, and paraded a beau with pride. Bridie saw no reason why women were supposed to feign disinterest in men. "The lads are just as well got as the lasses," she told Hannah. She was amazed at how American men also liked to dress up, wearing colours an Irishman would shrink from. Even Freddie Bowe-Spencer, for all his fancy ways, would never have worn such dandified ensembles.

The relationship between men and women here struck Bridie as more equal than at home, where voluntary segregation was practised. It all changes once they're married, though, she thought, noticing how Kathleen had no time to promenade in the evening. She didn't even eat with Danny, instead serving him when he came in at night and fell on his food, ravenous. Husbands seemed to be a liability. Single women had more independence, more disposable income and more fun, whereas marriage meant children and a grinding workload.

Dressing up and being taken to those Bowery beer gardens and dance halls she'd heard about was more to Bridie's taste. Not that Danny let her within a hen's kick of such places – he took the protective brother role too seriously for her liking. She was impressed by the assurance of these big, handsome Americans of both sexes, who walked confidently, refusing to be stared down. It was ungainly, perhaps, that stride of theirs, but it was liberating. Bridie practised the walk when no-one was looking, flinging out her limbs like a Yank.

Hannah, however, shrank incrementally, retreating inside herself. She longed for Doon, for the winding boreens where she wandered as a girl with her sisters, picking wild flowers which lived scarcely a day in jam-jars, and for the stream filled with tiny, pulsing brackeens where she fished with her brothers. She wanted to sniff air that smelled of misty rain and peat fires, of her father's snuff and her mother's soda bread.

There was no birdsong in this place. "Why were you bringing me here, Tom?" she reproached his shade, forgetting the constant scrabble to earn a living at home.

She felt hemmed in by the cheek-by-jowl accommodation. The whitewashed cottages of Ireland with their thatched or corrugated tin roofs were small, but at least families had their own front door. Here there were four families to a floor and the daily routine was conducted on intimate terms with their neighbours. They seemed to share a home, not just with Danny and Kathleen Ryan and their son, but with the thirteen other families in the tenement. Hardly a minute in the day passed without children wailing or quarrelling, drunks singing or shouting, men coughing or swearing, couples bickering or making love.

"Danny and I won't be in a tenement forever," said Kathleen. "We'll have a house of our own by the time this little fellow is knee-high to a grasshopper. He's a grafter, my man, he's never had a day sick off work. There's always another boatload from the old country arriving at the docks, younger, stronger fellows, but he keeps his head down and slogs away."

Bridie pulled a face behind her back. "She should give her tongue a rest," she mouthed at Hannah.

Hannah occupied a parallel plane of existence, however, only intermittently aware of the others. It seemed scarcely credible that Tom was gone but a baby planted by him was left behind to grow inside her. She rested her hands on her stomach, puzzling at what lay on the other side of it. Some people called a child a gift from God but this baby was no gift – it was a reminder of her transgression. Hers and Tom's. But hers was the greater sin because women were supposed to say no. She'd caught sight of Tom on these teeming New York streets a dozen times. She'd be walking along and a man might turn his face toward her, and for a split-second she'd think it was her man.

Hannah looks back towards Tom as the lifeboat jerks down the side of the Titanic. He seems a slender figure – boyish, even. He raises a hand in farewell and she drops Bridie's to wave back with both hers above her shoulders. Then she cups her hands around her mouth to amplify her voice.

"Goodbye, Tom!"

She's uncertain if he hears, but he smiles at her. Hannah tries smiling

*back, but feels too overwhelmed. She's distracted by Samuel Armstrong
standing next to Tom. Such a debonair figure, in his cutaway coat, blowing a
kiss to his wife. Just then the lifeboat tilts, the Atlantic dauntingly far below,
and she grabs Bridie around the waist. When she searches Tom out again, the
angle is too steep and his deck is out of sight.*

*Goodbye, Tom. Is that the best she could do? As the boat wallows by the
side of the* Titanic, *she jeers at herself for not managing something more
memorable. There wasn't even time for a kiss in all the commotion. She
assumed he was coming with her – it never occurred to her they'd be
separated.*

Sometimes Hannah thought the versions of Tom she saw on Canal
Street or Eldridge Street might allow her to say a more memorable
farewell, but the phantoms always evaporated before she could find the
words.

"I'm having our baby, Tom."

Those would have been words worth cupping her hands around her
mouth. She should have called them out to him as the lifeboat was
lowered, never mind who was listening. Would knowing he was to be a
father have made death easier – or harder? She hadn't wanted to say
anything until after he made her his wife, preferring to believe he'd do
right by her without pressure.

Hannah would have liked to be left alone to inhabit her reverie, but
the living pressed their claims. Bridie kept nipping at her heels about
communicating with Tom's mother in Bonavie. She knew Margaret
O'Brien by sight, a cottage loaf of a woman who only removed her apron
once a day – to go to bed – and twice on Sundays because of Mass.

"His mother will want to know the details of his last moments,"
Bridie urged. "It's only natural."

Bridie felt guilty she hadn't spoken out louder for the lifeboat to pick
up bodies thrashing in the water. She could have supported Hannah
when she pleaded with the rowers to turn back for the love of God –
weren't they all some mother's son? She could have said something
when there was a chance Tom might have been saved. Or someone else's
Tom. This was her way of making amends.

Hannah didn't want to write to the widow – she felt like an impostor.
Tom's mother was Mrs O'Brien, not her.

But Bridie persisted. "Come on, a field was never ploughed by turning it over in your mind."

Finally Hannah sat at the table, smoothed a sheet of ivory paper and chewed her thumb knuckle for inspiration. She crimped her forehead and wrote "*Dear Mrs O'Brien*". That was the easy part.

"Shouldn't you call her 'mother' or 'mother-in-law'?" Bridie read over her shoulder.

Hannah clenched the pen nervously, expecting it to trail ink-blots across the page. The nib scratched as she drew a line through the telltale words.

Tuesday, April 23rd, 1912

Dear Motherinlaw,

I am sure it is a Shock for You to be called that by me. I am sorry to Inform you that your Son Tom died on The Titanic. We were after buying a ticket as husband and wife to go to America. He was intinding for to write from Chicargo and Tell you about our getting Married. I know this will come as a Fearfull Shock and I am sorry for your Trouble.

The page was almost full and Hannah hoped not to continue to a new sheet. She looked up at Bridie. "Would that be enough, do you think? The pen is hurting my hand."

"Could you not tell the poor woman he was asking for her at the end? It might ease her mind."

"Sure he did no such thing!"

"*I'll find a place on another boat, never you worry, darlin'. God bless and keep you.*" Those were the last words he'd spoken to her. They were hers alone, she wasn't sharing them.

"There's no harm in a little white lie to soften the truth. And you'd best tell her about the babogue while you're about it. The woman has a right to know."

Hannah bent her plaited head to the table.

Toms last words were tell Mam and all the Lads in Bonavie I am thinking of them.

Your loving daughter
Mrs Hannah O'Brien (Hannah Godfrey that was)

How quickly she was growing accustomed to signing the name she wasn't entitled to use. The more times she wrote Hannah O'Brien, the greater her sense of ownership of it. She studied the missive. There was a thumb smudge on the word "inform" where Hannah had erased an extra syllable, and she'd lost her nerve about spelling 'affectionate' halfway through, substituting "loving". But her handwriting had neat spacing and looped aesthetically, as she'd been taught at the village school.

"You forgot to mention the little stranger."

"I don't like to tempt fate. I'll tell them when I'm further along."

She didn't want it going back to Ireland she was pregnant already – the neighbours would claim it was why she had eloped.

She licked the envelope flap, hoping that would be the end of her dealings with Tom's family.

10

Galvanised by his dinner with the Hudsons, Edmund Newton lay awake most of the night with his mind fomenting. He was seized, as the major had been – as many of the *Titanic* survivors would be – by the conviction his life had been spared for a reason. But what was that reason? To ensure such a disaster never happened again? To represent those who weren't saved? He kept returning to Major Hudson's advice to look in on the US Senate hearings and his own notion of volunteering to report on them for *The Times*. Perhaps his purpose, in being spared, was to monitor the inquiry; presumably its functions must include highlighting a campaign for increased safety measures at sea. Edmund dozed off at dawn, believing he had found his answer.

The following morning, sizzling with nervous energy, he wired collect to *The Times* in London. He offered services as a correspondent at the Washington hearings, pointing out his special status as a *Titanic* survivor, and reminding the newspaper of the letter sent from the *Carpathia* as proof of his journalistic potential. After his weekend of self-doubt and apathy, Edmund was fired by the idea of action.

As animated now as he had been lacklustre before, he waited a day for a response, fretting that the time difference was acting against him. To kill time, he walked around Pennsylvania Station, where eagles with outspread wings guarded the pillared entrance, and a 277-foot waiting room was tricked out like Roman Baths. It's all so imperial, he thought. He stood for a while on the station concourse to watch trains arrive and depart, but the crowds oppressed him. Edmund hurried back to the safety of his room, where he listened for the bellboy's knock with his commission from the newspaper.

By Tuesday he was tired of waiting. Amazing events might be unfolding at the hearings – he couldn't afford to sit about in New York. He decided to go to Washington anyway, he had nothing to lose. Besides, a train journey to DC, as Americans seemed to refer to their administrative capital, was part of the adventure. He dropped the major a line at the Waldorf-Astoria telling him of his plans. With time to pass before his train left, he lingered to study *Titanic* postcards in a metal rack. The publishers had responded quickly and were having a field day with pious and sentimental offerings. Young women in attitudes of theatrical grief were popular, against a backdrop of a ship with its lights blazing – although the vessel depicted was the *Olympic* and not the *Titanic*.

"You looking at the *Titanic* postcards, buddy? Some disaster." The stall-owner whistled through his teeth.

"I know." Edmund was at his most pompous. "I happened to be on the *Titanic*."

"Oh yeah? How come you survived?"

"By the skin of my teeth." Defensive, he turned away.

* * *

It was too late, when he arrived in Washington, to attend the public hearings. Edmund found a hotel and turned up on Wednesday morning. The April 24th session was jammed with spectators and reporters, just as previous ones had been, and a considerable delay ensued before the session could start while the sergeant-at-arms restored order. This was already the fifth day. These Yankees certainly get down to business in a hurry, thought Edmund. Alongside Senator Smith were six other members of the Committee on Commerce's *Titanic* sub-committee, selected for political balance rather than maritime experience.

Edmund recognized McLeod among the audience, the junior officer who had commanded his lifeboat, and nodded at him. But he was watching another officer prepare to take the stand. Fifth Officer Harold Lowe, in charge of Lifeboat 14, was sworn in to give testimony. A hush fell on the stuffy room as Lowe told of leaving it almost an hour before going back to look for survivors, although he'd been only 150 yards away in the nearest boat and it wasn't full.

"I had to wait until the yells and shrieks had subsided – for the people to thin out – and then I deemed it safe for me to go amongst the wreckage. I picked up four people."

"But your boat had, according to your own admission, a water capacity of sixty-five people?" said Senator Smith.

"Yes, but then what are you going to do with a boat of sixty-five where 1,600 people are drowning?"

"You could have saved fifteen!"

"I made the attempt, sir, as soon as any man could do so, and I am not scared of saying it. I did not hang back or anything else."

"I am not saying you hung back. I am just saying that you said you lay by until it had quieted down."

"If anybody had struggled out of the mass, I was there to pick them up; but it was useless for me to go into the mass. "

Edmund realized how lucky he had been to keep a cool head and swim towards Lifeboat 16.

He whisked back to the hotel and composed an article about the officer who rowed back to look for survivors. Senator Smith's prods at Lowe had peeved Edmund, suspecting him of anti-British sentiment. Nevertheless his blood had run cold on hearing the officer, who had taken composure to the point of callousness, speak of waiting until the drowning people thinned out.

He worked at a table in the hotel's lounge. Finishing off, Edmund glanced up to see a young lady reading over his shoulder. Caught red-handed, she smiled under the canopy of her hat. Edmund did not reciprocate the smile. Really, the citizens of this country lacked any concept of polite reserve.

"That's some yarn you're scribbling!"

"It's not a yarn – it's a newspaper report for *The Times of London*."

"That line where you call the ship The Widow-Maker – it's sure got a ring to it. You were at the hearings, weren't you? I saw you jotting away. He was a cold fish, that Lowe character."

"He was only trying to do his duty." Edmund didn't care to hear slighted a fellow subject of His Majesty's Britannic Empire.

"Duty!" She was dismissive. "Men always use that as an excuse. I was on the *Carpathia* too, you know." She tilted her chin to look up at him, the movement stirring marabou feathers on her hat. "You got a way with words. What's your name?"

"Edmund Newton. And you are?"

As she opened her mouth to respond, a bellboy entered the room. "Telephone call for Miss Dorothy Gibson! Miss Dorothy Gibson, telephone call!"

The woman held up a gloved hand. "Excuse me, I must take that."

* * *

Violet Markova was shown into an imposing salon smelling of beeswax, and left alone for longer than was polite. She was wearing her chinchilla again, although it was uncomfortably warm, because a woman needed armour dealing with the Armstrongs. There was ample time to survey a carpet with arabesques that swirled through the wool, lending an impression of perpetual motion, and surfaces crammed with ornaments, ginger jars, framed photographs and vases of flowers.

Adam Armstrong arrived as she lifted a Dresden china shepherdess from a side-table to check its base. "My great-grandmother brought that back from her wedding tour in Europe."

"I declare, how enchanting."

"She and my great-grandfather were particularly fond of German spas – every other year they took the waters." He advanced and shook the fingertips she extended to him. "I'm Adam Armstrong. My grandmother asked me to keep you company until she can greet you herself. She had no forewarning of, ah, the pleasure of your visit and finds herself detained."

Violet accepted the saffron brocade seat he indicated. Too right the old witch had no forewarning; she'd wanted to give her no reason to

134

avoid this confrontation.

"May I offer you some refreshment?"

"Thank you, no. Do you have time off school? Or perhaps you're tutored at home?"

"Sure I go to school, though I have weekend tuition too, but my grandmother thinks I should stay away from classes until after the arrangements. About my father, I mean."

"May I offer my condolences?"

He moved closer to Violet. "Do you know, nobody's said that to me? Everyone sympathises with my grandmother and she didn't care for Papa half as much as I do."

"You bear a marked resemblance to him."

Eager, he was about to question her, when the door opened and Rebecca appeared.

"Run along now, Adam."

"But grandmuh-mother, I'd prefer to stay. Mrs Muh-Markova and I were having a super chat."

"Servants have chats, Adam – people in our position have conversations. You may leave us."

With his hand on the doorknob, he flicked back his fringe and appealed to Violet. "Do you really see a resemblance?"

"A pronounced one, especially about the nose and mouth. You'll be as tall as your father – you may even surpass him in height."

The boy smiled. "You mmm-must see the library before you leave. Its walls have 13th century panels with the earliest known example of the Scriptures translated into Norman French. Grandfather bought them at auction shortly before I was born."

"That will do, Adam." Rebecca preferred people to believe their treasures were inherited. When he left the room, she turned face-on to Violet. "This is unexpected."

Violet Markova's arch manner sugar-coated a determined nature. "I hardly imagine so. You can't have expected us to vanish off the face of the earth."

Rebecca's face betrayed a desire that mother and daughter should do exactly that. Violet sailed on. "We have a lot to discuss, you and I. It was hardly appropriate for us to do so the other day, in view of my daughter's condition. She needs rest and quiet."

"Your daughter's condition is of no concern to me, as I believe I made abundantly clear." Rebecca turned her back on this overdressed china doll of a woman and walked to the fireplace. She adjusted a length of antique lace decorating the mantelpiece and waited for Violet to be intimidated into leaving. Rebecca mistrusted women who did not act their age.

Violet refused to be cowed by the ramrod spine or by the physical advantage Rebecca stole by standing while she was seated. "Come, now, Mrs Armstrong. My daughter is expecting our grandchild. Are you really accusing her of cheating on her husband? She's hardly more than a child, only eighteen years of age. She could no more be faithless than she could jump off the new Woolworth Building."

Rebecca spun about, chips of ice in her glare. "My son contracted the mumps two months after Adam was born. We sent him to the cottage in Newport to recuperate. The physician who treated him told us his chances of fathering another child were slight."

Violet pounced. "Slight or zero? The difference is substantial."

Rebecca's complexion reddened. "I object to your manner, Mrs Markova."

"I object to your inferences, Mrs Armstrong. Yesterday you used the term 'sterile' when you effectively accused my daughter of foisting another man's baby on her husband. Once more I ask you, slight or zero?"

"Slight," she conceded.

"In which case, fatherhood is not impossible."

"Not impossible, but improbable."

"That's for a court to decide."

"You'd drag my son's name through the courts?" Rebecca grasped the arm of a chair for support.

"I wouldn't drag the name of my grandchild's father through the courts. But I must do what's necessary to protect my daughter."

"This is blackmail! I shall consult my lawyer."

"As I shall consult mine."

Violet rose and they faced each other, the older woman breathing heavily. Violet gave no sign of stress, although her heart drummed a tattoo in her eardrums. Rebecca rang a bell at her elbow and a footman appeared.

"Laski, show Mrs Markova out."

* * *

Louis loitered by a 24-hour coffee stand, trying to drum up the courage to follow through with his plan. He had run out of money, having left his wallet inside the jacket he threw off to climb into the lifeboat. Monsieur Pires was paying the hotel bill but no wages were being forwarded to him. His employer was even less eager to take to the seas after the *Titanic* disaster, and until he arrived his secretary was free to kick up his heels in New York. But in the meantime Louis had to earn some dollars. He knew what he was proposing to do wasn't gentlemanly but needs must when the devil beckons. Taking a deep breath, he entered the reception area of the *New York American*.

The reporter lapped up his fantasy about rioting on the ship after the lifeboats were gone, with people "slugging it out and decking each other" – the reporter's phrase, not his; about seeing officers shooting passengers and crewmen alike to quell the disturbances; about a Chinaman letting down his pigtail so he looked like a woman and tricking his way onto a boat; about an Italian knocking over a mother with a baby in her arms and trying to take her place, until pinned down by three sailors. Was it all too excessive, he wondered? On the contrary, excess seemed most acceptable in this country. Louis's piece de resistance was his description of First Officer William McMaster Murdoch raising his gun to his temple, saluting and pulling the trigger before the ship went down. He considered giving this honour to Captain Smith but there were too many conflicting reports of his last sighting.

The reporter was avid as he scribbled. "Did you see any of the swells before they died? John Jacob Astor?"

"I spoke to him briefly. He wiped away a tear as he mentioned his wife."

"Dame by the name of Madeleine?" prompted the reporter.

"Yes, Madeleine. He said, 'Tell Madeleine never to forget me and never to doubt that I love her'." Louis hesitated, wondering if he should condemn the young woman to eternal widowhood. "He also said she should marry again. 'She's too young to wear black for the rest of her life,' said Astor. Then a wave washed him overboard and it was all I could do to save myself."

"How did you save yourself, buddy?"

Louis knew his account of shipboard pandemonium leaked like a sieve unless he claimed he'd been on the *Titanic* almost until the last. He borrowed Edmund Newton's story. "I climbed on a rail and jumped as the ship went down, then I swam like a man possessed. I made it as far as a lifeboat and by great fortune I was pulled on board. Two girls – Irish, I think – rescued me. All I remember is kissing their hands in gratitude and passing out. I looked for them on the *Carpathia* to thank them but I never did find my guardian angels. They must have been too modest to come forward."

"So you never got to give them a reward or anything?"

"No, to my eternal regret. Of course I lost everything when the ship went down, but I'd gladly press into the hands of my saviours every one of the dollars promised to me by your newspaper – 100, wasn't it? – if I could only identify them."

"Gee, maybe we could run an appeal for them to come forward and you could hand the money over?" The reporter had a vision of a follow-up story, complete with photograph, as Frenchie here was reunited with his guardian angels thanks to the *New York American*. Something with angels and colleens in a banner headline. The boss loved all that schmaltz.

Louis winced for his alibi. "I'm afraid I can't describe them. They may have been English, they may have been Swedish, I couldn't say for certain. Actually, I think there were three women involved in the rescue, and a young boy, and a . . . yes, a dog. Or was I hallucinating? Once I reached the lifeboat, everything becomes unclear."

"Too bad." The reporter snapped his chewing gum. "How about any of the other big-shots, they say anything to you? Did ya see the painter fellow, Frank D Millet? Usedta be a famous war correspondent, heard he was travelling with Major Butt, the President's aide. "

"I spoke to a hotelier called Armstrong."

Louis knew he hadn't, but who could call him a liar? There had been so many people milling around the boat decks, anything was possible in the confusion.

"Samuel Armstrong? The one who caused the scandal by divorcing his wife and marrying a little nobody?"

"Mrs Armstrong struck me as somebody. Most decidedly somebody."

"Sure, buddy, whatever you like. What did Armstrong have to say for himself?"

Louis reflected. Perhaps he could offer Nancy some consolation for the loss of her husband – even if his death was convenient for Louis. "He said his wife was expecting their child and called himself the proudest man on the ship. 'My only regret is that I'll never see my son or daughter. But a man couldn't have asked for a more devoted wife than Nancy and I know she'll raise our little one as a worthy successor to the Armstrong heritage.'."

"And like a true American?" the reporter coached him.

"Yes, like a true American."

"Believe we have a page lead here."

The newspaper's picture desk turned up a file photograph of Nancy and Samuel embarking on their wedding tour the day after their marriage, and splashed a story about the "bride-widow" being urged to raise the dead man's child like a true American. Louis's allegations about the First Officer's suicide caused outrage in London, while the Ambassador from Rome called on him to retract his slur against Italian men; the Chinese had no ambassador and registered no protest.

On Fifth Avenue, Nancy read his words and puzzled over them. Was it possible that Samuel and Louis Stubel had spoken before the Frenchman boarded her lifeboat? She had lost sight of her husband for a while in the mêlée. It seemed unlikely Samuel would have discussed her pregnancy with Louis – but the usual rules had been suspended during those last hours on the *Titanic*. But why would Stubel claim he was pulled from the water when he had climbed down a rope with a baby? It didn't make sense. Nevertheless Nancy clung to the consolation of Samuel's message: he had called her a devoted wife.

"Do you know this man, Louis Stubel?" Violet took the newspaper from her daughter's hands.

She hesitated. "We shared a lifeboat."

MARTINA DEVLIN

"You should invite him here – he could pass on Samuel's final communication to you in person."

Nancy remembered how Louis had looked at her – and how she had looked back at him. It unnerved her. "I really have no wish to hear Samuel's final message from his lips. It's enough to see it written here."

Little nincompoop, thought Violet. Surely she realized Louis Stubel's intervention couldn't have come at a more opportune moment? It proved Samuel knew Nancy was carrying his child and acknowledged paternity.

"His mother might wish to hear if he had any words for her. Where better for her to be introduced to him than in your home?"

"I'm not sure it's a good idea, Momma. I met Mr Stubel, you know – there was something about him I . . ."

"Didn't care for?"

"Not exactly." Nancy tried to blot out the intensity with which he had stared at her.

"What then? Violet inhaled, her diaphragm testing her dress fabric more than was advisable. She suspected she had sheltered her daughter too carefully. What did it matter if she had reservations about the fellow, so long as he was ammunition against the Armstrongs?

"I can't explain why. I just don't want to see him again, Momma."

* * *

The newspapers showed no sign of tiring of the *Titanic* tragedy. They dwelled on John Jacob Astor who once said, "A man who has a million dollars is as well off as if he were rich." On mining heir Benjamin Guggenheim, whose dying message for his wife was written down by a steward so he would not forget it: "If anything should happen to me, tell my wife in New York that I have done my best in doing my duty." A more imaginative newspaper parlayed it as, "Tell her that this is a man's game and I played it to the end. Tell her that no woman was left on board the ship because Ben Guggenheim was a coward." On the loss of streetcar magnate's wife Mrs George Widener's pearls, and a 1598 edition of Francis Bacon's essays recently bought by her son Harry, who said before he died: "Mother, I have placed the volume in my pocket –

the little Bacon goes with me."

Kathleen absorbed it all and repeated it to Hannah and Bridie, avid for their insights. Sometimes they humoured Kathleen, since they were under her roof, but at times Hannah wished never to hear the name *Titanic* again while Bridie grew crotchety at her sister-in-law's insatiable curiosity. No story was too far-fetched – her credulity was limitless.

"I saw Mrs Widener's pearls – they were the size of pigeon's eggs," Bridie confided, Kathleen's eyes dilating. "She had a matching tiara too. One of them purser fellows let me try it on. He sneaked me down a staircase made of solid silver to show it to me. It was locked in a safe but he had the key and took the tiara out and I had a wear of it. I felt like a queen." She checked Kathleen's expression for scepticism but her sister-in-law was mesmerised. This was no fun – it was like taking candy from a baby. Bridie was collecting Americanisms to drop into conversation, she wanted to become as Yankee as those bold-eyed girls she admired.

Rumours persisted that the *Titanic* had been an argosy, stuffed with jewels and antiques. People who struggled to pay the rent on one-room homes speculated about the extent of the cache lost with the liner. There was a certain satisfaction in dwelling on all those Mrs Wideners denuded of their pearls – even if they had other baubles at home.

"I hear some of them are crying more about losing their necklaces than their husbands," Kathleen told the front stoop gathering.

"You don't have to be a society lah-de-dah to like jewellery better'n husbands!" laughed a neighbour.

These women in the Lower East Side were not envious – instead they relished stories of waterlogged booty as a respite from the humdrum. They picked over them while they scrubbed their clothes or sweated at their irons. The disparity between rich and poor yawned. The multi-millionaires who sailed on the *Titanic* were the world's most affluent elite and not slow to flaunt their spending power. Gold plate gleamed on their tables, vintage wines were racked in their cellars, jewels hocked by indigent European nobles glowed on their wives' bosoms.

But their money had not saved them. The public had a ringside seat on the scale of their excesses and the *Titanic* tragedy gave them a rare chance to patronise their betters.

"A ballroom in his house wasn't much good to Astor when push came to shove," said Danny Ryan.

When they wearied of discussing lost treasure, there were the search vessels to speculate on. Would they find bodies and would they be identifiable?

"What if their faces are eaten away by sharks? Or if the flesh has all been sucked off by octopuses?" Kathleen moistened her lips.

"Kathleen, show some respect!" Bridie nodded towards Hannah.

Hannah was in a trance, wondering how she'd react if officials told her they had found Tom's body. She wouldn't like to be asked to identify it, after hearing about corpses bloated beyond recognition. But she would prefer, for his sake, that he had a Christian burial – somewhere herself and the baby would be able to visit and lay flowers in remembrance. Then perhaps she'd stop seeing Tom O'Brien's face in this city where he had never set foot.

* * *

The *MacKay-Bennett* steamed towards Halifax with a cargo of 190 bodies, among them a small blond boy of about two years. Also found by the search ship were the remains of John Jacob Astor, identified by the initials JJA on the back of his collar – although many were reluctant to discount the rumour it was on account of the extensive quantity of money in dollars, pounds and gold in his pockets. A further 116 disfigured corpses not suitable for embalming were committed to the deep. The *MacKay-Bennett* only carried enough coffins for a little over half of its cargo, and once again class distinctions were made. Second and third-class corpses were placed in canvas bags, with the coffins reserved for first-class.

The *Minia* was left behind to continue the search. "*I expected to see the poor creatures very disfigured but they all looked as calm as if they were asleep. None of us like this job at all but it is better to recover them and bury them properly than let them float about for weeks,*" wrote her wireless operator to his mother. The crew of a passing ship spotted the body of a man in white tie floating twenty-five miles away from the *Titanic's* distress position and contacted the rescue vessel. Blocked by heavy ice in the area, the *Minia* was unable to respond and Major Archibald Butt, the US president's aide-de-camp, went unburied. A memorial service was held for him at which President Taft's voice cracked with emotion as he delivered a eulogy.

An efficient system to aid identification operated. As each body was recovered from the sea, a piece of canvas with a number stencilled on it was attached. Into a ledger was entered a description corresponding to the number: hair colour, height, approximate weight, age and any obvious markings such as scars or birthmarks. With a witness present, an inventory was taken of pockets, money-belts, jewellery and clothes. Addresses on letters were noted, names on passports, numbers on passage tickets, personal photographs found in wallets – all recorded to assist in the identification process. Personal property was placed in canvas bags corresponding to the owner's number for return to relatives.

Bodies were retrieved floating high in the water, in spite of sodden clothes. Some wore layers of clothes as a protection from the cold and all had the lifebelts strapped on which kept them buoyant. In the pockets of most of the crew were tobacco and matches, besides keys to lockers and state rooms. A victim was recovered wearing underpants with H Lyon marked on them, but nobody of that name was listed as crew or passenger. "Imagine dying wearing someone else's drawers," observed a crewman. His shipmate was distracted by the corpse of a young woman wearing a diamond ring. He tried to assess his chances of sliding off the ring without being caught: it was risky but worth a try. He managed it when the older sailor felt nature's call. The thief felt no compunction. It was no use to her now. Finder's keepers. Besides, this was a hellish job, he needed some incentive.

Samuel Armstrong was easily identified by the team on the *MacKay-Bennet*. The silver cigarette-case with the monogram SFA, the gold hunter watch from his parents for his twenty-first birthday inscribed *Time and tide wait for no man*, the pigskin wallet containing a photograph of Nancy all helped to place him. But the dog-eared rectangle of paper which he had kept near him for nine years fragmented as the air made contact with it.

"What's this?" asked the officer noting personal effects. "Looks like some kind of sentimental token."

The man with a stolen ring in his pocket caught a scrap of paper with a train wheel on it. "I think it's a birthday card, sir. Isn't that word 'birthday'?"

The officer peered at the liquefying script. "Can't make head or tail of this. I'll just log it as 'paperwork, illegible'."

* * *

Samuel's family was among those contacted as the *MacKay-Bennett* sailed towards Halifax. The news was sent to his mother, and Rebecca ordered the butler to Novia Scotia to meet the ship and formally identify Samuel's body. It did not occur to Rebecca to consult Nancy.

"I should go with Powell. Someone of Papa's blood ought to identify him," Adam protested.

"Nonsense." Rebecca was crisp. "You are too young for such a charge and I am too old for it. Powell will serve the purpose adequately. He is loyal and discreet."

Adam locked himself in his room and howled, despising himself for his weakness and loathing his grandmother more. When he was a man he would move into his own apartment and never go near her, not even at Thanksgiving. She didn't love him – nobody cared about him. His mother thought only of planning themed parties he was too young to attend. And if he'd been important to his father, he'd never have vanished off for three months to the other side of the world with a new wife. "I miss you, Papa," he sobbed. "Why didn't you love me more?"

11

Powell waited at the quayside as the *MacKay-Bennett* sailed in on the morning of April 30th with her flag fluttering at half-mast. As soon as she appeared on the horizon he removed his bowler hat, holding it carefully between gloved finger-tips and tutting at spots of hair oil on the inner brim. Powell hoped to have Master Samuel's remains released into his custody and to depart later that day. The sooner Master Samuel was interred in the family vault the better. He had already checked out of the Halifax Hotel, leaving his luggage with the young man staffing an information bureau for *Titanic* relatives. The clerk, whom he had routinely tyrannised since his arrival, was equally eager for Powell's departure.

Halifax's usually bustling harbour was empty of craft. A naval band playing the Dead March from *Saul* met the vessel and the coffins were transferred by horse-drawn hearse to a temporary morgue at the Mayflower Curling Rink. Powell paced behind the hearse carrying Samuel Armstrong, through streets which were deserted following an appeal from clergymen for people to keep away.

Quite right, nobody wants to make a spectacle of this, thought Powell.

The curling rink was unrecognizable as a place of amusement. At the western end, benches were set up behind a wooden partition where embalmers went to work. Prepared bodies were carried from there to the main rink, where cubicles had been erected – identification would take place there. Powell waited in the observation room, watching everything closely in case Mrs Rebecca had questions. As he produced his letter of authorization from his employer, there was a commotion among the undertakers: one had found his uncle among the victims and collapsed.

Finally Powell was allowed to step up to a cubicle. An attendant pulled back the covering on Samuel Armstrong's face and Powell swallowed and looked away. He was pasty but it was Master Samuel all right, no mistaking him. His gorge heaved. He had known Master Samuel man and boy. It was Powell who taught him how to play chess and fasten his bow-tie, and later how to mix a martini. "It was a crying shame to see him laid out on a slab," he told the cook subsequently as she poured him a glass of Madeira, making clucking sounds. "At least I spared his mother that sight."

Powell took hold of himself and barked a series of commands, the singsong timbre to his Welsh accent surfacing – something which only happened in times of extreme stress. But his hair remained firmly moulded to his scalp. His mouth puckered as he noticed the casket in which the master was lying; it was quite unsatisfactory, much too plain for a gentleman of his standing. Mrs Rebecca would have something to say about such inferior quality wood. At least White Star had already made travel arrangements with shipping and railroad companies. Powell interrogated a clerk at Halifax Station and was told the coffin could be sent by express to New York for the cost of a first-class fare times two. Or if accompanied, the charge was a first-class fare.

"Which service would you like to avail of, sir?"

"Mr Armstrong's family would never dream of allowing him to make this journey unaccompanied." Powell's expression was forbidding as he passed over some notes. The sooner he was back in the United States the better. He'd had enough of church bells tolling continually. It was respectful, but his head was throbbing. Powell tipped a Negro porter and climbed aboard the train for Toronto, where he'd change for New York. He folded his compact frame into a seat, opened a battered volume,

Victoria, Queen and Ruler, by Emily Crawford, and settled down to his favourite chapter: how the young Queen fell in love with her cousin Prince Albert.

* * *

A Marconigram arrived from Powell. Rebecca was indignant when Adam suggested Nancy had a right to see it. "Don't speak to me of rights! I carried him in my body, I gave him life – any rights are all on my side."

"Grandmmm-mother, she must be told it's official." He almost mastered his stammer. "She is father's widow, after all."

The old woman tried to contradict him, but her features contorted into a grimace and she screwed the Marconigram into a ball. Her son's death, which she had accepted with equanimity initially, became real for the first time with those typed words from Powell. She did not cry, no-one had ever seen her cry, but she averted her head and left the room, skirts rustling with more vehemence than usual. Adam retrieved the rumpled sheet of paper dropped on the rug.

Tuesday April 30th, 1912

BODY RECOVERED. IDENTIFIED. FACE PERFECT. ACCOMPANYING REMAINS. ARRIVE TOMORROW 2150HRS. POWELL.

Adam decided to bring the Marconigram to Nancy. It gave him a reason for calling on her, and he had been looking for one since the *Carpathia* docked. He rang for Laski, the footman, and ordered the carriage brought to the front door, then went into the hall and lifted one of his father's walking canes from the rosewood umbrella stand. The cane's tap-tap-tap as he practised walking with it reminded him of Samuel.

* * *

Nancy held the sheet of paper, her face ashen. "I can't believe it. I won't believe it."

Adam looked nervously at this woman only four years his senior, for whom his father divorced his mother. Her loveliness swam towards him. A rope of pearls dangled to her navel and she wore a close-fitting gown in pale green, with contrasting dark blue sleeves and a diamond-shaped inset at the front. He knew nothing about fashion, this gawky boy, but he knew she was stylish. Her hair looped into coils at the side and was tied high at the back, a green ribbon around it, bandeau style. The effect was one of willowy length. It was a relief to see her in colours, for his grandmother's black oppressed him.

"Powell seems to think there's no room for mistake, ma'am." His voice startled him, dipping and soaring as though in the process of breaking. He had thought all that behind him, and coughed to hide his embarrassment.

"Who's Powell to know?" Nancy was scornful.

"Powell has known my father since Papa was younger than me. He wouldn't make a blunder, ma'am."

Nancy realized she had known her husband such as brief time – there seemed to be a horde of others staking prior claims. "Why are you calling me 'ma'am'?"

He scanned her face, testing whether she was teasing him. "What should I call you? Mrs Armstrong?"

"Why, Nancy, of course." It seemed shockingly intimate and his fumbling hands betrayed his confusion. "For your father's sake, I'd like it," she added gently. "He had a present for you, Adam – a puppy. He chose it himself in London. We carried it with us on the *Titanic*. I'm afraid it must have been lost."

Adam brightened. "What sort of puppy?"

"An Airedale terrier. It was male, with a damp little nose and a tail that wouldn't stop wagging."

"I should have called him Scamp." Anticipation lightened his eyes, but then they clouded. "Grandmother would never have let me keep him."

"We could have kept Scamp here and you could have visited him. I'm sure your father will buy you another dog. I'll remind him."

Adam's smile faded. This impossibly young stepmother of his really did believe his father was still alive. Could the tragedy have addled her brains? Perhaps she was mad; people did go queer sometimes, if they

148

were very old or had received a shock. His grandfather had been confused, in his final months, mixing him up with his father and warning him never to do business with abolitionists or anarchists. "Extremists, Sam. Never go into partnership with them." Adam glanced nervously at Nancy, but she seemed too young and engaging to be mad. "I have to get back now, I must change for dinner. Grandmother doesn't like to be kept waiting."

"Of course, come again." She folded into squares the Marconigram he had taken pains to smooth out.

"I should take that back for grandmother."

Nancy walked in a leisurely fashion to the fireplace, where she threw the paper into the flames.

"No!" he protested, rushing to dislodge it with a tongs, but it was consumed. "Now you'll get mmm-mmm-me in trouble!"

"My goodness, how you do take on! Samuel gets scarlet in the neck like that, too, when he's annoyed."

Adam backed away, forgetting his father's fox-head cane. In the hall he cannoned into Violet, sending beribboned packages from a shopping trip cascading from her arms.

"It's Adam, isn't it? How kind of you to call. Have you had some cake?"

Stooped over the packages, he raised a dazed face to hers. "Forgive mm-me, Mrs Muh-Markova, I muh-muh-must dash."

Violet frowned, unbuttoning her gloves. The boy seemed rattled. She opened the door to the sitting room where Nancy hunched over the fire, stirring it with a poker.

"What on earth have you been saying to Adam Armstrong, Nancy? I just collided with him in the hall and he looked like he'd seen a ghost."

"Oh, we were having a chat about Samuel. I told him about the puppy his father picked out for him. He seemed pleased."

Violet suspected there was more to their exchange than that. She pulled Nancy down beside her on a sofa and slid an arm around her waist. Nancy nestled there obediently, but Violet sensed an absence. Perhaps heartache over Samuel had unhinged her. Grief was a powerful emotion. But medicine was even more powerful, Violet held. She resolved to make Nancy an appointment with a physician specialising in nervous disorders. It would be a priority as soon as all this unpleasantness regarding Samuel's burial was settled.

* * *

Hannah forgot about the letter to her mother-in-law in Ireland as soon as it was posted, for there was a wealth of activity in New York to divert her. Every time she stepped into the street it was as good as a visit to the theatre. A heart could not stay flattened indefinitely amid this hustle and bustle. "*Ciao, bella!*" bantered the Italian barrow boys selling fruit and vegetables, whistling after her. They were even-handed in flirting with all the women.

Coloureds lived in the next apartment block. She couldn't help staring at their ebony smoothness and flashing semi-circles of teeth when they threw back their heads and laughed, which they did at any opportunity. The women walked with an undulating grace, and Hannah envied them the hoops that stretched their earlobes. She had one pair of earrings, Connemara marble discs bought by Tom, but they seemed tame by comparison. One dark-skinned man in a squashed slice of headgear – it might once have been a top hat – sold frankfurters from a wagon. He always tipped his hat to Hannah, and often she saw him jiggling dance steps on the pavement – the sidewalk, as she was trying to remember to call it – and singing a vaudeville hit.

"*Oh! You beautiful doll, you great big beautiful doll!*"

His name was Abe Cooling and he lived with his mother and his three grown-up sons. Once he asked her, "Is it true all those Englishmen wear monocles?"

"I've never been to England," she said.

He met her eyes in disbelief.

His mother, Ellen Cooling, rainbow bandana twisted around her head, seemed more like his sister. When she encountered Hannah she always flashed a grin that swallowed up her face and said, "Take Jesus with you for your friend." Hannah didn't know if Jesus would want to be her friend, with what she carried in her belly.

One day a Jewish peddler came to the door, long grey beard like dandelion fluff, selling belts and shoes. He scratched under his skullcap and muttered to himself in Yiddish when they turned him away, but thanked them politely in English.

"Did you ever imagine people could come in so many shapes and colours?" Hannah marvelled to Bridie.

"Never mind the colour of their faces, what about the fabric on their backs? I never imagined they could wear such glorious clothes for everyday, or that servants could look like lords and ladies. When I have my own shop there'll be no shortage of customers."

Hannah paid no attention – Bridie was weaving castles in the sky.

But Bridie didn't have far to look for those castles. Only a few blocks away from Danny and Kathleen's home were flagstoned boulevards, where women picked their way swathed in sables, bobbing plumes on their heads, where uniformed nursemaids pushed prams, where liveried footmen answered the front door of houses brimful of luxuries. This was the milieu which fascinated her: it was from here Bridie distilled her version of New York.

The Irishwomen treated their early days as a holiday, cushioned by some relief money distributed by the Society of St Vincent de Paul. Danny found out Hannah was entitled to it, as a pregnant widow, and Bridie brought her to the organization's office to stake her claim to the dollars. Left to herself, Hannah would never have gone looking for the money. It bought them breathing space to adjust to this astonishing country, where they no longer counted the hours by the Angelus bells struck without fail at six in the morning, noon and six in the evening. It was not that it was godless, here in America – rather, there seemed to be a panoply of gods.

After dark the city grew lurid with electric light, and the population jostled about its business long into the night. It was a far cry from following the hours of daylight at home, and Hannah wondered if it was quite natural. She found it hard to get her bearings here, with no streams or hills as landmarks.

But Bridie revelled in this polyglot, unpretentious city. New York was non-judgmental. Class differences seemed less rigid, It was cheekily, irrepressibly, gloriously modern. "Isn't New York swell?" she said to Hannah.

"Swell, indeed! You're turning into a Yank already with your

American talk!"

Bridie was intent on learning all their addictive abbreviations – bike, bus, pram; Americans seemed to shorten everything.

"I guess we're people in a hurry." Kathleen was complacent when they raised it with her.

Hannah winced: speed had wrecked the *Titanic*.

Day after day Hannah and Bridie wandered New York's streets, marvelling at the billboard hoardings advertising everything from hot dogs to face creams, and something intriguing called Dr May's blood-tonic. As for the fruit stands, they'd never seen so many unfamiliar varieties: nectarines, huckleberries, pomegranates, quinces. No wonder Danny called this a place of full tables, provided you were prepared to exert yourself.

There was want here too, of course, just like in the old country. Anyone with eyes in their head could see how many street urchins lived rough, scavenging in dustbins, while old folk without families to support them were soon destitute. But there was opportunity, all the same, for those who stretched out their hands to seize it.

Once the girls meandered as far as the piers downtown, where sailing vessels with their fretwork of masts were berthed. Bridie harboured hopes of going home on a holiday one day to show everyone – and someone in particular – how she'd made good in America. Another time they went with Kathleen to the Public Bath House in Allen Street, City-owned steam baths with private shower stalls, but it seemed immodest to them and they preferred to wash in a hipbath at home when Danny was at work. Kathleen looked at Hannah's stomach in the bathhouse, and asked Sadie Brolly, a neighbour who was an amateur midwife, to check her over. Sadie prescribed raw eggs and orange juice to build her up, which Hannah held her nose to drink.

Busy acclimatising to their new home, fascinated by how different life was 3,000 miles away from Ireland, there were days when they forgot all about the *Titanic* disaster. As time passed, life with Bridie became Hannah's routine. Sometimes she almost believed her own version of events: that she was a widow waiting for the birth of her first child.

Until a day came when her peace of mind was shattered by a letter postmarked Chicago. The correspondent was Tom's eldest sister, whose address was written on the back of the envelope – an address she knew as well as her own, for Tom had made her learn it off in case of emergency, although he could never have anticipated the scale on which it had occurred.

638 Sherman Place, Chicago, Illinois

Dear Hannah
We were shocked to larn of poor Toms death and nerly as shocked agin to larn from your letter to Mam he took a wife to himself nobody in Ireland knew a thing about it and Tom never told us he was bringing a wife with him to America but you have sufered a great hardship with this dredfull shipwreck and we are keen for to welcome you into the family in Tom's name you can have a home with us never let it be said we would trun our backs on someone down on their luck rite and tell us what train you arive on and somebody will meet you at the station welcome to the family
Your fond sister
Winifred Tobin

Hannah handed the letter to Bridie, whose lips moved as she read it. "I guess you're on your travels again," said Bridie.

* * *

Nancy held the white card edged in black as though it scorched her fingertips. It was an invitation to Samuel Armstrong's funeral.

"His remains should have been returned to you, as the widow." Violet's tightly-buttoned bodice heaved, indignant. This was the Armstrongs' way of demonstrating who called the shots. They may not have been able to stop his marriage but they could certainly take control of his burial.

"I won't believe it's Samuel until I see for myself, Momma. For all I know it could be some – some impostor they're burying. It might suit them to claim a corpse that's not recognizable any more."

"Darling, the butler has identified him."

"The butler! What do I care about a butler?"

Violet, who cared quite a lot about a butler, especially with regard to their lack of one, was dubious. "Nancy, the bodies have been dead for weeks now. Do you really want to subject yourself to an inspection? You must think of the baby."

"I am thinking of the baby. How can I tell my son his father died on the *Titanic* if I don't know it myself for a fact? Besides, the remains were embalmed – the corpse is preserved."

Violet shuddered at the idea of inspecting a corpse of some weeks' standing but, chewing her lip, finally agreed. It might bring Nancy to her senses. A doctor had to attend, however.

*   *   *

Nancy dressed carefully for this encounter with the man they said was her husband. She regretted the Poiret dresses lost on the *Titanic*, but chose a primrose tubular gown cut high at the waist, with seed pearls sewn onto the neck and hemline. It had a matching coat with swan's-down at the collar and cuffs. The ensemble was part of a collection from Worth which Samuel bought for her in London on the first leg of their wedding tour, and had shipped back to New York. "Yellow is Samuel's favourite colour," she told her reflection. She was still able to squeeze into her pre-pregnancy wardrobe, although her bust had started to swell.

Violet, in black velvet with cream silk lapels, squirmed when she saw her daughter's sunny outfit. "Are you sure you want to wear yellow to a funeral parlour, Nancy?"

"Of course." Nancy lifted the white gloves Roberge had laid out for her. "Why should I wear mourning? The man they brought from Halifax isn't Samuel. My husband's on another ship which hasn't yet made it to port."

Violet sighed and tweaked at the hat with ostrich plumes shading her daughter's face. She couldn't decide if the sight of Samuel in his coffin was likely to kill or cure Nancy, but she was as prepared as any mother could be. A bottle of smelling salts clinked in her reticule, while the expensive private doctor was to meet them at the Chapel of Rest.

* * *

The entire Armstrong clan was in attendance when mother and daughter swept in. Rebecca, whose air of martyred forbearance would have suited a Sistine Chapel painting, pointedly avoided rising to greet them. Instead she inclined her head in terse acknowledgement. Adam stood to go towards them, but his grandmother laid a hand on his arm. He bowed at the women and sat down again. With them was a tall, chic woman whose veiled hat covered her face; Nancy supposed she must be Samuel's first wife, from photographs she had seen in the society pages. A man with protruding eyes, dressed in a frock coat and striped trousers, sat behind the first wife, along with a woman who watched Nancy covertly. Nancy seemed to remember the man in tails was some kind of cousin of her husband's working in the family business. Noah Armstrong, that was his name. Samuel had introduced them once. Further back in the semi-circular tier of seats were several other men, also in frock coats.

It was clear from the sparse gathering that the Armstrongs were not an abundant family. Samuel had been an only child, as Nancy was. It had been something in common between them, although Nancy hadn't missed out on playmates the way her husband had. He had spoken to Nancy occasionally of his strict upbringing in the Park Avenue mansion: forbidden to whistle, fidget or slump when he sat, play games on a Sunday or read books except those of an improving nature.

Nancy became aware of a magnificent walnut casket, a replacement for the simple wooden box in which the body had been transported from Halifax. Lighted tapers flickered at its head and foot, and there was a sense of space around it. Powell, a crepe bow falling from his black silk top hat to his shoulder blades, approached the party and addressed Violet. "When would your daughter like to view the remains, madam?"

Violet glanced towards the doctor. "As soon as possible."

The medic cleared his throat. "I recommend we empty the room."

Powell's normally impassive face registered a ripple. "I don't see how we can ask Mrs Rebecca to leave."

The doctor peered at the matriarch. "Quite. Perhaps if we reduced the numbers of those present to the bare minimum?"

Powell went over to Rebecca Armstrong, murmuring in her ear, and her look of martyrdom intensified. He advanced towards Noah Armstrong and the other gentlemen. This group rose, Noah's wife shaking out her skirts, the men carrying their hats in the crook of their arms, and retreated to an ante-room.

While these preparations were carried out, Nancy thought about her wedding day. Something old, something new, something borrowed, something blue. How determined she'd been to fulfil the adage before beginning married life. The veil was old – her grandmother's – the gown new, paid for by the sale of an heirloom necklace of her mother's. She borrowed pearl earrings from the school-friend who acted as her bridesmaid, even though people said pearls were for tears, while something blue came from a gift of Samuel's. It was a blue ribbon attached to a brooch-watch "with a lapis lazuli to match your eyes, little girl" on the flip-up lid. Its dial was too tiny for her to read without squinting, but she didn't admit this to Samuel when he presented it to her on the day before their wedding. Later Nancy bought a matching strip of ribbon, tying it to his gold hunter.

Rebecca couldn't bear the feeling of being on the margins and crackled across. "Are you determined to look on his face?" she demanded of Nancy.

"Yes."

"Very well. As his widow, or should I say one of his widows" – her heavily veiled hat quivered in the direction of Cora Armstrong – "you are entitled. There were some items found in my son's pockets."

"Do they identify him?" Violet interposed.

"Yes. A watch, a wallet, a cigarette case and a piece of paper which disintegrated when it was opened. They said it might be a birthday card – utter nonsense, of course. All the writing had washed off. I recognized the watch at once, my late husband and I presented it to Samuel as a birthday gift. I have passed it on to Adam."

Hearing his name mentioned, Adam sprang towards the group. His mother was left alone, but Cora Armstrong was immersed in reviewing the arrangements for a costume ball she was organizing for a friend's birthday in a month's time. Fortunately it was to be held in Newport, since it might be regarded as tasteless to press ahead with it in New York, under the circumstances. Cora could spend weeks planning parties, drawing up invitation lists, devising coups, debating menus tailored for excess. The quest for novelty at these entertainments led to meals being eaten on horseback, or dishes floated by on miniature yachts. Cora was still smarting over a rival who held a dinner party for her set's pet dogs. It was the talk of the town.

"Your grandmother tells us you have your father's watch," said Violet.

He drew the gold hunter from his pocket. Its hands pointed to twenty past two. "The shock of immersion in the water must have stopped it, I guess."

Nancy looked at the bedraggled scrap of blue ribbon on the watch. She could just make out the capital T of *Time and tide wait for no man*. She turned towards the coffin.

"If everyone could please step back," said the doctor.

Nobody moved, but they lowered their eyes.

"I could take mmm-mother out, if you like – if there are still too many people here," volunteered Adam.

He glanced anxiously at Nancy. He had looked at his father's face already, and at least it was undamaged. He wouldn't like her to see anything gruesome.

"Quickly then, Adam," said his grandmother.

Cora Armstrong made a fuss about finding her parasol, although in reality she was thinking about her costume ball and didn't care whether she stayed or went. She was debating a Knights of the Round Table theme, if only she could locate a lute-player. Samuel would have complained about the expense, but Samuel hadn't balked at the cost of divorcing her and substituting a schoolgirl as Mrs Armstrong. He was even willing to have himself cited for adultery – paying some little actress to let her name be used – since it was the only grounds for divorce in New York State. She threw a contemptuous glance at the second Mrs Samuel Armstrong. That upstart couldn't organize a costume ball in a month of Sundays.

With the room as close to empty as he could expect, the doctor twitched his eyebrows towards the undertaker, who raised the coffin-lid. A face and upper torso were exposed, fingers laced across its chest.

Nancy took two steps forward. The watchers were braced for a reaction – a shriek, or some exclamation – but the silence was absolute as Nancy remained intent on the embalmed shell of her husband.

It was both Samuel and not Samuel. Nancy's yellow gown stroked the casket as she leaned forward. How odd, the surface of his hair was flat, totally without texture, and they had parted it whereas Samuel wore it brushed straight back from his forehead. Perhaps his eyes were more sunken than she remembered. Her hand stretched out to adjust the unfamiliar parting but she couldn't touch the corpse. Breath oxygenated her lungs in shallow gasps and pain blistered over her skin, so that she looked down at her hands expecting welts to have erupted. It was a surprise to see the flesh remained smooth.

Violet noticed how bloodless her daughter's lips were and left the knot of onlookers to tug at her elbow, trying to guide her away. Nancy stood her ground, shrugging off her mother. She wanted to absorb every detail of this version of Samuel.

He was wearing a new white wing-collar shirt and a black cravat. His jacket was black too. It was all so sombre – Samuel liked a splash of colour. The mortician working on him had covered the gash on his temple, disguising any evidence of violence in death. But there was no covering the waxen patina of his skin.

He was her husband and she would kiss him, Nancy decided. She bent towards his face. "Is it really you, Samuel?" she whispered. But before her lips connected with his cheek the colour leached from her own. As startling as a bludgeon blow, a spasm twisted her womb. Nancy tottered, ostrich feathers fluttering as she clawed at the air. Just as the doctor reached her she subsided beside one of the tapers, the gust of air from her collapse extinguishing it.

How unlucky, thought Rebecca, who was not superstitious as a rule.

12

Louis walked around New York, finding his bearings. His favourite building was the Flatiron, which seemed to him to be constructed with an aesthetic quality missing from its neighbouring skyscrapers. Still, while New York lacked the poise of Paris, possibilities seemed infinite in this swarming metropolis. He handed a coin to a newsboy hawking the evening paper and took himself off to a diner with a striped awning outside, red leather booths and counter stools to match inside. He ordered a slice of cherry pie and looked aghast at the waitress when she suggested coffee. American coffee was deplorable, but at least they knew how to bake fruit-pies.

Reading beneath a whirring fan which ruffled the news sheets, Louis paused now and again to consult a small English-French dictionary he had bought, and was struck by the number of benefits held in aid of *Titanic* widows and orphans. The public's pockets seemed inexhaustible when the ship's name was mentioned.

As he retreated to his hotel, he encountered Edmund on Seventh Avenue, just back from Washington after a telephone call from Major Hudson. The major had heard of a part-time opening which might interest the schoolmaster. In return for teaching the classics three mornings a week to the wards of Colonel Lars Sorensen, an old military friend who lived near the major in Washington Place, Edmund would be offered the use of a self-contained basement apartment in the colonel's house. The colonel thought Pliny was just the discipline his wards needed.

Edmund, perpetually worried about his finances, was pleased to accept. His travel plans could easily be deferred for a few months. He checked into the Station House Hotel again for a night, until he could move to the apartment, where a decidedly tetchy Marconigram from *The Times* waited for him, declining his offer of articles and asking him to desist from sending speculative pieces. Nothing from Minerva. At a loss how to spend the evening, Edmund walked across to the Excelsior Hotel to see if his sister might have written to him there.

On the pavement outside he spotted Louis. Bored and in need of company, he held out his hand. "Hallo, old man. How's America agreeing with you?"

"I have no complaints."

"Come and have a glass of Cain's brew with me," invited Edmund.

"Cain's brew?"

"Beer. That's what my headmaster at Dulwich College calls it – he's an abstainer."

They made for a saloon on the corner. Around them, Irish construction workers were drinking whiskey and beer chasers known as Sean O'Farrells at a spanking rate in their replica Irish society.

"They're in good humour now but they'll be fighting before you know it." Edmund nodded towards the labourers. "Give them whiskey and they'll kill each other for the fun of it. I've seen them in London." He ordered a pitcher of beer and asked Louis if he'd encountered any of their fellow survivors.

"No-one." Louis coiled his hand around the glass of cold beer. "And you?"

The beer loosened Edmund's tongue. "I stay in touch with Major Hudson. I heard through him that one of the ships searching for bodies found Mrs Armstrong's husband. The funeral took place yesterday – the major put in an appearance. Apparently the widow was too ill to attend." He lowered his voice. "That young lady's been through a lot."

There was silence as each man considered the lustre of Nancy

160

Armstrong and how much she had suffered.

At least she'll never have to count the nickels and dimes, thought Edmund, regretting gossiping about Nancy Armstrong in a saloon. Fortunately Stubel wasn't pestering him with questions; in fact, he hadn't uttered a word. The fellow was tactful, he'd grant him that. Sometimes you'd scarcely take him for a foreigner.

"Ever been to Washington?" he said. Louis shook his head. "Just come from there, observing the Senate hearings. It's a bit uppity, the Yanks investigating something that involves a British vessel in international waters."

Louis had no interest in the Senate hearings. The whys and wherefores of the *Titanic* sinking were irrelevant to him. The ship was gone, *c'est la vie*. Still, he feigned attention as he drank this lager which tasted bitter to him. A glass of red wine would be preferable but he knew better than to ask for one in a country which couldn't provide a palatable cup of coffee.

They parted company after Louis bought them each a finger of bourbon for the road. Louis sat in his room and contemplated Nancy Armstrong – now officially a widow. Was it possible to love someone he had exchanged no more than a handful of words with? Louis's intellect doubted it, yet his heart had no such misgivings. He knew it wasn't convenient to be in love, for he still had his way to make in the world. All the same, he longed to see her again – just to stand in her vicinity would be enough, even if they didn't speak. But Louis had no idea how he was to engineer such a meeting.

* * *

Nancy lay in the enormous bed she had never shared with Samuel and was force-fed chicken soup by her mother. Much of the time she slept – prolonged, comatose spells. The relentlessness of grief made her bone-weary. Her mother prattled at the foot of her bed, preparing tonics and counting out pills. Nancy was only hazily conscious of what was said.

Initially she refused to eat and Violet had to hand-feed her, coaxing her like a bird with titbits. It could take an hour to finish a bowl of soup.

As she fed Nancy – "just six spoons and Roberge will take the bowl away" – she told her of encountering Major Hudson. "He asked after you, darling." Nancy's eyelids didn't flicker. Violet judged it best not to mention the location of their meeting: the church where Samuel's funeral service was conducted, his young son reading the lesson in a voice that fumbled, the minister extolling the dead man's heroism as an example of Christian self-denial. Rebecca Armstrong was deeply moved by a spray of lilies sent by the President.

Violet noticed a finger of sunlight was troubling Nancy, her forehead puckering under its streaky touch. She adjusted the shade, wondering how to rouse her daughter.

"Nancy, you must get well for the baby's sake."

The girl's form remained inert.

"Don't you care about the baby?"

Nothing.

"You must remember it's Samuel's child as well as yours, darling. You have a responsibility to his memory to bear him a healthy child."

There was movement beneath the eyelids but they remained closed.

Violet sighed, straightened the quilt and turned away. The decorator was due to call with some nursery designs – perhaps they would perk up the mother-to-be. She looked back over her shoulder into the room. Propped against a battery of pillows, her daughter seemed tiny in the four-poster. Violet had let her imagination – and Samuel's money – gallop away with her, ordering a bed from a London firm of antique dealers belonging to one of those King Georges whose number she could never remember. Nancy's eyes were closed but Violet could tell from her breathing she wasn't asleep. She tiptoed away.

When she was alone, Nancy struggled to push off the blankets and ease out of bed. Her wedding ring rolled around on her finger, only the knuckle preventing it from falling off, while strands of hair detached themselves from her scalp and were marooned on the embroidered pillowcases. She looked older than her eighteen years – the blithe freshness of youth which had attracted Samuel leaked away. Still beautiful, she was no longer untouched. Nancy reached the window by holding on to islands of furniture along the way and twitched aside the blind to look out onto the street. Yes, that was the source of the noise she could hear above her mother's burbles. Pressed against the railings at the front of her house, a tour guide was pointing out her home to a group of out-of-towners. "This is the property bought by hotel nabob Samuel Armstrong for his child-bride Nancy Markova. He was lost on the *Titanic*, folks, and never got the chance to live here with her. The young widow, who was saved on board the *Carpathia*, is recovering inside these four walls after her ordeal. Samuel Armstrong surrendered his seat to a woman from steerage – no class distinction with him. That's the American way. Guess his widow must be real proud of her man. Next up, folks, we'll be taking a look at the Wideners' place. Young Widener was a book collector. He'd just bought a real fine book, I guess you could call it a literary gem, from Sotheby's in London-England seventeen days before being consigned to the depths, book and man alike. It was the *Rubaiyat of Omar Khayyam*, studded with more than a thousand jewels set in gold . . ."

Nancy wasn't proud of her husband's sacrifice – she was livid enough to spit at him, if only she had the energy. Fool! What did she care about gentlemanly gestures? That woman should have come to the boat deck earlier or waited for another lifeboat.

Nancy and Samuel are in a lifeboat waiting for evacuation. A thin man plucks at the sleeve of the officer loading it.

"Can my wife have a place, sir?"

"I'm afraid all the room on this boat is taken. Try the port-side." The officer turns away and barks an order to a group of sailors.

"Please find space for her, sir. I heard Captain Smith say women and children first. There are men on your boat."

"You're too late. If you'll just step back please – we're trying to lower away. We haven't much time." He nods at the sailors to push back this persistent little man.

Samuel jumps up. Nancy sees he is attempting to climb back on deck and clutches at his arm. "Where are you going, Samuel? I'm frightened!"

"Sweetheart, no gentleman could occupy a seat when a lady needs it."

"But I need you!"

"The lifeboats are a precaution, Nancy, nothing more. Chin up."

"No!" she howls, struggling to detain him. "No, you mustn't, I forbid it."

Samuel tries to free himself without hurting her. "Roberge will look after you. Be brave. I'll see you at breakfast, little girl."

"But you said we were safer on the Titanic than in one of these shrimps. Don't leave me, Samuel!"

He drops a kiss on her forehead, capturing her hands in the same downward swoop. "A lifeboat is the best place for you, Nancy." With that he pushes her gently away, steps out of the lifeboat and approaches the officer.

"This lady can have my seat." Samuel Armstrong bows in the direction of the thin man's wife.

The officer's expression is irresolute.

"If you please, ma'am." Samuel takes the initiative and extends his hand towards her.

She fixes her eyes on his patent shoes, pools of light reflected in them, unsure whether to move.

The thin man nudges her. "Go ahead – accept the gentleman's kind offer."

The officer shifts from one foot to another, impatient. "Come along then, I can't afford any more delays."

"But what about you?" The woman looks troubled, turning to her companion.

"I'll find a place on another boat, never you worry, me darlin'. God bless and keep you."

Nancy rested her forehead on the window-frame overlooking Central Park and whispered now what she wailed then. "Don't leave me, Samuel." But she knows he has – and he's never coming back.

*   *   *

Violet decided to ignore her daughter's reservations and set about tracking down Louis Stubel. She was determined to have the Frenchman quoted in the newspaper on their side, in case of a battle with the Armstrongs over Nancy's rights. Rebecca had slighted Violet at the funeral, leaving her in no doubt the family would not willingly be generous towards her daughter. Stubel's testimony about Samuel acknowledging paternity would be useful.

He was not difficult to trace, still at the Excelsior Hotel where White Star had billeted him on the first night. Louis was walking through the foyer when he heard his name mentioned at the front desk by a tightly corseted lady. He doffed his hat. "*Madame*, how may I be of service?"

"My name is Mrs Markova. My daughter is Mrs Armstrong, Mrs Samuel Armstrong. I believe you may have made her acquaintance on one of the *Titanic* lifeboats?"

Louis crackled to attention. "The charming Madame Armstrong – she's well, I trust?"

"She's taking the loss of her husband to heart, I'm afraid. Perfectly natural, of course, they were deeply in love."

"*L'amour.*"

He did not say it with the customary Gallic flourish, but in a fashion that struck Violet as almost accusatory. What an unusual Frenchman! Perhaps the sinking had robbed him of any appreciation of romance. Still, there was something beguiling about the way his lips framed the word *l'amour*.

"Yes, *l'amour*," she repeated, thinking herself quite the cosmopolitan. "Where would we be without the gentler emotions? Mr Stubel, could I trouble you to call on us? There is a small matter which I believe you may be able to help us with, if you'll be good enough to perform the service."

Louis hid his surprise – and his exhilaration. "No service is too much trouble for the beautiful Madame Armstrong and her equally beautiful mother."

"I'll leave my card, and look forward to receiving you in our home. I know my daughter is most anxious to renew her acquaintance with you."

A smile parted those chiselled lips Violet Markova had found herself admiring. This was better than Louis could have dreamed.

* * *

Back in Halifax, bodies were kept at the rink for up to two weeks to allow people time to claim them. Photographs were taken of every corpse; these, plus records, were retained and the body's burial location noted for possible future exhumation. On Friday, May 3rd, the Royal Canadian Regiment conducted 700 mourners to Fairview Lawn Cemetery. A kilted band of pipers played the inevitable "Nearer My God To Thee", and the remains of the *Titanic*'s dead were dispersed to

Catholic, Protestant and Jewish graveyards. Fairview Cemetery held 121 graves, the greatest number. Its central avenue led to the *Titanic* section, plots arranged along a slope – one curved line of graves leading to later claims that they had been trying to ape the contour of a ship's bow. In time, dark grey granite headstones would be installed with brief inscriptions.

Four ships recovered 330 bodies in all, many of whom were never identified. White Star sent printed lists of recovered bodies to its main agencies to seek out relatives. In Ireland, Tom's mother Margaret O'Brien received a letter on paper whose letterhead boasted the *Titanic* was the second largest steamer in the world. For all the good it had done her son.

Among those buried in Halifax were a number of unidentified victims. Charlie Chadband, the steward who winked at Bridie, was one of them. He was logged simply as white male, aged twenty to thirty. He had nothing to identify him – everything had floated off. There was nothing to categorise him as anything other than a member of the human race: neither nationality nor denomination nor name. Bridie never did remember to light that candle in his memory.

* * *

Bridie had expected Hannah to take up the O'Brien sisters' offer, but Hannah said she had been uprooted once and never wanted to go through it again. "They're strangers to me. I'll stay with you, Bridie, if you'll have me. If people were made to flit here and there the good Lord would have given them wings."

Bridie was willing, especially as the paternalistic attitude of her brother grew too overbearing for her to stomach. Always telling her what she could and couldn't do – he'd seen red when the Italian barber had tried to make a date with her. That Enrico was a fine cut of a man, but he used too much cologne. Still, Danny wasn't her father, he had no right to lay down the law to her. She was going to be twenty-one in August. She wondered how much it would cost for a room of your own. Hannah needed her but she needed Hannah too, to share the expense.

Sadie Brolly, midwife to the tenements around 33rd Street, called again to prod Hannah's stomach. Kathleen supervised in her bossy way, but a knock sent her to the door and Sadie whispered it was a wonder she'd condescended to marry Danny Ryan at all. There was a pecking order between those off the boat and the American-born Irish. "They say the men only know how to dig and the women how to wash clothes. But diggers and washerwomen are always needed." Sadie Brolly folded work-roughened arms across her chest, the nest of wrinkles beneath each eye quivering.

She had a pushcart selling matches, bootlaces and cakes of blackening, the contents of a huckster's shop at home. The tenement families made a point of giving her their custom, because it was her only way to keep body and soul together.

"Why are you on your own? Have you no family?" Bridie asked.

"I went ahead of my family. They were to join me later but weren't allowed in. Trachoma."

The name of the disease sent a shiver down Hannah's spine. She'd been riddled with anxiety during the medical examination before being allowed on the *Titanic*, when doctors had used button-hooks to turn her eyelids inside out. The US immigration authorities had a checklist of diseases debarring admission, one of which was trachoma, a disease of the eye marked by granular spots on the inner surface of the lids. The checks were called six-second physicals because the experienced medics were able to detect everything from anaemia to varicose veins with a quick look at an emigrant.

The girls studied Sadie with pity. Rejection on medical grounds was a body-blow to people who travelled long distances to the wharf, sometimes on foot, selling all their possessions in advance. Entire families abandoned the idea of emigrating if one member was turned away.

"Did you really come all this way on your own?" marvelled Hannah.

"I came with my daughter but she died a month after landing. There was a typhoid epidemic, sewage in the drinking water."

Sadie's face closed in. She'd been expecting her son-in-law and grandson to follow, but the boy suffered from trachoma and was refused passage. His father stayed with him, hoping to borrow the money to persuade an official to turn a blind eye, but bribery didn't work. Doctors checked again for trachoma at Ellis Island and any emigrant suffering from it was repatriated at the steamship's expense. So Sadie Brolly found herself on her own in New York, starting life over at the age of sixty-one.

Bad and all as my circumstances are, at least I have Bridie, thought Hannah.

There was safety in numbers in America – alone, you were vulnerable.

* * *

Life settled into a rhythm for Edmund in New York. He bought second-hand copies of Pope's translation of Homer and set about trickling it into the reluctant brains of Colonel Sorensen's wards. This left him plenty of free time to see the sights. From all the attractions he visited, he sent postcards to his sister Minerva. But something was missing. He fretted he might be doomed to be a classics master all his life. Here he was in America, in the youngest of the world's great cities, and what was he doing? Teaching about a dead civilization. He was ageing before his time.

Major Hudson paid a visit to his basement rooms. "How are you managing with Colonel Sorensen's wards? Able to drum the classics into their skulls?"

"I do my best."

"Boys like wars. I had a fondness for Caesar's campaigns as a youngster."

"I'm trying to make lessons entertaining for them. I have them translating a fragment of a play by the Greek dramatist Epicharmus. He wrote a comedy called *Orya, The Sausage*, around 500BC."

Privately, the major thought a few battles might do the trick. He'd have them translate episodes from the Trojan War – the single combat between Achilles and Hector would be a dandy place to start. But he was only a retired major, not a schoolmaster. He creaked in a cane-bottomed chair, trying to get comfortable. "Come to lunch with me at my club, Newton – I want to talk to you about my book. It's still a little early, but we can walk towards Madison Avenue and work up an appetite."

"Rather," said Edmund, who never needed to work up an appetite.

He slid his latchkey into his pocket, tightened his tie against his three-inch starched choker collar, and was ready for the Union League Club.

They ambled along, enjoying the dissonant sounds and smells of the city.

"White Star's annual report is just out. It recorded a profit last year of more than £1 million. But, of course, most of this was wiped out by the *Titanic* losses," said Edmund.

"There's money in travel – railroads, steamships, not sure about those automobiles, the drivers look damned uncomfortable perched so high up, but I suppose the same principle applies. Ways of getting around make money. I have shares in the Akron-Canton Railroad of Ohio."

Edmund thought glumly how he had no spare cash for investments.

"I'm making enormous headway with the *Titanic* book," confided the major. "Did you know that in Liverpool, where the ship was registered, the entire electricity supply suddenly failed shortly before nine in the evening on the day she sank? And in Cherbourg a grey-haired, shabby Frenchman approached passengers at the tender, whispering, "This ship, she is not safe. Do not sail on her, *je vous en prie!*" What do you make of that, Newton?"

"It's all hindsight at work, major. I never felt the least shadow of disaster when I looked at the *Titanic* – I thought her a magnificent product of British ingenuity and workmanship. They had some fitters and so forth from Harland and Wolff on board. I quizzed one while we were taking on passengers in Ireland. He'd just come up from the boiler rooms for some air. Proud as a peacock. Said she was the finest vessel he'd ever worked on. I think he regarded it as the pinnacle of his career, poor blighter. It was the finale to his career anyhow. They all died, those Belfast shipyard chaps. Don't think they even tried to get off."

"Let's speak of something more cheerful." Major Hudson waved his walking stick at the sunlit cityscape. "What do you make of our '*many tower'd Camelot*'?"

"It has energy – its citizens seem determined to prosper. And it's rather more imposing than I was led to expect." Edmund's eyes never stopped darting about whenever he walked through this vibrant city.

169

The skyscrapers left him stiff-necked from craning. Incapable of unqualified approval, he added, "I do find it bizarre how everyone constantly chews gum. It makes men look loutish, while it gives women a particularly coarse air, like animals at the cud. It'll never catch on in England."

"Mr Wrigley's made a fortune from it."

They crossed the street, avoiding a sweeper with broom and shovel clearing up horse manure. The major stopped by a handsome building on the corner of Madison and East 26th Street which would not have been out of place on a Parisian boulevard. "My club. Don't know about you, Newton, but I'm ready for a Scotch and soda."

*   *   *

After they parted, despite some very fine lamb's kidneys and a bottle of Chateau Larose, Edmund felt more disconsolate than ever. Even Major Hudson had a project to occupy him – but here he was in America, a pedantic teacher old before his time. In this frame of mind, he received a Marconigram signed Jules Brulatour from the Éclair Moving Picture Company inviting him to lunch at Delmonico's the following day to discuss a business proposition. The name rang no bells. But lunch at Delmnico's was lunch at Delmonico's. Brulatour would be paying, wouldn't he? He studied the Marconigram. "*As my guest,*" read the invitation.

The following day Edmund gave his name to the maître d', who checked down his list and led him towards a corner table. Although Edmund was early, a man in his forties and a woman twenty years his junior were seated with half-empty glasses apiece. The man rose at his arrival, while the woman unleashed a dazzling smile. She took the initiative.

"Mr Newton, we're real glad you could meet us. I'm Dorothy Gibson and this is my associate, Mr Jules Brulatour." She said her name as though it ought to register with Edmund.

"Sherry?" asked Jules Brulatour. "We're having it in your honour – we know how attached the English are to their sherry."

"Please."

170

Edmund considered them. The woman was dressed modishly in a rust and cream dress with a pleated neckline. Her mobile face and expressive eyes made her a head-turner, although she had an arch manner that Edmund found irritating. She kept tilting her head in a variety of poses. There was something familiar about her voice, however. As for the man, he had a restless gaze.

"Don't say you've forgotten me already, Mr Newton," said the woman. "We spoke at the hearings in Washington. You showed me your report."

The woman who had read his article over his shoulder? Her headgear had shadowed her face, so that all he could see was a mouth with a sensuous upper lip. He checked. Yes, that upper lip still looked ready to gorge on life's pleasures.

"Once seen, never forgotten, Miss Gibson." He reached for gallantry to cover his lapse.

She smiled. "Your newspaper report was wonderful. I've been telling my friend Mr Brulatour all about it. And we have something else in common, Mr Newton."

"What might that be?" Edmund could imagine nothing in common with this woman who widened her eyes dramatically after every sentence.

"We were both saved from the *Titanic*."

"*Saved From The* Titanic! That might work as our title." Brulatour leaned across the table, catching her by the arm in his excitement.

"You think so, Jules?"

Brulatour tapped the side of his nose. "Sure thing. It offers hope, see? Movie-goers don't like a story that's bleak, they want a happy ending."

Edmund cleared his throat. "I don't believe we met on the *Carpathia*, Miss Gibson, or, indeed, on the *Titanic* for that matter. I'm so glad you were rescued."

"Not as glad as me. I was travelling with my mother, we'd just finished a rubber of bridge and retired to our cabin when I heard a sickening crunch. We left on one of the first lifeboats, Number 7. I thought it shameful how few of the crew knew what they should be doing in an evacuation. It was a shambles. I said so to the *New York Times* when they interviewed me. The plug in our lifeboat didn't fit properly, we tried bunging clothes into it but the water continued to seep through, so someone had to sit on it all night."

"How did you manage to escape, Mr Newton?" drawled Jules Brulatour's New Orleans accent.

Edmund bristled. "I went down with the ship. But I'm rather a handy swimmer and was able to get clear of the wreckage. I swam to a lifeboat and was fortunate enough to be allowed to board."

"How amazing!" breathed Dorothy. "I never learned to swim but I'm sure going to take lessons now."

"I presume you're a newspaperman, Mr Newton? Miss Gibson mentioned *The London Times*."

"No, I teach classics at a boys' school in London. I attended the hearings as an interested member of the public."

"Swell. Why don't we order lunch and then we can talk about why we asked you here? I recommend the broiled sweetbreads."

"People eat lobster when they're at Delmonico's," objected Dorothy.

"Oh yeah? Well, Jules Brulatour eats sweetbreads."

Over a first course of salmon vol au vents, Edmund was amazed to discover the Éclair Moving Picture Company had a half-written script for a motion picture about the *Titanic* and planned to open it in theatres in the United States on May 14th – exactly a month after the liner's collision with an iceberg.

"I'm playing Miss Dorothy, the heroine, in the flicker," interrupted his hostess, as Jules Brulatour spoke of the need to rush it out while the *Titanic* story was hot property.

"The name fascinates folk now, but by next year they may have forgotten all about it. The public is fickle, Ed. Takes at least two months normally to get a motion picture on the circuit but we can cut a few corners."

By the time a plate containing paupiettes of fowl was in front of him, Edmund had learned Éclair was a French company with an American branch at Fort Lee, New Jersey.

"Miss Gibson is one of our most talented actresses, about to play the role of a lifetime," said Brulatour.

They exchanged a smile which made Edmund feel supernumerary.

"Congratulations. But, frankly, I'm mystified why you're telling me all this."

Brulatour and Dorothy disengaged their gazes with some difficulty.

"We need help with the script. Dorothy, I mean Miss Gibson, mentioned your gift with words. She sure was impressed with that humdinger article you wrote in DC, and the speed you cranked it out. That's what we need, a guy who's fast. We have special requirements you're uniquely placed to fill, Ed. You're a *Titanic* survivor, you have an insider's understanding of what happened that night. You seem able to work under pressure, and you can write. How about collaborating with us on our script, buddy? You'll find Éclair a generous employer. We'll make it worth your while."

"I have other obligations." Edmund's mind was whirling, but he spared a thought for the children he was contracted to teach. After all, Major Hudson had helped secure the position.

"We won't keep you from the classroom for long. Our feature is due for release in less than two weeks."

"The deadline is positively breathing down our necks." Dorothy rolled her eyes. "Everything's helter-skelter in the moving pictures business."

"But motion pictures are silent. Is the script so important?" Edmund asked.

"Of course, it sets the scene and defines the plot." Brulatour seemed shocked by his ignorance.

"Do say yes," coaxed Dorothy. "It'll be fun. You won't regret it."

Edmund found himself agreeably tempted. It had nothing to do with the delicious meal, or the chilled white wine which followed the sherry, or the elaborate confection of chocolate mousse, whipped cream and brandy sitting on a plate in front of him. It was the euphoria of being pursued. He was certain he knew nothing about scriptwriting and fairly certain he couldn't improvise. However, he allowed his mind to toy with the possibility of being a scriptwriter for a moving picture. He never went to the cinema, preferring the theatre, but Minerva would be impressed – his sister was a fan of the moving pictures.

Suddenly a thought occurred. "How on earth did you find me?"

"You gave the name of your New York hotel when you checked into the Washington place," said Brulatour. "I tried there but you'd moved on, so I slipped the porter a coupla greenbacks and he dug out your forwarding address." He winked. "Money talks in this part of the world, Ed."

Edmund's satisfying sense of being in demand puffed out. "I'll do it."

Brulatour pumped his hand while Dorothy clapped hers together.

"Welcome to the team, Ed!" said Brulatour. "I have a copy of the script outline in my attaché case. Go home, read it and tomorrow we'll set up a meeting. Dorothy and I motored up from New Jersey this morning but we're planning to stay over. Can we schedule you for a script conference first thing?"

"I don't see why not."

"OK, we're in business. Now Dorothy, you settle the check" – he tossed a handful of bills onto the table – "while I telephone my wife and tell her I'll be in New York for a coupla days." He stood. "If we're gonna be working together you better call me Jules."

"Are you my co-scriptwriter?"

"Not my department, Ed. You'll be swapping ideas with Dorothy. This is her baby. She thought of the idea for the film, persuaded the studio to run with it and she's the star. You and Dorothy will be seeing a lot more of each other over the next few weeks. You're gonna be eating, working and sleeping together." He laughed, seeing Edmund's expression pucker. "Maybe not sleeping – there's no vacancy in that department, is there, baby?"

* * *

Edmund went home and read the script. It was excruciatingly dull. How anyone could have made an event as cataclysmic as the *Titanic* disaster so turgid was a mystery. Where was the drama, the heroism, the self-sacrifice, the terror, the pathos? He tried to remember what his sister had told him about moving pictures. She seemed to like romance, that much he remembered. Romance was a foreign country to Edmund. He'd better get on to Minerva for some ideas. Would his funds run to a quick telephone call? He ought to splurge – these Americans were so full of vim they wanted everything done yesterday. After he spoke to Minerva he'd see about going to one of these flickers himself.

* * *

"Do come downstairs, darling. It's only respectful." Violet stroked back Nancy's hair.

"I'm too tired to get dressed, Momma."

"Silly goose, that's why we pay Roberge. I'll send her in to you."

"I'm too tired even to let someone dress me, Momma. Can't I just lie here?"

"You can't keep Mr Stubel waiting."

"Say I'm indisposed. He'll understand if he's a gentleman."

"Of course he's a gentleman – your own mother knows the difference. Louis Stubel is an aristocrat to his fingertips. Can't you make the effort for my sake? I invited him to call, after all."

Nancy closed her eyes.

"You must stir yourself, darling. The doctor said you were to take a little light exercise every day."

Considering everything that had happened to Nancy, it was a miracle she was still pregnant. All the same, Violet was growing impatient with her daughter. When Nancy wasn't spending all day in bed she was complaining of headaches or toothache, or convincing herself she had a racing heartbeat. A variety of specialists could find nothing wrong with her, although one wanted to extract two healthy teeth and another had microbes swabbed and grown from her throat, which he intended to make into a vaccine and inject into her. The real culprit, psychological causes, was not considered. Doctors reassured Violet, with their cant about toxins invading a patient's nervous system and poisoning it. She saw to it that her daughter was attended by a succession of men who washed their hands scrupulously and presented her with large bills, which she paid with Armstrong money.

Violet changed tack. "It hurts me to see you lying here so full of despair. A mother's heart is bruised by it – you'll understand for yourself soon enough. Won't you get up for a short while? Twenty minutes will do, darling."

Nancy caught one of her rose-scented pillows and pressed it over her face to block out her mother's wheedling. Why wouldn't she leave her in peace? She heard the door close as her mother conceded defeat, then let the pillow thud to the floor.

Violet pattered in high-button shoes to the sitting room, where Louis was evaluating their taste in art. Execrable: one chocolate box scene of bucolic sentiment after another.

"I'm so sorry, Mr Stubel, my daughter is unable to receive anyone. She's in a greatly weakened condition, I'm afraid. She sends her compliments and asks me to thank you for doing us the honour of paying a call."

"I understand." He bowed, disappointed. "I brought Madame Armstrong *un petit cadeau* but perhaps under the circumstances it might not be appropriate to offer it." He hesitated. "I must admit I was selfishly hoping to catch her expression when she opened it."

"A present might buck her up!" exclaimed Violet, overlooking the volley of bouquets delivered to the house. "May I bring it to her on your behalf?"

This wasn't what Louis wanted but he couldn't refuse. "It would give me great pleasure. I've left it in the hall. And now, I can no longer impose on your good will, Madame Markova – a lady has many demands on her time." He accepted the hand extended to him and kissed air half an inch from Violet's fingertips.

She accompanied him into the hall, where the footman waited with his hat.

"The trifle I mentioned is there." He indicated a bulky rectangular package. "Perhaps you'd be kind enough to tell Madame Armstrong that I hope the gift might be an heirloom for her son."

Violet judged it risqué of Louis to refer openly to Nancy's pregnancy but, apart from pink shading at the neck, betrayed no sign. She prided herself on being a woman of the world.

The footman carried the package as far as Nancy's dressing room, resting it against her vanity table.

"Not there, Watts, it'll scratch the gilt. Lay it flat in front of the Peking screen."

Violet waited until he was gone before opening the connecting door to the bedroom. "Now, Nancy, you really must rise for a few minutes." She clapped her hands together, trying to galvanise her daughter. "The

French gentleman has left a gift for you and I can't for the life of me imagine what it is. You simply mustn't leave me in suspense a moment longer. It's so gloomy in here. I'll open the drapes a little – it'll pep you up. Don't worry, I won't flood the room with sunshine, but you need some light, darling." She swept about, ignoring her daughter's mumbled protests. "Here's your peignoir, let me help you into it. Nobody's asking you to get dressed, Nancy, just slip into this and then come see your present. I wonder if it could be an antique? He mentioned an heirloom."

"I don't want to take presents from Mr Stubel, Momma. I don't know him. Samuel wouldn't like it."

Violet tied the neck of Nancy's robe, brushing her hair off her face. Then she linked arms and half-dragging, half-coaxing, brought her as far as the dressing room where Louis's package was waiting.

Nancy began to unwrap it.

"Here, let me help you, you're taking all day about removing a few sheets of paper."

Louis had mulled over possible tokens to bring Nancy, ranging from flowers to chocolates, but had finally decided on the offering which now lay across her knees. It was the *Titanic* plaque he had unscrewed from Lifeboat Number 16.

Both women were silenced. Violet regained the power of speech first. "Mercy, I'm absolutely appalled! What can the man be thinking of, giving you such a ghoulish memento? This is completely inappropriate. Nancy, child, I'm so sorry I dragged you out of bed to open it."

Nancy stared at the plaque. "I love it."

"You do?"

She nodded. "Samuel stood in this lifeboat and behaved like a hero. He laid down his life so others could live. That's something I can tell his son. And here's something I can show him. It's a symbol of my husband's courage, Momma. I'm grateful to Mr Stubel. Truly I am."

"Well, I guess it was generous of him. He could have sold it to souvenir hunters, they're desperate for *Titanic* keepsakes. I hear some of them have been hounding Captain Rostron for autographs. They say he's even receiving offers of marriage from predatory females, although he's already happily settled in that direction."

Nancy was stroking the raised lettering on the plaque.

"I wonder if it's quite legal," said Violet. "I mean, surely this is the property of the White Star Line?"

"It's mine now." Nancy's voice had a dreamlike quality.

"I expect Mr Stubel asked permission to take it. From Mr Ismay, probably. Yes, I expect so." Violet smoothed down her black dress.

"It's mine now," repeated Nancy, holding the plaque against her robe, where a rust stain was transferred to the chiffon.

"Very well, darling, if it means that much to you. I'm sure it was extremely kind of Mr Stubel. I imagine he realized it would have sentimental value."

"It's for my son – mine and Samuel's."

"Exactly. You must write and thank him."

"I'll invite him to tea tomorrow."

"Do you feel strong enough?"

"I heard the doctor telling you I was as strong as a horse and only staying in bed because I didn't want to get up, not because I couldn't. I want to have Mr Stubel to tea tomorrow."

"Then you shall, Nancy. I'll send Watts to his hotel with an invitation immediately. Or should I telephone?" Violet was still a little dubious about telephones. Nancy ignored her. "You're right, darling, a note is more personal. I'll send Roberge in to help you back to bed, you mustn't overestimate your strength, and I'll write to him." She swished away, fingertips assessing the coils of her pompadour, wondering what a Frenchman ate for afternoon tea.

13

"Have you seen our series of Alpine paintings, Mr Stubel? My husband's grandparents brought them back from their wedding tour." Nancy led him towards a triptych of unremarkable paintings in the furthest corner of the drawing room.

Louis followed, admiring the scalloped hem on her mourning gown, which matched the detail at her wrists. She had discriminating taste, he thought, not realizing the dress was chosen by her mother. She was too young for black, however. It bleached her face of colour and stole the shimmer from her hair. He found it barbaric that such a young woman should be condemned to widow's weeds for a year.

They left Violet spooning tea-leaves into the pot, moving to a corner of the room where she couldn't overhear them. Like her daughter, Violet preferred coffee but was loath to admit it in case it branded her unsophisticated. She was momentarily distracted from her tea-making by the sinewy grace of Louis's walk. Then she shook herself. She'd always been too brisk to waste time admiring handsome men. No percentage in it.

Louis realized, at first glance, how ill Nancy had been; her face had contracted to just the eyes. He was startled when they met again, thinking her – not older, exactly, but matured in a way he would have wished to spare her.

It had taken Nancy an age to dress. She stood, doll-like, while Roberge and her mother pulled on her combination, the one-piece garment which replaced the chemise and drawers. Over it went a corset which had to be laced up the back. Even before seeing the new hobble-skirt fashions in Paris, Nancy had resisted a voluminous froth of petticoats, favouring the sleeker outline, and so there had been only one petticoat to go on next. Finally came the dress which Louis admired for cut if not colour.

Now Nancy and Louis stood in front of paintings depicting the Alps in spring, summer and winter. No autumn: Samuel's grandfather hadn't cared for the season.

"Did you really speak to my husband, Mr Stubel?" Nancy spoke quietly.

There was a new-found naked quality in her gaze, so that some people found it difficult to hold it for long, but Louis looked steadily, aware of her pain. He saw a strand of her hair was twisted around an earring, and longed to untangle it. "Are you referring to the newspaper report, Madame Armstrong?"

"Yes. You said you spoke to him on the *Titanic*, shortly before it sank. I wondered why he would tell you about our baby. It seems odd. Samuel didn't know you."

"Perhaps he needed to share the news with someone. Perhaps he knew he might never get a chance to tell anyone else."

"Tea's ready!" trilled Violet.

"Coming, Momma. But why did you tell a newspaper about his last message for me? You could have given it to me yourself on the *Carpathia*."

"Mr Stubel is quite the art critic, Nancy. He practically lived in the Louvre, he told me. He's viewed the Mona Lisa countless times and a host of other wonderful paintings. Shall I pour?"

"Do, Momma. I can see Mr Stubel is struck quite dumb by the gauche pretensions of our Alpine paintings."

"If I might speak to you alone I could explain myself better," Louis murmured.

She gave no evidence of hearing his appeal, but after tea she said,

"Momma, I believe a breath of air may do me some good. I might try to persuade Mr Stubel to accompany us on a drive in Central Park."

"No persuasion is necessary – your wish is sufficient command."

"Bring Roberge with you as a chaperone, Nancy, I have some correspondence to catch up on." Violet had eaten too many iced fancies and needed to loosen her stays, as Nancy guessed would be the case.

* * *

Louis traced a finger across the writing on his twenty-pack of Fatima cigarettes and told himself he must not startle her by declaring his love. She was a pregnant widow. It was too soon to woo her, even supposing the difference in their stations could be overlooked. Yet chemistry crackled between them. He couldn't believe she was immune to it. She was so young, she would recover soon from that girlish infatuation with her husband and a new love would revitalise her. But he should tread carefully. She was vulnerable. The *maman* will be my best ally, he thought, I must cultivate her.

Nancy appeared in her coat and veiled hat and he stubbed out his Turkish-blend cigarette. They drove to the park in her carriage, Nancy and Roberge on one side and Louis rattling along opposite the ladies. Roberge contented herself with darting a succession of hostile glances, while Louis spoke of his favourable impression of the New York skyline. Rather than steeples, as in Paris, he described how the eye was met by a succession of towering buildings which struck him as etiolated churches with their domes, columns and spires. "They're temples in the sky," he announced, hoping to please with his analogy.

"I understand you're a secretary, Mr Stubel. Who's your employer?" Nancy was determined to keep him in his place so he would take no more liberties with her.

Louis stiffened at being reminded of his lack of status, but pride kept his face expressionless. "Until the day before yesterday I was in the employ of Monsieur Jean-Claude Pires of Paris. He was relocating to the Boston office of his family firm and sent me ahead with his luggage."

"What happened the day before yesterday?"

"I received a Marconigram telling me he died. It was most

unfortunate. He stayed in Paris rather than sail on the *Titanic* because he had a premonition of death, yet he died anyhow. A series of strokes."

"How unfortunate! Will you go back to Paris?"

"I must eat, which means I must find another employer." He gave a shrug. "But no, I don't think I'll return to Paris just yet. Your country interests me."

Nancy wondered if he'd have survived if his employer had joined the *Titanic*. Probably not: secretaries and valets were required to go down with their gentlemen. Shivering at the thought of his death, Nancy abruptly ordered the carriage stopped so she could walk a while.

"You mentioned something about explaining why you went to the newspapers with my husband's message for me?" Nancy prompted behind her parasol, which offered them some privacy from Roberge lagging a few paces to the rear.

"I know this probably sounds incredible but I simply forgot about it on the *Carpathia*. So much had happened, and I was in a state of shock. Later, when his words came back to me, I thought about writing to you. But the truth is I went to the newspapers first because I needed the money. Forgive me."

Nancy sighed. She hadn't the energy to be angry with him. Besides, Violet was delighted with such a public expression of Samuel's faith in her. Her mother was convinced it would improve their position with the Armstrongs.

"Thank you for the lifeboat plate," she said. "It will be an heirloom for my son."

"I hoped you would see it in that light. You anticipate a boy, then?"

Instinctively Nancy's gloved hand cupped her stomach. "A son, yes. But he'll never hear his father's voice or feel his arms around him. My son's father will be a ghost-presence in his life. It's such a waste."

Louis scuffed his heel against the grass verge, trying to restrain himself. But it was no use. "Love is never wasted, regardless of which direction it comes from," he said urgently, resting his gaze on her.

Nancy looked at him, retracted, and looked again.

"Madame, it is getting cooler." Roberge approached with a shawl for her mistress, but when she wrapped it around her she noticed Madame looked flushed rather than cold.

* * *

Hannah carried the pitcher of milk up the stairs, careful not to spill a drop.

"The very woman. Will I brew up some tea?"

"I wouldn't say no to a drop, Bridie."

She unpinned her hat and, while the kettle boiled, Bridie pricked herself idly with the hatpin.

"We can't trespass on Daniel and Kathleen's hospitality forever, Hannah."

Hannah's heartbeat slowed. It was too good to be true, that she could make a nest for herself here. Bridie was telling her it was time to move on.

"To be sure, I've outstayed my welcome. But I'll be sorry to lose you, Bridie. You're like the sister I never had."

"As I said to that eejit of an officer who wasn't for letting me on the lifeboat." Bridie laughed. "She's my sister, I told him – you wouldn't part sisters. I wasn't taking no from the likes of him."

"I can't see you ever taking no for an answer. You don't put up with anything you don't like."

Bridie threw the leaves into the pot with a violent flick of her hand, using her sister-in-law's apron to cover the scalding metal handle of the kettle and pour boiling water into the teapot. "People treat you the way you let them treat you. They'd grind you into the dirt if they could."

"Not everyone, surely," protested Hannah, astonished by her friend's rapid mood swing.

"Those that can, do." Bridie slapped cups on the table. "They couldn't care less about the likes of us, the people with power – they never have. The *Titanic* after going and sinking hasn't changed that. The last words Mama said to me were 'Maybe things'll be different in America'. They don't look that different to me. The world is ill-divided, whichever side of the Atlantic you're on. There's still them that has money and them that hasn't. Maybe the chances of getting a hold of some of that money are easier here, if you're willing to work, but that's the only difference. We have to get our hands on some of those dollars,

183

Hannah. We're due to start at the button factory on Monday – maybe in a few weeks we'll have enough put by to move into a room of our own."

"You want me to move in with you? You aren't throwing me out? I thought I was getting my marching orders!"

"Of course not. We have to stick together, Hannah."

Hannah stood and hugged her friend.

But Bridie pulled away, presenting her back to her friend. Words gushed out. "There's something I ought to tell you about myself, Hannah. Before you agree to share with me. Something I did that I suppose I should regret. But I don't, probably because I'm wicked inside and out. I was carrying a baby, same as you are, maybe a little further along. And I didn't want to go through with it. So I got rid of it, God forgive me. I don't suppose He will – I can't blame Him."

Hannah was nauseous. She'd heard about kitchen-table abortions but never met anyone admitting to one. Whatever about girls such as herself, who offended Our Lady by their lack of purity, girls who killed their own babies were the devil incarnate. So Father Byrne at home said.

"I'm not wicked, I don't care who says I am!" Bride spun around. "I did what I had to do. Or if I am, I'm no more wicked than Freddie Bowe-Spencer, who'll be a baronet one day and have half the county tugging forelocks to him. Bad enough that I had to clean up his mess, but all the sin can't be on my shoulders too. I won't believe I'm evil. I gave in to him because I loved him, and love is a good thing, it has to be. But I won't love any man ever again." She subsided, her breath coming and going in shuddering gulps. She wouldn't say another word about Freddie Bowe-Spencer. He was dead and gone for her, talking would only resurrect him.

Hannah swallowed past an obstruction in her throat. "What's done is done." She raised her hand to pat Bridie on the shoulder but failed to make contact, resting her fingers on her own stomach instead. Protecting the child inside.

"I suppose you'll stay here with Danny and Kathleen now. You won't want to be in the company of a woman who could kill her own child in cold blood."

Hannah's thoughts were too jumbled to answer. She realized Bridie, who had befriended her when there was no-one else to look out for her, deserved reassurance. Yet her tongue couldn't formulate any. She killed her own baby! It was repugnant.

The door opened. Danny paused, sensing an atmosphere. "What's going on? Where's the missus?"

Bridie's eyes begged Hannah. *Say nothing to him.*

"Next door, I think," said Hannah.

"That woman is never done céilí-ing." He unlaced his boots and sat heavily on a chair. "Any tea in the pot? My stomach thinks my throat's been cut."

* * *

Major Hudson paid a courtesy call on Nancy, intending only to leave his card. However, Violet sent the footman after him and insisted he stay a few minutes.

"It would rally the girl to see one of her *Titanic* friends. Do give me an opportunity to send for her. She's with the doctor but will be free shortly."

"I trust there are no complications?"

"Just a precautionary visit, major. He calls to her regularly in view of the precious cargo she's carrying."

The major wished he'd left it until another day to pay his call. Mothers were not a species an old Indian fighter was comfortable fielding. He wondered how this insistently curvilinear woman, boned and moulded into shape, could have given birth to such a willowy creature as Nancy.

A flurry at the door announced the arrival of another visitor. Rebecca Armstrong sailed into view, resplendent in a bird's-nest hat, complete with roosting bird. She was checked by the sight of the major, and Violet hurried to introduce them.

"Major Hudson, like the river," he said automatically.

Rebecca surveyed him. She was steeped in the intricacies of her lineage, knowing by rote the pedigree of each branch of the house and the marital connections spanning two centuries. She clicked through data, evaluating and discarding.

"Major Hudson, how do you do. You mean, of course, Hudson as in the explorer, a distant relative of the family. The river, indeed." She treated him to a chilly smile. "I believe our great-grandmothers were cousins – on the Fitzsimons side."

"You must mean my great-uncle Silas's first wife."

He guided her to a brocade seat into which she lowered herself gingerly, gripping the arms.

"Poor Deborah, yes, she died in childbirth when she was still little more than a bride."

Rebecca evaluated the major again. He was vintage American stock and knew his lineage, she approved of that. There were too many newcomers about, scheming to intermarry with the old guard.

Violet was thrilled by Rebecca's visit. It was tacit admission she acknowledged Nancy as Samuel's widow and the child she carried as one of his heirs. Her overtures to Louis Stubel had not been necessary. Rebecca had seen sense after all, sending Powell with grapes from her greenhouse following the funeral and having her calling card left on a brass tray in the hall with her handwritten compliments a few days after. A personal visit was quite an advance.

Realizing she had an acquaintance in her drawing room to meet Rebecca's exacting standards, Violet moved to lay claim to the major. "Major Hudson has been so kind to Nancy and me, we'd have been lost without him."

Rebecca took this as a barb. She was paying more than sufficient attention to this rather common woman and her seductress daughter. They flaunted her son's money – look at that enormous chandelier with the teardrop pendants hanging from the ceiling rose. It was positively vulgar.

The major cleared his throat. "I saw you at your son's funeral, Mrs Armstrong, but didn't like to intrude."

"Such a sad day," said Rebecca, who looked remarkably untouched by it all. "President Taft sent a spray of lilies, you know."

A door closing on the floor above and footsteps on the stairs signalled the doctor's departure. A few moments after, Nancy arrived.

"Mrs Armstrong, how charming of you to call. And Major Hudson, what a pleasure."

"Normally I never pay morning visits," announced Rebecca. "However, I was in the neighbourhood and decided to make an exception."

"Too kind. How's Adam?"

"He's back at school learning, among other things, about obligation; learning the family motto."

"*Be Mindful*." Nancy remembered Samuel quoting it. "Send him to visit me some time – he reminds me of his father."

Violet watched for Rebecca's reply. The older woman played for time by checking the watch which hung from her breast, her only item of jewellery apart from a wedding ring. "I don't see why not, although he has a lot of extra studying to catch up on."

Acceptance, thought Violet, and realized she'd been holding her breath.

Nancy was unconscious of the concession, preoccupied with re-positioning an American Beauty in a cut-glass bowl. Every day after breakfast, she made a ritual of arranging the long-stemmed roses in a blue oriental bowl. The blooms were delivered daily and stood beside a wedding photo of her wearing a filmy veil, her oyster charmeuse gown highlighting her tiny waist.

"What have you been doing with yourself, major?" Nancy's smile was automatic, but no less brilliant, over the rose-bowl. "Are you keeping busy?"

"I'm collecting stories for a book about weird coincidences attached to the *Titanic*. Many people had premonitions and refused to sail on her. There's an author I'm trying to track down, a gentleman by the name of Morgan Robertson. He wrote an obscure novella about a huge liner called the *Titan* which sank when it struck an iceberg – with devastating loss of life. It was published in 1898 and yet uncannily prefigures our own unfortunate experience."

Nancy's beautiful, near-sighted eyes attempted to focus on him. "Jiminy! You must meet our Mr Stubel, mustn't he, Momma? His employer cancelled plans to sail on the *Titanic* after a premonition of danger. It came in a dream three nights in succession."

"A premonition of danger? I was woken by one immediately after we hit the iceberg!"

187

"Mr Stubel's employer was forewarned in time to avoid sailing. Unfortunately he died several days ago – of a stroke, I believe."

"Extraordinary!" The major quivered with excitement. "I must meet him, you must introduce us."

Rebecca Armstrong decided Nancy and the major had lasted long enough without the benefit of her directing their conversation, and abruptly abandoned an exchange about the weather with Violet. She broadcast a complaint about a headache and despatched the major to fetch a packet of powders from a leather Gladstone bag in her carriage. With the major gone, Rebecca patted the seat next to her. "Sit closer to me, child, I want to take a look at you. Have you thought about a name for the baby? The Armstrongs always choose biblical names. Naturally it will be Benjamin if it's a boy, after my husband, but I suggest Esther for a girl."

Nancy faltered. "But I intend to call my son after his father."

"The Armstrongs never name their sons for themselves but for their grandfathers and granduncles. That is our family tradition. Adam was named for his grandfather and Samuel for his." All this was delivered in the tone of one who believed God's will came a poor second to Rebecca's.

"My son is to be Samuel, not Benjamin." Nancy spoke quietly but there was no mistaking the thread of determination.

Rebecca blinked. She absorbed Nancy, from the coils of her too-shiny hair to the grosgrain ribbon edging her chiffon gown – black, admittedly, but chiffon for mourning! – sinking to the crossed legs. At that, her chilly expression plummeted several degrees further south. A lady crossed her legs at the ankle, right over left, never at the knee. Who was this chit of a girl who had entrapped her son and now declined to be guided by her? She should thank her lucky stars the Armstrongs were willing to acknowledge her. New York society was closely knit and everyone knew exactly which rung on the ladder they occupied. Look at the alarm on that ridiculous mother's face – she realized how much her daughter risked in alienating her.

Violet followed their exchange avidly. Rebecca's insistence on choosing the child's name struck her as an endorsement. She couldn't fathom why her normally tractable daughter was digging in her heels –

for what difference did the baby's first name make so long as he had the Armstrong surname behind him? Her antennae warned of an imminent disagreement and she gushed to divert it. "It's too soon to settle on a name, Nancy. Mercy, I ran through dozens before I fixed on yours. I was determined you should be Melissa, then Alexandra, then Estella because I was reading one of Mr Dickens' novels at the time. Yet as soon as you were born I realized you could never be anyone but Nancy."

The woman talked nineteen-to-the-dozen and had nothing to say worth hearing, thought Rebecca. She wondered what could be delaying the major – she was ready for one of her headache powders.

The major was apologetic when he returned. "We searched every inch of your carriage, Mrs Armstrong, but there was no medication to be found."

She stood, setting the stuffed bird nesting in her hat a-quiver. "I must go home instantly. Is my carriage outside the front door, major?"

"Yes, Mrs Armstrong."

"Then be so good as to convey me to it." Without inquiring whether his visit was concluded, she added, "You may accompany me home. I should like to establish whether we have other family connections in common."

Meekly, Major Hudson prepared to take his leave. "You won't forget to introduce me to Mr Stubel?" he reminded Nancy.

"I'll send him to visit you, major. His story will be just the ticket for your book. Are you still staying at the Waldorf-Astoria?"

"Until the weekend, when I return to my apartment in Washington Square. I decided to have it redecorated, which meant staying on a little longer than originally intended." In fact, since the tragedy he found he needed people around him. The idea of being alone in his second and third-floor rooms in the neo-classical building was repellent to him.

"I'll telephone and ask him to call tomorrow. His name is Mr Louis Stubel."

A vibration of distaste quivered through Rebecca at the name of that man who was quoted in the newspaper – the one whose intervention persuaded her to give Nancy a second chance, although she'd never admit it to the Markovas. "Child, a lady in your condition should never wear heels. You'll end up with fallen arches. I should have expected your mother to advise you better than that."

Nancy looked at the inch-high heel on her satin slippers, before raising her eyebrows at Violet. Her mother gave an infinitesimal shake of the head.

They waited until the door was closed and they could hear Mrs Armstrong's imperious voice in the hall below, bullying Watts, their footman.

Finally Violet spoke. "I believe that visit is what we should consider a success. Mrs Armstrong seems willing to welcome you into the family."

"That rude interference counts as a welcome?"

"Of course, darling. We need her, you know. We've been living on credit since your return to New York."

"But I'm Samuel's widow. This house, its contents, these servants – surely they're mine?" Nancy was bewildered.

"Houses don't run themselves, Nancy, and servants expect to be paid; doctors too, for that matter. You have no income, none that I know of, until the will is read out. Samuel did make a will, didn't he?"

"Yes, but he wasn't satisfied with its terms. That's why we cut short our wedding tour. We learned about the baby in London and he wanted to come back to New York and speak to his lawyer. I think there might be a default in the will which settles a certain sum on any child born after his death, but I don't know how much. I thought Samuel and I had a lifetime ahead of us."

Violet took her daughter's hands between hers. "Some lifetimes have to be lived in a few months, Nancy. I need you to be strong now and try to remember what Samuel said about his affairs. Do you know how much control he had of the hotels? Is his mother head of the business or was it him?"

"There's a cousin, Noah Armstrong, who runs things on a day-to-day basis – he was there that day in the funeral parlour. But I know Samuel's mother has a lot of power, he was always complaining about it."

"In that case, Nancy, we must hope for clemency from Rebecca Armstrong. There's something I should tell you. We're living in a house bought in her name. We depend on her for the roof over our heads."

14

Major Hudson answered Louis's knock. "How do you do? So good of you to come at short notice. Allow me to introduce myself: Major Hudson, like the river."

"Delighted to meet you."

They were no sooner in his sitting room than the major leaned forward in his seat to pinion Louis. "I'm compiling an anecdotal book on *Titanic* 'coincidences' – although the more stories I hear, the less inclined I am to dismiss them as mere coincidence. Indeed, Mr Stubel, I'm becoming convinced the public not only needs but deserves to read this book. *The Jinxed Ship*, I'm calling it. What do you reckon?"

"I think such a title will certainly attract the public's attention."

"I'm not doing this for lurid purposes, Mr Stubel. Now, I understand your employer Mr Pires had some forewarning and cancelled his passage."

"He had the same dream three nights in succession: he dreamed he saw a huge liner, lights blazing, sink into the ocean – he heard the cries of the drowning as clearly as though they were just feet away. Monsieur Pires was so persuaded by his dreams that he decided not to travel on the *Titanic*, despite urgent business in Boston. His dream was correct, but it seems his time had come in any case. Last week, he died in his bath from

191

a stroke. Death came surrounded by water, *quand meme*. 'There are more things in heaven and earth' – isn't that one of your sayings?"

Major Hudson was mesmerised by the repetition of the phrase he had used to Edmund; did this Frenchman, too, acknowledge the spirit world? "Intriguing. I must make notes." He reached for a notebook, his pen racing across the page.

When they were finished he studied Louis. He was respectably turned out, properly polished shoes and a decent suit. The fellow had taste and poise. He had a trick of not quite looking the major in the eye, which the older man found respectful. It reminded him of the Cavalry, when junior ranks used to address themselves to a space immediately left of his eyes. "What are your plans? Will you return to Paris, Mr Stubel?"

Louis, who had also been assessing Major Hudson, reached a spur-of-the-moment decision. He would like to work for him until he had enough savings to set himself up in some line or other. He didn't yet know what that might be, but he was certain an idea would strike him in New York. Intuition, for which Louis had profound respect, urged him to stay in contact with the major. But how to persuade the major he needed a secretary? The trick was to have the major believe the idea originated with him.

Just then the door opened and a young man strolled in. Louis flicked his eyes over his dark green houndstooth suit toned with sherbet pink cravat and handkerchief and dismissed it as garish.

"Stuart, come and meet Mr Stubel. We're having a fascinating chat about the *Titanic*."

Louis stood, extending his hand, but Stuart nodded at him and pretended not to notice the gesture, instead strolling to the drinks cabinet and pouring a glass of sherry. "I'm starving, Pa, what time do we dine?"

"Soon as you like, my boy." Major Hudson turned back to Louis. "Well, I can't tell you how grateful I am for your mighty invaluable insights, Mr Stubel. Allow me to escort you to the elevator."

"There's no need, thank you. I can find my way back."

"French, are you? Off the *Titanic*?" asked Stuart. "Seem to remember hearing some of the chaps talk about a lily-livered Frenchman who dressed up in skirts to save his skin."

"Look here, Stuart, there was more than one Frenchman on the *Titanic!*" protested his father.

Louis faced Stuart, only the clench of a muscle in his cheek betraying his annoyance. "I climbed down a rope to return a baby to its mother. The boat was lowered away before I had a chance to return to the *Titanic.*"

"Say, I had forgotten that!" Major Hudson's jaw worked as he slapped him on the shoulder. "Well done, young fellow! Stay and have a drink with us. Stuart, this gentleman did a mighty fine thing. Pour some sherry-wine for Mr Stubel. Or would you prefer Scotch?"

"No, thank you, I'll intrude no longer. Perhaps I may leave the address of my hotel for you, in case I can be of further assistance? If I think of anything else in connection with Monsieur Pires's premonition, I'll write to you here."

"Not here, I'm moving back into my apartment in Washington Square, 12b, you can reach me there. It's high time I went home."

"I understand it's a most agreeable neighbourhood."

"It suits me. An apartment is more than enough for my needs. It's frowned on by some of the neighbours, of course. They think it criminal to turn the houses into apartments, but they're too large by modern standards. Better to convert them than let them fall empty."

After Louis left, Stuart announced he was taking a bath, retreating with the sherry decanter. Major Hudson read the newspaper in an aimless fashion, turning page after page without being able to settle to a story, until his eye was caught by an advertisement headed *CELEBRATED SPIRITUALIST.* Gripped, he read on.

Your loved ones are not lost! They have only crossed over to the other side. All that separates you from them is a veil. Mama Carmen can lift that veil and help you make contact with those you love! She is channelled by her spirit guide, who gives her unparalleled access to those in the other dimension with messages for you. This world-renowned psychic, newly arrived in New York, has been consulted by the great and the good including acclaimed British writer Sir Arthur Conan Doyle. MAMA CARMEN'S POWERS ARE GENUINE!!

The major felt a catch in his breath. "Jean directed me to this, I feel sure of it." He copied down the address, noting personal callers were welcome between three and six o'clock on Tuesdays and Fridays. Good, he'd call to her premises tomorrow. He had no hopes of Stuart sharing his interest, he was only a boy, too much life in him to think about the dead, but he did wish Edmund could be more open-minded about the occult. It would be companionable to have someone with him. Still, it was only a matter of time before prejudices were eradicated and spiritualism became accepted. The major stood to pour himself a finger of sherry and realized the decanter was missing. He frowned. Stuart was fond of a drink. Still, that was natural with young men – he'd knocked back a fair amount of grog in the mess himself, as a young buck.

* * *

The following afternoon Louis presented himself again at the Waldorf-Astoria. Louis reasoned that the more Major Hudson saw of him, the better his chances of making himself indispensable. Realizing how attached the major was to his theory about the *Titanic* as an accursed ship, he brought the newspaper clipping he had saved about a mummy on board. It had been a busy morning for Louis, who had made further inquiries about the mummy story with his contact on the *New York American*. Enthralled, the major announced he would write to the British Museum inquiring about it.

"Ah, you use a typewriter then?" asked Louis. "It makes correspondence look professional. Organizations such as the British Museum give priority to typewritten letters. I know this because I worked for an English banker."

"Can't use one of those contraptions." The major touched the wax on his moustache, which brought it to twin points. "Guess I could hire someone to do it for me."

"Allow me," insisted Louis. "But I'll need to borrow a typewriter since the one I used lies at the bottom of the ocean." He paused. "I could also type up some of your notes, if you like. It makes it easier to read through them and cross-reference."

"I couldn't impose on your time."

"My time is my own, *Monsieur*. My employer is dead, and I must consider what to do next. In the meantime I can help you, if you're willing."

"Well, perhaps if you'd just type up that letter to the British Museum – it's important to do things properly. I can send out for a typewriter for you." He hesitated. "Good of you to call, Mr Stubel. I should like to talk this mummy business over with you some more. But I'm just about to hail a ride – I'm going on a little expedition."

"I'll take up no more of your time. Perhaps I could call again later in the week and tell you a little more about this mummy, the priestess of Amen-Ra? She died hundreds of years before Christ was born, and was buried deep in a vault on the banks of the Nile. In 1889 four rich young Englishmen visited the excavations at Luxor and were invited to buy an ornate mummy case containing her remains. They drew lots for the privilege – and each of them met a horrible end. But I won't detain you any further. We can speak of this again."

Major Hudson was hooked. "I say, won't you join me? I'm headed for Fourth and 10th. We can chat as we go. It's so refreshing to meet a fellow traveller on the spiritualism road."

They were driven to the Lower West Side and found themselves in an area that was neither prosperous nor down-at-heel. The locals were on amicable terms with the police officer who stood on the corner, watching the traffic. Many of the houses had tubs with a few sulky flowers, and a small restaurant with gingham tablecloths and an Italian name above the door was doing a brisk trade. Louis jumped out to reconnoitre, reading Mama Carmen's name on a wooden plaque alongside a greengrocer's door.

"This appears to be the place, above the shop, *Monsieur*."

The major dismissed the driver and rapped on the door with the knob of his walking stick. It was opened by a girl in her mid-twenties, an apron wrapped twice around her middle. She looked at them in an accusatory fashion. "I bain't a servant, I'm just helping out as a favour. I'm an American and I serves nobody."

Major Hudson nodded. "I see. I wonder if Mama Carmen is at home?"

He felt in his waistcoat pocket for one of his cards, expecting to be asked to state his name and business, but dealing with strangers was obviously her mistress's stock-in-trade.

"Follow me." The maid scampered ahead up a flight of stairs covered in linoleum.

On reaching a small anteroom, Major Hudson and Louis were told to wait. Before the girl disappeared the major managed to press his card on her, which she studied dubiously. "You bain't like any major I knows."

"Do you know a great many?"

"My fair share, I should think. We get all sorts here."

As he waited the major noticed a framed testimonial to Mama Carmen's powers on the wall and peered. It seemed to be signed by – he squinted – the Tsar of Russia.

The maid reappeared.

"May I ask, is that letter from Nicholas II?"

"It could be from Nicholas the twenty-second for all I knows or cares. Mama Carmen tole me to say she'll see you now."

"Should you like me to wait here, *Monsieur?*"

"Just plain 'major' will do. Yes, wait if you would."

Major Hudson was led into a claustrophobic room in which everything seemed to be red – from the heavy drapes blocking out light at the window to the lamps which diffused a crimson glow. Even the walls were covered in matt red velvet. A wave of heat hit him, as though the room was fired by a furnace. A heavy, imposing woman of Hispanic origin rose at his entrance. Beside her stood a man whose thick black whiskers and overhanging eyebrows contrasted with his shock of white hair. The man had a pelican's beak of a nose with a knobble at the bridge, through which the bone gleamed beneath the skin. A ring with a tiger's-eye stone on his thumb lent him a showy quality. The woman, by comparison, exuded a charisma which had nothing to do with the silk shawl striped in vibrant colours draped over her dark gown. Her skin was sallow, her hair blue-black and piled high on her head, but her most arresting feature was luminous grey eyes. Wide-set and glowing, they were shadowed by semi-circles and gave her an air of one who could empathize with the pain of others.

"Howdy do, friend. You're welcome, yes, siree." The man's smile displayed large, tobacco-stained teeth. He held the major's card between his thumb and forefinger. "My name is Walt Keppel and this is my wife Mama Carmen. How may we be of assistance?"

"Good day to you both." The major bowed to Mama Carmen.

"Thank you for granting me an audience, ma'am. I am a widower of twelve years' standing. Recently I believe my wife contacted me from the other side. I was involved in a disaster of epic proportions and I'm convinced she intervened to save my life. It strikes me she wishes to communicate again – there may be some message she's keen to relay. I've been dreaming of her every night, dreams in which Jean and I have the most wonderful conversations, but when I wake in the morning I can't remember a single word. Naturally this is most disconcerting, and I thought I should seek assistance from someone attuned to psychic matters. I fear I'm just a hoary old soldier who's missing the relevant vibrations."

"Well, friend, if anyone can help you I can safely say it's my wife. Yes, siree, she has a rare gift. We're recently arrived in this fine city from San Francisco, where Mama Carmen had a wide circle of admirers."

He didn't add their departure from San Francisco had taken place at dead of night, ducking out just ahead of the bailiffs.

Mama Carmen took a step forward. "How did you lose your wife?"

His eyes misted over. "She died of TB. I tried everything to save her but her time had come and no power on earth could keep her with us. But I've been fortunate: she left me with a son, the living image of his sweet mother."

The medium's voice was melodious and as deep as a man's. "I sensed a great sorrow welling up in you from the moment you entered the room. It reached out to me and begged me to alleviate it."

The major gazed into her dilated pupils. "I spent too long apart from her when we were married, years I can never reclaim. I was in the US Cavalry and posted to the western states. Jean would have joined me, she was fearless, but I preferred to think of her safe at home on the East Coast."

"I see an aura surrounding you, a dark, oppressive aura signalling deep sorrow. My heart hurts for you."

The major was surprised, for a dozen years had given him plenty of time to adjust to the loss of his wife. He missed her, of course, but he enjoyed life. Still, if Mama Carmen sensed an oppressive aura perhaps he was carrying a burden of grief. "Can you help me make contact with her, Mama Carmen? So many times I feel as though I'm on the brink of communication, only for it to evaporate into thin air."

"Yes, I can help. You must place absolute trust in me – do you trust me?"

The major nodded. He felt an urge to surrender his will to this compelling woman.

"When you come again I should like you to bring a photograph of your loved one, along with some personal effect belonging to her – a comb or an item of jewellery. I can use it to help make contact. The more personal the object, the greater my connection will be. Come next Monday, we have a séance at eight o'clock." She passed quickly from the room, shawl floating behind her.

"You're honoured, friend. Mama Carmen doesn't usually invite strangers to one of her séances at the first meeting. I should explain our terms. I deal with the money side. Mama Carmen doesn't sully her hands with dollars. Obviously we have expenses, Mama and me. It's not that she charges a fee, her gift doesn't operate that way, but if you could see your way clear to making a contribution of, say" – he appraised the major – "fifty dollars, I think I can safely say you won't go home disappointed. Half the money up front would be appreciated."

The major produced his pocket book and Walt Keppel reached for the money with hands that trembled in their eagerness, bunching the notes.

"We'll expect you shortly before eight, friend. Ever been to a séance? No? I think I can safely say you'll find it quite an experience. Yes, siree, quite an experience. Don't forget the photograph and the other item my good lady mentioned. You'll get better results that way. You did the right thing coming to Mama Carmen, friend. People think they can handle the dead on their own but they never make good. To work in this area without a truly gifted sensitive is like" – he screwed up his eyes – "like looking at the stars without a telescope. You'll make some progress, can't deny it, but there's a limit to how much. You may muster enough of the magnetic force to call in a spirit but it probably won't be the one you want. It's directionless, see, like standing in the street and hollering a name instead of making straight for the home of the person you wish to contact."

"The magnetic force?"

"Yes, siree, the odylic force. My wife has it in bucketloads. It's what makes her one of the truly great sensitives. You'll see for yourself at the séance."

15

Bridie disliked it at the factory from day one. The six o'clock starts didn't bother her as much as the pressure to work seven days a week when the bosses demanded it. *If you do not come in on Sunday when asked you need not come in on Monday*, said a notice on the factory floor. Bridie felt entitled to at least one day free a week. Slavery was supposed to be abolished here.

By comparison, Hannah didn't mind the factory and was glad to earn as much as possible while she was fit to work. Besides, she liked the buttons, all shapes and sizes of them. Imagine there being so many types of buttons in the world! Buttons for gloves, blouses, coats, trousers, jackets . . . They reminded her of the elegant buttons on the uniforms of the *Titanic* officers, embossed with a flag and the shipping company's five-pointed star. Even Tom, with his aversion to uniforms, had allowed they were handsome.

"We have to get out of here," hissed Bridie, as they swallowed bread and butter sprinkled with sugar in their meal-break.

In theory they were allowed forty-five minutes in the middle of their shift but no-one took it. They knew they'd be sacked – on some pretext – if they did. Instead, workers gulped their food and returned to their stations as quickly as possible. Until the previous month, workers had eaten where they toiled – despite the lack of ventilation and the heat generated by the machinery – and records were doctored to dupe Labour Department inspectors. But an inspector had caught them red-handed and the owner had been reprimanded, so now the letter of the law was adhered to: a whistle was blown and supervisors made sure the workers left their places.

Bridie was fretful, crumbling her crusts. "I can't bear working here, I don't care how good the money is. There have to be other jobs in a city the size of New York."

"It's not so bad once you get used to it."

"Maybe I don't want to."

"What would we do instead, if we did leave?"

"I've heard of an opening in a laundry – Enrico the barber told me about it. Anything has to be better than this," hissed Bridie, under the suspicious gaze of a foreman in braces. The foremen disliked people talking, even during their meal-break. Chatter affected productivity.

"But Danny took the trouble to find us the job," protested Hannah. "And I need to earn money while I can, for when the baby comes along."

"I keep telling you, Hannah, there'll be compensation from the *Titanic*. You're a pregnant widow. If you aren't entitled to a few shillings then nobody has any chance of money from them."

"I don't know how to go applying for no compensation money."

"I'll keep you straight. Anyway, those Red Cross busybodies are doing a good job of keeping tabs on all of us. Once the money comes through from White Star you'll know all about it, never worry. Now, we have to come up with a way of persuading Danny to let us quit. He's such a bossy boots, he thinks he's my father. Dada was never as bad as Danny – at least I knew how to get round him."

"He has your best interests at heart. Cheer up, we get paid today."

Hannah was always anxious when Bridie complained about Danny, knowing she owed the roof over her head to him. Besides, she liked the factory well enough. Her fingers were nimble at the work, counting buttons made of cowhorn or wood and boxing them or sewing them on to cards in sets of six, eight and a dozen. Best of all was handling the mother-of-pearl and jet buttons intended for luxury items such as ladies' clothing. Bridie was unsettled by the constant roar from machines with clunking arms, punching pistons and clanking wheels, but Hannah could block it out and conjure up images of Doon.

That evening they queued for their first pay-packet, Bridie brightening at the prospect of money to spend. She was going to treat herself to something pretty on her way home – in New York you could shop late into the night, thanks to Thomas Edison lighting up the city. When she counted her money, however, she discovered only fourteen dollars instead of eighteen. Hannah checked hers and saw she was also short.

"There's been a mistake with our money," Bridie told the cashier. "We're due another four dollars each."

The cashier, black sateen shirt protectors over his sleeves, consulted a ledger. "No mistake. Your friend was fined for excessive lavatory breaks and you broke some buttons."

"Excuse me! They were split to begin with. And even if they hadn't been, you could get a haystack of buttons for four dollars. As for lavatory breaks, what else can you do if nature calls? Do you want us to squat down beside our work stations?"

"No need for crude talk. Shift along, you're holding up the line."

"But this is unfair! I want to see someone about it. I know when I'm being victimised."

"Shift along, I told ya."

Hannah pulled Bridie aside before she said something she might regret. She knew what her friend was capable of, in a temper. As they walked towards the stairs one of the more experienced hands, a woman with the red-veined nose of a tippler, caught up with them. "Don't look back. It's the head foreman, Zimmer, the one grinning like a Barbary ape. He always takes his cut from new girls, splits it with the cashier. He'll only pick on you for a couple of weeks, then your wages'll be left alone."

"I'm not putting up with it!" Bridie whirled around and stamped up to the foreman. His grin increased when he registered her fury. "You're a sleeveen and a crook, so you are! You'll come to a sticky end!"

Zimmer's eyes, webbed from squinting, narrowed into their creases. He didn't know what a sleeveen was but he caught the gist. "You mind your manners, girl, if you want to keep your job."

She caught him by the sleeve. "I know your sort. You'd steal the eyes from a corpse and go back for the eyelashes. Now give me and my friend the four dollars each you conned out of us, or I'll stand here screaming 'til the peelers come."

He shook her off. "I don't give two bits for your threats."

Bridie opened her mouth so wide her tonsils were visible and emitted a banshee's howl. Zimmer folded his arms, prepared to face her down, but at the manager's approach he put his hand over Bridie's mouth and bundled her away. Other workers hugged the walls, reluctant to get involved. Bridie bit the calloused flesh, thrashing about.

"You're hurting my friend! You've no right to do that." Hannah hung on his other arm, impeding his progress.

Bridie's teeth hit their mark. Exasperated, the foreman let go, and her renewed shrieks would have woken the dead. "All right, all right, here's your money." He flung some dollar bills on the floor. "Crawl for them, if they mean that much to you."

Bridie bent and retrieved the money, ostentatiously counting it. "You'll not make me ashamed of taking what's owed to me." She stuffed half the notes into a pocket of her coat. "Here's your money, Hannah, it's time we were going home."

Belatedly, Zimmer realized he was supposed to be the one telling them to leave. "The pair of yez can clear off, and don't think there'll be a job for yez to come back to on Monday, either."

Bridie laughed, sliding her arm through Hannah's. "Will we stop in at the soda fountain for a Coca-Cola on the way home, Hannah? I have a metal taste in my mouth. I think it might be blood."

* * *

Danny Ryan disapproved of swapping jobs after just a week, but he could see there was no returning to the button factory. Besides, he was secretly pleased Bridie had refused to kowtow to that foreman. "Fellows of his sort are so clever they'd meet themselves coming back," he told Kathleen. "It'll do him good to be pulled up short."

The girls were taken on as piece-workers in a hand laundry on the corner of Broadway and 23rd Street. Although its temperature was searing, and the experienced hands warned them it would be even hotter in July and August, Bridie enjoyed the work at the Clean and Brite. She proved deft with the iron and showed she could handle the requirement of ironing a shirt a minute. The manager soon switched her to the more costly fabrics. Bridie found she could earn up to $25, and never took home less than $19.50, but for that she worked a twelve-hour day, six days a week.

Sometimes the manager, Warren Vicosen, who admired her soft round arms, sleeves rolled above the elbow, would offer to sell her items that went uncollected by their owners. "You're the cutest little squaw," he'd tell her, and pinch her bottom if she didn't step out of his way quickly enough. Bridie picked up an embroidered shirtwaist at a bargain price. She knew she was meant to be saving but she couldn't resist it.

Hannah, less enamoured of the work, wondered why she had come all the way to America to labour from morning until night in a laundry, and go home with her hands scrubbed raw and the small of her back aching. That wasn't part of the milk-and-honey future Tom had outlined to her walking by fuchsia-studded hedgerows, birdsong spilling from them.

"I have to go to America, Hannah, there's no prospects in Ireland. No hope of advancement unless you have pull. I have the dollars from my sisters in Chicago. I'm leaving on the first sailing that'll take me."

Hannah's pace falters, heart shrivelling at the thought of being left behind. She has loved this little rhubarb stalk of a man from the start, loved him for the tender way he has with him, for all that the veins stand out like cords on his arms. He has promised to write, but she fears he'll forget about her when he reaches America, with those fancy girls she could never hold a candle to – sure how could she compete with American girls? She lowers her eyes to the dusty road and the birdsong takes on a mocking ring.

Then he catches her by the shoulders and the words stream out – words that transform everything. "Come with me, Hannah darlin'! I won't go at all if you don't come with me. I could no more leave you behind than I could cut off my right arm."

Hannah was less adroit with an iron than Bridie. Vicosen docked her wages after she scorched a pillowcase, and instead set her to toiling at one of the vast porcelain sinks with a washboard. She breathed air laden with particles of soda, ammonia and other chemicals, on her feet all day in steamy temperatures with her hands in hot starch, or her knuckles pounding against washboards. Perspiration dripped from her. The floors were made of cement and it often seemed to her as though she was standing on roasting coals. No wonder she wasn't gaining much weight, her child a neat bump high in her stomach. Looking at her workmates, it was clear long days of toil were ruining their bodies. Hers would be wrecked too, in no time. But sure what odds, who'd want her anyhow? Tom O'Brien was her first sweetheart and he'd probably be her last. Still, it was good to be independent. At home, working on the family smallholding with only the egg money to call her own, it took her months to stockpile what she could earn in a week here.

Running a mangle alongside her in the washroom was an eleven-year-old girl called Pamela Sadowska, the main wage-earner in her family after her mother was injured in an accident at the laundry last year. Children under fourteen were not supposed to be in employment but Pamela had lied about her age.

"I been working in the garment trade since I was old enough to pull a thread. 'S a fact," she told Hannah, bravado rippling through her round-shouldered frame. "I bain't too good at the reading and writing though."

Betsy Ettor, one of the American girls, was in the Laundry Workers' Union and kept urging Hannah and Bridie to join. "Accidents happen because we're tired," said Betsy. "What about Pamela's mother? She can't ever work again." Mrs Sadowska had suffered first-degree burns to her hands. "If we all band together in a union, we can push for shorter working hours."

"Vicosen says we'd only use our spare time for immoral purposes," giggled Bridie.

"Everything's a joke to you, Bridie Ryan. But children working like grown women is no joke. Who's to keep them out of the workplace if we women don't? Everyone knows the truant officers aren't able for the job. Pamela here should be in school."

"I'm too old for school!"

Bridie liked it at the Clean and Brite, but she felt the absence of pleasure keenly and had a sense of life passing her by. Where was the point in an embroidered shirtwaist if there was nobody to admire her in it? She discounted the manager, who had bad breath from constantly grazing on pickles – besides, he was married.

"We must get out more," she told Hannah, but after work her friend was content to sit at home gossiping with Kathleen.

*   *   *

Major Hudson set off for the séance at 10th Street, accompanied once again by Louis. The Frenchman insisted it would be prudent for the major to bring a companion and, since it was his first experience of a séance, the major was inclined to agree. It was unknown territory, after all, and back-up was a sound idea – Cavalry training had taught him that. He found himself already reliant on Louis, who had a most agreeable way of anticipating his needs. He could use some assistance with *The Jinxed Ship*. Was there any chance Louis Stubel might consider accepting a position with him? He would broach it on the way to the séance.

Three others were waiting ahead of Major Hudson and Louis in the vestibule. One was an elderly lady with a black veil over her face and the other a young woman with a resentful mouth. The third was a man with second-degree burns etched into his skin. The maidservant, who still wore the oversized apron but had added a lace cap to her ensemble in honour of the impending séance, showed them through to the parlour.

"I think perhaps you should join us, Stubel," said the major.

Louis had a profound distaste for clairvoyants, having drunk crème de menthe one evening in Paris with some psychics who chortled over the gullibility of the public. But he bowed and followed the major. The room had been cleared of all furniture apart from a circular table, chairs and a small side table with a lamp. As before, Major Hudson was conscious of a wellspring of heat when he entered, although there was no fire in the grate.

Walt Keppel rubbed his hooked ridge of a nose. "Welcome, friends, welcome. Mama Carmen is in particularly fine form, I think I can safely say no-one will go home disappointed. I'm going to pass around a container for your contributions and then we'll get started." He walked around with a crocheted bag, his tiger's-eye ring gleaming in the lamplight. He paused by Louis. "I see we have a stranger in our midst. Howdy do, friend. Did someone send you to us?"

"This is Mr Stubel, who's with me. Do you object, Mr Keppel? Perhaps I should have checked in advance."

"I guess not. I'll tell Tilly to bring in another chair." He appraised Louis from under his shaggy eyebrows. "Are you hoping to make contact with the spirits, friend?"

"I have no hopes in that direction."

"Still, I guess we'll have to charge you if you're intending to sit in on a séance."

"Allow me." The major extracted some bills from his pocket book and tossed them into the bag, which restored Walt Keppel's humour.

He flashed his horse's teeth. "Now for those newcomers tonight – I believe that's only you and your associate, Mr Hudson–"

"Major Hudson," Louis corrected him.

"Major Hudson. As I was saying, folks, there's one or two rules. Nobody must attempt to touch or waken Mama Carmen once she goes under, I cannot stress this too emphatically. It could be catastrophic for the sensitive if she's wrenched from her state of grace. Her body is tethered but her mind wanders free through the spirit world, see, guided by Ada, her spirit contact. I can't answer for the consequences if she's disturbed while this separation of body and mind are in train. Nobody must leave the room until the séance is finished. Nobody must leave their place at the table for any reason. You are, as always, at liberty to search the room and, indeed, my own person before we get started. We have nothing to hide. Mama Carmen doesn't need to indulge in special effects – she communicates with the spirit world through the genius of her talent alone. Major Hudson, did you remember to bring some personal effects belonging to your wife?"

The major produced Jean's portrait saved from the *Titanic*, and a brooch in the shape of a sprig of heather. "Will I be able to have these back?"

"Of course, Major Hudson. My wife just needs to run her hands over the objects associated with the dear departed and meditate on them before she starts. It helps her pick up psychic signals, see? You can bring 'em home afterwards. Now, friends, if you'd like to take your seats, I'll fetch my good lady."

He left the room, and the others stole covert glances at each other. It struck Louis how the acoustics of the room were muffled, so that when the elderly lady brought her fist to her mouth and coughed, the sound seemed to erupt from an unexpected quarter. Beside her, the young woman parted her mouth for a nervous whinny. When Keppel returned, Mama Carmen two paces behind him, a sigh born of anticipation and relief floated around the group. Her expressive eyes swept them. Louis wondered if he was imagining their quizzical light as they rested on his face, quickly replaced by a sympathetic glow. No, this was showmanship and he was allowing himself to be sucked in. He studied her carefully: a woman not to be underestimated, he concluded.

The medium's hair was loose, flowing down her back almost to her waist, a few streaks silvering the black, and she wore a simple white muslin gown, cinched tight by embroidered bands under the bust in a vaguely Grecian style. Her jewellery, however, was that of a barbarian princess: an enamelled necklace in the shape of a phoenix, beak circling her neck and wings extending across her breastplate, with a smaller version fastened around her left wrist and clunking when she moved her arm.

"If everyone could kindly place their hands on the table," directed Walt Keppel.

They laid their palms on the heavy velvet cloth which trailed against the rug underfoot, and their shadows leapt up the walls in separate flurries before spreading to an interlocking uniformity. Mama Carmen had still not spoken. Instead she seemed to be listening intently. She laced her fingers and stared at the gridlock of lines in her palms; within a few minutes her eyes glazed and her head slumped forward. A ripple passed through her body and it became rigid.

Her husband leaned behind him and adjusted the lamp until it was a whisper away from extinguished. They were almost in darkness, apart from a faint glow from the street-light beyond the curtained window. Suddenly an object flew through the air and landed on the lap of one of the circle.

The elderly woman gave a gasp. "It's a rag-doll!" she exclaimed. "It looks just like the one my little Pauline used to have."

The tinkling of a fairground tune was heard, seeming to emanate from several points within the room, and a breeze riffled the air, bringing a scent of toffee-apples. Slowly the table began to tilt, first one way, then the other. Louis watched to see if any of the others were manipulating it, perhaps using a lever under the cloth, but counted seven pairs of hands on the cloth including his own. It continued to sway, as though seeking to break free from its tether and levitate. All at once the table gave a shake and settled back. Out of the gloom emerged a voice. It was Mama Carmen's.

"No, I cannot help you and I don't believe you can help us."

She cocked her head, listening.

"No, I'll wait for Ada."

Again that focused demeanour.

"Ada is my spirit guide, I must wait for her. Your presence among us is agitating her. She won't come to me until you leave us." Her expression betrayed a struggle, a series of muffled raps rang out on the table, then a change stole over her features, smoothing and growing perceptibly calmer. She began to speak again, although not in the voice she had previously used. At first the voice was weak and incoherent, the words disjointed, but it gained in strength until a small girl's tones could be heard. "A long, long way . . . so dark crossing over . . . Lloyd butted in ahead of me but I hid 'til he went away . . . messages for many of our friends." There was a fluttering sigh. "A lady called Helena came up to me, such a pretty lady with ringlets. She stroked my cheek and said to tell George she's whole again, no marks. He must stop worrying about her – the flames didn't hurt. She says he did everything he could to save her, it was nobody's fault. He's not to blame himself."

"Sweet Helena, she reads my mind!" exclaimed the scarred man seated to Louis's right. "Is she happy? Does she have friends to keep her company?"

"Many close friends. She's at peace."

"I expect she misses her pony. Helena was always attached to her little Shetland. She used to feed him sugar lumps from her hand. He knew to nuzzle her pocket for them. I had to have him put down afterwards – I couldn't bear to look at him."

"Ponies go to heaven," continued the child's voice issuing from Mama Carmen. "Yes, they do, cats and dogs too. Helena says she hitches her pony to a trap and goes riding with him every day. It pleases her to have him with her. There's someone else here who has a message for one of our group. Does anyone know a lady whose name begins with the letter V? Victoria? Maybe it's Veronica? I can't exactly make out what she's saying to me. An old lady with white hair. Perhaps her name begins with a W and not a V. She has a little lace cap at the back of her head and a kind smile."

"Could it be my grandmother, Ursula de Meyer?" burst out the young woman with the sullen mouth.

"That's it, it's a U. She says she's called Ursula and that her granddaughter is here. The lady says to tell Florence she's grown up real beautiful, but she must be beautiful inside, too, and do the right thing. She says Florence will understand."

"Why must I do the right thing?" protested the woman.

"She says it seems hard now but it will be worth it in the end. The lady, did she come from the old country in a boat when she was a little girl?"

"No, she was born here."

"Oh yes, the lady has just corrected me, I misunderstood her. She says to tell you not to stay away from home too long."

"I was to visit friends in Kentucky next month. Does my grandmother advise against it?"

"She says you can go, but to remember you're needed at home."

Something fragrant drifted from the ceiling onto the table and Florence gasped. "Rose petals! My grandmother cultivated roses. It's a sign!"

The voice shifted an octave, a breathless note injecting it. "Muttie! Muttie!"

"Heidi, is that you?" cried the old lady.

"Muttie, I miss you!"

"I miss you too, Heidi. Is Papie with you? I worry about you being lonely without your muttie."

"I miss Muttie but I like having Papie. We've been playing hide and seek." A child's giggle sounded. "Papie never knows where to look for me, he's not very good at it. But he gives me candy when the game's over."

"Tell Papie not to give you too much candy, it will rot your teeth. Heidi, do you love your muttie? Do you?"

"I love my muttie very much," lisped the voice faintly.

Then the voice sounded, more strongly. "There's a soldier in our company who's escaped great danger. From a shipwreck, I think. Wait, someone is whispering the name of the ship to me. The *Ti* . . . yes, the *Titanic*."

Major Hudson gasped. "That's me, I had a narrow escape from the *Titanic*."

"I have a lady beside me. She's a beautiful lady with light hair and eyes that shine when she says the name Richmond. She says she loves you dearly and it was painful to be taken from you. She wants you to know she's watching over you and Stuart. She says your love is not dead, it's simply entered a new phase."

Major Hudson bowed his head, too choked to speak. Beside him, Louis glared at Mama Carmen: these were trite communications, she was telling the major nothing new – she could easily have discovered the few details with which she peppered the message. He had given her his card, after all, and was listed as a *Titanic* survivor.

"She says she was tempted to have you join her, beyond the veil, on that dreadful night when the ship sank. But your time has not yet come. There is something you must do before you and the lady can be united."

"I knew it," gasped the major. "I knew I'd been spared for a reason. Did she mention my book?"

The child's voice was replaced by a trained soprano's, dipping and soaring through a wistful aria from Mozart's *The Marriage of Figaro*. *"Dove sono i bei momenti…"*

Louis was startled, some timbre in the voice touching him to the quick. The singing stopped abruptly.

"Another lady and gentleman have joined me. The gentleman is of high rank and the lady says she sang in society. She says tell the clean-shaven man she sang this to him in his cradle. It was his favourite lullaby."

Goosebumps prickled on Louis's skin. He was the only clean-shaven man present. "Who is she?"

"She says all your life you've followed your head. Now all of a sudden you're following your heart. But there must be balance – too much of one and too little of the other upsets life's equilibrium. She says you were to be given your father's name, after they married, but they didn't–"

A series of angry raps sounded on the table followed by a crash as Mama Carmen's forehead hit it with a thump. Her husband snapped on the light and the circle pushed back their chairs, blinded.

"Someone fetch Mama a glass of water," Walt Keppel ordered.

Florence went to the anteroom and called for Tilly. Feet thudded downstairs from the floor above and the request was repeated.

Mama Carmen opened unfocused eyes and clutched at her larynx. "My throat hurts," she mumbled, voice grainy.

Tilly arrived with a glass of water. "I brung you something to drink."

"It strikes me Mama Carmen might need a drop of brandy," remarked the scarred man.

"My wife never touches intoxicating liquor." Walt brought the glass to her lips and she drank thirstily, fat drops spilling on her muslin gown.

By and by she looked around. "Was I of any assistance?"

"Your trance address was magnificent," her husband reassured her.

"Couldn't we continue?" suggested the scarred man.

"We must take care not to overtax Mama Carmen's strength," said the elderly lady. "I'm sure I speak for all of us when I say how privileged I feel to have witnessed such an impressive display of psychic powers."

"Ada did have more messages for you all but two other spirits burst in on us, a lady and her husband," said Mama Carmen. "They're connected with this gentleman here." All eyes swivelled towards Louis. "This couple has been desperate to make contact with our new friend for many years, and when the opportunity finally presented itself they had no patience to wait their turn."

"Who is this Ada?" asked the major.

"She works in heaven to redeem her murderer," said the old lady.

"Poor Ada was murdered at the age of eight by a neighbour," explained Walt. "His name was Lloyd Berry and he strangled her and six other little girls before committing suicide. Nobody ever connected him

213

to the murders – Ada's family even placed flowers on his grave. It happened in 1838 in Baltimore."

"Is he in hell?" asked the major.

"There's no heaven or hell in the after-life – that's a primitive notion based on reward and punishment," Mama Carmen chided gently. "He was full of anger and self-loathing and now he's being educated to love himself and hate his actions. He's learning from his mistakes and Ada is one of his teachers."

The scarred man caught her hand, pressing his forehead against it. "Mama Carmen, you've given me such reassurance. I can sleep easy now, knowing my wife is physically whole in the afterlife."

"The fire was a horrible experience for you, Mr Eugenides, but it was an accident and you mustn't continue to relive it. You must learn to re-engage with life."

"But to see her suffer excruciating pain for those months!" He shuddered. "The loss of her eyesight was a tremendous blow."

"At least you know she can see again," said Mama Carmen. "She told you there are no longer blemishes on her flesh."

"Thank God! And thank you, Mama Carmen, you've lifted a crushing burden from me."

The psychic traced the outline of a plum bruise rising on her forehead and winced. "Major, was there a message for you?"

His face was lambent. "I spoke with my wife for the first time in twelve years. You've shown me love can survive the grave."

She turned to Louis. "And you, do you remain an unbeliever?"

"Mama Carmen, this has been an education."

She frowned. "There was something in particular the lady wanted me to tell you but I couldn't catch it . . . the connection was severed. Lloyd Berry frightened Ada away."

Mama Carmen had not converted Louis. He was almost certain he had seen Walt Keppel reach under his chair for the rag-doll flung on the old lady's lap, and the raps on the table could have been made by Walt too. As for the fairground music, a hidden gramophone could take care of that, while the rose petals signified little. It was also possible the table tilting had been carried out by the Keppels – it wasn't a particularly heavy item of furniture. He was far from convinced Mama Carmen possessed extraordinary gifts. The messages were too vague, the sitters too eager to believe them. Conjurors' tricks, thought Louis. A production had been staged, a convincing one, but either the maid or her husband was helping Mama Carmen to hoodwink the naive. Louis was not prepared to accept he had witnessed anything paranormal.

Major Hudson entertained no such doubts. In the cab home, he enthused about Mama Carmen. "I must attend another séance – she's an extraordinarily talented sensitive. I was captivated, hearing her sing an aria in Italian. Her husband told me she speaks only English and Spanish, her native tongue. I should bring Stuart to communicate with his mother. Imagine if the boy could speak with her, what joy it would bring them both!"

Yet the singing resonated within Louis, for no reason he could explain. And how could Mama Carmen have known he was following his heart for the first time in pursuing Nancy? It must be a lucky guess.

16

The script conference, held in a sitting room in Jules Brulatour's suite, went well for Edmund.

"You got the common touch, Ed," Jules said, after hearing his ideas for *Saved From The Titanic*. "You sure burned the midnight oil on this baby – I like that. You'll go far. You really never done none of this scriptwriting before?"

Edmund didn't admit he'd filched his ideas from his sister. Among her suggestions was for Miss Dorothy Gibson to wear the dress in which she was evacuated.

"Oh boy, the press will lap that up!" said Jules.

Dorothy was particularly pleased because she had to pay for her own costumes, which rankled with her. She interrupted Edmund to complain how unfair it was that the studio refused to supply costumes.

"Never mind your griping, we got work to do," Jules slapped her down.

"Mary Pickford don't like providing her own costumes neither. She calls it a liberty," she insisted.

Jules rolled his eyes towards Edmund and mimed "blah-blah-blah".

"Lousy cheapskate! You must think I'm some schmuck. You studio chiefs make enough money out of us actresses without twisting the knife!"

217

"Twisting the knife! I'm making you a star, baby."

"I don't wanna be a star, I wanna be a lady.

"You ain't the only fish in the sea – there's plenty more dames."

"I wanna be a legitimate actress, on the stage. Motion pictures ain't legitimate acting."

"Flickers put that swanky gown on your back, baby, and those furs in your wardrobe. They paid for that French perfume you sprayed on the pillow before we hit the hay last night, and they're paying the rent on your apartment. So don't go shooting off at the mouth about legitimate acting to me."

"You big lug! You ain't got no empathy, that's your problem." Dorothy crossed the room and stood in front of Edmund, eyes pleading. "You got no idea how humiliating it is, being pestered on streetcars and asked for your autograph."

"You love the attention!" boomed Brulatour.

"I feel so exposed. I don't never know when an autograph hunter is going to ambush me. I ask this big baboon for a pay rise to compensate me but what does he do? He laughs in my face."

"I'm turning you into Éclair's biggest star! You should be on your hands and knees thanking me."

"A star! You don't even list me on the credits. It's all Éclair, Éclair, Eclair and the great Jules Brulatour. You started off as a buck-grabber, a middle-man selling Eastman film to the studios. What makes you the great motion picture expert?"

"Shut your trap, you ungrateful piece of skirt!"

Edmund tiptoed to the door.

* * *

The motion picture was rushed out in record time, debuting exactly a month after the *Titanic*'s sinking. Edmund had free tickets to distribute for the opening night and had the idea of inviting the Irish girls to clear his debt to them – and because he wanted to see Bridie again. He persuaded a Saint Vincent de Paul representative to give him their address and paid them a visit. Danny was still at work, and Hannah and Bridie were minding the baby while Kathleen paid her respects at a wake house. She had a weakness for wakes.

Bridie thought her eyes were deceiving her when she spotted Edmund Newton walk up Third Avenue. Her first instinct was to jump back into the room from her perch on the windowsill, in case he accused her of spying on him, but she was afraid he might walk on. Anything was better than monotony, even a chat with this long drink of water.

"Ahoy there, shipmate!"

He stretched his neck, seeking the source of the voice, and touched his hat brim when he recognized her.

"Slumming it, are you?"

"As a matter of fact, I'm looking for you, Miss Ryan. Mrs O'Brien, too."

"Well, come on up, fourth floor, mind your step on the landings, they're on the dark side."

Edmund was initially surprised by the faded grandeur of the tenement's brownstone frontage – a vestige of style which hinted that this rabbit-warren of rooms had once been home to members of the Knickerbocker class. But the longer he stayed there, the more the feeling grew that the building was wounded somehow.

The women were excited by his invitation to the premiére and the first night party. Bridie looked him over, wondering if she'd been a bit hard on him. Mind you, she preferred him without his spectacles – the way she remembered him from the *Carpathia*.

"Are you sure we'd be let in?" asked Hannah. "It sounds very –"

"Classy." Bridie supplied the adjective for her. "There's no place like America! I can't wait."

"Certainly you'll be admitted. I said you were my guests. Major Hudson will be there too."

Hannah's face was transformed by a smile, while Bridie's excitement gratified Edmund – who suddenly remembered he was the one meant to be grateful to the girls and not vice versa. "I haven't forgotten what you ladies did for me. I might never have got into the lifeboat but for you." Edmund patted the baby gingerly on the head, called him a sturdy fellow and pressed a silver dollar into his podgy fist. Daniel Junior let out a raucous squawk and Edmund backed off.

"Babies have never liked me."

"I'll walk out with you and show you where to get the streetcar," Bridie offered.

On the sidewalk, he offered her his arm. "Which way?"

"Let's take the air for a few minutes. Sure where's your rush?" Bridie wanted to do like the American girls and promenade with a man. She swung her hips, wishing she was taller to be more like them. Edmund glanced down at the head bobbing below his shoulder, and acknowledged she was a fetching little miss.

They negotiated their way past a dripping hydrant, an Italian fruit-seller who leaned on his cart and sang out the price of his wares, and a gaggle of street arabs who looked speculatively at Edmund's pockets. He wondered if every fruit-vendor in the city was Italian.

Bridie wanted fun tonight – and Edmund Newton was her best chance of some. "How about taking me to one of those Lobster Palaces? I bet you go there all the time." She forgot to look coquettish and was an eager girl instead.

Edmund was flattered she should think he frequented Lobster Palaces, but still had work to do on the script. He had already taken off more time than he could spare to visit the girls. "I'd like to, Miss Ryan, really I would, but I have an engagement. Perhaps another time?"

"Oh." Pause. "I don't suppose that major friend of yours needs a housekeeper?"

"I'm afraid not. Are you looking for work?"

"I have a place in a laundry but I'd like something better. I thought the Upper East Side might suit me. Will you let me know if you hear of anything?"

"Of course. How are you finding life in New York? It must be very different to Ireland."

"It is and it isn't. Here, I have a brother trying to tell me what to do instead of a father."

Edmund opened his mouth to explain young women needed an older male relative to protect them, but was distracted by the flash of Bridie's dark eyes. "I'm going to find a place of me own. I'm bone-weary of Danny laying down the law to me."

This alarmed Edmund. Women had weaker minds than men, which meant they also had weaker moral frameworks. Heaven knows what would happen to this feisty one if she sloughed off her brother's guardianship. "I think that might be a tad rash." He adopted his most measured tone. "You are very young, after all –"

"I'll be twenty-one in August."

"Precisely. Your brother has your welfare at heart."

Edmund strolled a little further than he had intended with Bridie. He felt more at ease with her than he usually did around women, although he couldn't look directly at her except when her attention was elsewhere. Girls unnerved him, even ones of an inferior class.

After they parted, Bridie took her time going home and there was a scene with Danny, who had arrived in ahead of her.

"Where were you?" he demanded

"Out."

"Out where?"

"Out walking."

"With an Englishman?"

The baby started to bawl, awakened by the raised voices, and Kathleen murmured in the background pacifying him.

"Questions, questions, a priest wouldn't ask you as much."

"What have you got to hide?"

"Nothing, Danny, I have nothing to hide."

"Couldn't you have found an Irishman to step out with? Sure the Lower East Side has more of them that the whole county of Limerick."

"Irishmen, Englishmen, they're all one to me."

"Well, they're far from all the same to me. But leaving that aside, I'll not have the family name dragged through the mud, Bridie Ryan. You'd never get away with that back in the old country and don't think you can do it here. You're making a holy show of us – only a certain class of girl goes out walking after dark."

"Are you calling me a hoor?" Her eyes heckled his.

He was checked by her appropriation of a word he would not have used in front of her. "I'm just saying, is all."

"Just saying what, exactly? That I have to sit in and be a good little girl, the same as if I was back in Ireland? You're my brother, Danny, not my father."

"You're living under my roof. I have a right to expect decent behaviour."

"Aye, and I'm paying for the privilege. Don't I hand over the dollars to your Kathleen, regular as clockwork?"

"Answer me this, at least. Did he try anything on with you?"

"Try anything on, is it? Jaysus, that fellow's a monk. If he saw a woman lying naked on the street he'd step over her." She relented and honeyed her voice. "Come on, Danny, what have I done that's so wrong? Here's me in the Land of the Free, and I can't exercise any freedom. I just wanted to stretch my legs and talk to someone who got off the *Titanic*, same as me."

Bridie had longed for something exciting to happen – for Edmund Newton to take her somewhere with lights and music. But all they'd done was go for a stroll. How could she be leading such a humdrum existence in the heart of this pulsating city? She might as well be back in Oola for all the benefit she had of New York. She continued, defensive. "You have to enjoy a bit of life while you can, God knows you're a long time dead. If I didn't know that before I set sail for America, I certainly knew it by the time I arrived."

The reference to the *Titanic* deflected Danny's annoyance. A matter of weeks ago he had thought his little sister lost, now he was bellowing at her for staying out late. "You always did want to be out and about mixing with folk, Bridie."

Kathleen, who thought brother and sister were alike, both as ornery as the other, judged it time to step forward and urge Danny into bed. Changing the subject, she chattered about a neighbour's toddler who fell from a third-floor window and landed with the agility of a cat.

Bridie joined Hannah on their mattress behind the curtain, stripping down to her petticoat.

"Listen, Danny," she called then, "why don't Hannah and I watch Daniel Junior tomorrow evening and yourself and Kathleen take a stroll? You never get out."

"I take her to Mass on Sundays."

"Come on, man, you can do better than that. Isn't it time you showed off your best girl to the neighbourhood? She has no fun at all."

"Fun costs money." Kathleen's voice was layered with regret.

"Go on, the pair of you! I won't take no for an answer."

While they were out, Hannah could mind Daniel Junior and Bridie would have a chance to slide off and see if there were any rooms to let in the area.

* * *

The girls were entranced by the movie theatre: its world of plush, its embracing warmth, its opulent darkness, won them over immediately. People rustled either side of them, waving to friends or chattering with anticipation, but everyone settled down as soon as the orchestra in its red-lit pit struck up. Machinery began to whirr, and Hannah and Bridie looked a long way down towards a flickering screen which sprang to life. Magically, it showed pictures which moved. A girl in a magnificent hat. A man in a sailor's uniform. A liner in distress at sea. Hannah and Bridie hardly dared breathe in case it disturbed the amazing vista. So engrossed were they, it never occurred to them they were watching a recreation of a drama they had shared in.

Dorothy Gibson gave the performance of her career in *Saved From The Titanic*. Fantasy blended with reality as she shivered in a lifeboat in a white evening gown with matching above-the-elbow gloves, a sweater over her dress. The theatre was absolutely silent, not a cough hacked, not a cigarette-lighter clicked, for the ten minutes of the picture's duration.

Its fast-paced story told of Miss Dorothy, returning home to the United States to be married to Ensign Jack of the US Navy. She wrote to her parents that she'd set sail on the *Titanic* from Cherbourg and telegraph her arrival time on Sunday night. Impatient for news, Jack went to a wireless post to communicate directly with the *Titanic*. While there, *Titanic*'s SOS was received and Jack was distraught, fearing his sweetheart at the bottom of the ocean.

Miss Dorothy was saved, however, and the sweethearts were reunited at home with her parents, where she described the collision with an iceberg. As she relayed it, the screen filled with shots of the ship foundering, and Miss Dorothy became agitated reliving the nightmare and fainted. The next day her mother visited Ensign Jack with an ultimatum: he must choose between her daughter and the sea. The mother feared her child's emotional health would suffer irrevocable harm if she had the worry of a seafaring husband. He had twenty-four hours to decide.

Jack was torn between love and duty. He confided in his captain and the commander pointed to Old Glory floating in the breeze, advising him a naval officer owed his allegiance to the flag.

The next day Dorothy's father arrived for his answer and Ensign Jack replied, "A sailor's first duty is to his flag and country."

Impressed, the father called in Dorothy and put her hand in Jack's, saying, "My daughter, there is your husband."

The theatre erupted into a standing ovation at the end, the audience's applause drowning out the orchestra. "A sailor's first duty is to his flag and country," Edmund mouthed along as the star-spangled banner filled the screen. It was the only line of his to survive the re-writes. Listening to the whistles of approval, he felt dazed. They like it, he thought.

Afterwards there was a party in Jules Brulatour's suite and ice-white *Titanic* cocktails were served by waiters dressed as sailors, while an orchestra played Alexander's Ragtime Band.

"You sure got a schnozz for publicity, Ed." Jules tapped the side of his nose. "That dress gimmick has everyone buzzing. We gotta get you working on another of our flickers. How do you feel about sinking your teeth into a western?"

"I haven't actually been west yet."

"No problem, go see a coupla flickers and you'll get the idea. Catch Bronco Billy, he's the real McCoy. You wanna see Joe Public jump when he turns his gun towards the camera and fires. What movie does that happen in, baby?"

"Never mind those cowboy movies. How do you think I look in the poster?"

They were standing in front of a poster for the moving picture, which Edmund had already sent to his sister in Nottingham. ÉCLAIR'S WORLD SENSATION screamed the lettering, with a tilting *Titanic* on an ice-floe-strewn sea. Inset was a photograph of Dorothy in her evening gown.

"You look serene and stylish, baby, same as always."

"I was as serene as a foghorn – I was hell-bent on getting off that ship." She patted Jules on the cheek. "Thanks for crediting me on the poster, Jules."

"You deserve it, baby. I see you got the bracelet."

She waved her arm, on which diamonds glittered, and made a kissing motion with her lips. "You're spoiling me."

Edmund couldn't decide if he preferred them as lovers or fighters. He cleared his throat and read aloud from the poster. "*Miss Dorothy Gibson, a survivor of the sea's greatest disaster, tells the story of the shipwreck, supported by an all-star cast, in the film marvel of the age.*"

The pair ignored him, Jules whispering in her ear and Dorothy giggling.

Edmund reached for some soft-shell crab from a passing waiter, and as he did he caught sight of Major Hudson and hailed him. "How's your book coming along, major?"

"In leaps and bounds now I've engaged a secretary – a French fellow by the name of Louis Stubel."

"I know him. He was on our lifeboat and I met him on the *Carpathia*."

"Think he'll be a tremendous help to me, Newton. I must find Stuart. I think he's looking for some, what is it you call them, starlets?"

He ambled away, and in an eddy of the crowd Edmund saw Hannah and Bridie standing in a corner. His first thought was how attractive Bridie looked. She was wearing a dress borrowed from the laundry – the owner would never be any the wiser – and her glossy curls pooled onto crimson satin. He started to go across to them, but was intercepted by a pair of Éclair executives.

The Irish women gorged on canapés, apart from the oysters – they didn't like the look of them. Too slimy, they agreed. They also disregarded the highballs after their first spluttering sip of one.

"Jaysus, this stuff makes Dada's *poitín* seem mild," choked Bridie. She hailed a waiter. "Hey, sailor, haven't you got anything for a lady?"

"Would you like a liqueur? Mr Brulatour says his guests are to have anything they want."

"Anything at all?" Bridie's eyes gleamed.

"Anything at all," confirmed the waiter, whose shoes were too tight and who was fantasising about kicking them off at the end of his shift.

"I'd like a dish of ice-cream." Hannah was greatly daring.

"Certainly, madam. I'll bring a selection of flavours. And you, miss?" He raised an eyebrow towards Bridie.

"I'd like . . ." she tapped her teeth with a fingernail, "I'd like champagne. I'm partial to a glass of it – this isn't the first time I've had it, you know."

The waiter swallowed a laugh. "One dish of ice-cream and one flute of champagne. Leave it to me." He eased through the crowd.

"When did you ever have champagne, Bridie?"

"Never, but I'm not letting on to that fellow."

He was back within minutes, their orders balanced on a silver salver.

"You just tip me the wink when you want refills."

They smacked their lips over their champagne and ice-cream. "What does it taste like, Bridie?"

"The bubbles tickle going down. Here, try some."

They star-spotted among the party guests, commenting on the gowns of the ladies who glittered like night stars – some of them even wore jewelled stars in their hair.

"Fierce immodest," they whispered to one another, part-envious and part-scandalised by dresses cut so low at the front you could see every curve of their bosoms, near enough.

"That's how it is in society but it would never do in Oola," said Bridie.

Major Hudson saw the pair staring, fish out of water but enjoying every second of it. He pushed through the throng.

"If it isn't Major Hudson-like-the-river," said Bridie, who didn't need champagne to be bold, but it helped.

He bowed. "Charmed to meet you again, ladies. You both look enchanting."

"You're looking fierce smart yourself, major," said Hannah shyly. Delighted, the major brought his fingers to his luxuriant moustache, proud of how dark it was, despite the salt and pepper sprinkling his hair. Hannah couldn't believe she was in conversation with such an elegant gentleman, in his starched evening shirt with pinprick diamond studs instead of buttons. The men at home never wore white, it was impossible to keep clean. Maybe a white collar for special occasions but that was the height of it. And here she was in a room where many of the men were in tail-coats. Even their shoes were shiny, not from polish but from some class of leather they called patent. She pulled at her dress, livened up with a swirl of lace. She must stick out like a sore thumb. Maybe she shouldn't have resisted Bridie's suggestion to borrow something from the laundry. Look at her friend, blossoming under the major's attention. Bridie's pretty face meant she fitted in anywhere.

"We can't have you crushed in this crowd," said the major. "Let me find you some seats."

Just then the major's elbow was jogged by a man alternating sips from two over-filled glasses. "Pa, I've brought you a Brandy Smash. Hall-oo, who have we here?"

Bridie and Hannah were confronted by a dandy of a man with bright blue eyes.

"Hannah, Bridie, allow me to introduce my son, Stuart Hudson. Stuart, this is Mrs O'Brien and Miss Ryan. We met on the *Titanic*."

Not the boring old *Titanic* again, thought Stuart. Still, it had thrown this little filly in his direction. Was she Mrs O'Brien or Miss Ryan? He hoped she was Mrs O'Brien – married women were often more accommodating. The single ones tended to expect a fellow to keep his promises. "Ladies, it's an honour." He handed both slopping glasses to his father and rocked back on his heels, fingers hooked in his waistcoat. "Listen to the music, it has my feet tapping. Won't one of you take pity on me and come for a whirl around the floor?"

"There's no room for dancing, Stuart. Your partner will be crushed to death."

"Nonsense, I see some couples have cleared a space near the band. Who'll risk it?" He smiled into Bridie's eyes and extended a hand.

She drained her glass of champagne, hiccupped, and reached it to Hannah. "I'm game."

"I bet you are."

His face was admiring as he swept her away, in a collision of chemistry and collusion of sexual intent.

Edmund Newton, who was on the point of stepping over to Bridie with the same suggestion, was exasperated. That Hudson puppy had beaten him to it. Look at him swinging her about to 'The Oceana Roll', he'd hurt the girl if he wasn't careful. Edmund fumed as he turned back to Dorothy, who wanted his attention while Jules was occupied with the studio's financiers.

"That just leaves you and me, Hannah." The major liked this raw-boned woman's gravity – his own Jean had possessed the same quality. Hannah had self-effacing ways, but the major noticed her. He was partial to her hair in that coronet of plaits, and to the freckles on her hands and dusted across her nose. "Shall I get rid of your ice-cream bowl?"

Hannah quickly scooped in the last mouthful.

"Now, why don't I find us both somewhere quiet to sit down for a chat."

"Have you heard anything about Mrs Armstrong, major? Is everything all right with her and the baby? I'm not asking to be nosy, but on account of being in the family way myself."

"You don't say! Congratulations, when is the happy event due?"

"November."

"Splendid." He seated her and then settled himself in a chair alongside her, lifting the tails of his coat. "That's something to remember Mr O'Brien by, isn't it? I understand from Mrs Armstrong's mother that she's due to give birth around the same time. It was a bit of a shock to her, seeing her husband's body, but she's a plucky thing and rallied. She's managing wonderfully well, considering. I imagine the baby's a great consolation, as it must be for you. You ought to be mighty proud."

Hannah was silent. Then she burst out, "Bridie wants us to share a room together."

"Don't you care for the idea?"

"I suppose. I have to think of the baby – she's not fond of children." The more Bridie talked about the two of them renting together, the more Hannah worried. She wouldn't be any help with the baby. She never dandled Daniel Junior or sang him lullabies, and when a bee stung him it was Hannah who grated an onion and applied it to the throbbing spot.

"She's not much more than a child herself," said the major. He liked

228

to make himself useful around women and racked his brains for some service he could perform. "Say, are you in a draught there? No? Well, can I fetch you something, a cordial, perhaps?" Hannah shook her head. Major Hudson was at a loss. Then he remembered these modern young women sometimes liked to boast about their jobs. "What do you do, here in New York? Do you work in one of those manufactories I hear all the young women are flocking to nowadays?"

"No, I have a job in a laundry."

"I see." He fingered his waxed moustache. "I used to be with the US Cavalry. Best days of my life."

"I knew you were a soldier, I didn't know you were a Cavalry officer."

"Yes ma'am, I was proud to be a Bluecoat. It was an honour to wear the uniform of the United States Cavalry. Until, well, until I had a change of heart." He missed the music of the bugle. There had been a bugler on the *Titanic* alerting first class to the dinner hour, but it had lacked the sweet urgency of the bugle call on a tour of duty.

"What happened, major?"

"The Battle of Wounded Knee happened, back during the Apache Wars. That's more than twenty years ago, but it's as fresh in my mind as the day it happened."

"Do you mean them Red Indian fellows? The savages? Mind you, I shouldn't call them that – Father Byrne at home used to say some of them took up a collection and sent money to people in Mayo during the Famine."

"No, they certainly weren't savages. They did some savage things, but not as savage as us." He scrubbed at an itch between his eyebrows. "I was seconded to the War Office as an aide-de-camp to General Nelson A Miles back in 1890. That autumn he sent me to the Seventh Cavalry to observe a Messiah craze sweeping the Dakota reservations. The Sioux Indians were restless and had started doing a Ghost Dance. Their medicine men told them a Messiah was coming and he'd bring happy hunting grounds with plenty of wild game, just like in the days before the white man. They wore shirts decorated with eagles and buffalo, believing they'd make them impregnable against the white man's bullets."

"Like the Irish when they went into battle against the Normans. We learned about it at school. They painted Celtic patterns on their chests and thought they'd protect them from arrows and blades."

"I presume they didn't?"

"No, the Normans beat us. But then we beat them by turning them into ourselves."

The major nodded. "Assimilation. The dance spread like wildfire through the Sioux villages and whites feared an Indian uprising. The order went out to arrest Chief Sitting Bull at the Standing Rock Reservation. He was killed in the attempt on December 15th. When news came of his death, Chief Big Foot led his people south to seek protection at Pine Ridge. The army intercepted them on December 28th and brought them to the edge of Wounded Knee Creek to camp. The next morning the old chief was carried from his wagon to a blanket on the ground for a powwow with our Cavalry officers. It was as clear as the nose on your face he was dying. The medicine man, fantastically painted, started doing the Ghost Dance, throwing dust in the air and shouting 'Ha! Ha!' We had a half-breed scout translating for us and he said the medicine man was telling the braves, 'Do not fear but let your hearts be strong. Many soldiers are about us but their bullets cannot penetrate us. If they do come towards us they will float away like dust'."

Hannah's gaze was riveted to the major who was staring into the middle-distance as he marshalled his memories. She thought of the cigar-store Indian she had traced her fingers over, touching it to check it was wood and not flesh.

"I don't know how or why it happened but a shot rang out. The warriors were jittery and reached for their rifles. Our troopers responded by firing into the Sioux camp and the women and children scrambled for their lives, only to be cut down in the crossfire. I saw a trooper lose his nose. Mighty queer thing, it dangled by a few sinews. It was chaos. The troopers fired indiscriminately, into their own lines as well as into the Sioux camp. When the smoke cleared there were three hundred and fifty dead, mostly women and children. Big Foot was among them. Only twenty-five soldiers were dead. That was the end of the Ghost Dance movement – and the Indian Wars." He ground to a halt, troubled still, all these years later, by the carnival of carnage.

Hannah's heart was pounding. "Why did they do it? It sounds like a

230

bloodbath."

"It was a bloodbath, Hannah, a massacre. Some laid the blame on the Seventh Cavalry, which wanted revenge for General Custer's death. He was a fool and a braggart, the Cavalry was well rid of him. But soldiers are loyal to their officers – I guess it's all about loyalty. Duty to the flag, like we saw in the *Titanic* film. Or to your family. Loyalty to your tribe, maybe."

Hannah bowed her head, absorbed, as the glow from his cigar moved from hand to mouth and back again, its sickly-sweet smell catching in her throat.

Loyalty. It was important, she couldn't deny it. Hannah's mind was made up: Bridie was entitled to loyalty from her. She would move into a room with her.

"I think I'd like to go home now."

The major felt for a shred of tobacco clinging to his tongue and pulled it away. "So early? But the party's only just cranking up."

"I'm a working girl, I have to get up in the morning. Money makes the world go round, major, and money is something I'm never likely to have except what I earn by the sweat of my brow. Maybe my life would be different if I had a few shillings. But 'If ifs and ans made pots and pans, what would the tinkers do?' I can't see Bridie. Is she still dancing with your son, do you think?"

"If Stuart has his way, she is. He'd dance the night away. Let me find Bridie for you and then we'll rustle up a hansom."

"We'll get the streetcar, major." Hannah was scandalised at the expense.

"I wouldn't dream of it, at this hour," he said. "I insist you allow me to send you home in a cab, I'll take care of it."

Major Hudson was disconcerted to notice an intimacy in the stance between Stuart and Bridie when he found them in the throng. *"Put your arms around me, honey,"* crooned the singer, and Stuart was warbling along into her ear. The major didn't kiss his wife until he offered her marriage. Before their engagement she was never unchaperoned in his presence, apart from when he made his proposal. Yet here was his son whispering in a young woman's ear. It was something impertinent by her expression – yet not too brazen, for she was smiling now.

The older man felt a sense of loss; he missed the intimacies between a man and a woman, and not just those of the bedroom. He tried to remain celibate, but something always weakened his resolve. During his stay in London he had availed of the services of several Judies. However, prostitutes were a stopgap that did nothing to satisfy his need for closeness. If only he hadn't promised his dying wife he'd never remarry. Doctors advised the husbands of consumptive women against conjugal relations, and a continuation of self-denial had seemed no sacrifice. At fifty-one the major still needed a woman; at thirty-nine he had imagined he would never look at another.

Stuart caught sight of his father and waved, Jean's smile reconfigured on his confident face.

"Scatterbrain," he said to his son, affection welling. "You'll dance the legs off this young lady. She needs to sit down. I hope my son isn't turning your head with his nonsense, my dear?"

"He could charm the rain into not getting him wet, that one!"

When the major returned with Bridie and Stuart, Hannah gave her a searching glance. Bridie seemed animated.

"You don't have to leave now if you don't want to, but I'm ready for me bed," said Hannah. "I could sleep on a clothesline."

Bridie hesitated. "It's not so late."

"Swell, you can stay on," said Stuart. "We can have another drink and a dance."

Bridie could see how tired Hannah looked. "I think I'll head on with you after all. The morning is early coming, and you need your wits about you with the heat off those irons."

"I'm going to escort these ladies outside," said the major. "Will you come with us?"

"*Kind hearts are more than coronets* – always your motto, eh, Pa? Tell you what, I'll scout round and rustle us up another Brandy Smash or two. I'll wait for you by the band."

"Do we need to see Mr Newton before we go?" asked Hannah. "It was kind of him to invite us to such a lovely party, we should thank him."

The major scanned the room. "I see him with the young lady who acted in the motion picture, but it would take a pickaxe to make our way through to him. I'll convey your compliments later on."

* * *

"You seemed to be getting on well with the major's son," said Hannah, in the hansom cab.

"He's a nifty dancer, so he is."

"He doesn't look a bit like the major. What's his name again?"

"Stuart. Said he'd take me to the moving pictures again some night."

"You're not going, are you?"

"I don't mind either way."

"You'd think, Bridie, you'd have learned from what happened with Freddie Bowe-Spencer." It was the first time Hannah had referred directly to him.

Bridie's eyes snapped. "It's not the same at all and you have no right to pretend it is. Anyway, who gave you leave to go throwing Freddie Bowe-Spencer's name about?"

"I'm just worried for you, Bridie."

"Because I danced a few jigs with a young fellow? Sure I danced half the night away with various lads on the *Titanic* and you never said a word."

"I didn't know you as well then. I didn't mind what happened to you. Besides, they were our own kind. The major's son is a gentleman."

"Ah, for God's sake give over! I won't go with him, if that's what you want. Sure I told you I'm not bothered."

"It's only yourself I'm thinking of, Bridie."

* * *

Edmund was hunting for Bridie, wanting to boast to her about how Jules Brulatour had promised him work on another motion picture. Perhaps he could become one of these people, with their inventive slang and can-do attitude. Edmund knew he was conservative – the premature onset of middle age had troubled him, even as a student. He wound up teaching because it paid enough to keep himself, his mother and sister. Minerva's offer of her first job at the end of 1911 had brought a glimmer of freedom and started him thinking about a trip.

Already his hunch was paying off. Where else but America would he have been offered a scriptwriting job with no track record? Tonight two "vamps" – "As in vampires, buddy – they'll bleed you dry but what a way to go," Jules Brulatour winked – had made it clear they'd like to see him in a more personal setting.

Edmund spotted Stuart with an empty glass in each hand. From his glazed stare, it was clear he hadn't stinted. "Don't suppose you know what happened to some acquaintances of mine from the *Titanic?*"

"*Titanic, Titanic, Titanic,*" spat Stuart. "The gramophone needle's stuck. The *Titanic* is a crashing bore."

Edmund ignored the outburst. "You were dancing with one of them. Did you see where they went?"

Stuart collected two more drinks from a passing waiter and downed one. "My father went off to tuck them into a cab, haven't set eyes on him since. Expect he's rustling up another damsel in distress – Pa has a Sir Galahad complex."

Edmund was ashamed. The girls were his guests and he should have attended to their needs, not left it to Major Hudson. Some of his euphoria as a hotshot scriptwriter leaked away. "I see." His lips tightened. "I noticed you seemed to be getting along swimmingly with Miss Ryan."

"You mean Bridie?" He swayed slightly. "Heck of a fine filly – I've arranged to see her again. Might bring her to a show. That should be worth a kiss. Or more."

Edmund was furious. Of course it was of no consequence to him who Bridie chose to keep company with, but she showed poor taste in succumbing to this fellow. Look at him, he was soused. "A gentleman learns his capacity and never surpasses it, Hudson. If he must drink to excess, he does so when he's alone."

"You Britishers think you know all there is to being a gentleman, don't you? But I bet you planned on getting all your schmoozing with the bosses out of the way first, then you'd move in for the kill with the little dark colleen at the end of the night. That it?" He sniggered. "Someone you reckoned might be experienced enough to lead the way. I bet you've never actually gone the whole hog with a dame, Newton. I bet you're too buttoned-up, you big cream puff!"

The barbs were so close to home that Edmund's hands balled into fists. If he wasn't Major Hudson's son, he'd knock this lout's block off.

17

N ancy was alone. Violet had gone home to Avalon on an overnight
trip to take care of household matters. She sat at her embroidery
frame, transferring to her sampler the legend *Two souls with but a single
thought, Two hearts that beat as one*. Samuel had quoted the lines to her,
kneeling on one knee to propose, after securing her mother's consent in
advance.

Louis was announced and she frowned, fingering a skein of thread. It
was inappropriate for him to keep calling, but her mother encouraged
him. She ought to be off-hand, to deter future visits. She considered
ringing the bell for Roberge to sit with them, since her pregnancy didn't
discourage this man from looking at her in an improper way. But she
stayed her hand, although she didn't care to examine the reason. It
certainly could not be because, in a guilty little kernel of her
consciousness, she enjoyed the frisson between them.

"*Madame*, if the opportunity presented itself, would you wish to
communicate with your husband?" Louis didn't bother with a preamble.

Nancy's hands trembled at her embroidery. "Yes."

"I can arrange it for you. I've made the acquaintance of a psychic
who achieves impressive results – I attended one of her séances. Her
name is Mama Carmen and I believe she'll be able to make contact with

Monsieur Armstrong."

Nancy was shaken by the suggestion of attending a séance. She had heard them whispered about in school, but never met anyone who attended one. Was it . . . diabolical? Did those who participated risk their immortal souls? She knew so little about spiritualism. If only there was someone to advise her. Could she trust Louis? Oh, but if it might be possible to contact Samuel! She had so much to ask him. What should I do, Samuel? How should I live my life?

Louis's gaze never left her face. He found it hard to remember she was a widow, for her eyes conveyed the colour of first love, the hopeful certainty of it.

"I could ask Mama Carmen to visit you here, rather than put you to the trouble of going to her. She's an extraordinary individual. She has a spirit guide called Ada who's a little girl of eight – it seems she was murdered more than seventy years ago and now she carries messages between this world and the next."

"Jiminy." Nancy's voice was tinny. She stuck her needle into the sampler and twisted the frame between her hands. If only her mother was there to decide for her. Except her mother would never permit her to attend a séance. Nancy thought of her husband and how he always knew how to behave in any set of circumstances. Deciding for herself seemed such a heavy responsibility.

"What did she tell you, this Mama Carmen?"

Louis remembered the voice issuing from Mama Carmen's throat which claimed to be his mother's, and turned towards the veined marble fireplace.

"I'm not sure . . . something about my parents, perhaps."

Nancy thought he was looking at the tongues of fire in the grate. "I know it's too warm for a fire but I find it comforting to have one."

Samuel had loved tending the fire, heaping it with logs and riddling it with a poker, although the press of a button would have had a servant on their knees performing such tasks for him.

Louis felt again how wrong it was that someone so young and beautiful should be in mourning. He had an urge to run his lips across her throat and kiss the pulse points on her neck. He knew it was too soon to make love to Nancy, but his heart refused to measure time in

236

conventional units. Six swift paces brought him to sit beside her on the horsehair sofa, and the impulsive movement charged the air between them.

Startled, Nancy dropped her needlework. As though this was the signal he had been waiting for, Louis leaned towards her – so close she could see the fine deposit of down on his skin.

Alarm coursed through her veins – and something else. "I don't know what you think you're doing."

"Shush!"

His rebuke was tender. He looked at her upper lip, whose bow reminded him of a Rosetti painting: there was passion in its arched curve, only a fool could miss it. Under his gaze, the lip parted from its fellow and Nancy's heartbeat quickened in a way it never had for Samuel. Gently, Louis cupped his palms around her cheeks, and brought his face towards hers.

Just then a spark shot out from the fireplace and struck the rug. They sprang apart, Nancy rising to her feet and Louis rushing to stamp on the spot before sliding the fireguard into position.

The moment had passed. Louis stayed by the fireplace, lifting china ornaments and replacing them without seeing them, while Nancy's racing heartbeat told her she'd had the narrowest of escapes. She should be grateful, she thought. But she wasn't.

By and by Louis spoke. "You asked what Mama Carmen told me? She said I was to have been given my father's name, but something prevented it."

Nancy kept her eyes fastened on the floor. "Is that true?"

"I have no way of checking. You see, I never knew my father."

Nancy risked looking at him, and he was so forlorn her decision was taken. Her son wouldn't know his father either, and she never wanted to see him look as dejected as Louis.

"Bring this Mama Carmen to me. We'll hold a séance here."

Louis didn't think the spiritualist could put Nancy in touch with Samuel Armstrong, but he did think she could make the young widow believe it. *It's not deception*, he told himself, *it's an act of kindness. Ma petite will know relief, and then she can let go of this husband of hers. One séance will not harm her.*

* * *

Louis made his way to 10th Street, to the rooms where the Keppels lodged.

"My wife never conducts a séance except in our home." Walt Keppel was adamant.

"But the lady cannot be expected to come here – she has suffered a great bereavement. She's very young, and expecting a child. She lost her husband in tragic circumstances."

"I dare say it's a pitiful case, but Mama Carmen must be among friends if she's to make contact with the other side. Those antagonistic to our cause shake the psychical harmonies and upset the delicate balance of my wife's gift."

"Madame Armstrong is a friend to your cause. She'd do nothing to disturb psychical harmonies."

"It's not just the people at a séance who matter but the circumstances. I'm the guardian of my wife's special gift. See here, I wouldn't be taking my responsibility seriously if I allowed her to go into unfamiliar territory. She feels safe in our own little nest."

"I'd pay extra for her inconvenience."

Walt Keppel's ears pricked up. Still, he hesitated. "Our lifestyle isn't lavish, as you can see. We're spiritualists, not materialists, reliant on our friends for the basics to help us continue our work. We're not interested in the luxuries of this world but in elevating ourselves spiritually through contact with the next."

"Very well, if you're determined against it. Perhaps I may persuade another medium to accommodate me."

"Beware, friend. It pains me to tell you there are tricksters practising in our field."

"*Monsieur*, I wish my acquaintance to meet Mama Carmen – I confess myself impressed by her powers. But I cannot ask a young lady in her condition to travel. You leave me no choice but to seek another medium."

"Mama Carmen and I will seek guidance from the spirit world on this. If you could give us half an hour to speak with our friends in the beyond, I should have an answer for you."

"Thank you. I'll take a walk around your neighbourhood and return after thirty minutes."

"Just out of interest, friend, how much are you willing to pay for a personal visit?"

When Louis returned, both Mama Carmen and Walt were waiting for him in the claustrophobic sitting room.

"My wife and I have discussed your request and we're prepared to make a concession. My wife is interested in the lady you mention. She thinks the disastrous circumstances in which she lost her husband may be the *Titanic*. That so? Right as usual, Mama Carmen. My wife feels for the survivors of this maritime tragedy – she wishes to use her powers to alleviate their suffering. We have this to suggest. Mama Carmen has many talents attuned to the afterlife. One of them is the gift of automatic writing. She's willing to visit your friend and see whether the spirits wish to communicate with her. It's effective, but less arduous for Mama in a strange setting with unknown psychical harmonies."

Louis considered. He knew nothing about automatic writing, but Mama Carmen was a professional. If she were to mount a performance he didn't doubt it would be a memorable one.

Walt mistook his reflection for reluctance. "It can be quite a sight to witness, friend. Once I saw my wife produce a passage from *The Koran* in that Arabic lettering they use. It sure looked impressive, with all those swirls and whatnot. Sometimes little Ada gets involved and then it's schoolgirl lettering, like you'd see scribbled on a slate. Nobody's ever disappointed by Mama Carmen's automatic writing. No, siree. The messages still come through, see, but the sensitive's hand is the means instead of her voice."

"Could Mama Carmen use her powers to set Mrs Armstrong's mind at rest? She's young for widowhood. She needs reassuring her husband isn't opposed to her taking another husband, in time." He held Mama Carmen's eye. "Is that possible?" Unblinking, she matched his stare. He placed a wad of dollar bills on a side-table. She looked at them, back at him, and nodded.

"I'm grateful, Mama Carmen. I look forward to seeing your talents in action again."

The Keppels agreed to present themselves at Fifth Avenue in two days' time, visibly impressed by the address.

* * *

"Kathleen, I need to borrow your red velvet Tam o' Shanter."

"But I only just got it, Bridie, I ain't worn it above twice."

"I'm meeting a gentleman about a job. You can't have me going out like a ragamuffin."

"What's wrong with the job you got?" Kathleen swatted some flies away from a bowl of oatmeal she was feeding Daniel Junior.

"Nothing's wrong with it for now, but I don't intend to be a laundress all my life. This gentleman might be in a position to help me."

"Does Danny know you're meeting a fellow? It's not that Enrico from the barber's shop?"

Bridie ignored her. "Where's the hat, Kathleen? I'll be late if I don't get a move on. I need your ruby hat-pin as well."

She disappeared behind the curtain which screened the beds from the room.

Kathleen heaved herself to her feet, realizing resistance was futile. If Bridie was determined to borrow something, she might as well find it for her rather than let her go grubbing through drawers.

Bridie dabbed her armpits with vinegar to prevent perspiration, covering the smell with lavender water filched from Kathleen. After that she slapped her cheeks to colour them, buffed her hair with a strip of satin and changed into her new shirtwaist. Kathleen's Tam o' Shanter, arranged at the back of her head, looked better on Bridie than it did on her. Even Kathleen was forced to admit it.

Stuart Hudson had arranged to wait just out of sight of the tenement house. Bridie had learned her lesson from showing Edmund off. He straightened when he saw her.

"You look swell. Where would you like to go?"

"Somewhere swish." She sighed happily in anticipation. "Oh wait, here comes Sadie Brolly – she's only after telling me it hasn't been a good week – too many people buying on tick. Buy something from her."

He bought matches, shoelaces and a length of purple ribbon when

240

Bridie admired it.

Sadie called Bridie back to her as they left. "It does my heart good to see a nice-looking girl like you with a lad to spoil her."

"Him? I'm only playing with him – I'm finished with men."

Shrewd eyes bored into Bridie's. "You'll never be finished with men, me girl."

Bridie caught up with Stuart. "You look like a gent who knows how to enjoy himself. Are you game to show a girl a good time?"

"Game as they come. Where should we go?"

"How about you take me to one of those ritzy uptown places I've walked past? A hotel, maybe, or a club?"

Not the club, his father would hear about it. "I expect we can find a hotel."

* * *

"Champagne, please."

Stuart nodded at the waiter. "Now, tell me all about this laundry where you work. Wouldn't you prefer to go on the stage, a cute gal like you?"

"Ah, leave off about work. Did you know champagne tickles your throat on the way down?"

"I did know that, as it happens. What do you usually drink, Bridie?"

"I'm not supposed to drink at all, the parish priest at home had us tormented about taking the pledge. He said Our Lady never touched a drop of alcohol in her life and neither should we. How he knows about Our Lady is anybody's guess. I think these fellows make up the half of it and foist any old yarn on the poor ignorant suckers. That's an American word, you know – suckers. Yes, I've had beer, and some of my father's *poitín*, a vile brew, and once I had a glass of sherry. It tasted like Christmas."

"Did it now?" Stuart was amused by her chatter.

The waiter returned and popped the cork, its foaming vapour exciting an "oooh" from Bridie, forgetting she was supposed to be sophisticated. The waiter poured two flutes and deposited the bottle in an ice bucket. Money made everything effortless, thought Bridie.

241

"Here's to you!" Stuart clinked his glass against hers.

"And here's to me too!" She knocked back a mouthful, choked and he patted her back.

"Easy does it, Bridie. You sip champagne, that's the trick."

"I knew that. I just had the hiccups as I swallowed."

"Sure thing, those hiccups can be a pest."

Bridie took a small sip, delighting in the sensation of bubbles on her tongue. She allowed her eyes to travel around the lounge. This was a classy establishment and no mistake. There were gilt mirrors everywhere, gigantic affairs with naked cherubs on top – she wasn't convinced it was quite decent to expose so many chubby bottoms. She must memorise everything to describe to Hannah and Kathleen later.

"So what do you want to know about the Clean and Brite? It's good wages, but the heat would make your head explode. The manager says I'm the quickest girl he's ever trained up."

"I bet you are. Here, let me top you up."

Bridie laughed, her mood as effervescent as the champagne she forgot she was supposed to sip.

* * *

Despite her attempt at discretion, Danny Ryan heard his sister had been seen out with a stranger and was waiting up to confront her.

"What will people think, Bridie?" was his opening salvo.

"I don't give a tinker's curse what people think!"

"Well, I do. I'm trying to make a life for meself here, a respectable life for my wife and son, and you're pissing on it." Bridie tried to push past him and prepare for bed but he caught her by the shoulders. "By God, I can smell the drink off you. That was no gentleman you were with, getting you sauced. So help me, if I catch up with him –"

"We weren't drinking – we ate little cakes with liquor sprinkled on them, rum babas he called them. That's what you smell."

"Don't lie to me! I didn't come down with the last shower of rain."

"Why should I travel all the way to America and have to stop in every night? I want a better life too."

"Not at the cost of your good name, surely?"

242

"Good name, bad name, a name's of no interest to me. It's just a word people know you by."

"Surely you'd never resort to evil?" He was aghast, the skin under his tired eyes pendulous.

She barked out a laugh lacking in humour, all her vitality from the champagne evaporating. "I'm tired, Danny, leave me go to bed."

"Not until you promise never to see this fellow again. He can only be interested in one thing from a girl like you. I'll knock the brains out of any man who interferes with you. I hope you're still pure, Bridie Ryan!"

"Oh, it's on to purity we are now – funny how it's only women have to worry about staying pure. You never hear a man criticised for losing it." Suddenly she slumped, too tired to bait her brother. "Listen, Danny, nothing happened. Your man talked to me, is all. Then he brought me home, proper as you like. It was nothing, for all you're building it into something. God knows I wish he did have designs on me, it might give me something to look forward to instead of a sweatshop."

"God forgive you, Bridie Ryan!" He pulled on his boots, ignoring his wife's calls, and slammed the door on his way out.

"Ah Bridie, what are you falling out with your brother for? He has your best interests at heart." Kathleen climbed out of bed and stood barefoot in front of her. "He'll only go to the saloon now and start drinking our savings."

"I won't have him telling me how to live my life!"

Hannah lay quietly, wishing the unpleasantness could be at an end. Perhaps if she said nothing they'd think she was asleep – although brother and sister had made a racket fit to wake the dead.

* * *

Violet tried to cancel the session of automatic writing but Nancy defied her mother in a rare flash of rebellion.

Violet summoned Louis.

"I'm surprised at you, Mr Stubel, I expected more. You must realize my daughter is an exceptionally vulnerable young woman, not just physically but emotionally. She needs protecting. This leaves her open to destabilising forces." Violet flapped a lace and ebony fan as she paced the morning room.

Startled by the force of her opposition, Louis cursed himself for not having smoothed the way first with her. "I assure you, Madame Markova, my only interest in this matter is your daughter's welfare."

"As her mother, I ought to be the best judge of my daughter's welfare."

"That goes without saying."

"Mercy, I don't know what my pastor will say about this tampering with unnatural forces. I've been a church-goer all my life. This automatic writing smacks of the devil. It's just an old snake of Satan's in a new suit of clothes."

"Only meet Mama Carmen and you'll see how far from being a fiend she is. Her single wish is to help people make contact with their loved ones."

"Money doesn't enter the equation, I suppose?" Violet's eyes tested his.

His hesitation was momentary. "Everyone must live."

"I knew it! My daughter is the widow of an extremely wealthy man, she's bound to be a target for the unscrupulous, the greedy and the downright corrupt."

Louis made one final effort to pacify Violet. "*Madame*, I have no intention of exposing your daughter to harm. I wish her nothing but happiness – she was kind to me on the lifeboat, a debt I seek to repay in any humble way I can. I thought only that Mama Carmen might help to dispel this sadness which threatens to engulf Mrs Armstrong. She was so reluctant to surrender her husband to death – we all saw how she refused to give up hope, long after his survival was impossible. I'm convinced if your daughter can make contact with Monsieur Armstrong, if she can be reassured death is not the end but only the next stage in a journey, she'll be reconciled to his passing and ready to embrace life again. Believe me, Violet, all I want is to give her peace of mind."

She felt a tingle. It was so long since a man called her Violet. Did this compelling Frenchman think of her as Violet, not as Mrs Markova, a middle-aged matron? She fluttered her fan, stirring up air. The atmosphere was close and she felt flushed.

"A worthy aspiration, Mr Stubel. But the child, when it comes, will moderate her grief."

Louis felt a twinge of jealousy for this infant who could accomplish what he was incapable of doing. "That happy event is some months away. We must not allow Madame Armstrong to mope until then. Unhappiness corrodes."

"I cannot stop this charade – my daughter is set on hosting it. However, I insist on being present. If there's any chicanery I'll spot it at once." She turned away, still thrilling to his use of her Christian name, which had been inadvertent on Louis's part. Vee-o-let, he pronounced it, curving his lips around the syllables. She touched a hand to her heated cheek: Violet Markova had believed herself past the stage of men reducing her to blushing confusion. She rang the bell for Watts, the footman. "You must excuse me. I have to attend to my daughter, Mr Stubel."

Louis bowed, frustrated by his stupidity in not making an ally of the mother before approaching Nancy about Mama Carmen. Violet pricked her ears as he said goodbye, disappointed at hearing herself addressed as Madame Markova. Could she have imagined the intimacy of that Vee-o-let?

* * *

Only Nancy, Violet, Mama Carmen and Walt Keppel were present for the automatic writing session. Louis was hoping to be invited, but Violet would not allow it. It was her way of punishing him for not broaching the subject with her first.

The event was an unqualified success. Nancy felt a catch in her throat, followed by a rush of gladness, when Mama Carmen took both her hands in her own. "I am a channel of communication between the living and the dead. Death is no barrier if love is strong enough. Would you have me stretch my hands through the partition on your behalf?"

Nancy nodded, rapt, but Violet didn't care for the way Walt appraised their home, lips drooping away from tobacco-stained teeth as his eyes darted everywhere.

The messages from the spirit world reassured Nancy. She kept the sheets of paper filled at breakneck speed by Mama Carmen when she went under, and read out Samuel's words to Louis later.

"*I am watching over you, Nancy. Believe me when I say you will survive this unhappiness and move into a brighter phase of your life in the earthly dimension. Joy lies in store for you again. You will marry another man some day, it is right that you should – you cannot go through life alone. But always remember me, too. Believe that time has no power to whittle away a love such as ours. We will be together in the afterlife, when you will be my wife again and I shall be the proudest of husbands. Nancy, my Nancy, I thought of you as I sank below the water – yours was the sweet face hovering before my eyes as darkness claimed me. Tell our child about me, let it know I love it. As I love you.*"

Louis frowned, thinking there was too much about Samuel Armstrong loving Nancy and being reunited with her – and not enough about her moving on and remarrying. He had heard automatic writing lent itself to self-deception, which made it particularly subtle and dangerous. But how did it work? Did the subconscious mind of the medium act in tandem with the sitters – some kind of telepathic thought transference?

"Samuel also had a message for you, Mr Stubel, from your grandmother. She said," – Nancy lifted another folio – "*I am sorry you lost something you prize so dear, liebling – that which holds the key to your identity.*"

Louis kindled with anger. Mama Carmen had exceeded her instructions. "How did she know my grandmother spoke German?"

"She transcribes the words dictated to her," said Nancy.

"Conjurers' tricks," snapped Violet.

Louis frowned, trying to gauge the spiritualist's intentions. "I remember hardly anything about my grandmother, except that she called me *liebling* and smelled of peppermints. I called her *oma* and she used to bake *apfel kuchen*. She said my mother sang like an angel and my father was . . . never mind what my father was." He was afraid Nancy would laugh at him if he revealed his *oma* said his father was a royal duke. "She died before I was four. The man who brought me up told me she arrived one day with me in her arms, when I was only months old. He said for the first year there was plenty of money and then it grew scarce. He could never remember where she came from. Some place in

Germany, presumably, since she spoke German. He had her buried in a pauper's grave – he said the money she left was needed for the living."

Louis's mind was racing. How had Mama Carmen known to mention his grandmother? He had no idea what she meant by losing something that held the key to his identity. Everything was lost on the *Titanic*, apart from his christening mug. Louis shook his head, unable to decide if Mama Carmen was a swindler. Her husband was a buffoon, but that didn't necessarily taint the lady.

As soon as he was back in his room, Louis hunted out his christening mug. He found the leather presentation case at the back of his wardrobe, but the catch was broken and the mug gone. It must have been damaged in the fall into the lifeboat. Louis crawled about on his hands and knees, using his fingers as a dragnet to draw them over every inch of the floor, in and out of the wardrobe, under and above it. Splinters lodged in his flesh, cobwebs clung to his thick blond hair, and a sticky patch disfigured the knees of his trousers before he conceded defeat. Bleakly, he rocked back on his heels. When had he last examined the mug? Not since the *Titanic*. He had assumed it was safely inside its case. It could have been lost or stolen at any time between the lifeboat and the major's apartment. Dry-eyed, Louis stared into space. The only tangible clue to his identity was gone. He studied a scratch from a rusty nail scored deep into the palm of his hand, found the nail in the floorboards and slowly, deliberately, scraped another cut.

* * *

The christening mug had been a gift to Louis's parents from his father's sister and it did, indeed, solve the mystery of his identity. Louis was the son of Archduke Johann Salvator, cousin to Franz-Josef, the Austro-Hungarian emperor. His father's titles included Prince of Hungary, Grand Ducal Prince of Tuscany, Knight of the Golden Fleece and Lieutenant Field-Marshal in the Imperial Army. Louis's glittering heritage, however, was diminished by his mother's lineage – Ludmilla Stubel was a shopkeeper's daughter. And Louis was illegitimate.

Their affair set tongues clacking in 1880s Vienna; Archduke Johann's involvement with Ludmilla, who sang and danced with the

Vienna Court Opera, was a scandal. Despite pressure, the archduke refused to relinquish her and renounced rank and privileges for Ludmilla's sake, assuming the name John Orth. He bought an estate in Chile through his agents and the couple set sail for South America. From the moment their vessel left port neither passengers nor crew were sighted again. Rumours whirled like snowflakes: he was spotted in Japan, where he became an admiral in the navy; in Argentina, where he was a rancher; in the gold fields of San Francisco, where he made a fortune and blew it in one night's gaming. The mystery remained unsolved, but shipwreck was their likeliest fate.

Louis was born in 1889, the year before they married and set off on their voyage. He was a puny, premature baby, and doctors advised his parents the long sea passage would overtax his strength. The couple left him with Ludmilla's mother, intending to send for their son when he was stronger and they were settled. They were never heard from again. Ludmilla's mother moved to Paris, but when she died nobody guessed at the identity of the precocious blond boy she doted on – although the old lady told the concierge a rambling story about his illustrious forebears. The concierge didn't believe her. But when she was dying he accepted the money she gave him to take on this small boy with a christening mug whose rubies winked cold fire.

* * *

The letter from Ireland was as antagonistic as it was brief. Its hostility was laid bare for all to see on the envelope, which addressed her as Miss Hannah Godfrey instead of Mrs Hannah O'Brien. Her pulse slowed when she saw it on the table after work. Her eyes consulted with Bridie's, before she slit the envelope with a breadknife.

From Arnold and Sheehan, solicitors-at-law, Cappamore, County Limerick.

Dear Miss Godfrey,
We understand you have lodged an insurance claim with regard to our client's son, Mr Thomas O'Brien of Bonavie, County Limerick. Our client,

Mrs Margaret O'Brien of the same address, has reason to believe her son was never married to you. Unless you can produce proof of marriage, the compensation money from the Titanic disaster should rightfully go to Mrs O'Brien as the legal next of kin. We await your cooperation in this matter.

Yours faithfully,

Jeremiah Sheehan

18

Hannah passed the letter to Bridie. "My good name's in tatters. It'll be the death of my mother when this gets back to her. When I was growing up, time and time again she said they could take away everything we owned but we were never to let them steal our good name."

Bridie's snort showed her opinion of good names but she nodded imperceptibly towards Kathleen, listening greedily as she burped the baby. "Come outside for a stretch of the legs, Hannah. My head is pounding after the day we put in. It must be close to boiling point in the Clean and Brite."

"Not bad news from Ireland, I hope?" Kathleen's button eyes were eager.

"You'd be the first to know," said Bridie, bundling Hannah out ahead of her. "Sure we'd rely on you to help us through it."

"It seems odd they didn't use her married name, whoever it was writing to her," Kathleen fished as they went out.

"Old friend from years ago, they wouldn't know about her marriage," Bridie tossed back.

On the street, she slid an arm around Hannah's waist. "Remember what I told you before. All you have say is you were married on the

Titanic and your marriage paper went to the bottom of the ocean along with everything else. And the priest who conducted the service was lost the same way. "

"I know – that's what I wrote my mother and I'm sure she told the O'Briens. But they don't believe me. This solicitor's letter as good as calls me a liar." She gouged her eye sockets with her knuckles. "I am one."

"Well then, here's what we do. We say I was your bridesmaid. I'm willing to stand up in a court of law and swear on the Bible I saw yourself and Tom legally married on the ship."

"You'd do that for me? Perjure yourself on my account?" Hannah's reddened eyes grew round.

"Certainly. I may as well be hanged for a sheep as a lamb."

"You mean" – Hannah was hesitant about naming the abortion – "that other business?"

Bridie nodded. "I'm a bad lot and I'm done for one way or the other, Hannah. Someone may as well have the benefit of it. Anyway I don't count it much of a lie. You told me yourself Tom O'Brien promised to marry you, as sure as night follows day. He just ran out of time."

Still Hannah vacillated about letting someone do on her behalf what she'd never dare herself.

"It's not as if you're claiming his name for the money, Hannah, although there's no doubt it'll be useful. You want your child to have a father's name on its birth certificate, instead of 'father unknown'."

"That's true, I'm doing this for my baby, and for Mama – to spare her shame." *And for myself.*

"So we'll find one of those lawyer boys ourselves and have him write back to this Jeremiah Sheehan of Arnold and Sheehan. Him and his threats! Our Yankee lawyer will be able to threaten with the best of them. We'll tell him he has no right to make insinuations about your good name." Bridie liked that word 'insinuations'; Warren Vicosen, the manager of the Clean and Brite laundry was always using it to customers who turned up late to claim clothes he'd already sold on.

Hannah brightened. "A Yankee lawyer wouldn't take any nonsense, would he? Only he'd be fierce expensive."

"Never you worry about that. Aren't you earning top dollar these days, a working girl like yourself? And sure I have a few bob put away for a rainy day. If push comes to shove, I won't see you stuck."

＊　＊　＊

The Red Cross recommended a lawyer and Hannah and Bridie took time off work – not without a barrage of complaints from Warren – to visit his offices on Lexington Avenue at 64th Street. Sidney Malpother was a rangy man who rubbed a tension knot at the base of his neck as he listened to Hannah. She had been coached by Bridie and, although queasy with nerves, kept reminding herself she was doing this for the baby. She didn't want it to be illegitimate as well as fatherless. When her story was finished, the lawyer sighed and said it was a straightforward business which could be cleared up quickly. One of his clerks drew up an affidavit which Bridie signed, confirming that she, Bridget Ryan, had witnessed the marriage of Hannah Godfrey and Thomas O'Brien on board the *Titanic* on Saturday, April 13th, 1912. A letter was sent to Jeremiah Sheehan of Arnold and Sheehan with a copy of the affidavit, trusting this now put an end to the matter and warning of unspecified consequences if further defamation of his client's good name should occur.

On their way out, the clerk asked for an address to forward the bill. Hannah insisted on settling up there and then.

"Mr Malpother told me to give you a discount, on account of how he lost a niece on the *Titanic*," volunteered the clerk. He wrote "*Paid in Full*" in swirling copperplate on her invoice and handed Hannah a copy.

Bridie hurried her along to the omnibus, so they'd only be docked for two-and-a-half hours' pay instead of three.

＊　＊　＊

Edmund Newton had not expected to like America quite so much: its clamouring energy, its reckless extravagance, the sheer insolence of the city. Back home in England, people complained it was too young and had no history. They said Americans insisted on having everything too big to compensate – buildings, mountains, department stores, even steaks. They said the country made grandiose claims for itself, insisting in its Bill of Rights that all men were born equal, but treated its coloured population as a sub-standard race.

Edmund observed how all the shoe-shines were dark-skinned and were called "boy", even the old men. He noticed innovation and modern were favourite words, while out-dated was a term of abuse. But he saw other things too. That the people were taller and better-fed than their European counterparts, and the class system was less pronounced. Of course he wouldn't want to live here permanently, but the metropolis was interesting, scriptwriting was challenging, there was Major Hudson for company – and Bridie Ryan was in New York.

Edmund fell into the habit of lounging in a wing-backed chair in the major's sitting room several evenings a week. Sometimes they played a rubber of bridge, but usually the cards were dropped and they fell into discussion. They had a tangential way of conversing, leapfrogging from topic to topic, but sooner or later they gravitated back to the *Titanic*, as though everything reminded the major of the ship.

"What does the *Titanic* show us?" The major would set the ball rolling, the lamplight penetrating deep into his eyes.

"The triumph of the intellect over brute force," said Edmund, who contended he used his wits to reach a lifeboat.

"Luck helped, Newton."

"True, but so did helping myself."

His gaze was drawn to a framed print showing two prize-fighters, naked to the waist, squaring up for a bare knuckles fight. *Mendoza and Humphries at Stilton, Huntingdonshire, May 6th, 1789*, was stamped at their feet. Sometimes a man had to take the gloves off and fight to survive, thought Edmund. The *Titanic* had taught him that.

It was the kind of conversation Major Hudson had dreamed he might engage in with his son, but Stuart showed little bent for teasing out philosophical riddles. All he seemed to want to do was go to the theatre – still, his mother had adored the opera, it was only natural their son should have inherited Jean's highbrow tastes. (Stuart was indulging those highbrow tastes at that moment, borrowing a friend's opera glasses to compare whether the blonde in the second row or the brunette at the back had the shapeliest figure.)

The major's book about the hoodoo aspect of the sinking worried Edmund, who wondered if his friend was becoming obsessed. He was on to the Hope Diamond now, claiming its presence on board could have sunk the *Titanic*.

"Why should a gem sink a ship?"

"Not just a gem, Newton, it's the Hope Diamond – there's a curse on it. It was bought from Mr Cartier last year in Paris for Evalyn Walsh McLean by her husband Ned. She's an heiress, you know. Daughter of an Irish immigrant. The diamond's history is bloodstained: the last woman to wear it was a sultan's favourite in a harem in Turkey, and she was stabbed to death during the Turkish rebellion. Marie Antoinette wore it before her. The stone is cursed and all who wear it are dogged by tragedy and premature death. It was found in India and is said to glow with a rare, violet brilliance."

"It's glowing at the bottom of the ocean now," shrugged Edmund. "That's if it ever was on board."

"I have the Keppels looking into it for me. Mama Carmen is trying to make contact with the sultan's concubine, who wore it last. Of course, she may not speak English," he added doubtfully, "but Mama Carmen says we shouldn't let that deter us. The spirits have a knack of getting their message across, regardless of language barriers."

Edmund didn't like the sound of the Keppels and tried to discourage his friend's interest in the occult, but the major was not to be reasoned with.

"It's absurd that man's survival beyond the grave should be indicated by moving tables and levitating plant pots," said Edmund.

"But it's the force propelling the object which fascinates us, not the object itself. That's simply the sign of a presence."

Edmund tried another tack. "Do you think these Keppels are genuine?"

"I'm not a fool, Newton, Walt Keppel is a man on the make. But his wife has a rare talent. I hear Jean speaking through her."

"Communication between the quick and the dead is impossible."

"Oh ye of little faith! There are powers in the human psyche we barely grasp."

"Major, it strikes me this fascination with spiritualism is based on a fear of death so overwhelming that people like you refuse to believe in death at all. You're all hoping for immortality by making immortals of your loved ones."

"Wouldn't you wish for immortality, Newton?"

"The ancient Greeks had a word for that: they called it hubris. I'm prepared to live my life and call it a day. Whatever happens afterwards can take care of itself."

Major Hudson tapped the tip of his cigar into a brass ashtray. "Perhaps it's for the best. A successful séance depends on mental harmonies. The sensitive is finely attuned to atmosphere and negative vibrations interfere with their ability to connect to the spirit guide."

Edmund stared, worried. He wondered if he should have a word with Stuart. No, it ought to be Louis. All that loafer Stuart thought about was chasing skirts. Irish ones, at that, he thought crossly.

* * *

The tenement house was even drearier than Danny and Kathleen's, despite crumbling fluted columns either side of the doorway. It was on Third Avenue and 29th Street, no distance away, but the girls felt nervous of venturing too far into the unknown. The room Hannah and Bridie arrived to inspect was meagre. It was the back room on the top floor, and a succession of odours jostled for position – mildewed linoleum, soiled mattresses and musty curtains, as well as the sweetly sour taint of gas from the bracket. There was no running water and the fire escapes, laden with washtubs and furniture, presented a fire hazard. Below them, doors banged and voices were raised, while outside cats yowled and streetcars and cabs clattered past. It cost more than a third of Bridie's and Hannah's combined wages.

"Take it or leave it," said Herb Sousa, the landlord's agent. He had damp lips like twin slugs, and a dented bowler hat worn pushed back from his forehead. Sousa worked for Rebecca Armstrong, who owned eight tenements, and he added 10 per cent to the rent quoted because he was dubious about letting to women. They'd be unable to earn as much as men and subsequently the rent would be less secure. Sousa looked pointedly at Hannah's belly.

Bridie knew they were being asked to pay above the going rate but she also knew they had no choice. She caught Hannah's eye. "It doesn't look much now but we can do something with it. That corner is perfect for a crib. See how it catches the evening sunshine?"

Hannah preferred it with Danny and Kathleen. She had burrowed into their home and adapted to their lifestyle with the tenacity of an expectant mother who longed to fit in somewhere – anywhere. But Bridie was her family now. Where Bridie went, she went. "Yes, that corner is bright. There's a shop Kathleen showed me where you can buy material to curtain off a sleeping area. I saw a yellow print that would remind you of the May flowers in the fields at home."

"Will you be able for the stairs?"

Hannah had been obliged to pause on two of the landings before continuing her ascent to the fifth floor.

"The exercise will be good for me. Anyway the higher rooms are quieter, with no feet tramping above us. There's less chance of the baby being disturbed."

"We'll take it," Bridie told the agent.

Herb Sousa was in no hurry to respond. He rooted around in his pocket for a plug of tobacco, examining tooth-marks on the black wedge. Fuzz from his pocket was scraped away with a thumbnail before he bit off a corner and lodged it in his cheek. He had all the time in the world – plenty more in line if these women didn't want the room. Still, he was getting a little extra from them. "I'll need a week down in advance and I'll be round to collect every pay day. You say you work in a laundry? What day you get paid? Friday? Well then, Friday's our payday too. Fall behind with the rent and you're out on your ear, no second chances. Them's my instructions from the owner and she never makes exceptions. The money's to be ready by Friday evenin' or you're on the street next mornin'."

"Today's Saturday so we'll only pay you six nights in advance," Bridie haggled.

"I always have seven up front."

"In that case you'll have to leave it until Saturday week before calling again for money. I thought you wanted to catch us on payday?" She winked at Hannah. "The fancies we might buy with our wages between

Friday and Saturday are nobody's business!"

Sousa pushed the shiny bowler so far back it seemed to defy gravity. "Suppose six nights in advance will do. But I'm takin' a chance on you girls and I hope you don't go lettin' me down." He counted the bills Hannah handed over, licking his thumb as he leafed through them. "You Irish? Fine-lookin' squaws, the Irish. Just off the boat, right?" A thought occurred to him and he wrenched his gaze away from the dollars to rest it on the girls. "There's to be no hanky-panky in this room, you better be respectable girls. No doin' business with gentlemen callers. Don't think I won't hear about it because I will, quick as a wink. This is a respectable lodging house and Mrs Armstrong won't tolerate nothin' bringin it into disrepute."

"Mind your manners," Bridie flashed. "You've no call to be making nasty insinuations about my friend and me. I told you, this lady lost her husband on the *Titanic*. She has enough on her plate without gombeens like yourself heaping on the insults."

"No offence, I was on'y sayin'." In the face of Bridie's indignation, the agent backed down. "Just layin' down some ground rules. You're good-lookin' dames, stands to reason you'll have offers. And she wouldn't be the first widow who had to earn her money where she could, with a kid on the way."

"What's he saying about me, Bridie?" Hannah was mortified.

Bridie stood toe-to-toe with the agent. "Have we a deal? Is the room ours?"

Herb Sousa spat a tobacco-stained globule on the floor. "It is. Now you're to behave yourselves and—"

"Where's the key?"

"Here it is." He laid it in her outstretched palm. "Remember what I —"

"Well, then, if the room's ours, I'll thank you to clear off immediately. You're not welcome here."

Involuntarily, he stepped back a few paces. Then he puffed out his dented dignity. "I'll be back Friday for the rent. See you have it."

"We hear you about Friday. But you've no call to be in this room a minute longer so take your filthy mind and the rest of you while you're at it, and beat it."

He hesitated, his jaw hanging slack, before banging the door after him with a thud that shook the timber window frame.

"He's a bad article, that fellow, only out for what he can get."

"You can't go falling out with everyone, Bridie," Hannah warned. Hannah wasn't clever like Bridie, she had no quick-witted retorts, but she had commonsense. "It's a long road that has no turning – you might need the people you insult one day."

"Fellows like that – I can't abide them."

In the hiatus that followed, Hannah looked out at the alleyway that was their only view of the wider world. It had been raining earlier, the deluge a welcome balm from the summer heat radiating out from concrete. She saw a discarded umbrella with broken spikes, like bat's wings, and some ragged urchins racing newspaper boats in gutters filled with water. The cloudburst reminded her of home – which seemed infinitely more than an ocean away.

Bridie joined Hannah at the window. "Well, now. We need to buy a kettle and some cups so we can make ourselves a drop o' tea, and we should see about the material you mentioned. Yellow, was it, you wanted? You can have the stars and stripes if that's what takes your fancy."

"It was odd, though, the name he used – about the owner, I mean."

"I never heard any name, Hannah – I was too busy trying to stop myself taking a swing at him. That would have spoiled our chances of the room altogether."

"He said the owner was a Mrs Armstrong. You don't think . . .?"

"Unlikely. Sure a city the size of New York must be thick with Armstrongs."

"I suppose so." Still, Hannah remembered something Danny Ryan said as she read Samuel Armstrong's obituary in the newspaper: *"They own hotels, factories and tenement blocks, these people – they'd rent us back the sidewalks we walk on and charge us for the air we breathe if they could."*

They clattered downstairs, past a landing on every floor.

"A teapot," said Bridie, black curls bouncing on her shoulders. "We need a teapot as well as a kettle."

They went to the ironmonger's first, where poles laden with polished metal objects tinkled in the breeze.

"Do you think we could run to a skillet, Hannah?"

Hannah nodded and smiled. It was fun buying provisions for their new home. A shadow crossed her face as she remembered the plans she once nursed for setting up home with Tom.

It took no time to spend their money. They walked more slowly as they carried home their purchases, which included a tin chamber pot with a pink flower painted on. Bridie laughed when Hannah asked her to move the roll of material for a curtain from her left shoulder to her right.

"It's bad luck to carry something into the house on your left shoulder."

"That's only an old *piseog*, Hannah. Still, no point in courting bad luck."

She shifted her package to the right shoulder.

"We'll go back tomorrow morning to Danny's for our few bits and pieces. If we go at ten when they're at Sunday Mass, we should be in and out without running into either him or Kathleen. No point in another scene."

The girls had not gone to church since that first time after arriving in New York. They felt too guilty for it, each in her way, although Danny and Kathleen were scandalised.

It was evening time, and they had already spent a day working in the laundry, but the pair set to with a will and aired the room, scrubbing it with carbolic soap and ammonia, and stringing the curtain. In one corner was a kitchen area with a gas bracket, over which they suspended the kettle by driving a piece of wood into the wall. They would keep their food in a packing case which could double as a seat. But there was no food, they realized. While Hannah rested her ballooning ankles, Bridie ran out and bought a pitcher's worth of milk, half a pound of tea, a pound of sugar, a tin of potted meat and a loaf of bread.

As they ate their supper, Bridie outlined her plan to save up and buy an electric iron, an innovation just introduced that year. "Perhaps we can bring home work from the laundry and earn a little extra that way."

"That's not why you want one of them contraptions. You're just mad into everything modern."

"Well, isn't this the modern age? We have to be part of it, Hannah."

"We shouldn't get carried away – money runs away fast in America."

That night they slept in their coats until their next pay packet would buy them blankets. It felt like home already.

* * *

Weeks passed without contact between the girls and Danny and Kathleen. Hannah felt uneasy about it, on account of their generosity in welcoming her into their home, while even Bridie half-expected her brother to loom up at her one night outside the laundry and demand her return home. She was nervous of a letter of reproof from Oola – parental authority was capable of stretching across the Atlantic – and knew it had been wrong to do a flit, even if they had left dollars on the deal table. Missing Daniel Junior, Hannah wanted to slip off one evening and visit them, but she was nervous of goading Bridie.

"Did we have to do it this way – just vanish on them without a word?"

"Danny would've cut the legs off me rather than let me walk out. He has a temper on him that would scare Lucifer himself."

He's not the only one in that family with a temper, thought Hannah.

If only she didn't feel she ought not to go back into a Catholic church, after sinning with Tom and telling lies to the lawyer. She'd love to light a candle and pray the bad blood between brother and sister would be swept away. Perhaps it was time to think about making her Confession.

* * *

Unusually, the stars were razor sharp in the New York sky – the street-lights tended to obscure them. But tonight a phalanx of stars gleamed so bright in the blue-black sky they reminded Bridie of the night she escaped from the *Titanic*.

"Penny for your thoughts," said Stuart.

"I was remembering someone who taught me how to tickle trout at home."

"I'll bet that someone was a man who was madly in love with you."

She shrugged, dismissive. Love tainted was not worth having.

He passed her a stick of chewing gum and they walked up Broadway, a warm breeze on their faces. Stuart whistled as he walked, and Bridie noticed he was almost always whistling a tune. He sang a snatch of "Come to me, my melancholy baby" and Bridie smiled, for nobody could be miserable walking around Broadway at night, ablaze with lights and a babble of voices curling through the air. She looked at the continuum of windows and doors, marvelling there were enough people in the world to occupy them.

The Weber Theatre was doing sensational business with a programme built around the *Titanic*, which drew immense crowds for footage of the ship's launch, as well as the *Carpathia* and her '*hero skipper in realistic poses*'. Bridie, however, declined Stuart's offer of tickets for it.

"As true as God, I'm *Titanic*-ed out," she complained.

"Begob, Oi'm Toy-tanicked out," he mimicked her accent.

"Hould your whist!" she played up to him. A girl could have a laugh with Stuart Hudson.

"I see The Unsinkable Molly Brown presented a loving cup to Captain Rostron on behalf of the survivors."

"Did she? I never asked her to do anything on my behalf. She had shoulders on her like a navvy, that one. Mind you, the man deserves anything he gets – I liked him."

"Better than me?" Already Stuart had a lover's instinct towards jealousy.

"Maybe. Who says I like you anyway?"

"You don't have to be so blamed casual about it. Didn't I bring you roses?"

Bridie patted her hat, where a rosebud was threaded though the band. She was pleased enough with them, but flowers died. She wanted something more concrete from Stuart Hudson.

"Maybe you're not the only fellow buys me flowers."

Stuart was accustomed to girls of Bridie's sort being grateful for his attentions and was uncertain how to handle this nonchalant miss. "Who else buys you flowers?"

"I'm not saying."

"Is it Edmund Newton?"

"Maybe."

"That uptight Britisher!"

"Ah, he's not the worst. He invited us to his premiére and the party after it. It was lovely."

He seethed beside her and she took pity on him. "Isn't that where I met you? We should be grateful to Edmund Newton."

He tucked her hand into the crook of his elbow. "I suppose you were working in the laundry again today. It sounds hotter than hell in there. I don't know how you bear it."

"I bear it because I must, what choice do I have? A girl's got to work, that's why I came to America – to work and save and better meself."

"And are you saving your nickels and dimes, my wild Irish rose?"

"Not as fast as I'd like. There's all sorts of temptations to spend your money on here. This hat, for example – you haven't said yet whether you like my hat, Stuart. I had to fix the brim after I bought it but it looks grand now."

"Haven't I admired it? How rude of me. I love your hat, Bridie, nearly as much as I love you."

"You're some chancer, dripping honey from your tongue to a poor girl who might take you seriously, if she didn't know any better. You could talk the rain into not getting you wet, Stuart Hudson!" She was laughing as she said it, but her grip on his arm tightened.

It occurred to her he was dressed more colourfully than she was, and with more attention to detail. Still, she could hold her own in this jacket bought cheap from the laundry manager – although obliged to submit to a soggy kiss for the privilege. It had electric blue frogging, and she mourned the lack of an electric blue hat to complement it. Bridie wore vivid flashes of colour in her clothes in the United States which would have caused comment at home.

Arms looped, Bridie and Stuart sauntered along, Stuart adjusting his leather gloves and admiring his long, narrow hands. The major had hands like shovels and split every pair of gloves he put on, but Stuart had inherited his mother's neat bone structure.

Their date had started with a visit to the motion pictures in a theatre on 42nd Street – Bridie was addicted to them since *Saved From The Titanic*. Stuart had a soft spot for westerns, with their villains in black hats and their heroes in white, their barmen taking down mirrors any time a shoot-out looked imminent, their doe-eyed heroines standing by their men. Bridie liked them too, but she preferred the romances. Happy-ever-afters made her chest tighten. She enjoyed anything with Mary Pickford in it, although Lillian Gish was fast becoming her star of preference – she cried during *Two Daughters of Eve*.

But Bridie had no time for romance now, she needed to be single-minded. She leaned into Stuart and winced.

"What is it, Bridie?"

A plaintive note entered her voice. "I don't like to bother you, Stuart, it's not important."

A police officer passed, whistling, his night-stick tapping the sidewalk, and cast them a speculative glance. He made a rapid evaluation: the man was over-gussied, the girl was punching above her weight. He could leave them to their own devices.

"Tell me what's wrong. I want to know," insisted Stuart.

Bridie crinkled her heavy, dark eyebrows. "I'm covered in scorch marks all along my arms from the iron. I had to rub half a bar of soap into them before I could leave the room to meet you. The irons are so hot, you need eyes in the back of your head when you use them. You can't look away from them for a second. Most of the other girls working in the laundry are fine big lasses who can manage, not a bother on them, but I'm not as strong as they are."

"I wish you didn't have to work there, Bridie." Stuart tilted back his straw boater and frowned.

"Sure what choice have I got? A girl has to earn a crust."

"What did you do in Ireland?"

"I was a seamstress."

"Could you not get work as a seamstress here?"

"I could, but it doesn't pay as well as the laundry. I'm saving up, you see, Stuart. I'm going to open an account in the New York Bank for Savings. Imagine swanning into a bank and having the tellers bowing and scraping to me!" She stopped walking. "Don't laugh if I tell you."

"Why should I laugh at someone who wants to open an account with the New York Bank for Savings?"

Even though Stuart had difficulty keeping a straight face, he was beguiled by Bridie. He was not in love with her but he was certainly smitten by her. It was appalling that such a fragile creature, with her mobile face and lilting voice, should have to work in a furnace to pay her way. If only he was twenty-one, he'd lend this feisty little thing the money she needed to escape from that death trap. That's when he had access to his inheritance from his mother. It was worth $60,000 a year. But next February was months away – it might as well be years.

"I'd like to open a milliner's. As sure as eggs is eggs, I could make a go of it. I just know what works with hats and what doesn't – how to add a feather here and bend a brim there. But it takes money to find premises and pay rent on them, never mind buy stock. I'll be old and grey by the time I have the dollars saved up. Still, that's my dream and I'm not going to give up on it. If we can't have dreams, what's the point? We may as well lie down in the street and let people step over us 'til we die.'"

There were others like her in the tenements – her brother Danny, for one – who grasped that to get ahead they had to work seven days a week, save up and start their own business. But Bridie had noticed how some people's dreams wore as threadbare as their clothes and she was determined this would never happen to her. She even had a name for her shop: Alicia's Modes. Alicia was Freddie Bowe-Spencer's mother, the woman whose violet creams they used to scoff. It was such a cosmopolitan name, whereas Bridie sounded rural and insignificant – both conditions she was bent on escaping.

What a rum notion, thought Stuart, whose ambition was never to do a hand's turn in his life. Still, he was impressed by her determination, a shaft of starlight silvering her face as she spoke.

He wanted to hug her to him there and then, but they were standing in a public thoroughfare. If only they could go somewhere private. That was another niggle: he wished he had somewhere to bring her. He couldn't ask her back to the pa's apartment, not with the old boy always hanging about the place. He had suggested taking a hotel room once, but Bridie had given him a look that would make the angels weep. "The last promise I made Mama back home in Ireland was that I'd never go into a hotel room with a man," she had lied sweetly.

"If I had any spare cash to invest, I'd come straight to your door with it," he said now. "I wish I did."

"If wishes were horses then beggars would ride," Bridie sniffed. "Sure

I know you'd help me if you could, Stuart, but I have to help myself, don't I? I'd best leave you now – I'm in early at the laundry tomorrow."

"I thought we might go for some chow. I know a place near here, the Breslin. They serve a terrine de foie gras I wanted you to taste."

For a moment she was wistful, for even semi-smart restaurants in New York had orchestras and she loved to dance. "Sounds wonderful but we'll have to do it another time. I ought to be catching the streetcar. I'm not my own boss the way you are. Don't walk with me, I'd prefer to go on my own."

"You're not angry with me, Bridie, are you? Let me take you to the streetcar, at least."

"No, I have to be independent, remember?"

His evening curtailed unexpectedly, Stuart listened to the retreating drum of her footsteps and wondered whether to have an early night. It was warm and mild, however, still well before midnight, and he didn't feel like going home. He might try out one of those black and tan saloons a fellow at the club had told him about, where whites and coloureds mingled. "Bully music, and the drink's strong and cheap," his friend had said.

On the ride home, Bridie wondered if she was wasting her time with Stuart Hudson. It wasn't the young men who had money but the older ones. She'd give him another few weeks, and if he didn't come through she'd have to move on. A girl couldn't expect to keep her looks forever.

19

Hannah was anxious about Bridie's excursions with Major Hudson's son, but when she said so Bridie called her a Nervous Nelly. It was stifling in the room, so Hannah took an aimless walk around the neighbourhood. The shadow of a flock of birds fell across her face and she remembered the scavenging seagulls as she and Tom had boarded at Queenstown.

Gleaming in the afternoon sun, the gigantic ship is motionless as she slowly ingests passengers and mailbags. She continues to lie still as the tenders supplying her ebb away from either side and come together to accompany one another back to Queenstown. A black puff issues from a blowspout and now the Titanic stirs herself, lazily nosing to one side and slowly swivelling to face once more the harbour mouth. Hundreds watch from the headlands as, silhouetted on the horizon, she pauses to drop her local shiphandler, then steams away with steady purpose and is lost to sight around the crook of bay. The New World is out there, waiting.

Doing her best to recreate Ireland in America, Hannah stopped at a fruit and veg stall to buy a head of cabbage for the following day's dinner, and the stall-owner threw in an apple for free. Strolling home, she thought how disconcerting it was not to be able to smell the soil of America – only concrete dust. She passed the house where the

267

industrious Germans lived, who started learning English the day they arrived – she knew their tenement from the flowers grown in window boxes: red, white and pink blooms which looked like begonias, although she didn't suppose they were called that here. Everything had different names. It was odd not to see a bevy of butterflies gorging on the flowers – she hadn't laid eyes on a single butterfly since disembarking. Hannah admired the Germans for taking time to sow flower seeds – she was too tired after a day's labour to give herself more work. Maybe when the baby came she'd plant flowers for both of them. The heat was wearing her down. On these stifling summer nights, neighbours had started sleeping on roofs or windowsills, despite the stories of people tumbling to their death while unconscious.

"How you doin', sugar? Ain't seen you in some time."

A woman with skin like polished mahogany sat on the doorstep of her tenement block. Her smile was blinding. It was Ellen Cooling, whose son sold frankfurters from a wagon and thought all Englishmen wore monocles. She was the woman who was always telling Hannah to "take Jesus with you for your friend".

Ellen nodded towards Hannah's belly. "Li'l girl you carryin'."

"Is it?"

"Sure is. Purty li'l girl. Her daddy be real proud of her."

"My baby doesn't have a father." Hannah shrank inside herself.

"She got two mommas." Ellen cocked her head, jangling the enormous gold hoops in her ears. "She got you and your friend, the sassy one. That's twice as much as some folks got."

"Would you like an apple?" Hannah wanted to pay her back for mentioning Tom.

"Why, thank you, sugar." Ellen buffed its red skin against her apron and bit in. She wore a raucous printed bandana knotted at her forehead and was missing the first joint of her little finger. The flesh puckered there, turning inwards. Hannah felt she could look at Ellen forever, with her velvet skin and colourful display.

An Oriental went by on his way to a fan-tan game, hugging the walls to avoid attention, and both women stared at his moustache, like coils of wire, and his curved fingernails six inches long.

"They good cooks," said Ellen. "Mmm-mm, you wants to taste their pork and noodles! They sure looks funny, though."

Hannah leaned against the wall. She knew Ellen lived with her son and three grown-up grandsons, and they had to pay higher rents than the whites. This was on the grounds that whites would refuse to live in the same house as coloureds, or even a house recently occupied by them, so the agents argued the rental value of the property was impaired.

"You wants to come on up for a cup of coffee?" Ellen threw away the apple core.

Hannah hesitated. She had never been in a coloured person's home. Danny Ryan was dismissive of them, calling them "work-shy darkies". Mind you, he didn't like the Chinese either – they were "rat-eaters and cat-eaters'" while the Italians were "wastrel dagoes" with their passion for the Penny Lottery. He reserved his most scathing contempt for the English. Kathleen used to shrug her shoulders and continue swapping recipes and gossip at the washing lines with her neighbours in the tenements, irrespective of their origins. But Danny was insulated from other nationalities at the building site, which had an exclusively Irish hiring policy.

"Won't Abe mind?" He was Ellen's son.

"Abe and his boys gone out. Drinkin' that dang jungle juice, Jamaica Special, or somethin' like that. Jus' me at home all on my lonesome. Come on, I got peach cobbler."

The room had a caged songbird chirruping by the window and jam-jars of silk flowers in a riot of colours erupted from every surface. Hannah studied a print of a bearded man in a high silk hat, hanging from a nail in the wall, while Ellen poured coffee. A black ribbon was tied to the frame.

"That's President Lincoln you lookin' at, sugar – the Liberator. He a real good man, too good for this world. He done all he could for his coloured children, saved us from our bondage. President Lincoln was next to the Lord. I named my son for him." She lifted a tea towel protecting the peach cobbler from buzzing flies, and cut a chunk. "Eat up, sugar."

Hannah lifted her spoon and tasted a mouthful, then quickly scraped the plate.

"Good, huh? I used to work as a cook. That's how I come to lose part of my finger."

"What do you do now?"

"Cleanin' jobs, mos'ly. Don't like cookin' for folks not my kin no more. I was a good cook, I got the fig-yure to prove it." She ran her hands over her generous expanse of hips. "My poppa always said a woman without flesh is like a dinner without meat. Not enough there to satisfy a man."

"Is your father still alive?"

"Lord-a-mercy, no, he dead and gone to his eternal reward these thirty years or more. He was Irish, same as you. Talked a bit like you, too. Kinda sing-song."

Hannah was startled. Danny had told her no self-respecting Irishman or woman would mate with a darkie. "Apart from anything else, their kids end up a smoked colour – they're neither-nor," he had said, consigning them to an intermediate race.

"You look real surprised, sugar!" Ellen laughed, an eruption which began deep in her chest and escaped in choking eddies from her throat.

"You don't look Irish," stumbled Hannah, looking at Ellen's gleaming skin and the glimpse of corkscrew hair at the front of her turban.

"I'm dark," agreed Ellen, "but my poppa was from a place called" – she wrinkled her nose – "Ballyhaunis. You ever hear tell of it? He said there weren't much to it but I always thought it sounded kinda cute. Ballyhaunis. He said it was green there, and it sure rained a lot."

"How did he meet your mother?"

"Momma was a freed slave, sugar. She come to New York from a plantation down Georgia way. Think she used to miss it, sometimes, but you're not a-s'posed to say that. She taught me how to bake that peach cobbler you just et. My parents wasn't married, she and Poppa jus' shacked up for a time. Then one day he ups and moves to Montana to work in the mines. Come back the onst to see us when I was ten or thereabouts. He a fine-looking man, usedta sing some real sad songs 'bout Ireland an' all. But he went back to Montana and I never did see him again. Seamus Moloney, that's what my poppa was called. Not that he give me his name."

"He didn't give you much, did he? Not even his name."

"He give me Jesus. He made sure me and my brother was baptised

270

Catholics, same as him." A framed Sacred Heart picture was produced from under the bed, complete with votive light. "My boy Abe don't like it on the walls – he say it spooks him. I likes to take it out when I'm on my own." The picture reminded Hannah of the kitchen at home. "Come to church with me some time, sugar. It's a real friendly place."

"I used to go. But I can't any more. I've committed terrible sins, you see. Mortal sins, probably. "

"Jesus washes all stains clean. Don't be afraid of being a sinner, there ain't none of us without sin." Ellen laughed her expansive thunder-roll. "He been in my heart these long years now. Ain't nobody got a better friend than Jesus."

* * *

Hannah thought about what Ellen had said about Jesus being a friend to her. But she needed to settle what was outstanding between them first: she had to confess her sins. Women died routinely in childbirth – it was foolhardy to risk it with sins on her soul. *Is it really disloyal to Tom to admit we sinned, and to ask for forgiveness,* she wondered? *Why are you trying to stay loyal to the man who led you astray in the first place? If I never met him, I wouldn't be in this pickle.*

After two days of dithering, Hannah plucked up her courage and went to Confession in St Dominic's, a little church two blocks from where she lived. Father Killoran grew grim as she told him what she had done, but he listened without interruption.

"I committed sins of the flesh with a man, Father, and now I'm carrying his child," she said, unable to utter Tom's name.

She told him about lying that she was his wife, and about letting her friend Bridie perjure herself by claiming she had witnessed their marriage. She wept in the musty darkness, and after a stern but not unsympathetic lecture, the priest gave her absolution.

"Your friend needs to come to Confession and it's your duty to bring her here," ordered Father Killoran, but Hannah knew she had no chance of persuading Bridie to repent.

"I'll do my best, Father," she said, before launching into the Act of Contrition. "*Oh my God I am heartily sorry for having offended thee and I*

271

detest my sins . . ."

Afterwards, the relief was overwhelming. Hannah took to stopping in at St Dominic's whenever she had the chance, and often she went out of her way to pass it for the pleasure of a minute or two inside. Sometimes she went with Ellen, who always asked her to read from a battered *Lives of the Blessed Martyrs* she carried in her pocket, a gruesome St Sebastian on the cover with a dozen arrows protruding at improbable angles from his body.

"Don't you read or write, Ellen?"

"Nope, never had no schoolin'. 'All the teachers interested in teachin' us was how to be good slaves,' my momma say. My momma, she born a slave, though the master free her, and she always tole me there ain't nothin' like freedom. I never got no schoolin' cos she was 'fraid they'd learn me to be a good slave. Now you read me about that Saint Catherine lady, please, the one the pagans tied to a wheel."

Soothed by the incense-fuelled solemnity of its atmosphere, drawn to the sensual poetic of the ritual, Hannah started going to Mass again on Sundays while Bridie stayed in bed. She loved the extravagance of Catholicism, the mysticism, the ceremony; the way Catholicism and Irishness appeared to be mutually reinforcing values here in America. She would have been quite content if only the priest hadn't told her she had a duty to bring Bridie to Confession – short of manhandling her there, she had no idea how to bring it about. Bridie didn't worry about sins the same way she did. Hannah suspected Bridie might be sinning with Stuart Hudson – or intending to, anyhow. Lustful thoughts were just as bad. When she raised the subject with Bridie she laughed at her, and said Stuart had to deliver first. "That much I learned from Freddie Bowe-Spencer, Hannah."

* * *

Adam arrived to visit Nancy with a gift of some flat pumps from his grandmother. Exquisitely wrapped, they were the right size but ugly.

Nancy supposed it was a kind gesture. The seamstress who had altered a selection of her dresses and was now working on a layette of diapers, crib sheets and tiny night-slips could have the shoes.

Nancy set them aside and looked at Adam. "Jiminy, can it be possible you've grown another few inches since I saw you last?"

"I seem to be shooting up like a beanstalk." He started to bite a nail and then stopped himself. "Grandmother wants to invite you to our house."

"That's kind."

"It's not exactly a social occasion – it's for the reading of the will. She says she's sorry it's been delayed so long. There were complications – the contents of the will seem to have surprised grandmother, she needed to make certain arrangements."

Nancy thought how pleased Violet would be that a date was finally set. She was always saying it was high time everyone knew where they stood financially.

"I've had a cracking idea about what to do with my money, if I'm allowed access to any," confided Adam. "I intend to fund a competition offering a prize for the best life-saving device for ships at sea. I'll name it in Father's memory: The Samuel Frost Armstrong the Third Award. With Roman numerals, of course. What do you think?"

He was anxious, twisting his hands behind his back, and Nancy wanted to ruffle his hair for Samuel's sake, but also for his own. "That's a fine idea. Your father would be proud of you."

Adam relaxed. "I'm going to write to Senator Smith, too, asking him to push for laws to give passengers an automatic seat in a lifeboat when they pay for their passage. I think a plan should be hung in each cabin showing where their lifeboat is situated and the fastest way to reach it."

"Senator Smith – is he the politician heading the inquiry into the sinking?"

"Yes. But you know he submitted his report to the Senate ages ago, at the end of May." He looked at her curiously; Nancy had been letting the swirl of events pass by her. "It cost the taxpayer $6,600. I managed to get hold of a copy – it ran to pages and pages. I'm afraid" – his voice was conspiratorial – "my schoolwork suffered because I devoured it."

"What did it say? Whose fault was the sinking?" Anger propelled Nancy upright.

"Well, the senator said there should be a medal for Captain Rostron."

"What else?"

"He wanted the mmm-maritime comm-muh-community to investigate rules about how vessels are built and equipped."

Words, words, they were a lava flow. "Adam, why did Samuel die?"

"The *Titanic* was going too fast, proper lookout wasn't kept and there was poor organization in loading and lowering boats. He said there was no discrim-min – no discrimination against third-class."

"I should think not, with gentlemen like my husband giving away their seats!"

"He criticised the captain, but only a little. He was over-confident and that was one of the direct causes of this unnecessary tragedy. That's what the senator called it, an unnecessary tragedy." Adam fell silent, unnerved by the way Nancy's lips were moving, although no sound escaped from them. He thought it best to say no more about the report, which had been received with hostility in sections of the British press – who referred to the senator as an "ass" and his speech as "shoddy eloquence". After a time the boy ventured, "Shall I tell grandmother to expect you at the reading of the will?"

Nancy was unresponsive. Patiently, he repeated the question.

"Yes. But you must tell her I'm bringing a confidante. Tell her I'll be accompanied by Mrs Carmen Keppel."

"I'm not sure grandmuh-mother would approve of outsiders attending."

"She's not an outsider – she's a wonderful woman who has my complete trust."

* * *

For convenience, Louis was now occupying a small bedroom in the major's apartment while they worked on the book. The Frenchman quickly grew accustomed to his employer's idiosyncrasies. Major Hudson always kept a thousand dollars in gold nuggets locked in a drawer of his desk in case of emergencies and slept beneath a portrait of his illustrious ancestor Squire Percival Hudson. A forebear of the squire's had played host to Queen Elizabeth I, taking her hunting, but she accidentally killed his favourite stag and decamped in such haste that her favourite bed covering was forgotten. Squire Percival brought it to America with him and the counterpane was still in the family, behind a glass case in the sitting room. Louis admired it dutifully.

"I slept under it once and dreamed of the Ghost Dance," said the major.

They worked in Major Hudson's study, with its towering glass-fronted bookcases and collection of animal heads. Louis would blow smoke-rings into the frozen snarl of a tiger's jaws when he was alone, and ponder how he was to win Nancy. He had overstepped a boundary that day, when only a spark from the fire had stopped him kissing her. Nancy was wary of him now. Whenever they met she put physical obstructions between them, standing behind sofas or tables. He had only once managed to get her on her own. "They married you to an old man," he had told her. Her lower lip had trembled, yielding, but before he could take it any further Violet's footsteps had tapped outside.

Common sense told him to bide his time until Nancy's baby was born. A woman pregnant by one man couldn't listen to another's declarations. After that, he would ease out the spiritualist and take her place. But common sense tended to dissolve before the intensity of his feelings for Nancy.

In the meantime the major kept him busy with research. Every time he drew the major's attention to something which bolstered his theory about the jinxed ship, his cheeks grew rosy and he became exuberant. Louis watched him, wondering if he was quite well. There was a glitter to his employer's eyes which struck him as unhealthy. When Edmund mentioned his concerns about the major to Louis, he was quick to pay heed.

"It's not just his mono-fixation," said Edmund, "it's the Keppels who worry me."

Louis raised an eyebrow. "Why?"

"They must be out for what they can get."

"They charge a fee for each session but they haven't asked the major for any further contributions."

"Do you believe them to be genuine?"

Louis hesitated. "They are certainly plausible."

"Not the same thing, is it, old man? The major tells me you introduced Mrs Armstrong to these people too."

Louis fell silent. It had been a mistake to bring Mama Carmen to Nancy, for the young widow was growing increasingly reliant on her.

"Come now, Stubel, do you honestly believe this Mama Carmen person has special powers?"

Louis traced the ball of one thumb along the other with careful attention. There had been no further arias or messages from his grandmother, probably because Nancy and the major were more important clients. "No, I don't think she has special powers. Perhaps she is intuitive, that's all."

"Stubel, you owe it to the major to keep an eye on these Keppels."

* * *

Violet would never have permitted Mama Carmen to make such inroads into her daughter's confidence if she hadn't been distracted by the feelings Louis Stubel triggered in her. Even when she discussed her reservations about Mama Carmen with him, it was on the Frenchman she concentrated.

"Nancy sees too much of her," she said.

"Mama Carmen is conducting séances here?"

"No, but she visits constantly. My daughter sends the carriage for her. Usually she comes on her own but sometimes she brings that odious little man. Nancy disappears to her room with the Keppel woman and they" – what did they do exactly? – "talk, I suppose. I know Nancy has given this person gifts."

"Valuable gifts?"

"Not particularly. A shawl she admired and some baubles. But where will it all end? I fail to understand how Nancy can be drawn to this person."

Louis tried not to stare at the artifice of her hairstyle, a meringue of stiffened frothiness. He found himself contrasting it with Nancy's soft waves. "Perhaps it's Madame Armstrong's condition which makes her vulnerable. Women who are *enceinte* can take strange fancies."

"The poor child feels unsightly, I know – she's spoken to me about it."

"A daughter of yours could not fail to be beautiful, *Madame*."

A clock ticked away the seconds. Louis thought his gallantry meaningless, while Violet hid shining eyes in her lap. So, he acknowledged what was between them!

Louis continued, "I advise you not to put any obstacles in the way of their meeting. It will make Mama Carmen seem like forbidden fruit."

"I'll do whatever you suggest. I appreciate your concern, Mr Stubel – a woman alone feels so helpless at such times."

A surge of optimism energised Louis as he realized he could sway Violet, perhaps counteracting Mama Carmen's influence through her. "A woman who listens is lost," his foster father would often say in Paris, as he drank absinthe at the kitchen table.

*　*　*

Nancy drowsed, a cushion under her feet so they were higher than her ankles, which her mother insisted was beneficial. As well as everything else, Momma was now the authority on pregnancy. She realized her mother and Louis had a rapport, perhaps even an understanding, and the knowledge bothered her. Anyone could see Violet grew animated in his vicinity. Her mother had always basked in the presence of men, a forced edge of gaiety defining her manner, but with Louis it was pronounced. Gradually it was dawning on her that Violet had a romantic interest in Louis, and any difference in age or station didn't register with her. Only yesterday she had seen them whispering together in the window seat of the morning room. There had been something confidential in the way their bodies inclined towards each other. Could they be lovers? The possibility shook her.

After Louis left, petulant because her back was hurting where the baby kicked, Nancy remarked, "Do you think Mr Stubel is satisfied with his position with the major? Perhaps we should try and persuade him to come to us. He would make a competent butler – he has a gift for service."

"Louis Stubel would be competent at anything he turned his hand to – he has a gift for understanding what's needed in any given situation," her mother replied. But a faint colour creeping, like a high water mark, above the neckline of her gown betrayed her. The taunt had not gone unnoticed.

Nancy lay on her day bed, knowing she had to get ready to go to the Armstrong mansion on Park Lane for the reading of the will, but the heat left her too lethargic to move. She told herself it was the age difference between her mother and Louis which made her intolerant of any relationship between them. He's twenty-three – seventeen years younger than Momma. It's impossible, she thought, disregarding the eighteen-year age-gap between herself and Samuel.

The knowledge she felt attracted to Louis tapped for admission at Nancy's consciousness. She tried to ignore it: she was a pregnant widow, deprived in tragic circumstances of a husband she believed she loved. It was too soon to notice other men. Yet what about the time, horrifyingly, when they had almost kissed? And the time after that when Louis Stubel had leaned past to reach something, so close his breath had tickled the back of her neck, and her body had responded to his – her blood stirring in a way it never had with Samuel? She was aware of him staring at her whenever he had the chance, shameless about it, and the urgency in his eyes unsettled her.

She had mentioned him to Mama Carmen one afternoon.

The medium had caught Nancy's hand to ensure her undivided attention. "With him, a woman would live in extremes. Joy and despair would be her bedfellows."

Remembering Mama Carmen's words, Nancy flapped her hand to stir up some air around her face, and wondered if the joy would compensate for the despair.

*   *   *

Violet was preparing to accompany her daughter. She tried on a citron-coloured hat which Miss Traas, her milliner, had persuaded her to take home to see whether or not she cared for it. By which she meant whether her face looked too lined for its frivolity. Of course she couldn't possibly wear anything so flimsy to the Armstrongs, but she was unable to resist twirling in front of the mirror. Violet hoped to feast on a vision of herself transformed into a version that was a decade younger, in a hat with curled feathers so becoming Louis would be smitten by her. Could she get away with it? Yes, she could! She must have the hat, even if she was supposed to be in semi-mourning for her son-in-law and it was

278

fiendishly expensive. Nancy wouldn't see her financially embarrassed.

Violet realized Louis was in no position to buy her hats, and in any case he was too young for her. Just by a few years. "But he has such a mature air, probably because he's European," she told her reflection. She was rejuvenated by Louis's attention and allowed her thoughts to meander along an agreeable path whereby Louis took her in his arms and told her he loved only her. In her heart, Violet knew they could not make a match. His beauty acted as a drug with her, however – not just the grace of his physical appearance but the inflection of his voice which flicked words upwards at the end of each sentence to send them on their way, and the intent way he appraised everything from a ruffle of lace to the brushstrokes on an oil painting.

At the age of forty Violet had fallen in love for the first time. Her marriage had been arranged; initially she had tolerated and eventually she had despised her husband for his lack of financial acumen which had reduced their standard of living. From time to time she toyed with the notion of a lover but opportunity and inclination never coalesced. Violet had not expected love to enter her life in her middle years, and was as intoxicated by it as any schoolgirl.

She removed the hat, replaced it in its box and lifted a less playful black substitute. Then she swept into Nancy's room. "Time for us to go to the Armstrongs, darling. I can't understand why you're so insistent on bringing that Mama Carmen creature with us."

Nancy pulled herself to her feet. "Samuel may have left a coded message for me in his will – she can help me decipher it. She has such insight."

Violet was exasperated. It was ridiculous of Nancy to insist on associating with this woman. For now, however, she had to concentrate on dealing with Rebecca Armstrong, never a chore for the faint-hearted.

* * *

Rebecca took one look at Mama Carmen and suggested she might be more comfortable waiting in the servants' hall.

"I won't stay for the reading of the will unless my friend is present," said Nancy.

Rebecca tried to stare her down but failed. It seemed to her as though all social distinctions were being levelled. Heaven knows where it will end, she thought. She had no choice but to concede. "Very well. But I take exception to this – grave exception."

"As you like." Nancy was serene.

"I sense in you someone who has suffered a succession of losses," chanted Mama Carmen, fixing hypnotic grey eyes on the matriarch.

Rebecca was amazed to find herself addressed by this person.

"Your burden is heavy, Mrs Armstrong – but there are those in the spirit world who would ease it for you. You must slow down."

The impertinence of this nobody! "Slow down? I was brought up to believe Satan finds mischief for idle hands." Rebecca whipped about and led the way to a room with deep-set bay windows forming a succession of alcoves. A lawyer in a wing-collar shirt was waiting there, along with Adam and the Armstrong cousin Nancy recognized from that day in the Chapel of Rest. Noah Armstrong, that was his name. Wasn't he the family trust's administrator or something?

She turned her attention to her stepson. "Hallo, Adam, how are the plans for the lifeboat prize coming along?"

"I've made some progress, Nancy. Perhaps I could tell you about it later?"

"I'll look forward to it."

His grandmother frowned. Who had given the boy leave to call her Nancy? And what prize were they talking about? "Don't cough, Adam, it's nothing but a nervous habit. Shall we proceed? Do sit down, everyone. Mr Bennington, we're ready for the reading."

The will was short. Samuel Frost Armstrong III left everything he possessed to his son Adam, the estate to be administered on his behalf by his grandmother until he reached his majority. There was no mention of Nancy or the child she was carrying.

Nancy listened to the words spoken by the lawyer, trying to hear Samuel through them.

Violet was scarcely able to believe her ears. "Isn't there a default in the will? I understood there was some arrangement whereby a posthumous child was entitled to a settlement."

The lawyer shuffled his pages. "Mr Armstrong discussed inserting such a clause and telegraphed me from London to that effect, but he omitted to take the necessary steps."

"What about my daughter? Surely as his widow she's entitled to a proportion of his estate?"

"There is provision for her. Mrs Armstrong is entitled to stay on in the house on Fifth Avenue for her lifetime or until she remarries, whereupon the property reverts to Mrs Armstrong Senior as the legal owner. There is an allowance of $5,000 a year, also conditional on her remaining single."

"That's it?" Violet felt dizzy.

"That's it."

"Nothing for the child my daughter is carrying?"

"I'm afraid not, madam."

"This is outrageous! We will appeal it."

"Your daughter was married to Mr Armstrong for only three months, Mrs Markova. Some might say the use of a handsome house for life and £5,000 a year is a lucrative dividend on a short-term arrangement."

Nancy said nothing. She was thinking of the wedding photograph which stood beside the rosebowl in her dressing room. The bride's lily-of-the-valley bouquet rested on a chair, her eight-feet-long train gliding out of the picture. People said the bride was the belle of the season, but Nancy knew there was a nervous light behind her blue eyes.

Mama Carmen spoke up. "Mr Armstrong regrets not changing his will. He intended doing so on his re-marriage, but in the excitement of the wedding tour it slipped his mind. He did wire his lawyer's office about it, but was told he had to sign the necessary papers in person."

"You seem remarkably well-informed." Rebecca's tone was steely.

"Of course. I had this from Mr Armstrong himself."

"When were you speaking to my son?"

"Two days ago, during a séance."

Rebecca and Violet exchanged glances.

"I think we've heard all we need to from this person," said Rebecca. "Mrs Markova, you seem to be a sensible person. I suggest you and I adjourn to the library to discuss a proposal I should like to put to you."

Rebecca preceded Violet from the room, her moral superiority back in place.

281

20

One Sunday there was a knock and Danny, Kathleen and the baby stood outside Bridie and Hannah's room. Kathleen held the collar of their son, who was walking a few steps now, while Danny whipped off his cloth cap as the door was answered, black hair plastered flat on his head. Bridie was amazed: her brother rarely awarded himself a Sunday off. After Mass he'd always go into work if the extra hours were on offer.

"Come in."

Danny avoided Bridie's eye. "God bless all here," he said gruffly.

"This looks cosy," puffed Kathleen, "don't it, Danny?"

He nodded, and Bridie knew there was to be no scene. Her brother had swallowed his pride to pay the visit.

The small boy toddled, crowing, to Hannah and head-butted her thigh. She dandled him between her legs, laughing as his podgy fist reached for her coronet of plaits. "I've missed you, wee man."

Bridie tickled her nephew under the chin but quickly lost interest. "Hannah, will you make Kathleen a cup of tea while I slip out for a jug of something to wet the brother's whistle? They have Guinness Stout or Dublin Porter on draft at the saloon – which would you prefer, Danny?"

"No need for either." His protest was half-hearted.

"There's every need."

"Well, Guinness if you're determined."

Her rapid departure sent a cool blast of air into the room.

"Thank goodness everything's jim-dandy again," said Kathleen.

Danny had been like a bear with a sore head since the girls flitted. That Bridie was a bit of a madam, but she was stimulating, and she'd put up with worse than her for Danny.

In addition to the beer, Bridie brought back a Home Rule for Ireland cigar. Lavish with happiness, she'd added a striped candy cane for her nephew and a walnut cake because she knew it was Kathleen's favourite.

As they were leaving, Danny felt in his pocket. "I was nearly forgetting, Hannah. I have another letter here for you from your in-laws, they seem very attached to you." Hannah accepted it unwillingly. At least they had addressed her as Hannah O'Brien this time. He removed his cigar from his mouth and looked at the glowing tip. "The English have finished their inquiry. A whitewash, just as you'd expect. I've been following it in the Brooklyn Eagle." In addition to the Senate hearing in Washington, another inquiry had been conducted in London. "The English were determined to let White Star off the hook from the start. The shipping line paraded eleven sea captains – eleven! – before that Mersey Commission in London, all of them testifying that when the weather was good and there was ice ahead, they always went full steam ahead until ice was sighted."

"Why would they do that, Danny?" asked Bridie.

"To keep speeds up – rich folk like to go from A to B in jig-speed. And they like those mailbags full of their business deals to do the same. If that Mersey fellow heard evidence he didn't like, he ignored it."

"Even if they did prove Captain Smith was at fault, it won't bring Tom back," said Hannah.

"But at least we'd know. Knowing counts for something. And it might make us a few shillings. Negligence, isn't that what the lawyers call it, Danny?" Bridie's eyes gleamed, grasping the significance. She forestalled Hannah's protest. "It's not about money, of course it's not, but we're entitled to something for what we've been through. What if the sinking wasn't an act of God, what if it was someone's fault?"

Hannah knew she'd need all the money she could lay her hands on to give the baby a decent start in life. But she felt compromised for having wrangled with Tom's mother over who was entitled to compensation, and guilty about lying to stake her claim. She slid the envelope postmarked Chicago into her pocket without looking at it.

"Aren't you going to read that, Hannah?" asked Kathleen.

"Time enough. There's never any good news in letters, so there isn't."

* * *

The letter lay for a week without Hannah opening it. Bridie was riddled with curiosity, and once or twice thought about steaming it open.

"Are you ever going to take a look at that?"

"I might and I mightn't."

Hannah would have liked to throw it in the fire unopened. However, she had an uneducated person's respect for the written word and hesitated to take such a destructive step. Finally she opened it one Sunday, in a church pew after Mass at St Dominic's. Whatever it contained could harm her less in such surroundings, she reasoned. The echo of the congregation's *"Ora pro nobis"* reverberated in the air as she slit the envelope and checked the signature. It was from Tom's favourite sister, Winifred. Then she read the words Tom's sister had written to her, and her blood rushed through her veins with such force she thought it might burst the membrane of skin. Winifred must despise her if she believed her capable of such a thing. Shocked, she stared at the stained-glass window above the altar until her eyes were dazzled by rainbow arcs shooting off it in the sunlight. The window depicted the adoration of the Magi: Baby Jesus, complacent in yellow curls, receiving their gifts of gold, frankincense and myrrh.

Hannah wondered if her child would resemble herself or Tom. Would it have her red hair or his sallow complexion? Even though it was Tom's child as much as hers, she hoped it would have nothing of the O'Briens in it. Not after what she read in Winifred's letter.

She lifted the envelope to tear it in two and something slid out of it. It was a sepia photograph taken three years earlier. A film of tears glittered in Hannah's eyes at seeing Tom's face again: a smiling face, squinting against a beam of sunlight – not strained, as it looked during that last night on the *Titanic*, biting back a retort to the officer who was short with him so he wouldn't spoil Hannah's chances of a place on the lifeboat. His hair was longer in the photograph, beneath the cap he always slid a salley rod inside to keep his brim firm.

August 24th, 1911: another glorious summer's day. Hannah rubs buttermilk into her skin before she sets off, to keep the freckles at bay. The train is crowded when it pulls into Limerick Junction and there is nowhere to sit.

"Would you like this seat, miss?"

Hannah accepts a seat from the fellow with a salley-rod in his cap. He has a humorous way of tilting his face, and sends a couple of shy smiles winging her way during the twenty-mile journey. She's glad she washed her hair in vinegar that morning to make it shine. Hannah smiles back, hoping he might speak to her again. The train is slowing for its final stop and still he hasn't plucked up courage. Hannah sighs, thinking instead about how much she may get for the basket of eggs she has to sell and what the money will buy. But as the train chugs into Limerick's arched station and she stands, he moves across to her.

"Can I carry your basket for you, miss?"

Her fingers reached out to graze the edges of the paper square containing Tom O'Brien's image. There was his long nose reaching almost to his upper lip. She couldn't believe she'd forgotten his nose. Just as she couldn't believe Tom's flesh and blood would be capable of suggesting a transaction as unnatural as the one mentioned in the letter.

* * *

"Say, Stuart, why don't you stay in and dine with your old pa tonight? We haven't eaten together all week."

"Gee, I'd like to, sir, but I have a date."

"I see. With anyone I know?"

Stuart turned away from Major Hudson, ostensibly to adjust his cravat.

"I shouldn't think so."

"It wouldn't be that little colleen, by any chance?"

Stuart continued primping. "Don't quite follow you, Pa."

"I wasn't born yesterday, my boy. You made a fuss of her at the premiére, and one of the chaps at the club mentioned seeing you with a dainty little dark-haired creature on Broadway the other night."

"Yes, it's with Bridie." Stuart tried to sustain his father's gaze but was defeated. He shuffled his feet.

"Disappointed you chose to lie to me, Stuart. What was it your mama always said to you about truth?"

"Beauty is truth, truth beauty." Stuart spoke unwillingly. He didn't know if it was another of those superimposed memories or if he remembered his mother quoting Keats to him.

"Exactly. I could forbid you to keep your date, but I'd prefer you to break it of your own accord."

"Why, what have you got against Bridie? She works hard, a darn sight harder than either of us. All I'm doing is showing her a good time."

"That's not all you're doing. You're giving her expectations – expectations you're neither willing nor able to keep."

"How do you know I won't keep them?"

His father looked steadily at him. "You are twenty years of age, Stuart. I understand you need to kick back and enjoy life while the sap rises, but not with Bridie Ryan. New York is full of girls, find another. She didn't come through the *Titanic* to land in trouble. Let her find a decent fellow of her own sort, instead of filling her head with nonsense in lobster palaces and vaudeville theatres, or wherever you bring her."

"But it's exactly because she came through the *Titanic* that she's determined to enjoy life. I can show her a good time, so why shouldn't I?"

"Because you'll spoil her for her own sort. She won't want to step out with a working man after being accustomed to what you have to offer – stands to reason. You'll turn the girl's head."

"I never had you down for a snob."

"I won't let you trifle with that girl. She's too full of life to have you suck it out of her because you're bored hanging round in New York, waiting for the new term to start at Yale. How about if we take a trip to Oyster Bay? Remember the fun we had there when your mother was alive? With the Punch and Judy shows and everything?"

"I hardly think Punch and Judy shows constitute my idea of fun."

Stuart stalked from the room. He returned almost immediately, collected the brandy decanter and a glass, and made to leave again.

"Just a minute, Stuart. If you're staying in, I suggest you send a note to the young lady so she isn't left standing. Louis will deliver it if you tell him where you arranged to meet her."

"You treat me like a child."

"Stuart, I'm only trying to do what's best. Come on, be a man about it, and when it's all done and dusted you and I can plan that trip. Your old pa doesn't see enough of you."

"That's because you're always off communing with the spirit world, wasting your money on charlatans who tell you what you want to hear. At least if I spend mine on a cute girl I get some benefit from it."

"Let me remind you it's my money you're spending, Stuart."

Frosty, he reached a pad of writing paper to his son, who debated treading it underfoot but reconsidered when he saw the older man's expression. His pa hardly ever laid down the law, but when his dander was up it was best to cooperate.

* * *

Louis Stubel approached Bridie outside a theatre on 42nd Street and handed over a note. Her lips moved as she read the message that Stuart sent his apologies but he was unavoidably detained.

"Major Hudson asked me to give you this." Louis proffered fifty dollars.

"What's it for?"

"Any inconvenience."

Bridie itched to tear the bills into ribbons and hurl them at his feet. She contented herself with grinding her teeth as she pocketed the cash. It was a tidy haul, after all, more than two weeks' wages. "Does Stuart know he's sending me money?"

"I couldn't say."

Bridie presumed the eleventh-hour cancellation, plus the money, meant she had seen the last of Stuart Hudson. Her mouth twisted, waspish. "Still hanging around after Mrs Armstrong, are you?"

Louis swept her with a chilly look. "I hardly think my associations are any of your concern."

"A cat can look at a king in this country. Or a queen come to that. But it doesn't mean she'll take him on to her lap and feed him titbits."

* * *

Bridie decided she might as well go home and keep Hannah company.

Climbing through the near-darkness of the windowless stairwells, conscious of tension behind all those closed doors on each floor, of other lives being lived, she wondered what would happen when Hannah's infant arrived in two months' time. Would it remind her of her own unborn baby? Would it be painful to be around? She hadn't paid much attention to Daniel Junior, for fear of resurrecting memories best stifled. Bridie reached the top floor, thinking that at least Hannah would be pleased her date had fallen through. But Hannah was out.

Bridie was sitting, hands wrapped around a cup of cocoa with a film over the surface, when Hannah arrived home. Only the street light outside relieved the gloom.

"Date finish early, Bridie? Are you losing interest in that young Hudson fellow already?" Hannah hoped this was the case, "It's pitch dark in here – let me turn on the lamp."

"It's more like he's lost interest in me. He stood me up."

Hannah's hands stilled at the gas bracket. "Without so much as a word of warning?"

"I think his daddy said I wasn't good enough for him. That French fellow off the boat was sent with a message. From Stuart, it was, but if you ask me the major had a hand in it. Up swans Frenchie, cool as you like, and gives me a note saying Stuart is unavoidably detained. Then he reaches me fifty dollars from the major and more or less tells me to stay clear."

"Do you like Stuart, Bridie? I mean really like him?"

Bridie went quiet for a time, comparing Stuart with Freddie Bowe-Spencer. "He has no silence," she said at last. Freddie's silences had been companionable. She shook herself. "No use crying over spilled milk. We had a few laughs, Stuart and I. What did you do tonight, Hannah?"

"Visited with Ellen."

"She invited you into her house? Negroes don't know their place."

"What *is* their place and who are we to decide it for them? Sure we're fresh off the boat, whereas Ellen was born and bred here."

"She's as black as a pair of riding boots!"

"Don't let's fight."

"Of course we won't, *alanna*. Anyway, I'm just being contrary because my date was a washout. Your friend is right not to know her place – I don't intend ever to know mine.

Hannah's eyes strayed towards the Huntley and Palmer biscuit tin where Winifred's letter was stored. "I read that letter at last. Tom's sister Winifred has offered to take the baby off my hands when it comes. She says she'll give it a good home. Herself and the husband have no child of their own." She brooded, before bursting out, "Imagine her thinking I'd hand over my child! She must have me down as heartless."

"Maybe she meant no harm? She could have thought she was doing you a good turn. Not everyone wants to raise a child on their own."

Hannah's agitation subsided. "Well, she did send me a photograph of Tom. It'll be something for the baba. Here – look." She passed it over to Bridie, who admired it dutifully. "And she said her way meant the child could have a father as well as a mother, but my way meant only a mother. But if I don't know what's best for my own baby, I don't know who does! Ellen says I should pray for them."

"You've discussed this with Ellen?"

"Prayed with her about it. We lit a candle at St Dominic's. Ellen says I shouldn't judge Winifred too harshly. But I can't help myself, Bridie, I get so indignant when I think of being asked to parcel up my baby."

"What exactly did Tom's sister suggest?"

Hannah wrinkled her broad, freckled forehead as the words flooded back. "I can promise the child a good home. I have money saved. I'll make sure it goes to school and get it apprenticed to a trade when the time comes, so it has the means to earn a decent living. I intend no disrespect, but you're only starting out in this country. Raising a child won't be easy for you. We'll do right by Tom's child, Patrick and me. I have my three sisters here, and it won't be short of family."

"She spoke fair."

"I suppose."

"There's some women would welcome the offer." Bridie wondered if she would have carried her own child to term, had she known a good home was waiting for it after the birth. She remembered that climb up the Hill of Oola, the inches-long baby in her arms. It had weighed hardly anything. She had tried not to look, but the towel wrapped around it had fallen away as she laid it in the hole. Its head had seemed too large for its thin red body. She thought it might have been a daughter. Her unformed face had peeked out at Bridie from the grave. Reproachful.

"There's too much bad blood between us all now, after those accusations from the solicitor in Cappamore. I'm better having nothing to do with the O'Briens."

"You can't blame the sisters in Chicago for a letter that came from Ireland."

"They're bound to take their mother's side in any argument." Hannah looked suspiciously at Bridie. "You don't want me to give away the child, do you? You're not afraid of it cramping your style?"

Bridie hesitated for a beat before assuring Hannah the baby was welcome in their home, and in that pause Hannah's worst fears were realized. She went to bed without further conversation.

* * *

Violet had refused to give Rebecca Armstrong an immediate response to her proposition, although her mind had reeled at the implications of the deal.

"I guess I'll have to sleep on this and let you know," she had told Rebecca, to the older woman's displeasure.

"It's a generous settlement – more generous, some might say, than your daughter deserves."

"My daughter is carrying your grandson and is due your respect, if not your money."

They had agreed she could have two weeks to think it over. Nancy had pressed her for the details of what she and Rebecca had discussed in private, and even the normally circumspect Mama Carmen had alluded to it on their carriage drive home, but Violet had been guarded. "It was nothing significant," she had said, dismissing the proposition which caused her ribcage to strain against the lacing on her gown.

It was unsafe for her to debate Rebecca's terms with Nancy, since Violet could not trust her to be discreet around Mama Carmen. Violet wanted to be the one to persuade Nancy to a particular viewpoint, not that foreign woman. First, she had to establish what her own stance was. She would confer with Louis.

She sent him a message inviting him to call. Preparing for his visit, Violet changed into a mauve morning gown and daubed Ambre Antique lavishly on the pulse points at her wrists and neck. The air in the salon was heavy with its scent when Louis arrived.

Violet outlined the details of Rebecca Armstrong's arrangement and he listened without comment until she finished.

"It's a liberal offer, although a most unusual one."

"Do you think I should accept? I mean, that Nancy should accept?"

Louis stroked his chin. "There are advantages and disadvantages. If you accept, your daughter will want for nothing for the rest of her life. It depends on how willing she is to abide by the terms."

"Exile is a cruel word, but exile is what it amounts to. Rebecca Armstrong is seeking to expel my child from these shores, using her money as bait. If Nancy is prepared to live outside the United States for the rest of her life, Rebecca will settle a lump sum of $5 million dollars on her. It's a fortune. But if we stay, we depend on the Armstrongs for the roof over our heads. If Nancy is to be banished, naturally I go with her. No price is too high for a mother's love, even expulsion." She paused for dramatic effect. "Besides," added Violet, who had never left the United States, "I'll soon adapt to life in Europe, I'm more European in my habits. But I can't imagine why she's intent on making outcasts of us. I, for one, welcome Samuel Armstrong's baby – even though all my friends insist I'm too vivacious to be a grandmother."

"If you stay in New York, I imagine she must acknowledge Mr Armstrong's child and receive you all socially. Perhaps that's not to her taste."

"I don't care a hoot if she acknowledges us or not," Violet lied. "Mercy, I'd just as soon lead a quiet life – I'm not one for social gatherings."

"Was that her only condition?"

"She says we shouldn't apply to White Star for compensation for Samuel's life. None of the best families are doing it. Not the Astors, the Guggenheims, nor the Wideners."

Louis could bear the lack of nicotine no longer and his fingers prised a cigarette from the packet. "Do you mind?" He tamped it down, his brain grappling with the Armstrong offer. "But the claims against White Star are mounting every day since the hearing closed in London. The major said millions of dollars' worth of claims have been entered by survivors or their families."

"Are you intending to make one, Mr Stubel?"

"Of course. But I wouldn't suggest you do likewise if it jeopardises your arrangement with the Armstrong family. Five million dollars in the hand is worth an uncertain settlement from White Star in the bush."

"So your advice is to take the money? We could go to Paris, perhaps."

Louis paused, needing time to reflect. Were his chances of wooing Nancy better in the United States, or outside them?

Violet picked up her ebony and lace fan from a side-table and began agitating the air. "Oh, do advise me, Mr Stubel. Rebecca Armstrong said her offer was only valid for two weeks."

"I think you should accept the offer, but don't let yourself be rushed into leaving too soon. You need to plan your movements carefully, and Mrs Armstrong will take time to recover from her confinement. Why not agree, but delay it until next year?" That should give me time to pay court to Nancy, he thought.

"We can't. There's no money forthcoming until we have our liner tickets booked – the condition is we're gone by Christmas."

"She's a tough negotiator, Mrs Armstrong's mother-in-law."

Tough as stringy chicken – she wouldn't tear in the plucking, thought Violet, but she didn't like to express such a sentiment. She was a lady, she wasn't meant to know anything about plucking chickens.

Louis decided it might suit him better to court Nancy abroad – there'd be fewer friends to advise against the match. "There are many places where you might put down roots and make a home. London, perhaps, might suit you. I could even accompany you there and help you settle in."

293

Violet's pulse speeded up and her fan fluttered in time with it. This was precisely the overture she had been waiting for. Careful, you're no débutante and he'll never mistake you for one. She was being propositioned subtly, every instinct told her it was so. She must signal that his overtures were far from unwelcome. But it had to be a delicate tango of advance and retreat. "You'd come with us, Louis?" Her use of his name was deliberate. "You'd leave the major and lend a hand to two helpless women trying to establish themselves in London?" She allowed herself to look into his tawny eyes, glancing quickly away and then back again.

Louis read the invitation in hers and recoiled, but he had the presence of mind to control his reaction: he couldn't wound the older woman's pride by flaunting his preference for the younger one. It was only vanity and boredom that persuaded her to flirt with him – her feelings couldn't be engaged. Louis had found it no hardship to flatter Violet. She was fleshier than he preferred, but she had a veneer of coquetry which he responded to and a seam of practicality which he respected. Crucially, she lent him access to Nancy.

All of a sudden, however, he was less surefooted. "I should be *desolé* to lose contact with you, Madame Markova, and with your daughter. You have opened your home and shown me nothing but kindness and hospitality."

She moved a few paces closer, waiting. He took her hand and bent his lips to it, but Violet had daubed scent too liberally and he coughed.

Violet's eyelashes fluttered shut and her lips parted as she waited for him to rain down further kisses, touching his mouth to her flesh . . . But he released her hand abruptly.

"Of course I'd accompany you, if I weren't a humble working man who must earn his bread. Alas, I'm not free to go."

She opened her eyes, breathing shallowly. Was Louis Stubel still too much the gentleman to accept what was freely offered? Surely he must realize she was a vibrant woman in the prime of life!

He turned away and strolled to the window. "How is your daughter today? May I be permitted to offer her my compliments?"

"She sleeps late these mornings, her condition requires it. I'll be glad to pass on your good wishes."

"I should like to do it myself."

Violet blinked at his impudence, and doubt nibbled. Was it possible Louis Stubel preferred the child to the mother?

Louis interpreted her change of mood and intervened quickly. "But it's my visits with you, Madame Markova, which brighten my life. You are what we call *sympathique* in France. When we meet, I feel a connection between us. As for your daughter, I didn't mean to take a liberty. It's simply that I feel a responsibility towards her – we shared a lifeboat."

"I can be responsible for my own daughter, thank you."

She was tart, and he decided not to risk pressing her. "Very well, it's of no consequence. I'll take my leave – I have business to attend to on Major Hudson's behalf. He is keen for another séance with Mama Carmen, a personal one this time, and I must arrange it."

"Mama Carmen is kept occupied, these days, between my daughter and the major."

"She'd have less opportunity to be occupied on your daughter's account if you weren't living in New York."

Violet tapped the fan against a thumbnail, assessing what he said. "The way my daughter feels about that person, she'd pay her a retainer to accompany us wherever we went – and, I declare, Mama Carmen would come, too. To Timbuctoo, if necessary."

"Mama Carmen is much attached to Madame Armstrong."

"Much attached. But attachments can be broken."

When Violet was alone she buried her head in the rustling silk of her lap and wished to God she was twenty again.

21

The shadows under Mama Carmen's eyes were more pronounced than ever, accentuated by a burnt orange pashmina which Louis recognized as one of Nancy's. This was a personal séance for the major, so that Mama Carmen's powers could be trained exclusively on him. Walt Keppel dimmed the lights and the foursome sat, two facing two, hands flat on the tabletop. Traffic grumbled outside, an occasional beam of light piercing a gap in the curtains.

Mama Carmen's breathing accelerated, then slowed down, and she entered her trance state. The table pulsed and swayed under their fingers and an erratic rapping was heard on its surface, which they took to be evidence of the psychic power gathering. A voice emanated from the medium that was neither Mama Carmen's nor Ada's, her spirit guide. It was male and guttural.

"What do you want?" it demanded.

"Evidence of life after death," answered the major.

"How would you have me prove it? Like a performing animal, by describing the contents of your wallet?"

"We ask no party tricks of you, sir. However you choose to prove it will satisfy me."

The voice softened. "What would you have me tell you?"

"Who are you, friend?" asked Walt. "Are you little Ada's . . . pupil?"

"Am I her murderer, is that what you mean?" A laugh was hacked out. "Yes, I'm Lloyd Berry, I stole Ada's life force. But the afterlife allows us space to atone for our mistakes."

"Could you describe the afterlife?" asked the major.

"We live as on earth, but in a heightened state of consciousness. The sunlight is brighter, the birdsong sweeter, the grass greener. There is no rain, no winter, no unhappiness. All is harmonious."

"But you miss your loved ones on earth, surely?"

"Not in the way you miss them, because we know we'll be reunited. And we can watch over you, so we know how your life is progressing. We celebrate your triumphs."

"You do?"

"Sure. Have you ever felt a moment of inexplicable happiness? There's no obvious reason for it, yet your heart is lighter?"

"Yes," the major marvelled, "I know that feeling."

"That's a loved one on the other side communicating their joy in the milestones of your life."

"Are you familiar with my wife, Jean Hudson? She's a Scottish lady."

"I don't know her. I'm not interested in women, they talk too much. Talking, always talking, it makes me want to put my hands on their throats and squeeze until . . ." There was a choking gasp, before the voice continued, more moderately. "I don't know the lady."

"I hoped you might have a message from her."

"To say she loves you? Pah! These communications make me sick. I will not be a conduit for them."

Throughout the major's exchange Louis watched Walt Keppel, wondering if he was a ventriloquist. Was his mouth moving? He couldn't decide. It was possible – yet it would take intense rehearsal between him and Mama Carmen for her lips to mouth words coming from her husband.

Keppel leaned forward and nodded in the direction of Mama Carmen's taut figure. "Ask something for yourself," he whispered to Louis.

"Do you know any relations of mine?" asked Louis, still hoping, despite his scepticism, for some clue about his identity.

A shape began to glow across Mama Carmen's features, dilating and altering its contours, until it settled in as the face of a young woman. Her hair was intricately coiled and blonde, her features overlaid with a sweet melancholy. Louis felt himself tremble, looking at the face, and despite the room's warmth a block of ice settled on his chest, crushing him. He heard the major's sharp intake of breath and was dimly aware of his own hands clenching and unclenching.

"Who are you?" Louis choked out.

The face curved its lips into a half-smile, and a voice tiptoed through Louis's brain.

You know who I am. Mine is the first face you saw.

Transfixed, Louis gazed at his mother.

Love takes courage. Your father and I learned that. There is a price to pay for love. You must be willing to pay it, whatever the cost. But first you must leave your love to find her again. You must go home.

"To Paris?"

Vienna.

The glow dimmed and Mama Carmen stirred. The opaque film over her eyes cleared and she pressed her fingertips against a furrow between her eyebrows. "It felt shorter tonight. What did our little Ada have to say?"

"We didn't have a visit from Ada, Mama." Walt adjusted the lamplight. "It was that fellow who murdered her."

"Lloyd Berry broke through? He's never managed that before. In the past I've been the only one who could hear his voice." Mama Carmen betrayed consternation.

"We had a manifestation, Mama. The face of a beautiful young lady was superimposed on yours for forty, maybe fifty, seconds. Clear as day. It seemed to be directed at our friend, Mr Stubel."

"Did she speak?"

"Nope."

It was then Louis realized none of the others had heard the apparition's words.

"It was quite unique." The major cleared his throat. "I feel privileged to have witnessed it. Yours is a truly unique talent, Mama Carmen."

"Mama Carmen's only rustled up two previous manifestations,

friends. This is a rare feat, yes, siree, a rare feat."

Mama Carmen's eyes, pupils engorged so that black swallowed up grey, turned to Louis. She cocked her head, earrings jangling, and watched him closely. "What did you make of it, Mr Stubel?"

"I don't know. I saw something but I'm not sure what it was."

"Aren't you? Listen to what your heart tells you instead of your head."

Pinioned by the gleam of those black pupils, he put out his hand to ward off her gaze. "My head has served me well in the past."

"Equilibrium, Mr Stubel. We must make space for both. Hasn't that message been passed down to you by the spirit world already?"

"It's been passed down to me – by what or whom I couldn't say."

"Mama Carmen," Major Hudson broke the current between them, "is there any chance my wife could be persuaded to take part in one of those manifestations? I'd trade the world to see her dear face again."

"I can promise nothing, major, but I can intercede for you."

"It would require considerable effort on Mama's part, major. She'd be out of circulation for some time – her other clients might feel the loss of her attention," Keppel hinted.

"I wouldn't dream of allowing Mama Carmen to lose out. Perhaps you and I can adjourn to discuss financial arrangements."

*   *   *

Edmund juggled working on script outlines with teaching the colonel's wards. It left no time for the tour of the United States he had intended, but he was experiencing the country in a different way by working there. Éclair was interested in his classics knowledge and contemplating a series of swords-and-sandals epics, since box office receipts showed the public had an appetite for spectacle. "We think we'll do Samson and Delilah." Jules manipulated his cigar from one side of his mouth to the other with his tongue.

"That's biblical, not the classics."

"Whatever. Picture it, Ed: slave girls, warriors, kings, and a dance so erotic it bewitches a king into promising a false woman anything her heart desires. The audience will lap it up!"

"Aren't you mixing it up with John the Baptist and Salomé?"

"See? That's exactly why we need your specialist knowledge, Ed. Off you go and research this Delilah dame. Dorothy would kill for a role like this. Remember, we need plenty of belly-dancing scenes."

It was baking in Edmund's basement apartment and, with the windows open, dust from the street kept swirling in. The studio had torn up all his background work about the feud between the Israelites and the Philistines for supremacy in the land of Canaan. All they wanted was to show Delilah seducing Samson into revealing the secret of his strength. Sexual interplay, was that all anyone was interested in? Brulatour and Dorothy were obsessed by it, Stuart Hudson was an alleycat when it came to it, and even the major was forever droning on about his dead wife, although Edmund had seen the way he looked at the Irish girls. Was he the only man in the world who thought there was more to life than the birds and the bees?

He threw down his pencil and mooched over to the sofa. A pair of trim ankles clicked past the window above it. Ankles like Bridie's, he thought. His temperature notched up another degree. This was a ridiculous climate – surely it should be cooler by early October. If Éclair would be advised by him they'd adapt *The Odyssey* and leave all that googly-eyed nonsense with dancing girls to those oily East Europeans muscling in with their studios. *The Odyssey* had the loyal Penelope waiting patiently for her husband in Ithaca – now that was his idea of a love story. And it should appeal to the shop-girls who paid over their nickels at the picture palaces. He'd suggest it when he was finished helping Delilah emasculate Samson.

Edmund returned to his desk, but the sight of those ankles had unsettled him. Stuart Hudson was probably ogling Bridie's. But Stuart Hudson hadn't invited anyone to a premiére. Oh no, he simply slid in on Edmund's coat-tails and took advantage of a silly girl's susceptibility to wine and music. Anyone could do that. Stuart wasn't working in what Jules Brulatour liked to call the dream factory – he didn't have to work at all. He had time on his hands to chase girls.

He wished he could pay another call on Bridie. But it would give her expectations. She had nothing to offer except her looks and a certain animal energy – Edmund didn't fool himself he was a catch but he did have financial security and some status, if he said so himself. Supposing, just supposing, he was to take her on: would it be an unequal match doomed to failure?

* * *

"Let's visit Kathleen," suggested Hannah.

A flooding problem had forced the laundry to close a few hours early and they had an unexpected holiday.

Bridie pulled a face. "I haven't the energy to face her inquisition. I'd rather look at some of the swanky shops – Macy's or Bloomingdale's." She loved prowling through them, savouring the fine clothes and household goods. Saving the best until last, she gravitated towards the hat department, dreaming of the day she'd own a milliner's.

"I'm always waiting for someone to ask me to leave when I go in there," Hannah admitted.

Bridie tossed her head. Maybe it was as well if she went on her own. When Hannah was with her, she acted like a frightened rabbit if they stepped through the doors of anywhere but Frank Woolworth's five-and-ten-cent stores. One day Bridie would have the money to shop in Bloomingale's – and then wouldn't she spend like it was going out of fashion! She'd have more gowns than there were days in the month. The world would sit up and take notice of Bridie Ryan, even if Stuart Hudson was too much of a daddy's boy to carry on seeing her.

"I wanted to talk to Kathleen about having a baby." Hannah was pensive. "I don't have long to go now. I'm nervous, Bridie – women die in childbirth every day. What if I died here in America? What would happen to my baby?"

"Time enough to bid the devil good day when you meet him. Sure you're as strong as an ox – what could possibly go wrong?"

"You never know. My mother's sister was strong too and had six children no bother, but when the last baby died inside her, she died too. Childbirth is uncertain. I just want someone to set my mind at rest. Please come to Kathleen's with me."

Bridie had an instinctive revulsion to the idea of listening to Kathleen and Hannah witter on about babies. She wanted nothing to remind her of that tiny form in the earth. "Don't ask me, Hannah. You go on and I'll see you back home later." Conciliatory, she added, "I'll pick us up some fish for supper. It's light, you won't have any trouble digesting it. I know you've been having bother sleeping at night."

"It's the baby kicking at me." Hannah tightened some hairgrips in her diadem of plaits. All Bridie thought about was fun and frocks – her and her Bloomingdale's. It wouldn't have killed her to say hello to her sister-in-law while her brother was at work. Daniel Junior was always pleased as punch to see them, trying his best to speak and chirruping out a stream of unintelligible words, bless him. He might as well be the chimneysweep's nephew as Bridie's, for all the interest she took in him. Hannah felt in her pocket. She had a few cents she could spare to buy the lad some of that sticky candy he liked.

* * *

Hannah had Daniel Junior on her lap and smiled as he left palm prints on her blouse.

"I hear the *Titanic* folks are running advertisements in the New York Times, inviting claims for lost possessions and so forth," said Kathleen, who remained fascinated by the sunken ship.

"So I believe."

"Have you put in a claim?"

"Not yet, but I suppose I will. We have until next January. Bridie says we have to get our due. Sure I hadn't much to lose. The only thing I regret is an Irish linen tablecloth. I had notions of Tom and me sitting either end of a dinner table, and all our childer along the sides."

"Don't tell them you only lost a tablecloth, add in the table and chairs for those insurance people. They can well afford to pay you."

"They'll know right well we had no table and chairs with us – our baggage allowance would never have run to it," laughed Hannah. "There was an old shawlie from Connemara had too much. 'Only ten cubic feet allowed,' the officer kept repeating. She was in a desperate state, since she had no money to be paying the extra, until a fellow from Donohill volunteered to take some. God knows what the old dear had with her. Bridie thought it must have been a couple of calves by the shape of one crate." Then she grew grave. "The few odds and ends I lost are neither here nor there. It's Tom I want back, a father for my baby. But he's never coming back and that's an end to it. It'll just be the two of us now, my babogue and me."

"I feel for you, honey. I'd hate to think of having to manage without my man."

Hannah heaved a sigh. "Bridie's very good to me, but she's not one for babies. I don't know what will happen once it's here. Sure we'll just have to take each day as it comes." Daniel Junior wriggled off Hannah's lap and staggered away to play with a set of farm animals Danny had whittled for him. "Tell me, does it hurt very badly, having a baby?"

Kathleen's button eyes gauged her. "No more than a woman can bear."

"But every woman is different. What one finds painful is water off a duck's back to another."

"True. But when it comes to birthing babies we all get the strength from somewhere. It just comes to us, I don't know how or why."

"What if something goes wrong? What if I die?"

"You just gotta have faith, honey."

Hannah pictured herself on her knees in St Dominic's. It was easy to have faith there, but it would be a different kettle of fish during labour. And what would happen to her baby if she died during it? Would the O'Briens snatch it for themselves and never tell her child a word about its mother?

"If anything happens to me, would you and Danny look after my baby, Kathleen? I couldn't depend on Bridie – she means well but you know how she is."

That one wouldn't lift a child to put it in a bucket of water if it was on fire, thought Kathleen. But she concentrated on reassuring Hannah. "Nothing's going to happen to you. You're just taking fanciful notions, is all. It's natural in your condition. You didn't survive the *Titanic* to die in childbirth, Hannah O'Brien."

"I suppose not. I remember Mama slipping a knife under the mattress when she helped out with childbirth. She said it was to cut the pain."

"Sadie Brolly swears by it. But I thought that was only an old wives' tale. When I had Daniel Junior my ma pinned a medal of St Gerard

Majella on my nightdress – he's the patron saint of mothers. She said every time I had a contraction I was to squeeze the living daylights out of that medal."

"Did it work?"

"I screamed the roof off and snapped the medal clean in two by the end of it. But I had Daniel Junior to show for my trouble. To be honest, Hannah, you forget about the pain as soon as they lay that baby in your arms. I'd do it again tomorrow. Now tell me, what's that sister-in-law of mine up to? Breaking hearts or just the rules?"

Hannah laughed. "Sure you know Bridie, she's always gadding about."

Kathleen smiled. She didn't give a whoop about Bridie, for all she was Danny's sister, but she missed having Hannah around. "I do. That one's as independent as a hog on ice."

* * *

Violet accepted Rebecca Armstrong's offer on Nancy's behalf but didn't tell her daughter, realizing she needed to approach her with caution. Nancy was not the compliant girl of a year previously, for which she blamed Mama Carmen. The spiritualist was bent on causing a rift that would be to her own advantage.

She intercepted Nurse Ivana Spatz with Nancy's morning cup of milky chocolate. A formidable individual, Nurse Spatz had instituted a regime which included cod liver oil and endless quantities of milk. Violet carried in the hot chocolate, shaking Nancy gently awake. While she stirred, mumbling, Violet opened the drapes and eyed the street scene. A horse-drawn omnibus was standing near a lamp-post, a man holding the halter. From it descended a flock of ladies, hems sweeping the dusty sidewalk, hats and veils protecting their complexion from the diminished October sunshine. One of them held a boy in knickerbockers by the hand. The child was dragging his feet, looking longingly towards Central Park where the trees were amber and russet.

I'll miss New York, thought Violet. Still, the world has many attractions.

A chink of cup against saucer told Violet that Nancy had surfaced.

"Darling, I loved your letters from Egypt. I'd give anything to go there after your confinement. You could bring me to all the places you visited with Samuel."

"But what about the baby? Egypt would be too hot."

"We could bring Baby as far as Europe with us and leave him in a kinder climate with his nurse. Perhaps in Sicily or Cyprus. Of course we wouldn't dream of setting off until the doctor said you were quite well after the birth."

Nancy took another sip of chocolate, her hair escaping from its night-time plait and spreading golden brown tendrils across the pillows. She remembered her honeymoon. "You're such an inscrutable being, I'll take you to see the Sphinx," Samuel had promised, on only the second occasion they met. And so he had. She had not felt inscrutable; she had considered herself an ignorant schoolgirl beside this urbane man, but he had mistaken her silence for something more profound. On their wedding tour they had stayed in the Mena House Hotel, almost under the shadow of the pyramids.

She licked chocolate from her upper lip, tasting the blistering heat of Egypt. Nancy concentrated, conjuring up the hotel's lounge with its potted palms. Next she filled it with khaki-clad officers in puttees and gun-straps, paying court to ladies in flower-bright silks who flirted discreetly behind their fans. She sent turbanned pages scurrying with messages, setting others to work stirring the languid air with whisks made of peacock plumes. She had traditional afternoon tea served, complete with scones and preserves which the flies buzzed around, while outside the fronds of palm trees drooped and the brown Nile trickled through a flat landscape.

Now Nancy was travelling through Cairo's streets in a carriage driven by a Nubian, two runners using staffs to knock people out of the path of their wheels. Barefoot native men in white or blue cotton robes and fez caps, the women veiled in black, swarmed the bazaar. How it had fascinated her, that maze of shops located down labyrinthine laneways, owners cross-legged on the street with their wares piled up inside. Nancy could almost hear the discordant tumult from the braying tangle of animals and the yelling of fortune-tellers, marmoset merchants, sweetmeat pliers and zither players. "*It is all so lavishly exotic,*" she wrote to her mother on a postcard, paraded around Violet Markova's cronies so often they never wanted to see an image of the pyramids again.

Nancy carried her fingertips to her mouth and left them there, dragging at the lower lip: Egypt might recreate Samuel and his love for her. And it would take her away from Louis, who activated feelings she didn't understand and didn't want to, either. "Can you make the arrangements, Momma?"

"Leave it to me, darling." Violet dropped a kiss on her forehead.

Step one was accomplished: her daughter was willing to leave the United States, and there had been no mention of the Keppels. Step two was to keep her daughter out or they'd lose the $5million promised by Rebecca Armstrong. But the world was a large place and those millions would make it an interesting one. She must approach Louis about accompanying them, perhaps as a tour guide or interpreter. Was that quite respectable? Violet found she didn't care.

* * *

Meanwhile the compensation case against White Star was rumbling along. Despite the purple prose of newsprint, the *Titanic* was carrying cargo worth hundreds of thousands, not running into tens of millions. Still, the contents were itemised, receipts produced. There was an Aladdin's cave of orchids, hosiery, furs, soap, lace collars, wheels of cheese, bolts of cloth – even seventy-six cases of a patent medicine called Dragon's Blood. But not the Hope Diamond, or indeed, anything to justify the ship's swelling description as the repository of all riches.

To save time, passenger claim forms were mass-produced with spaces to be filled in.

"*That on or about April 11, 1912, claimant took passage at Queenstown, Ireland, under contract entered into with the petitioner, on the said steamship Titanic . . . including in the property so lost and destroyed, as aforesaid, certain luggages and personal effects, the property of the claimant . . . said property was never salved or recovered, and an itemised list thereof, with estimated value of each item at date of loss, is annexed hereto . . .*"

Hannah and Bridie had little of value to insert into their forms. They wrestled with their consciences – Hannah for longer than Bridie – then claimed for a modest array of dresses, some Limerick lace, a spare set of petticoats, Hannah's tablecloth and Bridie's grandmother's silver candlesticks, pressed on her by her mother.

On October 18th, 1912 the White Star Line formally petitioned the Federal District Court in New York to grant limited liability in all cases. The claimants, whose lawyers now formed a loose coalition, opposed the petition, arguing that the more generous English Admiralty law should apply. The accident happened on the high seas where no jurisdiction obtained, they said. In such cases the governing statute should be that of the country where the ship stood registered.

Ultimately the Supreme Court made a decision. It ruled that an American court could only apply American law and White Star was entitled to limited liability. Payments to survivors and victims' relatives would not be overly generous.

* * *

"We've decided to accept the Armstrongs' offer. We leave for Europe and then Egypt after Nancy has her baby." Violet watched Louis narrowly, hoping he might betray some dismay at the prospect of a separation.

His face was immobile. Behind it, he was thinking: Egypt? What's the woman thinking of! I thought it was London. I could find work in England but there's nothing for me in Egypt. I must have time alone with Nancy before she goes. She has to understand she should be with me.

"You're stoical about our departure."

"I can't criticise you for accepting $5 million. I've no doubt you do it in your daughter's best interests."

"You're right. I'm sacrificing myself by going into exile with her." Violet sighed, almost convincing herself she'd miss Avalon, New Jersey, and the bridge circle snubbed for the past year.

"I'll miss you." His eyes were clouded with regret at the prospect of Nancy leaving.

His unhappiness galvanised Violet. "Will you come away with us? We need you. I need you."

She injected the last three words with a nuance which Louis failed to catch, busy wondering how he could reach Nancy before the flurry of departure plans engulfed her. It was virtually impossible for him to engineer time on his own with her now, so close to her due date.

"You wish to employ a secretary?" He was only half-attentive.

Violet crossed the short distance between them, sinking onto the sofa beside him, so close their flanks touched. Startled, he tried to stand up, but she laid a hand on his arm. He watched as though from a great distance, wondering what she'd do next.

Violet pressed one hand to the nape of his neck and tangled the other in his hair, bringing her face so near it blurred before his eyes. He could feel the heat of her body through their clothes. Her lips were warm and moist and they parted against his. It was a pleasant sensation and he automatically returned the kiss.

"Momma!" squeaked Nancy.

They broke apart. Louis shot to his feet, moving so abruptly that Violet fell back against the cushions.

"Nancy." She scrabbled to straighten up. "I thought you were taking a nap."

"Evidently."

Furious though she was with her mother, it was at Louis that Nancy shot a look of reproach. *How could you?*

Mute, ashen, he left the house.

22

Nancy splayed her fingers against her face, as though pushing her features back into place. She was seething with jealousy. Its white-hot energy pulsed through her, replaying that embrace. She had stood like a peeping Tom as her mother and Louis kissed, her senses absorbing how the woman's body curved towards the man's, lips clinging. It seemed to Nancy that she could taste the salt of his skin during the intensity of that kiss, feel the texture of his fair hair between her fingers.

It should have been me.

The thought shocked Nancy. "Samuel," she cried, "where are you?"

But there was no Samuel, just a juddering sensation of desire for another man. She tried to think of something else but again and again she saw Louis's mouth against Violet's, her mother's eyes closed in pleasure, his hands stretching towards her waist.

There was a tap on her door. "Go away, Momma!" She hurled a cushion at the door.

"I want to talk to you, darling."

"I don't want to talk to you."

"You have to talk to me sooner or later, Nancy."

"Later's fine by me."

Scalding tears poured from Nancy. She was fat, ugly and a widow, and her nineteenth birthday was still a few weeks off yet. Her life was over. She'd never regain her figure, no man would look at her again, and her mother had kissed Louis Stubel. Kissed him with her mouth parted and her face flushed like a girl's. Stop! She couldn't bear to think about it.

She rang the bell for Roberge. "Take the carriage to Mama Carmen's and bring her to me. Tell her it's urgent. Say I have nobody left I can trust except her."

* * *

"I need to make contact with Samuel."

"Would you like me to try some inspirational writing?" Mama Carmen didn't know what was agitating the girl but it couldn't be good for her baby to be so distressed.

Nancy nodded. "Can you ask him what I should do? Everything seems so difficult without him to help me."

"What you should do, my dear, is rest quietly until your baby arrives. After that you'll be too busy caring for your child to worry about what you should do." Mama Carmen kneaded Nancy's hands with her large, square thumbs.

"I don't care about my baby," said the girl. "I don't know what to do, I feel totally alone."

"You don't mean that about your baby, and you're not alone – you're surrounded by people who love you."

"No, you're wrong. Nobody gives a hoot about me. Samuel's mother wants rid of me – she's offered Momma $5 million to take me out of the country, and Momma wants us to go. Momma thinks I don't know but I do, Adam Armstrong told me. Nobody asks me what I want – nobody ever did except Samuel and he's gone. Please get in touch with him for me, Mama Carmen. I need him. I want to be with him."

Mama Carmen's antennae twitched at the mention of $5 million. She certainly didn't want the girl spirited away, she preferred her here in New York where she had access to her. She must discuss this development with Walt. But first Nancy had to be pacified, she was working herself into a state.

"Sweet child, you will be with your husband one day, but you have many, many years of life ahead of you first. It's not yet time for you to join him. He wouldn't want to deprive you of the years still waiting to be lived by you."

"Nobody will ever love me the way Samuel did."

"You're a beautiful woman, Nancy – many men will love you, if you let them. But you must be quiet and sensible for a time, and do nothing to injure the precious cargo you carry." Mama Carmen put a finger under her chin. "Can you do that? Can you put your baby first? You must be a brave girl."

Nancy raised a swollen face to Mama Carmen's. "That's what Samuel said to me – that I had to be a brave girl. It was one of the last things he said, when I was in the lifeboat and he was getting out. He must be telling me what to do through you. Is that possible?"

"Not only possible, child, but likely. I am a lightning conductor for messages. Spirits who want to pierce the walls between our worlds use me to make contact. I have no doubt your husband is eager to send you reassurance. He loved you very much, I know that."

"Do you?" Nancy was grasping at straws, desperate to believe she had been loved once, even if no-one would ever love her again. "How do you know it?"

"I've always sensed it strongly during my journeys into the other dimension. His love for you communicated itself to me as something warm and reassuring, like a hot bath after being caught in the rain."

Nancy frowned. She wanted romance, passion – not a hot bath. "Is that all?"

"Let's try some inspirational writing. I sense your husband is near." Her dark eyes were mesmerising. "I believe Samuel wants me to be with you, Nancy, so I can help you in his place. He wouldn't want us to be separated by – circumstances."

"You mean this trip to Egypt? I don't know if I want to go away with Momma now, I hardly trust her any more. I know, we can ask Samuel about it. He'll tell me what to do."

* * *

Louis was in despair. He returned to Washington Square and climbed into bed, pleading illness. The major sent Mrs Burdich to his room with beef broth but he was unable to touch it. "Do you have stomach ache?" she asked.

He shook his head. How to reply that every bone, sinew and nerve-ending in his body ached? Nancy had seen him kiss her mother, and his chances of courting her were in tatters. He couldn't imagine why she had launched herself on him – perhaps she was going through the change of life. His brain hadn't properly registered what was happening or he'd have pushed Violet away, not kissed her back. He tried to remember what was said between them immediately before she glued her lips to his, but all he could bring to mind was Nancy's stricken face. The summer-sky eyes had registered his betrayal, a shoal of emotions darkening them. Wait! Did her reaction mean she cared for him? No, she despised him! Brimful of remorse, he pushed his face into the pillow. The self-sufficiency he had learned as a child, wearing it as armour against the world, was well and truly breached. Louis Stubel knew at last what it was to be heart-sore.

* * *

Bridie, smarting about Stuart's defection, took to flirting outrageously with Warren Vicosen – who stopped eating pickles, a habit of which his wife was unable to cure him. It was in this mood that she glanced up from her ironing and, through the open doorway into the shop, saw Edmund Newton with his arms full of shirts. He was looking past Vicosen, writing out a docket, to where she worked, face rosy from exertion and hair escaping its pins.

"I believe I see my cousin," said Edmund. "Would you object if I had a moment's conversation with her?"

The manager did object, but he couldn't say so to a customer with the sort of plummy accent which made him feel like an oaf. "I can only spare her for a minute, we're behind today. Bridie, your cousin wants a word." His intonation on the word cousin conveyed some scepticism about their relationship. He was under no illusions his cute little squaw was a honeypot for men, and forward enough to make full use of it.

Bridie was curious. She rolled down her sleeves, gave her black curls a pat and walked towards Edmund, swaying her hips like an American girl. "It's yourself." She leaned against the shop counter.

"Miss Ryan." He shook her hand, formal, and she winced to see him notice its callouses.

"So what brings you here?"

"Could we step outside? It seems a little public in here."

Bridie preceded him to the street. "It's a lot less public here, of course."

"I didn't like the way that fellow was earwigging shamelessly."

"Ah, sure Warren doesn't have a life of his own – he has to eavesdrop on other people's."

Edmund felt at a disadvantage, towering above her. He stepped off the pavement, trying to lose a few inches, and was immediately beeped at by an automobile bearing down on him. A man on its running board shook his fist and Edmund jumped back onto the footpath.

"Have you a death wish? This is New York, not Oola – you'll be flattened!"

"Where's Oola?"

"It's the village I come from."

"What's it like? Do you miss it?"

Bridie flicked her eyes over his face. No-one ever asked her about Oola or if she was homesick for it. "It means the apple orchard, *na hÚlla*. It's a small little place, but it has a hill with a Fiddler's Stone at the foot of it. That's a rock shaped like a chair, thousands of years old, maybe, where the fiddler would sit to play his music."

"And did you play on the hill as a little girl?"

"We used to race each other to the top and play roly-poly down it. On a clear day there's a view at the top of two counties, Tipperary and Limerick, that would make the breath catch in your throat with the utter gorgeousness of it . . ." Her voice tailed off. Bridie was disconcerted to find herself speaking with nostalgia of the homeland she thought she despised. She coughed. "What can I do for you, Edmund Newton? You didn't hunt me out at the Clean and Brite to listen to me sing the praises of a freckle of a place you'll never visit."

"No, but you look different when you talk about it. I came to see you because I heard from Louis Stubel about a visit he paid you on behalf of

Major Hudson." He waited, but Bridie stared at the ground, although he could tell she was listening intently. "It must have been beastly for you. I told the major you deserved better. I mean to say, we all came through the *Titanic* together, we're shipmates – we ought to look out for each other." He unhooked his spectacles and polished them with a handkerchief, awkward in the face of her continuing silence. "Anyway, I just thought you might have taken a knock and I wanted to check you were all right." Still nothing from Bridie. He was sweating now, convinced he had erred.

Bridie was thinking how much younger he looked without his horn-rimmed barricade.

"I brought you something to cheer you up." He rummaged in his pocket and produced a tiny package wrapped in tissue paper.

Now Bridie did tilt her head back on its neck to look up at him. "You brought me a present?"

Edmund nodded, the tips of his ears pink. She reached out both hands, the way a child receives a gift.

"Any chance of you doing some work today?" yelled Warren Vicosen from inside the laundry.

"In a minute!" she called back. "Mother of God, if this is how he behaves with people on piece-rate, can you imagine what a slave-driver he'd be if I was on his time?" Bridie untied a wisp of green ribbon and the tissue paper fell open to reveal a padded box. Inside was a St Bridget's Cross brooch, an asymmetrical cruciform fashioned in silver. Her mouth parted with pleasure.

"Do you like it?" Edmund, unaccustomed to buying gifts, was anxious.

"How do you know about the St Bridget's Cross?" she asked.

"I knew an Irish lady once. She was the cook for the family next door to us when I was growing up. She used to feed me sometimes, in the afternoons after school. I never seemed to get enough to eat – I suppose I was sprouting like chickweed. Minerva was just a baby and my mother was preoccupied. The cook's name was Biddy and she told me about the St Bridget's Cross. It was made of reeds, wasn't it?"

Bridie nodded, tracing her smallest finger across the brooch. Freddie Bowe-Spencer had asked her about the cross, noticing its omnipresence in every cottage. "St Bridget made the first one, to explain what a crucifix was. We get a new one every year on her feast-day, February 1st."

"Bridie Ryan, if you don't quit yakking with your boyfriend and get back in here pronto you'll be out of a job," bellowed Vicosen, seething with jealousy.

"I have to go. Thanks a million for the brooch."

Edmund's shoulders relaxed. She liked it. "It's nothing. I always intended to get you something when my ship came in, so to speak. I do owe you, you know."

"You owe Hannah more than me."

That stumped Edmund. Hannah didn't move him the way Bridie did. "Um, yes, I'll have to think of something for her."

"She's having a baby soon – she'll need plenty of things for it. A pram would go down well."

"Right. Well. Right. I'll give it some thought."

Frugality was a habit with Edmund. His happy-go-lucky father had not paid into a pension for his wife, preferring to enjoy life in the present rather than worry about the future. Edmund had witnessed at first-hand the consequences of such an easy-going attitude, when the family was left penniless after his early death. Edmund took the lesson to heart: no-one would ever be able to accuse him of squandering money. Still, he should be able to run to a secondhand pram for Hannah.

"Better get back to work," said Bridie.

"I say, can we meet again? What time do you –?"

"Have to go or old Vicosen will have kittens on the counter. Thanks for the brooch, and for speaking up for me to the major."

"He meant well, you know. He had your best interests at heart – he was trying to protect you."

"He was trying to protect his son from me, more like. He made me feel like a cheap gold-digger. Anyway, what's done is done. I don't believe in looking back." With that she was gone.

"You took your time, missy!" Vicosen resurrected the jar of pickles from under the counter.

"Family business, couldn't be helped." Bridie dimpled up at him, trying to retrieve his good humour. "My, you look distinguished when you're cross, all stern and masterful. Don't be angry with me, Warren, just wait 'til you see how hard I can work for the rest of the day."

She set to with a will, but she was wistful as she ironed, thinking of her mother. She missed her, all of a sudden. Her mother had been in service but had left to marry. "No mistress will tolerate married servants," she explained to the young Bridie. She used to talk about the expense of being in service, with a uniform that had to be paid back out of her wages: a black dress, two aprons, two pairs of Lisle stockings, two caps, two sets of white collars and cuffs – all deducted weekly from what she earned. But sometimes the butler would bring out a bottle of gin from the cellar and they'd have a sing-song in the kitchen. Once, he produced a bottle of French wine.

Bridie decided to send her mother a Sunday-going-to-Mass hat as soon as she could save the money. She had her eye on one in brown felt with a rolled brim and two opposing plumes of speckled cockerel feathers. Josie Ryan would cut a dash in the village of Oola in that. It would be lovely to sit and have a cup of tea and a gossip with her mother, even if it was her fault Bridie had fallen for Freddie Bowe-Spencer, with her talk of sandwiches sliced as thin as an angel's eyebrows, served on china with gold paint at its rim.

And what was Stuart Hudson but an American Freddie Bowe-Spencer? At least now she understood what it was men wanted. They were all the same – Irishmen, Englishmen, Americans, there was no difference. They desired her and they'd use flattery, false promises, even the odd present to get what they were after. But if they wanted something from her, they should give something in return. That was only just. Freddie hadn't played fair by her, for all his soft words. Yet she had taken something from her encounter with him, all the same.

"The only lessons worth learning are the ones that come with bruises," said Bridie.

One day she'd have her milliner's shop and she'd be beholden to no man, no matter how many Freddies and Stuarts she had to humour along the way.

Edmund was waiting outside the Clean and Brite when she emerged with Hannah after work, arms linked as they discussed the sausages they'd have for supper. They were always famished after a day at the laundry.

"I see you're wearing my brooch." He was thrilled to notice it pinned to her coat collar.

"It's a dainty thing," she allowed.

"Like you." Striving for gallantry, Edmund cast an uncertain look at Hannah.

"Don't mind me," she said. "Just treat me as though I'm invisible."

He fell into step beside them.

"I don't see why you're bothering with us – sure I heard you were surrounded by women at the *Saved From The Titanic* party."

Bridie was teasing, but he thought she was serious.

"I must admit I was on the receiving end of some flattering attention. But those women are only interested in a chap when he's in the limelight – not when he's slogging away at a script that may or may not be turned into a moving picture."

"What about Miss Dorothy Gibson? She was lovely. Do you ever see her?" asked Hannah.

"Miss Gibson and Mr Brulatour are taking a trip together – for project development purposes."

Bridie and Hannah erupted in peals of laughter. Neither of them had a notion what project development might be, but they had seen how it was with Jules and Dorothy.

Edmund stiffened. These women were easier handled in ones, in pairs they became unruly. He could slap down a class of adolescent boys but he was ham-fisted when it came to dealing with females. He remembered some advice of Minerva's. "Talk to a girl as though you're talking to me," his sister had urged. "Just be natural with her. Think about what might interest her and chat about that."

"I'm working on a script for a moving picture set in biblical times," he began, diffident, but their faces turned instantly towards him. "It's about a beautiful, unscrupulous woman and the warrior she betrays. Her name is Delilah and she sells the secret of his enormous strength to his enemies, who blind and imprison him."

"What happens to her? Does she get her comeuppance?" Bridie was eager.

"Or does she repent and help rescue him?" came from Hannah.

"What does Delilah wear? Is she a princess? I expect she's dripping

319

with jewels."

"I hope it has a happy ending."

Edmund continued talking about Samson and Delilah until they stood outside the girls' tenement house. They shuffled, wondering if they should invite him in. There was only food enough for two but they couldn't cook a meal without asking him to join them.

"I'd hate for you to think badly of Major Hudson, Bridie. He's distracted at the moment – he goes to séances to make contact with his dead wife."

Hannah and Bridie blessed themselves.

"I can't help worrying this is delayed shock after the sinking," continued Edmund. "These psychics are nothing but highway robbers taking money from the vulnerable and the gullible."

"The dead are best left where they are – dead and buried," said Bridie. "No good can come of it."

Hannah wondered what she might say to Tom if he contacted her from beyond the grave. Do you want me to give our baby to your sister in Chicago? What if she didn't like his answer? No, it was better if the dead didn't tell the living how to conduct their business. "Are you stopping for a bite to eat, Mr Newton?" she asked.

"Another time, thank you. I should go home and work on my script. I have an appointment with Mr Brulatour next week and I want to be a hundred per cent satisfied with my outline before we meet."

The women were impressed. Here was a fellow rushing off to work on the script for a moving picture, but he made time to walk them home from the laundry. As they mounted the stairs, Hannah pausing at each landing to nurse a stitch in her side, she said, "He's sweet on you, Bridie. It wouldn't do any harm to encourage him."

"He has no money, for all his talk of scripts and moving picture stars – he needs elbow patches on that jacket of his. Besides, can you see Danny's face if he heard I was keeping company with an Englishman? He'd let a roar out of him you could hear all the way back to Oola."

Mind you, thought Bridie, the day she let her brother tell her how to live her life was the day she rolled over and died.

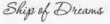

*　*　*

You're hanging around that Irish girl like a lovesick puppy, Edmund scolded himself on the streetcar.

He had no time for romance, he had his way to make in the world. This connection with the Éclair Moving Picture Company was a gilt-edged opportunity. A chance like that only came a man's way once in his life. However, he felt something for Bridie, he couldn't deny it, and perhaps he should be grateful to Major Hudson for vetoing his son's liaison with her. He knew he could never compete with that cocksure dandy, women were pushovers for fops. But he'd be foolish to idle on the sidelines while another Stuart Hudson nipped in. Except, then what? What did he want from Bridie Ryan? Marriage? He thought not. If he was ever to marry, which was by no means certain, he'd prefer an English rose, not a thorny Irish girl who mocked him.

I don't know what I want with her, Edmund Newton lied to himself. But he did know he wanted no other man to have her. And this time he really would punch Stuart Hudson on that fluffy jaw of his if he laid a finger on her again. He'd had his chance and flunked it.

*　*　*

Hannah was leaning over a sink in the Clean and Brite, scrubbing at a stain on a shirt-front, when she felt a stab of pain. She ignored it, about to lather on more soap when the pain jabbed again, more viciously than before. She clutched each side of the porcelain basin, perspiration springing in beads along her forehead, and waited for it to ease. It worsened. By now she was pallid. Her breath panted and dark spots floated across her vision. Pamela saw her drop to her knees, still clinging to the sink, and raced off to find Bridie.

"What is it, Hannah? Is it the baby?" Bridie crouched beside her. Hannah was unable to speak, caught in the vice of another spasm. "It's too early for the baby by a couple of weeks. Maybe it's a false alarm. How are you feeling, Hannah, do you think it's coming?" She massaged between Hannah's shoulder blades.

Warren, pickled cucumber in hand, left the shop front to see the cause of the disruption. "She can't go havin' a baby here, she'll haveta be moved." He rounded on Bridie. "You said she ain't due for another coupla months. She ain't 'sposed-ta do this at the laundry. What'll the customers think?"

"Babies don't pay any attention to 'sposed-ta's." Bridie mopped the moisture from her friend's face with her apron.

"She better not go having no baby on my floor. You get her outta here, ya hear?"

"Call us a hansom, then. She needs to be in bed."

"You got the money to pay for one?"

Bridie threw him a quick glance of assessment. Should she say no and hope he'd pay for the ride to get rid of them? "I'm not sure. Oh God, maybe we shouldn't move her. It might be bad for the baby."

"Her waters ain't broke yet, there's still time," said Warren, who had three children. "I'll pay the cab and take it outta her wages."

"Thanks for nothing." Bridie leaned in towards Hannah's ear. She hadn't cried out yet, apart from one muted moan. "Hannah, can you hear me? We have to get you home. Will you put your weight on me? Come on, *alanna*, you have to be brave, then you'll be in your own bed, all tucked up. I'll send for Sadie Brolly. There's nothing she doesn't know about having babies. Easy, now, Hannah, hold on to me and I'll get you outside."

"Take her out the back, I can't have no customers seein' her," ordered Warren.

"You mind your business and we'll mind ours. Where's that cab? Go on and whistle one up for us."

Bridie guided a doubled-over Hannah through the shop, despite Warren's protests, because it was the quickest way to the street. A carriage for hire was pulling up, hooves clattering.

"Third and 29th , quick as you can, but mind the potholes!" shouted Bridie, easing Hannah in.

"I don't want her comin' back to the laundry, even if it ain't time for the baby yet. We can't go having no more dramas, they're bad for business. And you're on borrowed time yourself, missy, ya hear? I ain't forgotten you told me she wasn't due 'til the New Year."

322

Bridie ignored him. She could handle the Warren Vicosens of this world with one hand tied behind her back. Right now she needed to concentrate on Hannah, no longer able to stifle her groans.

"Here, where do you think you're goin', missy? You put your pal in the cab and get back to work. I can't be two girls down or we'll be late meeting orders."

"Don't leave me, Bridie!" Hannah cried out.

"You get back in here or you won't have no job to come back to."

Bridie looked from Hannah to Warren, biting her lip.

23

"False alarm, it happens from time to time," said Sadie. She had pushed her handcart into an alleyway, asking another trader to keep an eye on her stock, before rushing to Hannah's bedside. Hannah's pains had stopped now, and a draught of Sadie's bitter tea made with herbs was helping her to sleep. Sadie's fingers had explored their way across her belly, concluding the child was not yet ready to come into the world. "That girl should rest, though, she's been working too many hours in the laundry. She shouldn't be spending so long on her feet, so she shouldn't. She's got veins in her legs that'll trouble her for the rest of her days. How many hours a day does she work? Twelve or thirteen? That's too many, Bridie – you have to get her to cut down."

"We'll have no problem there, the manager made it clear he doesn't want her back. I'm sacked too by the looks of things."

"That could be a blessing in disguise for your friend – sure she's too far gone to be bending over a washtub. It's a mercy she hasn't lost the child. You're to mind her well from now on. I'd say it should be another week or two before there's a baby in your life. I'll make up another batch of my tea and you're to give it to her every day until her waters break. That'll keep her straight."

Bridie nodded, willing to do whatever Sadie said. The old woman was believed to have the gift of healing on account of being born on Good Friday and christened on Easter Sunday.

* * *

Ellen Cooling waited for two-and-a-half hours by the communal front door. Her vigilance was rewarded as Bridie hurried out to buy bones to make soup for Hannah.

"'Scuse me," Ellen stepped from the shadows.

Bridie started, before recognizing the woman. "Well?"

"I'm worried about Hannah. I thought somethin' mighta happened her. She missed Mass this mornin' and that's not like her, and then I thinks to mysel' her time must be near. Everythin' all right with her and the baby?"

"She had a close call at work yesterday. She's resting up but she and the baby are fine."

"Will you give her this for me?" Ellen passed over a banana cream pie. "She needs buildin' up – birthin' a baby is mighty tiring. I knows it, I birthed four of my own."

"I'll tell her you called. I'd ask you up to the room only Hannah's sleeping."

"I wouldn't put you to no trouble, I jus' wanted to reassure myself 'bout Hannah. I'll get along now. Take Jesus with you for your friend."

Bridie watched her sashay away, shamed by the other woman's dignity. It was too late to rectify it and bring Ellen upstairs for a cup of tea. "Hannah told me your pies are wonderful," she called after her.

Ellen stopped. "Ever'body likes my bakin'. They's always houndin' me for my recipes but I ain't got none, I jus' throws in a pinch of this and a dollop of that. I always says 'Praise the Lord!' as I puts a pie in the oven, and out it comes jim-dandy. That's my secret. 'Praise the Lord' – he never lets me or my pies down."

"Hannah's off work, resting up – she won't be going back until afterwards. I'm sure she'd be glad of some company during the day. If you can spare the time."

Ellen flashed Bridie a blinding smile.

* * *

Ellen went straight to the parochial house, where she refused to be dissuaded by the housekeeper into delaying her business until the following day.

"I needs to see Father Killoran tonight, beggin' your pardon, 'm," she insisted, scrupulously polite.

"Is it urgent?" The housekeeper thought Father Killoran was entitled to a few hours' peace after the week he'd had.

"Anything to do with Jesus is urgent, 'm."

The housekeeper conceded defeat, showing Ellen into the parlour where the priest sat listening to a sentimental air on the gramophone.

"Take a seat, Ellen. How are Abe and his boys?"

"Abe has taken up with a woman, Father. He shoulda oughtta know better at his age, but this Jezebel, she turned his head. She got a gold tooth and she's never done smilin' to show it off."

"It's natural for him to want some female companionship, Ellen, he can't be all that old."

"He be forty-three on Christmas Eve, Father, old enough to know better. Not that men ever learn sense where those flashy light-skinned gals is concerned, the kinds that could pass for white. I don't got nothin' agin him havin' hisself some female comp'ny, but there's plenty nice steady coloureds aroun', he don't need to take up with no trash. It's his fondness for liquor makes him prone to these no-good types. Billin' and cooin' with 'em, and orderin' up rum punch to beat the band." Ellen Cooling was implacably opposed to the twin evils of fornication and alcohol and believed them interlinked. If there was more sobriety there'd be less sinning with the flesh – nobody could tell her any different.

Father Michael Killoran laced his fingers together across his soutane and waited. It wasn't Abe Cooling and his lady friend that brought Ellen into his parlour, but she'd tell him in her own time.

After some huffing and puffing, she confided in him. "It's about that Irish gal was saved off the *Titanic*, Father, Hannah O'Brien. She gonna have her baby any day now. Would you go and visit her? I'm powerful worried about her."

"Are there complications with the baby?"

"No, I'm not worried about that, she be able to produce babies easy as shellin' peas. But that gal needs Jesus and you can bring him to her."

"Why do you think she needs Jesus now, in particular, Ellen?"

"That gal been through a lot and she's a long way from home, Father. She got another big test coming down the track, havin' her baby after its poppa done gone and drownded. That's when folks need Jesus, when life goes trippin' 'em up. You don't got Jesus then, that other fella's like to muscle in."

"You mean Satan?"

"Sure do. You got to make sure that gal has Jesus, Father Killoran. I'm countin' on you. She's off work now, got a scare with the baby coming too early mebbes."

"I guess I could look in tomorrow evening, Ellen."

"I sure would be obligated to you, Father. I'll bring you over one of my upside-down pineapple cakes. Li'l bird tole me they your fav'rites."

"My housekeeper would have my guts for garters if she thought I was accepting cakes from parishioners – she's fierce possessive about feeding me." He was wistful, having tasted Ellen's baking at a Sunday School fundraiser. "How about if you slip it into the Sacristy after Mass one day? Don't come to the house with it, whatever you do."

* * *

"Mama Carmen is going to do something special for me, Stubel."

Louis looked up, wary. "Really, major?"

"Yes. Remember that impressive manifestation at her last séance? I asked if she could rise to one on my behalf. Yesterday she told me the spiritual harmonies would soon be aligned and she'd be in a position to try for me. Imagine if Jean could be materialised for me! It would be a miracle to see her image again."

"But you've had messages from her. She's spoken to you regularly through Mama Carmen."

"It's not enough. I want more – I want my wife back. I know that's not possible, not permanently, but there's a chance she might inhabit

Mama Carmen's body for a short while. I've heard about these corporeal manifestations and Mama Carmen is willing to risk it, although Keppel has warned me it can be hazardous for the medium. Oh Stubel, I long to see Jean's face and hear her voice again! I'd trade anything for ten minutes with my wife. The more contact I have with her in these séances, the more I want. It's a compulsion with me now, I can't rest for thinking about it." The major's eyes were feverish and his hands were trembling, tobacco from his unlit pipe spilling onto the buffalo-skin rug at his feet.

He's drugged with this spiritualism, thought Louis. "Has Mama Carmen definitely promised you this?"

"Walt Keppel says there are no guarantees but he thinks she can pull it off. I've left them some jewellery of Jean's to help Mama inhabit my wife's sphere, as she puts it. I was wondering whether I should invite Stuart back from Yale for the séance? He missed a lot of time last term on account of me, but if there's a chance of getting reacquainted with his mother . . ."

"Your son didn't strike me as a gentleman interested in mediums."

"Guess he's too full of life to think about the afterlife." The major fidgeted with matches. "Keppel's to let me know when Mama Carmen feels ready to try the manifestation. Apparently she has to gather her strength and prepare for it, because it saps her energy. You'll come with me, won't you, my boy? I could use a friendly face there when it happens. Don't know how I'll react, you see. This is something I want desperately, don't get me wrong, but it's bound to be strange. Jean's been dead for thirteen years."

"Certainly, major, I'll be glad to accompany you."

* * *

Nancy slid out of bed and walked barefoot towards the door. It was three in the morning and she was sleepwalking. She passed Nurse Spatz, sound asleep in her truckle bed in Nancy's dressing room, and pattered along the passageway to her mother's room. Violet didn't rouse when Nancy walked to her bedside and looked down at her. But she woke, heart hammering, when she heard the girl drag a trunk from her armoire and pile clothes into it. She wasn't folding them, simply tossing them in.

"Who's there?" Violet sat up, tumbling pillows onto the floor. "Mercy, is that you, Nancy? What on earth are you doing?"

There was no response.

Violet turned on the lamp and threw back the covers, winkling her feet into slippers. Her daughter continued mechanically taking clothes from the shelves and dropping them into the trunk. As Violet drew near, she could tell from Nancy's vacant stare she was sleepwalking. She hadn't done it since childhood, in the aftermath of her father's death.

"Nancy, can you hear me?"

"I'm busy, Momma."

Violet remembered she shouldn't startle Nancy. "I can see that, darling. What are you doing?"

"Sending you home, Momma. You can't stay here any more."

"But who'll look after you? A girl needs her mother when she has a baby."

"Oh, I'll be just fine. I have Mama Carmen and Nurse Spatz."

"Don't you want your momma?"

Nancy continued adding clothes to the pile until they overflowed onto the Oriental rug.

"Don't you, darling?"

"Momma's in the way. Momma needs to go back to Avalon. Momma's taking all the visitors for herself."

Nancy panted as she struggled to close the bulging trunk. Violet tried to guide her away, worried about the exertion, but she shrugged her off and persisted.

"What visitors am I taking away from you, darling?"

"Louis. Momma's taking Louis away from me."

Violet was dismayed. Were she and Nancy rivals for the same man?

A crash alerted her to the fact Nancy had abandoned the trunk and was at her dressing table, pushing bottles and jars into a tapestry Gladstone bag with a blind sweep of the arm. Most were missing their target and shattering on the wooden floor.

"Stop that, Nancy, you'll cut yourself!"

Nancy turned at the sharp note in her voice, stepping on a flake of broken glass. A thin stream of blood appeared, but she was oblivious.

Violet was at a loss. Glass might be embedded in her feet. If she led her away, the splinters could be pressed further into the flesh, but if she left her she might tread in more.

"Nancy, I need you to do something for me. I want you to stand perfectly still. Remember how you used to play Stiff Statues with your school-friends? Can you do it again? There's a prize for the one who manages not to move the longest. Darling, will you play Stiff Statues with me?"

Nancy nodded.

Violet backed away, eyes fixed on her daughter, and jammed her finger on the bell by her bedside. What was the matter with those servants? Where were they?

Eventually the jangling penetrated Roberge's sleep. The maid threw on a robe and raced down the stairs, plait thumping between her shoulder blades. It must be Miss Nancy going into labour.

Her hurtling entry into Nancy's bedroom disturbed Nurse Spatz, and together the women made their way to Violet's room. Violet held her finger to her lips, nodding towards Nancy. "Your mistress has cut her foot." She spoke in a hushed murmur. "Roberge, sweep up the glass around her before she steps in any more. Nurse, see to that cut. The blood doesn't appear to be heavy but we can't take any chances. Careful, she's sleepwalking and we mustn't startle her awake. If we can get her back into bed she'll fall sleep again."

Nurse Spatz bent and lifted Nancy's foot to examine the graze, while Nancy continued playing Stiff Statues. "Do you have a tweezers, madam?" she whispered.

Violet ransacked a drawer as Roberge swept up the glass with a dustpan and brush.

"Got it!" The nurse held up a sliver of blood-coated glass. She pressed a cloth to the foot to stem the flow, and tugged her patient towards a chair. The girl wouldn't budge.

"Nancy, well done. You've won Stiff Statues. I'll find a special prize for you. But you must be very tired after standing still for so long. Why don't you let Nurse Spatz help you sit down while I get your prize?"

Nancy allowed herself to be brought to a seat, where the nurse bathed and dressed her cut.

* * *

Violet could not sleep. After settling Nancy, she scolded Nurse Spatz for snoring through the first part of her charge's nocturnal adventure, then ordered Roberge to fetch her some warm milk. Roberge, who was due to rise at seven and would have liked to try for another hour or two of sleep, trailed off, grumbling under her breath. Violet tried to recall what the doctor told her about sleepwalking when she'd consulted him after her husband's death. She thought the subject's actions indicated suppressed wishes which they could not express when awake. Nancy had come across an old top hat of her father's in the attic and was discovered one night with it positioned on a console table, scolding her poppa for breaking his promise to take her riding. Next morning she remembered nothing. This continued until Violet brought her to a doctor who prescribed a change of scene. They paid a visit to Nancy's relatives in Maryland, where the girl ran wild with her cousins and slept the night through.

It was worrying that Nancy's sleepwalking should resurface, especially with her baby almost due. What if she went for a stroll one night and had an accident? She could lose her footing on the stairs and tumble to the bottom. Violet drained her milk and decided on two courses of action. Nurse Spatz and Roberge would take it in turns to sit up all night at the foot of Nancy's bed – she didn't care how much her daughter protested, she could not be left alone. And Violet would approach a specialist for advice.

Nancy had betrayed no preference for Louis Stubel until now. She seemed to tolerate his visits rather than enjoy them. Could Violet have misinterpreted that competitive desire to pack her up, bags and baggage, and send her away?

"Momma's in the way. Momma needs to go back to Avalon. Momma's taking all the visitors for herself . . . Louis. Momma's taking Louis away from me."

No, she hadn't misconstrued it. She wondered if Mama Carmen was planting ideas in Nancy's subconscious.

* * *

The specialist steepled his fingers and adjusted his expression to pompous.

"A psychic barrier is lowered during sleep and this is when emotional conflicts can surface. Some subjects work out their conflicts in dreams, others use the trance state to project them. During this phase, in which they're neither asleep nor awake, the subject is able to communicate opinions they might otherwise feel inhibited to express. Do you follow me so far, Mrs Markova?"

"Yes, doctor, I understand my daughter is experiencing stress and this is the reason for her sleepwalking."

"Good. Now I must ask you whether you engaged in conversation with your daughter while she was in the somnambulant state. What she said is crucial to understanding the cause of her nervous tension."

"No. I simply led her back to bed."

"I see. Well, it's likely to recur. You must try to persuade the young lady to communicate with you, as a means of discovering the reason for the strain. I also recommend you bring her to me for a course of therapy. I guarantee, Mrs Markova, that we will cure the subject. I've written extensively on this matter and conducted a series of tests. I've detected a pattern whereby the behaviour is latent for some years and then manifests itself at times of change or trauma. The loss of a parent, switching schools, being placed in an orphanage – all these have a tendency to precipitate episodes."

"My daughter is a grown woman, doctor."

"Young ladies are susceptible to this problem where there's a lack of a strong male figure in their lives, or when a new one enters it but there's a problem accepting him. Would this be a factor for your daughter, can you tell me?"

"Not at all."

Domineering mothers were another cause, but the specialist was too tactful to mention it. "Strange, it's generally the case. The point to remember is that sleepwalking is a way of acting out unconscious wishes through locomotion rather than through symbolism, as in dreams."

"Is it likely to continue while those wishes are unfulfilled?"

"I believe so. Psychiatric opinion is divided as to whether it's an illness, precisely, but it is certainly a symptom of something amiss in the subject's life. It's an expression of clandestine anxieties. Or urges, if you like."

Urges. Violet's already taut mouth tightened further. "I see."

"If you'd care to make an appointment with my secretary on your way out, I'd be delighted to take on your daughter's case, Mrs Markova. Don't worry about it a moment longer, I assure you she's in safe hands. I will unlock these urges and translate them for you."

"Doctor, you're too kind." Violet gave her gloves a vicious tug and swept through the reception area without pausing by the secretary.

* * *

Major Hudson parted his hair and applied a little of Stuart's pomade to keep it sleek. He was meeting his son at the train station and planned to bring him somewhere decent for dinner, hoping to mend fences with the boy. He had stormed off to Yale after that business with Bridie, and it pained the major to be at odds with his son. If only their differences could be resolved with a treat, the way they were when Stuart was in knickerbockers. If he was twelve, he'd offer to take him rabbit-hunting and they'd be the best of friends in no time. Still, Stuart had agreed to a weekend in New York and his father was grateful for the opportunity to smooth over their disagreement.

"I'm sure I wouldn't be such a bull-moose as a father if you were with me, Jean," he told his reflection. Then he smiled. For of course Jean was with him constantly – Mama Carmen assured him of it.

Stuart insisted they eat at Sherry's. He was inclined to be sulky initially, finding fault with his beef goulash and sending it back to the kitchen. However, after his father presented him with a handsome cheque over coffee – "Treat yourself to something, dear boy" – he relented.

"I had Mrs Burdich prepare your room. I don't know if you intend staying with me in Washington Square or if you'd prefer to go to your club, but I wanted everything ready for you."

334

"May as well bunk down with you, sir." Stuart was mollified by the size of the cheque. He decided to go to the races the next day, he was feeling lucky. If he won he'd settle a few bills. "Got any plans for the weekend, sir?"

"I'm going to a very special séance tomorrow night. Oh Stuart, if only you'd come with me! I feel confident your mother may be about to manifest herself. Mama Carmen has the power of materialisation! I saw it with my own eyes – the face of another woman was transposed on her own. My boy, it was awe-inspiring."

Stuart was shaken. "Mama's face? Mama's face appeared?"

"No, another lady's. But I'm assured she can call up your mother. She's been storing up psychic energy for weeks. Her husband tells me she's ready now – I can't wait. It seems fated the timing should be right when you happen to be in New York for a weekend. Do come with me, my boy! Come and meet your mama again."

"Pa, you have to let go. My mother's been dead for thirteen years. Why won't you let her rest in peace?"

"I'm not disturbing her rest – she wants to make contact with us. She has insights to share."

"Gee, Pa." Stuart was at a loss. His old man was going gaga. "Look, sir, you're always suggesting we take a trip. How about if we go to Oyster Bay, right now, tonight? That's where you wanted to take me before, remember? Let's get clean away from New York and spiritualists and all this ouija-board business and spend some time together, you and me. You can tell me about your Cavalry days. I want to hear all about" – he cast around in his mind – "those sweat lodges the Indians used to build. They were meant to purify the body, weren't they? Let's do it, Pa. Let's just hop on a train and leave!"

"They purified the mind and spirit as well as the body. I'm delighted you want to hear about them, Stuart. I always thought my Indian stories bored you. We can talk about this any time you like, and I'd love to take a trip to Oyster Bay, but not until after the séance. It means the world to me, son. Don't ask me to give it up."

Stuart drained his glass of burgundy, beaten. He recognized the obstinate note in his father's voice.

The major leaned across the table and caught his son by the wrist. "I know you think I take spiritualism too seriously, but if you only understood how much it means to me you wouldn't try to talk me out of it. The spirit world is all around us, it's integrated with ours. Our eyes are closed to its presence and I have to find a way to open them." A zealot's fanaticism blazed from him. "It's why I was saved from the *Titanic*!"

* * *

Father Killoran checked the piece of paper in his pocket. Fifth floor, back room – this must be the place. He tapped on the door which was ajar. Bridie appeared in the jamb, her expression frozen in surprise when she saw a clerical collar. Regaining her wits, she stepped back to allow him in, the habit of deference to the clergy indelible in her. She knew Hannah was spending a great deal of time at St Dominic's and assumed she had invited him. Still, she might have warned her.

"You must be a fit girl taking those stairs every day." Father Killoran produced a spotted handkerchief and mopped his forehead.

"Sure you get used to them." Bridie snatched up some stockings left out to be washed and cast an anxious eye around the room for other debris.

"Who's that, Bridie?" Hannah's voice called from behind the curtain.

"It's the priest from St Dominic's, Father –" Bridie realized she didn't know his name.

"Killoran," he supplied, rocking on his heels, hands laced behind his back. "I'm here to see the patient."

"Father Killoran!" gasped Hannah. "God, Father, I feel desperate to be lying in bed like this and you in the house. Won't you sit yourself down and I'll throw on some clothes? I'll be out directly."

"You're supposed to have bed rest," objected Bridie. "Sadie Brolly said so."

"Sadie Brolly's no doctor. Come in to me for a minute, Bridie, while Father Killoran catches his breath."

Behind the curtain, a furious exchange of whispers ensued. Hannah stood her ground, until Bridie helped her pull on a skirt over her nightdress and add a shawl to it. Hannah left her waist-length auburn plaits dangling, too tired to raise her hands above her head to pin them up.

"Bridie was just on her way to the grocery store," Hannah said pointedly, when she was sitting opposite the priest. Bridie lifted her hat and jammed in a hatpin. "Bridie, bring back something sweet for Father Killoran to have with a sup of tea."

"Ah no, nothing for me, I'm due home for my dinner shortly."

"Go on, Bridie, a slice of apple strudel from the bakery would be just the ticket. I've money under the pillow you can use."

Father Killoran beamed. Apple strudel was one of his favourites, especially from the Jewish bakery half a block down.

Bridie lifted the coins and went out, glad to escape.

"Now, Father, I'll put the kettle on so you can wet your whistle." Hannah grasped the side of the chair trying for purchase to stand, but her pregnant bulk left her struggling.

"I'll do it, you sit where you are."

The priest whistled, chirpy as he thought how dismayed his housekeeper would be if she could see him. She wouldn't let him do a hand's turn in the house. When the gas was lit under the kettle, he settled down in front of Hannah and made conversation. He had an easy way with him and there was no strain between the two, although Hannah wished she wasn't wearing her nightgown – even if a shawl was wrapped modestly across it. Bridie's taking her time with that cake, she thought, but the priest turned down the gas when the kettle boiled and maintained a steady stream of chat.

"Now, Hannah," he said at last, "I know it isn't long until you're due, and it might not be easy for you to get to Confession before then, so if you'd like me to give you the sacrament I'll be glad to do it. I'm not saying there'll be any problems with the baby coming, a fine strong girl like yourself should have no trouble, but there's no harm in covering all the bases. Would you like that?"

"I would, Father. Just make sure the door is closed there, if you wouldn't mind, so Bridie doesn't burst in on us."

Hannah insisted on going down on her knees, even though Father Killoran assured her the Confession would be no less valid in a seated position, and began the words learned by rote since childhood. *"Bless me, Father, for I have sinned . . ."*

The queue for the wooden confessional boxes had snaked into dozens upon dozens at Queenstown, in the days leading up to their voyage. People hadn't wanted to risk the passage without absolution. But Tom had refused to line up with her, saying he had nothing on his conscience. "What we do together is no sin, Hannah me darlin' and don't you let anybody tell you different."

"*... it's two weeks since my last confession.*" She paused, intending to make a clean breast of some uncharitable comments about Warren, the Clean and Brite manager. Suddenly she blurted out, "Father, I'm plagued by wicked thoughts about Tom's sister. She wants to take my child away from me."

"Tom was your husband, is that right?"

Hannah bowed her head, neither agreeing nor disagreeing. "The thing is, Father, Winifred and her husband can't have children and they're after my baby. She's offered to rear it. I never replied when she put it to me, I was that angry with her. I thought it was a monstrous thing to suggest. Was that a bit hard of me, do you think? Should I have written back and thanked her, but explained why it was impossible? I suppose she meant well, though I was that upset I could hardly sleep nights, turning it over in my mind."

Father Killoran reflected. "You said she had a husband, this sister-in-law of yours?"

"That's right."

"Has he a job, can he keep a family?"

"It's two jobs he has. He works in the docks and as a night watchman, beyond in Chicago. That's where they live, Father, it's where Tom and me were planning to go when we sailed for America."

"He sounds like a steady fellow, the husband."

"I suppose so, Father, I don't know much about him." Hannah was puzzled. Why was the priest asking all these questions about Tom's sister and her husband?

"I dare say they're a good Catholic family?"

"Winifred wanted to be a nun before she got married, so Tom told me."

"So this husband and wife would do their best for the child. They'd raise it in the faith and give it a decent start in life."

"I'd raise it in the faith too, Father."

"Of course you would, Hannah, no better woman."

Father Killoran paused, wondering how best to proceed. He knew Hannah lived with Bridie, who was a flighty one and kept company with men, and when the baby arrived its mother would have to leave her with someone and go back to work. It struck him that a selfless act on Hannah's part would be in the infant's best interests, although naturally he'd have to make inquiries about the couple via his opposite number in their parish in Chicago. "No better woman," he repeated, playing for time. "Hannah, has it ever occurred to you that God sometimes asks us to make sacrifices?" Hannah's forehead pleated as she tried to follow the priest's reasoning. "Remember the example of God the Father, who showed there's no greater love than for a man to surrender his only son. Saint John tells us, 'For God so loved the world that He gave His only begotten Son, that whoever believes in Him should not perish but have everlasting life.' Hannah, I think God is giving you the opportunity to show how much you love him by making a sacrifice of your own." Hannah's mouth plopped open in an oval of protest. "Hear me out, child. The Lord moves in mysterious ways. No-one knows that better than myself – he was calling me to the priesthood for years before I listened to his voice. I wanted to have fun and spend money as I earned it, and I refused to take what my heart told me was the true path. Then one day I was at the gym watching boxers training. I intended to have a good bet on a match and was curious to see where my money was going. One of the boxers took a blow to the side of his head and fell down stone dead inches away from me. As suddenly as that, I realized how everything can change in an instant, and I stopped listening to the din of the world and started paying attention to what God had to say. Do you think you could do that, Hannah? Could you listen to God's voice?"

"Father, God's not telling me to hand over my baby to Winifred. I know he's not, he couldn't be that cruel!"

"Do you know that in your heart, child? Or is it what you want to believe? Think about it, Hannah, take as long as you like. Just think about it. The answer will come to you." He patted her hand. "You're a good girl, I'm confident you'll do the right thing. Now, start your Act of Contrition and I'll give you absolution. For your penance, say the *Memorare* and three Hail Marys. *Ego te absolvo . . .*"

Bridie met the priest halfway down the stairs. "Father, I have your apple strudel here. I was delayed at the bakery." She did not add it was through flirting with Enrico, whose barber's shop was next door.

Father Killoran rested a hand on his middle. "Bridie, there's a sight too much cake has gone into this stomach over the years. Maybe it's as well you were held up. Will we see you at the St Dominic's on Sunday for Mass?"

"Maybe." She was evasive.

"Excellent, I'll look forward to it. A pretty face in the congregation is always welcome."

Bridie climbed the last flights. "Sorry I was so long, Hannah. Jesus, Mary and Joseph, what's the matter? You look like you've seen a ghost."

"Father Killoran heard my confession."

"Well, whatever you said has him in high good humour and you in flitters. Come on, *alanna*, let's get you back into bed and then we'll have some of this apple strudel the priest hadn't time to stay and eat. He's not the worst, that Father Killoran. I'd say he was a bit of a divil in his day, before he took the cloth."

Hannah allowed herself to be tucked into bed and fed tea and cake, which tasted like sawdust, for there was a clamour inside her skull threatening to overwhelm her. Maybe her baby was the price she had to pay for being saved from the *Titanic*. Or the penalty she owed for lying about being married to Tom O'Brien. Could Father Killoran be right – was God asking her to sacrifice her child?

24

"Say, Stubel, remember that special séance the Keppels were preparing for me? It's happening at 8 o'clock tonight. I know it's a Saturday and you might have plans, but won't you consider coming along with me? It promises to be a cracker of a session. You did say you'd join me, some weeks ago."

Louis hesitated. He was due to call to Fifth Avenue for pre-dinner drinks. Violet had been unusually insistent about needing to see him. He was hoping he might be invited to stay for dinner, where he was sure to encounter Nancy. She'd been avoiding him since that kiss with her mother – an embrace neither he nor Violet had mentioned. Or repeated.

"*Je suis désolé*. I have arrangements made, major."

"Of course you do. You're a young man with a social life, why would you want to spend Saturday night with an old warhorse like me? Don't give it another thought."

Despite the gracious retraction, he looked so disconsolate that Louis felt a pang of pity. Major Hudson was never less than a gentleman. Self-interest tussled with a sense of obligation.

"I could meet you there, if you like. At eight, did you say?"

"Would you? That's decent of you. It promises to be an unforgettable experience. Mama Carmen's been limbering up for weeks now, doing all

341

sorts of preparations, just like an athlete. I'm on tenterhooks." He held out his hand and shook Louis's. "Thanks, Stubel. Appreciate it."

*　*　*

Louis saw Nancy in the hallway as she left some letters on the tray for posting. Startled, she turned away but he intercepted her.

"Could I speak to you privately for a moment?"

She wanted to refuse but, aware of the footman's watching curiosity, agreed.

Nancy led the way into the little parlour where she liked to sew. Her gait was inelegant: everything about her had ballooned, and she was self-conscious about this as she steered a course to a high-backed chair. While Louis waited for Nancy to make herself comfortable, he studied the tapestry she had worked, now mounted on an easel. *Two souls with but a single thought, Two hearts that beat as one.* Forget-me-nots were embroidered around the edges, meeting either side of a pair of entwined hearts. She was still such a schoolgirl, his love – marriage and widowhood hadn't cured her of it. When she was his, the schoolroom would be left behind forever.

"Mr Stubel, what can I do for you?"

He bowed. "I hope you're well – I see you're blooming."

"I find the time passes slowly. I'm not able to go for carriage rides in the park any more. Still, not long now. It's November already."

"November already," he agreed, thinking how trite their conversation was when he longed to reveal what was in his heart: that even carrying another man's child she was precious to him.

"Mr Stubel, was there something in particular you wanted?"

"Only the indulgence of a few moments' conversation. I see so little of you."

"I understood you were my mother's particular friend – I have no wish to intrude on your intimacies."

He winced. "I'd be your friend, Nancy, if you'd allow me."

She coloured, hearing her name on his lips, and the flush made Louis bolder.

"I understand you may be leaving New York. I'll miss you."

342

"I appear to be an inconvenience to my husband's relatives – worse than that, an embarrassment. One they're willing to pay handsomely to escape. Momma and I are to set sail after my confinement."

"How do you feel about sailing again, so soon after the *Titanic*? Surely it can't be easy?"

His sympathy pleased her. Her mother seemed to think she was a behaving like a wayward child when she protested she hadn't the heart to set foot in another vessel. "It frightens me, to tell you the truth. I did suggest Canada or Mexico, we could reach them by train, but Momma prefers further afield."

"If it were up to me I'd take you to Canada or Mexico. I'd bring you anywhere you commanded, at the crook of a finger. I'd spend my life making you happy." Louis was grave, knowing she could ring the bell and have him ejected, yet unable to stay quiet.

Nancy listened in bewilderment. Could he really find her alluring, beached whale that she was? She allowed her eyes to meet his and felt again that undeniable tug of attraction. She tried to conjure up Samuel's image as a barricade, but could not shut out hazel eyes limpid with appeal.

Louis sensed he was reaching her and crossed the room to where she sat, bending to lift her hands in his. He flipped them over and dropped a whisper-soft kiss on the soft curve of a palm. Then he did the same to her other palm. Still holding her hands, he fell to his knees and – moving so gradually it was almost slow motion – flitted his lips across hers. As their mouths connected he felt the sadness in her and pulled back, his eyes searching hers.

Her heartbeat was thudding. It had never been like this with Samuel and it panicked her. She had felt docile when Sam had kissed her, almost an observer. Even in the marriage bed she had been a bystander to their union. Ladies inspired passion but did not participate in it: that was the correct way. Yet with Louis, something was smouldering into life. How could this be right? She was soon to become a mother. Bewildered by her whirling emotions, Nancy's eyes swam with tears. Gravely, Louis reached out a forefinger and scooped up a teardrop as it trembled on her lower lashes, bringing it to his mouth to share the salt of her unhappiness. In that moment she was lost.

A knock on the door made him spring to his feet and put distance between them.

"Enter," said Nancy, head turned away.

It was Watts, the footman. "Mrs Markova wonders whether you and Mr Stubel intend to join her for pre-dinner drinks."

"Tell her we'll be along directly."

The door closed and Louis was by her side in an instant, guiding her face towards his with his fingers under her chin. "Nancy, I meant to wait until after you were a mother before speaking words of love to you. But my heart bursts the restraints I keep trying to place on it. I can't measure time in ways recognized by the world beyond this room. A minute in your company is worth a year in another's. But the reverse is also true. For a day in which I don't see your face is wasted for me, and stretches remorselessly."

Nancy was simultaneously panicked and enchanted. "We can't do this now – my mother is waiting for us."

"Let her wait."

"You know how impatient she gets. She'll come bursting in on us if we keep her sitting around."

'Very well, *chérie*. But we must talk again soon – we have so much to decide. I want your promise on it."

"I promise."

Louis tucked a strand of hair behind her ear and traced his thumb along her jaw-line. Then he helped her to her feet. "You mustn't worry, Nancy. There is no problem we can't overcome together."

Violet was glacial when they arrived in the salon. "I had to drink my glass of sherry on my own, Mr Stubel. I was under the impression you'd accepted an invitation to a pre-dinner cocktail with me. But I learn from one of the servants that you've been closeted with my daughter for some considerable time." Rebuke crawled from her eyes. Give me an explanation I can live with, they pleaded.

Nancy intervened. "Don't blame Mr Stubel, Momma. He was on his way to you when I waylaid him. I wanted to ask his advice about our travel plans."

"But *I* wanted his advice, Nancy."

"On what, Momma?"

Violet opened her mouth and shut it again. She couldn't tell her daughter it was about the sleepwalking episode. There had been no significant repetition of the sleepwalking – Nancy had climbed out of bed on two further occasions but Roberge or the nurse had been on hand to persuade her back under the covers without wakening her. The sound of the dinner gong rescued Violet.

"Mr Stubel, forgive us, we've offered you no refreshment. But as you can hear, it's long past the cocktail hour. We must detain you no further."

He had offered no explanation for his desertion of her, and Violet was punishing him for it.

"Momma, I think we ought to invite Mr Stubel to share our dinner. Won't you, Mr Stubel? It's only devilled kidneys, you were probably used to much fancier fare in Paris, but I'd like it if you could join us."

Louis hardly dared look at Violet, whose annoyance was palpable, as he accepted. During the meal he orbited between the women, trying to pay them equal attention, and forgot his promise to meet Major Hudson at 10th Street.

* * *

It was just before eight o'clock when Major Hudson handed his silk hat, cloak and cane to Tilly Cather.

"Chilly tonight, isn't it, Tilly? Winter's breathing down our necks."

"My pappy always says the winter don't bite 'til after the New Year."

"Your father is right. Still, there's an east wind tonight that would keep a man indoors unless he had good reason to be out. Has Mr Stubel arrived yet?"

"Ain't seen hide nor hair of him."

"I guess he'll be along presently. No need to show me up, I know the way. Here's something for you, Tilly. Wish me luck tonight." He slipped a bill into her hand, before making his way upstairs to the vestibule.

Tilly unfolded the green note. A ten-spot! "Best of luck to you, major!" she called after him. She felt a twinge of guilt climbing the back stairs to an attic room directly above the parlour where the séance was to take place. Major Hudson was a gentleman, unlike some fellows with

345

fancy manners. In the attic floorboards was a warp where a gap had developed, corresponding with a hole gouged in the ceiling below it. Tilly settled herself by the opening and waited.

* * *

Mama Carmen was glittering with crystals, around her neck, in her ears and on both wrists.

"They helps to steer the od force, yes siree, like a lightning conductor," explained Walt. The major looked baffled. "Remember how I told you about the odylic force, a magnetic influence that helps sensitives channel into the other world? Sure you do, major. Some German baron or other discovered the od force and wrote about it more'n sixty year ago."

"Do you mean Baron von Reichenbach?"

"Yes," Mama Carmen answered. "People who are sensitive to the od force perceive a halo or aura around others. I see one about you now, major, it's a golden halo. You're protected by one whose love for you has survived the grave."

She returned a diamond necklace of Jean's he had lent her. It was a valuable piece, and he had wondered if he wasn't being a dunderhead, but had dismissed the suspicion as unworthy of Mama Carmen's talent. Her unprompted return of the jewellery confirmed he had been right to place his confidence in her.

"Thank you for the loan, major, it's a magnificent piece. I had a real sense of your wife when I held it in my hands. I saw her wearing it on her last day on earth. I felt the TB that attacked her body, and her regret at leaving you and your son, as soon as it touched my skin. Any object associated with human trauma will retain a certain atmosphere which can be transmitted to the sensitive mind."

The major had told Mama Carmen about his wife asking to try on the necklace, a family heirloom she wore on their wedding day, on the day she died. Its dazzle had struck an incongruous note of celebration on her wasted body.

"*Do you remember our wedding day, Richmond?*"

"*Of course I do, my dearest, it's etched on my memory. Happiest day of my life."*

"You made a poor bargain in me. I couldn't give you the family of strapping sons you wanted, and now I won't be around to keep you company in old age. I suppose you regret ever asking my guardian for my hand in marriage."

"I regret nothing, Jean. I'd do everything exactly the same."

His wife's smile blazes out, but afterwards she drops her head back on the pillow, exhausted by their conversation.

He stroked his knuckle across the satin-lined box containing the necklace, wondering how many years it would be before Stuart's wife wore it on her wedding day, as his mother would have wished. The boy was young yet, there was plenty of time.

"Shall we proceed, major?" asked Mama Carmen.

He placed the necklace box reverently in his coat pocket. "Wonder where Stubel can have got to? Don't suppose we could give him another few minutes? He's usually extremely reliable."

"We could delay a little longer, friend, but the vibrations are attuned in Mama Carmen right now. Yes, siree. There's no telling whether they might fade if she has to wait too long before getting down to business."

Normally Major Hudson would have told them to go right ahead, but for some reason he needed the company of a friendly face during this séance. It made no sense to him, but the fancy was there. More than a fancy – an instinct, he corrected himself. Instinct was a quality he had prized during his Cavalry days, a man's survival could depend on it. "I really would prefer to wait."

Authority echoed through his words and Walt Keppel looked at Mama Carmen, who nodded.

By nine it was clear Louis would not be joining them. At a quarter past nine the major was resigned to his absence, and the Keppels dimmed the lights in preparation for the séance. Upstairs Tilly had dozed off, and only a succession of particularly sharp raps on the tabletop alerted her to her duties.

She peered through the hole in the floor into the room below, and at a signal from Walt Keppel dropped a sprig of heather onto the table. The major reached out and smelled it, and his demeanour showed he was moved, although his face was in shadow. Tilly's eyes strayed to Mama Carmen's crystals, pinpoints of lights cascading onto her shoulders, and

347

she wondered if she could buy some crystal ear-bobs with Major Hudson's ten-dollar bill. She heard Mama Carmen's voice addressing Ada, and then the piping voice of a child said she had "a pretty woman with a sing-song voice beside her who wanted to talk to the gentleman". Tilly yawned, before remembering she was meant to have the slide projector tilted to fall on Mama Carmen's face. The angle was wrong. She tugged at it, trying to adjust its position, and a creaking from the floorboards betrayed her presence.

The major glanced up. "What's that?"

"Mice!" hissed Walt Keppel. "Ignore them, friend – it could be catastrophic to interrupt Mama Carmen at this juncture."

The major continued looking upwards. Tilly froze, trying not to blink the eye that was glued to a knot in the floorboards.

"The lady says you and Stuart must try harder to get along. It pains her when you don't like each other so good," Ada's voice issued from Mama Carmen.

The major's attention was drawn back to the medium. "He's at that age where a young man bucks against authority, Jean. I try my best with him, but could be I'm a little heavy-handed. Can you suggest anything?"

"She says you should spend time with your son, try and share his interests."

"He did want me to go to the track with him this afternoon but I'm not a gambling man. I could have made the effort, I guess. I ought to be a better father to the boy." Major Hudson dragged his hand across his forehead, feeling clammy. The room was stifling. He groped in his pocket for a handkerchief.

"The pretty lady says you're a wonderful father to that laddie and you mustn't be hard on yourself."

The major mopped at his face with the linen square, having trouble concentrating. What was Jean saying about a 'laddie'? How odd, she'd never referred to Stuart in that way. He blinked rapidly, trying to regain his focus. There was a dull ache in his central chest area. Heartburn, he thought. He had eaten too quickly before leaving for the Keppels'.

"Jean," he gasped, "I'd give the world to see your face again. If it can happen, today's the day. You know what day it is, don't you?"

There was a pause. "The lady says it's a special day, a date she could

348

never forget. She says she's gathering her strength to bridge the gulf and come to you."

His indigestion increased and numbness penetrated his nervous system. "Twenty-five," he gasped.

Again a pause ensued before Ada's voice trilled, a little uncertainly, "Yes, Richmond, twenty-five!"

Fiery darts were shooting down his left arm now and the room blurred. Shouldn't have eaten those chicken livers, he thought, fighting to control the pain. "Twenty-five," he wheezed out again, vision blurring, unable to see the phosphorescent light begin to play across Mama Carmen's features. The pain would not be held at bay. Jean's pale oval face materialised on Mama Carmen's in the instant before he lost consciousness, but he did not see it. Major Hudson was dying from a massive heart attack. His last thought was that it was twenty-five years to the day since he and Jean had met at a supper dance in Arizona, when she was visiting cousins and he was an awkward young Cavalry officer with newly sewn captain's stripes. It was November 1887. He did see her face, not superimposed on Mama Carmen's, but smiling at him above her dance card as she pencilled him in for a polka.

"I should warn you, I'm rusty on a dance floor, miss."

"Unless it's a Highland reel I'm no prima ballerina myself. We'll just have to sink or swim together, captain."

Tilly jumped as the major's head hit the table with a crash, and she knocked over the projector. Old Keppel would give her what for. But all was confusion below. Keppel was turning up the lamp, and Mama Carmen was supporting the major's head, her ear pressed against his chest. Mama Carmen mentioned a doctor and a juicy word erupted from Walt Keppel. The projector continued to run, a faint outline of Jean Hudson's face on the wall behind Mama Carmen's seat.

"Let me listen," Keppel said. "He's dead as a gate-post, Mama." He looked directly at Tilly's spyhole. "You go on downstairs now, Tilly, you hear? We'll call you if we need you." He waited a moment, listening for the sounds of her departure, but she rattled the projector as though leaving, then wedged her eye against the hole again.

Walt Keppel riffled the major's pockets as he lay warm but not breathing.

"Hurry, Walt!"

"Going as quick as I can, Mama, you bet. Now, what we got here? A hundred and eighty bucks. Sweet." He whistled between his teeth as he emptied the wallet of all but one twenty-dollar bill and slid the snakeskin pouch back into the major's pocket. Next, his fingers held the major's chased silver half-hunter watch by the chain, considering. "Too risky, it can be identified."

He pulled out the satin-lined case and Tilly's eye dilated at the diamond shimmer which made Mama Carmen's crystals seem tawdry.

"Walt, we can't. Cash is one thing but that necklace is an heirloom for his son's wife. I won't have it on my conscience."

"It don't need to go on your conscience, Mama, it can rest itself on mine. I can take the weight, yes, siree. Walter Keppel can take the weight for a bauble fine as this."

"But what if they trace it to us? It'll mean jail for sure."

"You don't suppose our old soldier boy told anyone he was going to be such a danged fool as to hand over his necklace to us, do you? Couldn't believe it myself when he did. I think we should take a calculated risk with this, Mama. I have a hunch we can pull it off." His eyes gloated over the diamonds.

"We don't need to – the Armstrong girl will be generous to us. Already she trusts me more than her mother."

"That momma ain't gonna let go her gal's money without a fight. I say we don't look a gift horse in the mouth."

"I don't like it, Walt, I have a bad feeling about this. Leave the necklace. Please." Her hands were laced together, knuckles taut.

He cocked his head to the side and thought for a few moments. "Normally I have the utmost respect for your bad feelings, Mama, I surely do. But shucks, a plum just fell in my lap and I'd be a dang fool to climb back up the tree and attach it to the branch. My mother never birthed her no fools."

The diamonds disappeared into his pocket.

*   *   *

Louis spent the meal hoping Nancy would engineer a reason to be alone with him. By the time they adjourned to the salon for coffee and liqueurs, however, he realized it wouldn't happen. Violet was watching them jealously and would never permit it. Still, at least he knew for a fact now that Nancy reciprocated his feelings. She was confused – it was natural – but her body had responded to his. His instincts were right. Certain that all obstacles would be overcome soon, he fetched demitasses of coffee for the ladies and sat on long after it was polite, consuming so much caffeine it ricocheted through his bloodstream. Finally Nancy's genuine yawns and her mother's sham ones embarrassed him into taking his leave.

Major Hudson never entered his thoughts. Louis remembered him for the first time as he arrived back in Washington Square. "I'll tell him I was detained." He blotted out the wistfulness with which the major had asked for his company at the séance as he turned his key in the lock. He intended to help himself to one of the major's Cuban cigars, which he'd smoke in his room while he retraced every second of his evening with Nancy – saving those precious minutes in her parlour until last, when his eye fell on a rectangle of paper on the hall floor. He lifted the envelope and read his name on the front. A tattoo of alarm drummed as he opened the hand-delivered message.

Major Hudson taken ill at our house. Come at once.

Walt Keppel.

Louis whistled down a carriage and offered the driver double fare. Soon he was outside the greengrocer's in the Lower West Side. "Wait for me, I'll make it worth your while," he told the cabbie.

Tilly Cather was subdued, the blotchy patchwork around her eyes told she'd been crying. "Such a gentleman, he was," she snivelled, answering the door.

Louis took the stairs three at a time and was met at the top by Walt Keppel. "Where is he?"

"Friend, this is a sad time. A tragic time, I might venture to suggest."

"Where is he?" Louis repeated.

Walt led him into the parlour, where Major Hudson lay outstretched on the floor, his head resting on a crimson cushion, hands meeting across his front. The table and chairs were shoved against the wall to make space. The scene was serene but the major did not look peaceful.

"On the floor?" Louis rounded on Walt.

"We called out a doctor and he said the major was a goner. Ain't nothing anyone could 'a done to save him. His heart just exploded in his chest. Mama Carmen and I wanted to move him to the bed in our room but the doc advised against it. Less pulling and shoving at him the better, sez the doc. Make him as comfortable as you can, respectful like, and then let his loved ones take him home, he sez."

"Where is Mama Carmen?"

"Mama's badly shook by the experience, yes siree. She's resting."

"A medium shaken by death? Surely it's her stock in trade. I've heard her claim concepts of life and death have no significance."

Walt's teeth flashed in a nervous rictus. "That's true, but she was mighty partial to the major. Not wanting to press you, friend, but what arrangements can you make for conveying the gentleman elsewhere? No disrespect, but he can't lay on our parlour floor indefinitely. It discommodes the household."

Louis looked Walt over with disdain. "Naturally I'll bring him home. I have a carriage waiting outside. I need to speak to the driver about how to handle this. Stay with the major, he shouldn't be alone."

"I been staying with him," whined Walt. "Mos'ly," he tacked on.

But *you* left him alone, hissed Louis's conscience.

The driver was reluctant to carry a corpse. "It's bad luck, buddy."

He kept shaking his head, but Louis opened his wallet and rained its contents into his hands, and the man's fingers closed atavistically over the notes.

As he raced back to the open doorway, Tilly appeared. "We gots to meet," she whispered. "I gots to talk to you."

"Later." He was impatient. But something made him pause on the stairs. "When and where?"

"Tomorrow, it's my afternoon off. Two o'clock in Times Square. Don't tell no-one."

* * *

Back at 12b Washington Square, Louis rang the doorbell hoping Stuart might be at home. It shrilled through empty rooms. He was still

352

out. There was no help for it – he and the carriage driver would have to manage Major Hudson by themselves. The dead weighed heavy.

"This is a real fix. I don't like it so good," the driver hacked out, knees wobbling under the load.

Louis ignored him, concentrating on banging none of the major's body parts as they negotiated the steps to the front door. His employer's limbs were starting to harden, and he had a horror of hearing stiff flesh thud against a door frame or wall.

"I ain't going no further," said the cabbie, as soon as they were through the door. He lowered the major's legs to the floor, leaving Louis no choice but to let his torso sink to the tiles too.

"We can't leave him like this, it's undignified. The major was in the United States Cavalry, he helped settle the West."

"That don't cut no ice with me, buddy. Settle the West or leave it to the Injuns for all I care, I'm outta here."

"There's more money in it for you."

"Money wouldn't pay you to do this job."

"The worst is over. Come on, I can make it worth your while."

Still the driver was resistant. Louis cursed softly in French beneath his breath. "His bedroom is on the next floor. Just one more flight."

"Sorry buddy, like I said – I'm outta here."

"He has a son. Do you want him to come home and find his father dumped like a parcel in the hallway?"

The driver had a son whom he had not seen for eight years. He had walked out on his wife and child when the boy was only seven. He imagined a lad of tender years happening upon his father's corpse. "Show me the money."

Louis flew upstairs for what he had saved from his salary before the driver changed his mind.

Finally they had Major Hudson laid on his double bed. The major's skin was blue-white now but his moustache bristled as energetically as ever. Louis fetched the buffalo-skin rug from the major's study and draped it over his torso – it seemed appropriate, somehow. Then he patted one of the stiff hands and sat down to wait for Stuart.

25

At two the following afternoon, Louis Stubel slumped on a bench in Times Square, a green oasis surrounded by business institutions. Exhaustion anaesthetized him to the cold: he hadn't slept the previous night, and the morning had been swallowed up dealing with undertakers. Stuart had staggered in at three in the morning, regurgitating several pints of port and he hardly liked to speculate what else, after seeing his father's body. Louis had watched the boy dispassionately as he had dropped to his haunches, heaving. His shoes had been speckled with vomit. All the same, Stuart had shed tears for Major Hudson.

Tilly Cather arrived a few minutes late. She stood among the pigeons admiring Louis's patrician beauty, proud to meet such a fine gentleman – even if his interest in her was perfunctory. He stood when he noticed her, bowing and calling her *mademoiselle* in that accent she found so appealing. Shattered though he was, it was second nature to him to compliment a woman on her appearance and to smile into her eyes with a suggestion of intimacy offered and more to follow. The whites of his eyes were veined red, but she had never seen a man fill a jacket as well as he did.

"It's no weather for sitting about," said Tilly. "I could sure use something to keep the cold out."

Tilly held out until her fingers were curled around her second glass of hot port.

"They looted him as he lay dead there, poor gentleman. Turned out his pockets and helped themselves. It was pitiful – I couldn't sleep last night thinking about it."

"You mean the Keppels?"

She nodded, puffed up with self-importance at being the bearer of such news. "It ain't right taking advantage of the dead, they deserve our respect. Cleaned him out, they did. Them two vultures shouldn't be let away with it."

She waited for Louis to agree but he seemed distracted. He was remembering how he had discreetly mentioned to Stuart that he had been obliged to outlay some considerable expenditure in transporting Major Hudson home. Stuart had shrugged he was strapped for cash, but no doubt the executors of his father's estate would meet his expenses. Louis had only a few dollars to his name, and no idea how long it would take before money was freed up by the major's estate. Would there be a reward for turning in the Keppels?

"Don't you agree it's sinful?" Tilly insisted.

Ah yes, sin. Walt Keppel was a most objectionable man, and Mama Carmen a charlatan – although those messages from the woman she claimed to be his mother continued to unsettle him – but sin wasn't something that cluttered up Louis Stubel's thoughts.

"They're packing to leave. I heard them mention Detroit. Will we go to the cops before they make their getaway?"

His brain raced. Nancy might be dragged into the mess if a police case was undertaken to expose the Keppels. Mama Carmen was capable of calling her as a character witness.

"Let me order you another hot port, Tilly, it's wintry today. You know, I can't help thinking it might be as well to let them clear off. Least said soonest mended, isn't that right?"

* * *

The funeral at St George's Church in New York City the following

Wednesday morning attracted a capacity crowd. Officers who had served with Major Hudson in the Third Cavalry Regiment were present in full dress uniform, along with a great many *Titanic* survivors. President Taft sent an attaché, and Union League Club members were out in force in top hats and tails. Edmund Newton had taken Stuart under his wing, loyalty to his friend suspending animosity. Heavily sedated, the boy was automaton-like.

A change in organ music tempo drew Edmund's glance to the back of the church, and as he looked two familiar figures detached themselves from the throng. They hovered, unsure where to sit. It was Hannah and Bridie. Hannah was due any day and Sadie Brolly had advised against attending.

"I liked him, I want to be there," Hannah had insisted, so Bridie had taken a few hours off work to keep an eye on her – Warren Vicosen had allowed her back to the Clean and Brite because she was his best presser. And because she had let him run his hands over her body for a few minutes, before wriggling from his grasp.

Edmund was about to start down the aisle towards the girls when Louis materialised at their side and directed them to a seat. At that, a flurry indicated the service was about to begin. Edmund bit his lip and returned to his place.

Captain Arthur Rostron from the *Carpathia* – in time he would be knighted for his service at sea, and become Sir Arthur Rostron – delivered the oration. He was in New York and Washington for a round of public functions, with presentations of everything from testimonials to illuminated addresses. The captain had been reluctant initially, saying he had hardly known the major, but Edmund had persisted: his friend had admired Captain Rostron and would have been honoured for the hero of the *Titanic* to play a prominent part in his funeral service. During his speech in front of the Stars and Stripes-draped coffin, Captain Rostron described Major Richmond Hudson as an officer and a gentleman. "The term has become something of a cliché, perhaps, but in the major's case it could have been new-minted for him."

He spoke of how gallantly the major had helped load *Titanic's* lifeboats and about his exemplary behaviour in the lifeboat. "This was one of those occasions in life when men have an opportunity to show their mettle – and Major Hudson seized it with both hands."

Everyone agreed afterwards he struck exactly the right note. Even Rebecca Armstrong pronounced the captain a most distinguished individual, and was nettled she hadn't invited him to Samuel's funeral.

"An artist was commissioned to make a plaque of his head for the Hall of Fame in New York City Hall. It's the first time this honour has gone to a Britisher," Adam had whispered during the oration. He was awestruck by the Congressional Medal of Honour glinting on the captain's uniform – the highest honour the Federal Government could bestow.

Rebecca was too enthralled to rebuke him for whispering in church.

* * *

"I'm going to ask him," announced Bridie.

"He'd be too busy to be bothered with the like o'that," said Hannah.

"Ask a busy person to do something, that's what my mother always says. I'll ask him straight away."

"Leave it until the crowd dies down."

"We may never get another chance. This could be just the leg-up your babogue needs. God knows, it deserves a bit of luck. I'll go over to him now."

"He's talking to that woman with the fluffy hair Louis Stubel pointed out to us. Mrs Markova, isn't that her name? She's young Mrs Armstrong's mother. You can't interrupt them, it might be important."

"Just watch me."

Bridie bowled up to Captain Rostron on the pavement outside St George's Church, where Violet had buttonholed him. Violet was on her own, for Nancy was too heavily pregnant to venture outside the house. She sent a wreath, however, along with a card inscribed "*Gone But Not Forgotten*", and wept for Major Hudson – remembering him escorting her down the *Carpathia*'s gangway when they docked in New York.

"Naturally I wrote to you, captain, but I just had to express my thanks in person for the care you took of my daughter on board your ship. She told me you even gave up your cabin for her."

Surrounded by a fan club of women, Captain Rostron tried to fend off Violet's insistent gratitude. Another woman intervened to ask for his autograph, but he declined modestly. "It doesn't feel right, madam, in view of the occasion. Sad day and so forth."

Bridie insinuated herself into a chink in the gathering. "Captain, I was on the *Carpathia*." She was breathless from pushing. "I was one of the people you rescued off the *Titanic*."

"How do you do, miss, I trust you're recovered?"

"My friend is about to have a baby. She lost her husband on the *Titanic* and you picked her up in the same lifeboat as me. Will you be the baby's godfather?" Bridie nodded towards Hannah, hanging back.

Captain Rostron was flummoxed. "It's a great honour to be asked, of course, but I hardly think I'm equipped to –" He tailed off, aware of a fascinated knot of spectators.

"It's a *Titanic* baby she's having – a *Titanic* orphan," said Bridie. "Well, a half-orphan. You'd be bringing good out of something bad."

"I'll do it." The captain snapped to decision, beckoning Hannah. "My name is Arthur Rostron. And you are?"

"Hannah O'Brien, sir."

He shook her hand. "Mrs O'Brien, it will be a pleasure to stand for your child. It may have to happen by proxy, I do spend rather a lot of time at sea – part and parcel of the trade, I'm afraid." He laughed, and his serious face was transformed. "If I give you my address, you must write to me and tell me when it arrives and what you're naming him or her. It looks set fair to happen any day now."

"Can I give him Arthur as a middle name if he's a boy? I ought to save the first name for his father, Thomas."

"Proper order. It would be an honour, Mrs O'Brien – and if it's a girl, my wife's name is Ethel."

"Holy Mother of God, you can't saddle the baby with a name like Ethel!" muttered Bridie, when the captain was once again engulfed. "That'll have to be a middle name too."

Just then they saw Violet Markova a little distance away and Hannah took her courage in both hands. "Begging your pardon, ma'am."

"Yes?" Violet barely glanced at her, busy watching Louis Stubel organize carriages to convey mourners to the cemetery.

"I don't mean to presume, ma'am, but I wanted to send my good wishes to your daughter, Mrs Armstrong. I know we're due around the same time."

Violet's gaze flickered over Hannah. "How do you know my daughter?"

"We were on the same lifeboat, ma'am."

"I see. She wanted to come today – she was fond of Major Hudson. He's from one of New York's finest families, you know. But she stayed at home on doctor's orders. It's been an extraordinarily draining year."

"Of course, ma'am. The major would be the last in the world to want Mrs Armstrong risking herself or the baby."

Edmund touched Bridie's elbow. "Hello, I didn't expect to see you here."

Bridie bridled – Edmund had the knack of bringing out the worst in her. "What, we don't have the common courtesy to pay our respects to the major?"

"Not at all. I meant simply you and Mrs O'Brien are working girls. It's not easy to take time off from jobs."

A disturbance drowned out his words as a frantic-looking man leaped from a cab and broke into a run towards them. It was the footman, Watts. "Nurse Spatz says you're to come home at once, madam! Mrs Armstrong has gone into labour. She's calling for you."

A path was cleared for Mrs Markova to reach the carriage. Louis Stubel hurried up to see what the commotion was about, and had to be physically restrained by Edmund from leaping into the carriage with Violet. "Babies are women's business, Stubel. Leave it until later."

Bridie checked on Hannah and knew from the dark circles under her eyes that she should bring her friend home. But she adjusted the comforter at Hannah's throat – "Can't have you catching a chill" – and lingered in the hopes of glimpsing Stuart. Just as she was about to give up, he passed close to where they waited. The young man was almost unrecognizable in mourning. Stuart was always turned out in something jaunty, but in a black suit and silk top hat he looked lost, Bridie thought, as though his identity had been misplaced.

The coffin was loaded into a coach and six dark plumes nodding on the horses' heads.

"Goodbye Major Hudson-like-the-river," whispered Hannah.

Bridie squeezed her hand, still watching Stuart. Did this mean he'd be able to meet her again – or didn't he care about her any more?

* * *

Violet arrived home to find the doctor in charge of the household, Nurse Ivana Spatz shadowing him. A tension born of waiting permeated the Fifth Avenue house. The servants went about on tiptoe and everyone spoke in hushed tones. Nancy bore down all day, as instructed, but the baby did not come. The labour went on through the night and the following dawn, and when her pains had lasted for almost twenty-four hours the physician used chloroform. A son was born soon after but Nancy was unconscious during her child's first minutes of life.

Violet accepted the fretting scrap of humanity swaddled in a downy white blanket from Nurse Spatz. "I suppose you must be Samuel Armstrong the Fourth," she said. "Don't think you can call me grandmomma."

The baby opened his rosebud mouth and discharged a piercing bawl. She handed him straight back to the nurse, who hushed him with soothing strokes to his back.

In the hiccupping aftermath Louis's voice could be heard from the floor below. The words were indistinguishable but his agitation was unmistakable. The nurse, who sensed something untoward between the Frenchman and this haughty woman, let fly a disapproving glance. Violet whipped out onto the landing.

"How is she?" Louis was at the foot of the stairs and called up the question. Frowning, Violet continued to descend. "I'm in agony. I must know – is Nancy in danger?"

At the use of her daughter's Christian name, Violet's teeth ground against each other. Apart from anything else, the servants could hear. "Mrs Armstrong is sleeping." Her voice was clipped.

"But how is she?"

"She has just given birth, Mr Stubel, how do you suppose she is?"

"Is everything all right? I insist on knowing! I want to see her!"

Violet inhaled, deep and slow, as she stood holding the curved sweep of the banister. She searched his features, trying to find some consolation there. What she saw was the face of a man in love. With another woman. Her hopes cascaded about her feet, splintering into shards. Nerves already overstretched by the tension of her daughter's labour, she rounded on him. "My daughter's condition is none of your concern. I believe you've outstayed your welcome, Mr Stubel. Watts will show you out. Good day." She mounted the stairs.

"Violet, wait!" he called. She ignored him. "Madame Markova, forgive me! I'm frantic with worry. Come back! Please!"

She kept climbing, taking extreme care as she placed her feet on one stair tread after another. In her mind's eye she saw these feet swell and bunch. She would grow more arid and unloved with the passage of years. Love had played a mean trick on her, dangling an image of what life could be like before snatching it away. Violet closed the door of her bedroom and sat on the edge of her bed. She caught a glimpse of her reflection in the mirror. She was looking at a grandmother – and a fool.

26

Louis kneaded a tension knot at the back of his neck. He only had a day, two at most, left in the major's Washington Square apartment before he'd have to leave. Stuart was quite explicit that his services were no longer required. It was back to the Excelsior Hotel, Louis supposed, unless he could reach Nancy and persuade her to go away with him. They could leave the baby with Violet and try Canada, South America, anywhere. But was she well enough to travel? And how would he gain access to her, now that Violet had grown hostile?

Louis had hardly any money and no job. But he did not see these as obstacles. Give him fifteen minutes alone with Nancy and he could convince her to elope with him – there was passion between them, perhaps even an understanding. He had sensed it from the first and now she had admitted it too. Louis cudgelled his brains. A *fait accompli* might work. If he showed her a ticket to Buenos Aires, would that persuade her? Except he could not afford to buy first-class tickets to any such destination, and he could not ask Nancy to run away with him on a shoestring.

Suddenly Louis remembered the thousand dollars in gold nuggets Major Hudson kept locked in his desk. The key to the desk was hidden in the glass case which housed Queen Elizabeth I's counterpane – the trusting major had volunteered that information as well. Louis walked stealthily to the sitting room, ear cocked for Stuart. He was in the bathroom adjoining his bedroom and generally spent an hour at his grooming. Louis could hear water running. He approached the case containing the richly embroidered bedspread with intertwined ERs. Stretching out a hand to open the lid, he froze when the sound of running water stopped. Was Stuart finished in the bathroom already? He listened intently. Louis tried the case and the lid opened. He felt around among the folds of the counterpane but there was no metal object. Perhaps he had misunderstood the major. But no, he had definitely said the Virgin Queen was the key's custodian. A door opened nearby and he jumped, still holding the lid. The jolt dislodged the bedspread and metal glinted behind it. Louis snatched the key.

"Say, what do you think you're doing?"

Louis dropped the lid, a crack spidering through the sheet of glass. "I was admiring your family heirloom, Mr Hudson."

"You've broken the glass, you clumsy fool!"

A pinprick of sweat sprang above Louis's upper lip. "I'm sorry, you startled me. Naturally I'll pay for the damage."

"Well gee, naturally. How much longer do you suppose it will take you to wind up my father's affairs? I intend to close up the apartment and take a vacation. I need a change of scene."

"I hope to finish today."

"Excellent. Chop-chop, don't let me hold you up."

* * *

Edmund had been wrestling with his conscience since meeting Bridie at the funeral. He wanted to go and see her. But to what end? Was he simply amusing himself – or did he envisage a future with her, despite what he felt acutely was their difference in station?

Major Hudson had pressurised his son to stay away from Bridie, realizing how little Stuart could offer the girl. Shouldn't he, Edmund Newton, be a gentleman about it and steer clear too? He stared at the script he was meant to be working on, words ghosting in front of him, and threw aside his pen in disgust. It was impossible to concentrate when so many questions were buzzing around in his head. He decided to take a walk. His feet led him to a streetcar stop and he stepped on one heading downtown. Almost without conscious thought, he found himself walking down Third Avenue towards 29th Street.

He knocked on Bridie and Hannah's door.

Something in the set of his jaw persuaded Hannah to haul herself to her feet and reach for her shawl. "I'm going to light a candle in St Dominic's."

"You'll not be able for the stairs again," Bridie warned.

"The exercise will do me good." Hannah smiled at Edmund as she passed him.

"Did you lose your job, Miss Ryan, for going to the major's funeral?"

"I did. Hannah was bent on going and I couldn't let her do it on her own. But Vicosen wouldn't take me back this time. Ah, sure, what odds? There's plenty more jobs in New York. I have a dollar or two put by to see me through. I'll be working again in no time."

"How would it be if you didn't have to work again? How would it be if I took care of you? Would you let me do that?

"Take care of me, is it? And what would you be wanting in return?" Bridie's cheeks were stained red as she prepared to work herself into a temper.

"Why, marry you, of course." Edmund was aghast that any other connotation was taken. He was such a nincompoop. He hadn't phrased his proposal in romantic language. Women liked to be wooed. But he didn't know how to flatter a woman, least of all one who laughed at him as Bridie Ryan did.

Bridie was flabbergasted. This long string of an Englishman wanted to marry her! Nobody had ever proposed to her – not the men who kissed her, not the man who planted a child in her belly. And now this fellow with whom she'd never shared a dance, let alone an embrace, was asking her to be his wife. "Why would you want to marry me?"

"I'd like to look after you."

"Why?"

Edmund hesitated. Because she was in his blood. Because he couldn't bear to think of another man touching her. He didn't know how to express any of that. "Marriage would be good for you – it would settle

365

you down," he blurted out.

Her ringlets bounced on her shoulders as Bridie tossed her head. "I don't see what business it is of yours whether I'm settled or not."

"I want to make it my business."

"You can want all you like. You haven't given me one good reason for marrying you, since you came barrelling in here telling me how I should live my life. It's all about what you want, I may as well be that table for all the account you're taking of my wants. If that's how the English court a girl, they have a lot to learn."

Edmund slid his finger under his collar, which had begun to throttle him. Bridie was right, he was making a dog's dinner of his proposal. He should have worked out some form of words to say instead of catching her unawares. Women liked to be softened up first. But he was knee-deep in the proposal now and there was no backing out. What was it men said in these circumstances? *You cannot fail to have noticed that my regard for you has developed into a deeper affection. No – that my esteem for you has ripened into love. How about, my sole hopes of happiness lie in your hands?*

Was that what she expected? Did she count on him comparing her to a summer's day, to wax lyrical about her eyes, her hair, her ruby lips? The trouble was he didn't know what women wanted or how to relate to them – he should have asked Minerva for advice before wading in like the clot he was.

"I admit I'm no ladies' man. Flattery doesn't fall easily from my lips. But that doesn't mean I lack feelings. I was under the impression it was a compliment to a woman when a man asked her to be his wife. Even if he repulsed her, she couldn't fail to see she was being honoured."

"So it's an honour to ask me to be Mrs Edmund Newton, is it? Well, I think it's honour enough to be Miss Bridie Ryan. You should be ashamed of yourself, creeping up on a girl and proposing marriage to her without so much as a by-your-leave."

Edmund was bewildered. This was the polar opposite to how he could ever have imagined a proposal scene being played out. A dignified withdrawal to lick his wounds in private seemed the only recourse. "If my advances insult you, I'm sincerely sorry. Naturally I'll remove myself from your presence at once."

"No, wait." Bridie sighed. The poor eejit was doing his best, she knew that – he didn't have it in him to be flowery. "Sure I know you mean well. It's just you caught me on the hop. Come in and sit down and give me a chance to draw breath, and maybe we can talk about it again by and by. I never thought you were the marrying kind."

"Neither did I." Edmund moved stiffly, pride wounded, and accepted a seat.

"You see, you missed a golden opportunity there to say 'until I met you, Bridie, and you changed my mind'." She laughed, to show there was no rancour.

Edmund smiled, self-conscious. "I can call you Bridie then, can I? The trouble is I spent too long with my head in books when I should have been learning how to relate to other people. The only woman I'm comfortable with is my sister. Sadly, my mother passed away last year."

"I'm sorry to hear it. Tell me about your sister."

Bridie settled herself on her windowsill perch. As she nodded and inquired, her mind was ticking busily: should she accept Edmund Newton, reject him, or keep him dangling?

* * *

Hannah was also asking herself questions about the future. She lit a candle and sat in a pew to consider her dilemma. What would be best for her child? She stroked her stomach. "Should you stay with me or should I send you to your Aunt Winifred?" she asked the baby inside her.

Ellen Cooling slipped into the seat behind. "How you makin' out?"

"Only middling, Ellen. I have a decision to reach and I'm asking God's help with it."

"Jus' right, sugar, take Jesus with you for your friend. Jesus never give nobody a wrong steer."

"I always seem to be going to Him with my troubles – he must be sick of the sound of my voice."

"Now don't you go talkin' all dispirited like that. He'll listen, he always does. You want me to listen too?"

"It's about my baby, Ellen. I'm not sure if I'm good enough to keep it. An offer has been made for my child, one I ought to give serious thought

367

to – Father Killoran says so."

"You know, when I was a li'l girl here in New York city, there was special horse-cars with a sign on the side. *Colored People Allowed In This Car*, they said. That means all the cars with no signs is off-limits to us. One day I axed my momma, 'Why's I not good enough to ride in all them other streetcars? Why jus' the ones with the sign painted on?' And you know what she says? 'You *is* good enough, Ellen, and don't let nobody ever tell you different'."

"So you're saying I'm good enough to keep my baby?"

"We coloured folks had to take the gutter end of the sidewalk for long enough. But we never got used to it. Don't you let yourself go gettin' used to the gutter end neither."

* * *

Louis managed to remove the thousand dollars in gold from the major's desk when Stuart was at the barber's. He felt qualms as he did so, but suffocated them. He needed this money to help him make a start with Nancy. The only risk lay in Stuart raising the alarm, but he was banking on Major Hudson having kept his son in ignorance about the emergency cache. He must have realized someone of Stuart's spendthrift habits would go looking for it. Stuart would have lunch at his club after his visit to the barber's, and wouldn't be home until late afternoon, so Louis had some hours yet to smuggle the nuggets out of the house. In the meantime he would hide the money under a loose floorboard in his bedroom, go to Nancy and persuade her to abscond with him.

Louis chewed a thumb knuckle, trying to second-guess possible impediments. Nancy might be a little reluctant to leave her baby so soon after its birth: very well, the child could come with them, if it pleased her. Violet might try some histrionics: he would be respectful but firm with her.

* * *

The Frenchman stared at the footman. "This is preposterous, there must be some mistake."

"No mistake, sir. Mrs Markova has left instructions you're not to be admitted."

"But didn't she receive my bouquet?" Surely she has forgiven me.

"The flowers were passed on to Nurse Spatz, sir."

Louis frowned. He had sent a posy of violets to soothe Violet's ruffled spirits. He had taken care to construct a message saying no doubt the house was awash with floral tributes for the new mother, but there was another mother who should not be overlooked. Clearly her pique – he saw it as nothing more serious – had not yet evaporated. "Give this to Mrs Armstrong and wait for an answer please, Watts." He took out a notebook, tore off a page and scribbled a few lines, before folding it and passing it to the footman, along with a five-dollar bill. "Don't tell Mrs Markova I'm here."

Watts opened the note as soon as he closed the front door.

Nancy, I must see you. It's a matter of the utmost urgency. Don't turn me away, I beg of you. Yours if you'll have me, Louis.

Pushy fellow, thought Watts, lifting the brass salver and depositing the note on the tray.

Nurse Spatz answered his knock. A newborn's thin bleat could be heard behind her, along with Nancy's tearful complaint, "I don't know how to quieten him."

"The gentleman asked me to wait for an answer," said Watts.

The nurse left the door ajar and moments later was back. "Mrs Armstrong says she's not at home to that caller."

Watts repeated the message to Louis.

"Perhaps she's tired today. I'll return tomorrow."

"Sir, if you don't mind my saying, save yourself the trouble. My orders are not to admit you again."

"Orders from Mrs Markova?"

"No sir, from Mrs Armstrong. I heard her myself. Tell him to stay away, she said."

"I don't believe you." Louis thrust past Watts and raced upstairs. He hesitated outside several doors, unsure which was Nancy's room. A baby's mewl solved his dilemma and he turned the handle on the door opposite.

Nancy was lying on a daybed holding an infant while a nurse leaned over them. Caught unawares, the women stared at him.

"Nancy, we must talk."

"Louis! I – I don't think we have anything to say to each other. Momma's told me everything."

Watts's hand was on Louis's shoulder but he shrugged it off. "What has she told you?"

"That you forced yourself on her that day I saw you together. And that you don't care which of us you have, so long as you get your hands on our money."

"Time to leave," said Watts. "The mistress wants you gone."

"Nancy, you can't believe that! You can't believe I want you for your money."

"I don't know what to believe any more. I'm tired, Louis. I want to be left alone." She turned her face to the wall.

The colour drained from Louis's face, even as he was manhandled by Watts. "Speak to me, Nancy! Don't push me away. Remember what I said before? Together we can overcome any problem."

Exhausted and confused, she lay inert.

Louis was bundled out by Watts, who shoved him through the front door and threw his hat out after him. He bent to retrieve it from the step, dusting it down. Instead of placing it on his head, he turned it between his hands studying the hatband, where the hatter's name was printed on a length of grosgrain ribbon. Focus though he would, he couldn't read the name – there seemed to be something wrong with his eyesight. Everything was blurred. Finally, still holding the hat by the brim, he walked away.

* * *

Louis examined a map of the United States in Major Hudson's study, trying to decide where to go. New Orleans was a French settlement, but he had no desire to be among his countrymen. Boston was full of the Irish. His eye fell on Philadelphia. It was a prosperous place by all accounts. Very well, he would go to Philadelphia. The major's nuggets would help him make his way there. As he packed, he began to have misgivings about the nuggets. They were so distinctive. What if they could be traced back to the major? Prudence recommended they should be converted into paper money. But if he walked into a bank with them he would arouse suspicion. Louis wondered who he could turn to for advice and remembered the newspaper reporter at the *New York American*. He lifted the phone on the major's desk.

"I'm making an inquiry on behalf of a friend. He needs to exchange some gold nuggets for paper money – is there somewhere he can go without drawing attention?"

"Are we talking about a considerable quantity of gold?" The reporter was not fooled by the reference to a friend.

"About a thousand dollars."

"There's a fellow in Brooklyn I came across who handles that sort of business. I can let you have his address, but don't tell anyone how you came by it. This fellow's not strictly legitimate, if you catch my drift. It's black market, so he'll charge your friend for doing it."

"How much?"

"Couldn't rightly say. But beggars can't be choosers, right, Stubel?"

* * *

Stuart Hudson waited for Bridie's answer, tapping his cane on the ground.

"Is it not a bit early to start spending your father's money?" She had hoped to see him again, with the major no longer there to keep them apart, but now she looked at him with active dislike.

"Life goes on – my father would be the first to say so. What do you think of my proposition?"

"It's an attractive one," she admitted.

"Gee, you can do better than that, Bridie. A generous one, I'd call it."

"Generous, yes, some people might call it that all right."

"So your answer's yes?"

"I have no answer to give you yet. I need time to think about it."

"What's there to think about?" Impatient, he flexed his shoulders inside his suit jacket.

"I've had another offer."

Stuart stared. "Who from?"

"I'm not at liberty to say."

"It's probably that manager fellow from your laundry. Well, if you can compare an offer from him with an offer from me –"

"It's not him."

"Who then?"

Stuart was so persistent that eventually she named Edmund Newton.

"He wants to marry me," she told him, shoots of pride springing up with the words.

Stuart's cane clattered to the floor. "The schoolmaster wants you for his wife! And what have you told him?"

"I haven't given him my answer." She tossed her head. "He's more of a gentleman than you are – he isn't hounding me for one."

Stuart had enough of his father in him to look uncomfortable as he mentally compared their two proposals. "I'll leave my offer on the table until Sunday. If I don't hear back from you by then, I'll take it you're intending to become Mrs Edmund Newton. More fool you," he couldn't resist adding. "He'll turn you into a dutiful little wife – you'll never achieve your potential with him holding you back."

"And your offer is all about helping me achieve my potential? Not a thought for how you can benefit?"

Two pink discs flared on Stuart Hudson's cheeks. "Until Sunday." He bent for his cane. As he straightened, a look of appeal swamped his eyes. "I do care about you, Bridie, honest I do. Say yes."

27

Hannah's moans could be heard as soon as Bridie opened the street door. She bolted up the stairs, calling "I'm on my way, Hannah. Everything's going to be all right!" It was the third Thursday in November and the baby was already past its due date. Hannah had complained of stomach pains over breakfast, but insisted it was indigestion and not the onset of labour. Bridie wanted to stay at home with her but she had the offer of a day's temporary work that might lead to a permanent position, and Hannah had persuaded her not to pass up the opportunity.

"I'll send for you if I need you," she promised. "Sure you're only a couple of blocks away."

Bridie had stopped off at Ellen's on her way to work, asking her to look in on Hannah. Now she burst into the room, to find Hannah breathing in ragged gasps and Ellen wiping her forehead with a towel. She was in the last stages of labour. Her contractions had started almost as soon as Bridie left.

"Hannah!" Bridie flew to her side. "Is the baby coming at last?"

"Yes! It's killing me!" shrieked Hannah, and bit down on a roll of cloth Ellen offered her.

"She ain't fully dilated yet," said Ellen, "But you're doin' good, sugar.

Real good." She brushed away some hair from her forehead.

"I'll get Sadie." Bridie backed away.

"Don't go, Bridie! Hold my hand!"

Bridie went to her side a little fearfully, but she took her friend's hand between both hers and kissed it. "I won't leave you, alanna." Hannah's nails dug into her flesh as a wave of pain washed over her, but she didn't flinch.

A rush of wetness between Hannah's legs soaked the sheet beneath her.

Ellen looked at the spreading dampness. "Aint no time to go gettin' no Sadie now." She reached under Hannah's nightgown. "Yup, I can feel the top of its head. This baby's near ready to be born."

"Do you know much about babies, Ellen? I haven't a notion. I could fly like the wind for Sadie – I'd be back before you knew I was gone, Hannah."

"No! I'm starting to push! Stay here with me! Ellen know what to do, don't you, Ellen?" She was panting and red-faced.

"I've birthed more babies than you've had hot dinners, little lady. Now everything's gonna be fine and dandy. You just push when I says to push. Bridie, fetch me some towels, clean ones, mind, and boil up a big pot of water."

Bridie shot across the room, while Ellen murmured a comforting stream of words.

Time seemed elastic to Hannah. She knew her baby's head was emerging from between her legs and her labour was progressing rapidly. But in her mind the pace slowed to a standstill. She pushed and panted, clinging to Bridie's hands, but her dazed eyes saw Tom O'Brien instead of Bridie Ryan. She smiled through the pain. "Tom, I dreamed I lost you," she gasped, but all Bridie and Ellen heard was a muttered jumble.

Tom O'Brien watches Hannah's minnow craft make its inching progress towards the ocean, adrenaline coursing through his veins. I managed to get my girl into a lifeboat! She'd have been just as happy back in Doon if I hadn't talked her into trying our luck further afield – I'm the one who put her in danger. But at least I've done right by her.

As Hannah's boat steers for open sea, the Titanic's *deck tilts dangerously, groaning, and sets him reeling. He braces himself against the ship's rail, the* first shockwave of fear skidding through him. But the gentleman next to him, the American who surrendered his seat to Hannah, radiates poise. Immaculate in white tie, only his fair hair looks ruffled, and even that is soon rectified as he unconsciously smoothes it back with one hand. Tom wishes he could match his composure.

Samuel Armstrong is debating a return to his suite: he could sit on that well-upholstered sofa, pour himself a cocktail and wait for the abyss like a gentleman. Where is his valet? He hasn't seen Pfiffor since just before handing Nancy into the lifeboat. Oh yes, his man said he would go back to their stateroom to pack because there was talk of transferring to another vessel. At least I'll have company, he thinks. Pfiffor would mix his martini just so, and the façade could be maintained until the end.

Unaware of Tom's scrutiny, he produces a slim silver case and extracts a cigarette, tamping it on the back of his hand. He rummages through a pocket for his lighter.

By a churning effort of will to impose a similar sang-froid, Tom manages to strike a match on the sole of his boot. He offers it, a tremor in his hand. Samuel rests two fingers lightly on the Irishman's hand as he shelters the flame, and Tom sees he has buffed nails.

"Thank you," he says, without particularly noticing Tom.

"Thank you," Tom responds, in a tone that causes Samuel Armstrong to squint at him though a spiral of smoke. "My Hannah got your seat."

"Good. I'm glad."

Tom wants to say something else, something to express his gratitude adequately, but just then they hear a noise that spreads consternation: water gurgling up the forward companionway from the deck below.

They glance at each other in concern; there is a heavy pitch forward now. Though it is only a matter of some feet, they retreat instinctively to the rail at the end of the deck, overlooking the after well deck. They find themselves peering down at a chanting throng — a hundred-strong crowd offering responses to the Rosary. They are the Third Class, overlooked in every sense.

Tom rubs his fingertips against the rosary beads his mother pressed upon him as he left home, the prayers soaring up to him and further above, soothing in their familiarity. He isn't intending to go down without a fight but he might as well have absolution. Just in case. He nods at Samuel, who nods back.

"Good luck to you," says Tom.

"*Same to you.*" *Armstrong understands his need to be among his people.*

After a difficult descent, watched by eyes astonished that anyone should be coming down *from topside, Tom O'Brien staggers towards a priest with a thatch of white eyebrows who is giving general absolution.*

Samuel has stopped watching his receding shape. He doesn't believe in God – not even as shipwreck looms. Samuel regards religion as hocus pocus. Suddenly he remembers the Airedale terrier he bought for his son as a peace offering, because Adam took the divorce to heart. The kennels are probably flooded – poor beast must be drowned by now, he thinks. Samuel became a father a few days short of his 22nd birthday, and he sometimes feels he had less control over the boy's upbringing than he'd like. It was easier to allow his mother to sweep in, to inculcate Adam into the family ethos, than to stand up to her. Damn it all, the senior Armstrongs have as much charity in them as the stone baptismal fonts and stained-glass windows they donate regularly to churches. No, he won't pray now, not to the God they worship. They rounded on him over his plan to divorce Cora and replace her with Nancy. "Divorce is vulgar, Samuel. There was never a vulgar bone in an Armstrong body," his mother said. At thirty-six, he is unpleasantly aware he pays more attention to his mother than other men of his age. Still, he defied her for Nancy's sake. She reacted with a sense of personal injury. "All very well for the old girl – she wasn't yoked to Cora," he mutters. Cora, who wore a hairshirt of martyrdom if he so much as kissed her.

Samuel realizes he is wasting time revisiting grievances. The ship is sinking fast – he shan't go down with it! He must find a way to survive – he has every reason to live. He loves his bride and wants to share her lifetime. They have only spent three months together, nowhere near enough time. Only a week ago she paid a visit to a doctor in London (secretive little minx, she claimed a new ballgown required another fitting). That evening, pouring him a glass of bourbon, Nancy's eyes glowed above the crystal decanter as she whispered he was to be a father again. "You've given me another chance," said Samuel, pressing his lips to Nancy's hand. He brought her to dinner at Simpson's in the Strand, admiring her hourglass shape as she preceded him up the narrow staircase to the dining room for saddle of mutton, to which the English had a fanatical attachment.

Samuel's brow clouds as the irony of his situation impinges. This pregnancy is the reason they are hurrying home from their wedding tour. He needs to reach New York to meet his lawyer and amend his will. Everything is tied up in trust for Adam, with no provision for another child. They left New York in a tearing hurry, in his eagerness to put at least one continent and preferably two between his bride and the scandalmongers. Samuel squares his shoulders, purposeful: he'll find that designer fellow, Andrews, and ask him the best place to go if he should stand any chance. He must survive. Another son, this one with a woman he loves – that's worth living for.

* * *

Tom O'Brien isn't satisfied with a general absolution from the priest. God helps those who help themselves, he thinks, shouldering his way to the front of the throng. "Bless me, Father, for I have sinned."

Father Thomas Byles turns towards him in surprise. There is no time to recite individual sins. The priest pats Tom on the shoulder. "Say the sin into your heart, my son – all of you! – tell God you're truly sorry and recite the Act of Contrition. Have no fear, his forgiveness is infinite. Ego vos absolvo a peccatis vobis, in nomine Patris et Filii et Spiritus Sancti . . ."

It is a little after two as Tom walks away from the prayers.

"Irish!" calls a Cockney voice. It's Charlie Chadband, the steward. "Girls get off OK?"

"They did. Thanks for showing us that ladder. The girls would've been too late for the boats if you hadn't given us a head-start.'"

"Seemed a shame not to give 'em a fighting chance."

Charlie is tying on a lifebelt found abandoned on a bench. Some people are taking theirs off, claiming the bulk will hamper swimming. Movement is awkward in them, with their six cork blocks in separate pouches, front and back.

"Ain't you got one of these?"

Tom shrugs. "Gave it away to a girl. She didn't manage to get in a boat and was in a bit of a state."

"Maybe you're as well without. I'll tell you this for nothing, mate, if I get out of here alive I'm never going to sea again – fiver a month or no fiver a month."

"First and last time for me an' all."

They smile faintly and clasp hands, neither daring to meet the other's eyes.

Just then the ship gives a great lurch. Tom's jaw sags. Over Charlie's shoulder he sees a towering wall of water bearing down on them, propelling before it an assortment of furniture. It is a writhing, foaming charge of death. "Look out!" he cries. The ship suddenly upends, pivots wildly, and both men are pitched through space to the sea.

Tom O'Brien learned to swim one summer as a child, splashing in the pond in a farmhouse near his home. The fellow who taught him promised it was a skill he'd never forget. Tom's legs and arms know to kick out as soon as they strike water. But kicking is ineffectual. He is caught in a whirlpool, suctioned down by the ship's descent.

The lights snap off and bedlam reigns. Charlie surges to the surface of the ocean, spluttering and disorientated. His flailing hands strike against something buoyant and he clings to it blindly. He can't see, but the noise is deafening, with people screaming all around him – a boiling mass of seething, terrified humanity churning up the water. Armageddon has come early. He is oblivious to all but the struggle to survive. He can discern a dark hump – there's something about the shape – it's an Engelhardt! It's overturned, there was no time left to launch it. He strikes out for the turtle-top. Some men have already reached the squat wooden boat and are sitting on top, exhausted. The din is frantic, a cacophony of fear and blind panic. Charlie guesses some swimmers are being hacked away from lifeboats. He forms a strategy, mind racing in his compulsion to live. "I'll tip you all in if I can't get on," he'll threaten, and they'll have to let him board. Charlie tries to straddle the floating keg or crate that holds him up, thinking to paddle it to the Engelhardt, but upends and hurtles back to the water. He hits the crown of his head against a clunking piece of debris and sprawls unconscious, the water closing over his nose and mouth. And still the lifebelt hoists his torso afloat.

* * *

Tom's body tumbles and pirouettes the long fall to the ocean floor. He has managed to take a deep breath before being pulled under, and if he can hold it long enough might be able to break free and strike out for the surface. But the force of the vortex imprisons him, spinning him downward until his lungs are strained almost to breaking point.

Half a mile away, Hannah is sobbing. "Tom, we must go back for Tom!"

Far below, he is conscious only of his heartbeat roaring in his eardrums.

"I wanted to tell you about our baby, Tom, I never got the chance," she cries, as pain sears his lungs and he thinks they must surely explode.

Tom O'Brien's jacket – with a fistful of earth in its pocket from the home farm in Bonavie – is dragged from his body by the water's powerful updraught. He is not concerned with Hannah as the last seconds of his life recede at breakneck speed. Or with her desire to tell what is too late for him to hear. He can hold his breath no longer. The bubbles of his last breath are yanked savagely from his body and salt water punches into his lungs.

Hannah is nowhere in his thoughts – he is incapable of organized thought now. He loved her, wanted to build a life around her, yet there is only one face in his mind as he loses consciousness. His lips move, forming a word.

"Mama!"

* * *

"Congratulations – Mama!" Bridie's voice rose above a baby's indignant wail. "It's a beautiful baby girl." Ellen held the child wrapped in a towel, cooing at her, while Bridie stripped off Hannah's soaking nightgown. Bridie was careful not to look at the infant – nervous the sight of a newborn baby might remind her of a tiny bundle buried on the Hill of Oola. Not wanting to think about it but seeing it in her mind's eye anyhow. "We're going to get you all cleaned up, Hannah, and then you can nurse your little girl."

Hannah accepted her daughter from Ellen and absorbed the rose-pink mouth, the bloodied forehead with a faint frown feathered on it, the nose she already thinks she recognizes as Tom's. Exhaustion melted away. "She's perfect. My daughter is absolutely perfect. Imagine, I'm a mother!"

"What will you call her, Hannah?"

"I don't know – she would have been Tom if she was a girl. What name would you choose, Bridie?"

"Marian. If she were mine, I'd call her Marian."

Hannah paused, still peering fixedly at the tiny, screwed-up face. "Marian," she said. "Or Marion? "Yes, I think she'd like to be Marion." She looked up at Bridie, then Ellen, her face radiant. "Marion Ethel

O'Brien. My little American."

"Happy birthday, Marion." Tentatively, Bridie drew nearer to the baby. She stretched out her index finger towards the minuscule fist, which clamped shut on the digit with an atavistic grip. The tiny mite yawned, opening eyes that were unfocused, not seeing the woman bent over her. As Bridie stared at her, some maternal chord she hadn't known lay dormant within her rustled.

Hannah's voice was muffled as she kissed her baby. "Guess what day it is, Bridie. It's one of those American celebrations – Ellen's been telling me about it. What's it called again, Ellen?"

Ellen leaned over from the other side of the bed and beamed at the baby. "Today is Thanksgiving Day. Your li'l girl a Thanksgiving baby."

* * *

Louis finalised his arrangements in a numb state. He refused to think of Nancy, to say her name or allow her face to appear before him: he knew he had to disengage from her, just as she had shucked him off. *I managed well enough before meeting her and I'll manage again without her.* He told himself his heart was bruised but not permanently damaged as, with careful deliberation, he packed it in ice.

Three hours before the Philadelphia train was due to leave, he caught a hansom across the Brooklyn Bridge to the address he had been given. The house he was looking for was located next to a boatyard. A man with a hare-lip answered the door.

"Bleever sent me," said Louis.

The transaction was swiftly completed and Louis found himself back on the street with a bag of dollars instead of gold nuggets.

He did not immediately hail another cab to take him to the train station. Instead he wandered along to the boatyard, pushing against the double doors with the tip of his boot. They squeaked and gave way. He peered in but it was too gloomy to see anything. He stepped inside and took a few moments, blinking, to adjust to the half-light. Louis sniffed stale air overlaid with a slight saltiness. It seemed empty of people, but towards the rear of the room he noticed a group of low, bulky shapes. As though prodded forward, he made his way to them. Lengths of canvas

were thrown over the oblongs, and he lifted the edge of one to
investigate what it protected. It was a lifeboat. Louis flung off the
covering, knowledge prickling the hairs on the back of his neck before
his eyes confirmed it.

He was looking at one of the salvaged *Titanic* lifeboats.

Like a man demented, he raced from shape to shape, hurling the
coverings on the ground. Before him were fourteen *Titanic* lifeboats,
mouldering away. Only two had their original nameplates and many
were missing oars, but there was no disguising their origins. Louis
searched until he found Lifeboat 16. He stood looking at it, reliving
those hours spent on board wearing Nancy's ashes of roses cloak. Then
he stepped inside and felt along the bottom. The wood was still damp to
the touch, and he fancied it was moisture from the Atlantic Ocean,
although it could simply have been from the Brooklyn atmosphere.

He did not know what he was searching for until his knuckles
connected with something solid. He lifted out a suede bag and a gold
christening mug emerged. It was too dim to discern the initials LSS but
the pads of flesh at his fingertips groped over the hole where a ruby had
been embedded, and reached the mounds where two more clung to their
setting.

Louis cradled the christening mug against a cheek, the metal cold
against his flesh. This was where his identity had lain, all these months:
it had rolled between the planks of a lifeboat and wedged itself into a
dark crevice. Waiting for him. He tucked the christening mug into his
overcoat pocket, shooting glances left and right in case he was observed,
and quickly made his way back out to the sunlit street, Louis went
straight to Pennsylvania Station. At the Left Luggage lockers, he
collected his bag. There were still twenty minutes before the
Philadelphia train was due to leave, although it stood alongside the
platform. He leaned against a hoarding, watching passengers board,
wreathed in coils of steam from incoming and outgoing trains. A
sandwich-board man shambled past with a Coca-Cola advertisement on
his back: *Demand the genuine. Refuse substitutes.* Coloured porters bustled
around, trunks were wheeled to the luggage car and whistles sliced the
air. It was a scene of organized chaos. "All aboard for Philadelphia!"
came a shout from the conductor. "Last call for Philly and all points

south!" A clang, a shudder, a door banging shut, a great burst of steam and the train slowly shifted forward, gained speed and writhed from the station.

Louis picked up his bag and turned for the exit. He needed to go back to Washington Square and return the Brooklyn dollars to the major's desk, His ardour for Nancy had clouded his judgment – he would not steal from a corpse, as the Keppels had done. All his life he had felt excluded: the only proof of having belonged, once, was an initialled christening mug. But pushing through the station doors, he realized a sense of belonging was not just a birthright. It was a choice. A man could live apart from people, or he could decide to live among them. His heart had chosen Nancy Armstrong. Now he must use his head to find a way for them to be together. It would not be easy but the prize was worth the struggle. Louis touched his christening mug and was comforted by its outline. This relic of his old life would help him keep faith in the new.

Suddenly a word reverberated through his head. Vienna.

You must leave your love to find her again. You must go home.

"*To Paris?*"

Vienna.

* * *

"You can have it back now." Edmund darted an anxious glance at the red-haired bundle on his knee, which he was holding as though nursing a bag of eggs. Babies leaked, he knew that much. It was only a matter of time before there was a damp patch on his good broadcloth trousers.

Bridie laughed at him. "You don't look like a man who's been around children much."

"On the contrary. I helped raise my sister, Minerva. I even chose her name – Roman Goddess of Wisdom, you know."

"That was twenty-odd years ago."

"It's very small, this baby. I hope I don't drop it."

"It's she, not 'it', and she's only three days old. Of course she's small."

"Here, Edmund, pass Marion over to me, she's probably ready for a feed." Hannah took pity on him and reached for her daughter, settling her against her shoulder.

"Will we take the air, Edmund?" Bridie pinned on her hat as she spoke.

They meandered as far as a small patch of grass where a bench invited them to sit. It was a crisp, autumnal afternoon, the sky reddened by a sun just failing to break through. They were companionable there, side by side, her shoulder brushing his upper arm. Edmund felt bathed in a glow of well-being. This must be love – imagine, all these years he had thought love to be delirium, a burning, thrashing sensation, when it was a soothing blanket of warmth. Love struck him as an absence of care, of struggle, of agitation. He thought how their life together would be one of peaceful, uneventful happiness. A set of church bells pealed and he was on the brink of slipping his hand around Bridie's waist when she spoke.

"I'm grateful to you, Edmund, for the offer you made me. Any woman would be honoured to be your wife. But I can't do it. I can't say yes to you."

His confidence, which had soared as she began, lost altitude. He swallowed. "I know you don't love me now but you could grow to, in time."

"I could," she agreed, more from pity than conviction. "But it's not marriage I'm looking for, at least not yet a while."

"What then?" He was mystified, for what else could there be for a woman?

"I want to open a milliner's shop. I want to be my own woman."

"I could never agree to my wife working. It wouldn't be seemly. People would think I couldn't afford to keep her."

"I know. That's why I'm sorry, Edmund, but I can't marry you."

"It means that much to you, having a shop?"

She nodded.

"Shops go bust all the time. There's more to business than filling a shop with fancy goods and waiting for customers to beat a path to your door."

"I understand that."

"Where will you get the capital? Start-up money's needed. You can't expect credit straight off, without a record."

"It's my dream, Edmund. We all need one." Bridie reached out a hand towards Edmund. It hovered in the air before falling back into her lap. "What will you do now, yourself?"

"I've had an offer to go to a place called Hollywood. Jules Brulatour wants me to take a look at some land he's thinking of buying – he plans to expand the studio and build a series of permanent sets for his moving pictures. Other studios are setting up there. First, though, I told Stuart I'd finish his father's book for him. I owe the major that much."

Bridie lowered her eyes at the mention of Stuart's name.

Edmund was bleak. He found himself with the superstitious feeling that the gods had created happiness and subsequently regretted it – punishing those who experienced joy.

After Edmund had taken his leave, gracious despite his disappointment, Bridie made her way to Washington Square, awed by the grandeur of the houses. Mrs Burdich admitted her to 12b and left Bridie waiting in the hallway while she went to inform Stuart he had a visitor. She clomped back to Bridie.

"Young master says he'll see you in his father's study."

Stuart was playing the phonograph and drinking burgundy when she was shown in. He offered her a glass from the near-empty bottle but she declined. "Gee, I forgot, you're the girl who only drinks champagne," he teased. "We can have some now, if you like, I'll ring for old Burdy to fetch a bottle."

"No, don't, Stuart. I want to talk to you."

He emptied his glass at a swallow and pulled her down beside him on the brown leather Chesterfield, a tango throbbing in the background. "I'm so lonely, Bridie, I can't bear it here on my own. I've missed you so much."

He began nuzzling her and she relaxed into his embrace, enjoying the sensation of his tongue flickering against an earlobe. Clumsy with drink, he scratched her neck with his tie-pin, and she sprang to her feet.

"Stop pawing me, Stuart. You're tight and it's only three o'clock."

"I'm bored, Bridie. I didn't know what else to do but have a glass of wine or two. I hate being on my own. It's so elderly in here, there's no life or energy about the place. I'm going to sell all these old relics of Pa's." He stood and emptied the dregs of the wine into his glass. When he turned to face her again, his tone was wheedling. "What do you say, Bridie, are you game? I have the money now to make your dream come true. Remember how you used to tell me about it when we'd stroll along Broadway, happy as larks? We could have fun together, you and I."

"We could have fun," she agreed. "But I have to dance to your tune if I play with you."

"It's a fair bargain, you agreed it was."

"It's not one you'd have dared make while Major Hudson, God rest him, was alive. But his corpse is hardly cold and you're up to tricks that would make your father spin in his grave."

"Are you turning me down?"

Bridie twirled a curl, taking her time before answering. "You're willing to set me up in a little place as your mistress. I'll have trips to the theatre and holidays, and you'll give me an allowance and take care of all the bills. I'll want for nothing, those were your words. I can have a maid, just like a lady, and you'll open an account at a dressmaker's for me. All I have to do in return is be nice to you."

"Would that be so difficult?"

"No, it wouldn't be hard at all. You said I could save my allowance if I liked and, if I put enough by, after a few years I'd have earned the price of that milliner's shop I always wanted. If I still wanted it then, you said."

"New York is full of girls who'd jump through hoops for an offer like that."

"It is." She folded her hands in front of her in a curiously demure stance.

"So, yes or no, Bridie? You've kept me dangling long enough. Look, I have a gift for you, to show good faith." He crossed to his father's desk, rooted in a pigeonhole and produced a cameo ring of his mother's.

"See? I promised you pretty things."

Unable to help herself, she slipped it on her finger. It took real willpower to tug it off and set it on the arm of the sofa. "No."

"It's that Catholicism of yours, isn't it? You're frightened it's a sin. It's not a sin, it's natural."

"It's not sins that frighten me – it's selling myself. I can give myself away but I can't put a price on my head. I don't know if dreams really do come true in America, I suppose they can't come true for all of us. But I might be one of the lucky ones and I'll never know unless I try."

"I can help you make your dream come true."

"No, you'll only hold me back. It's a house-pet you want, not a woman, Stuart Hudson. Good luck to you. Try to live up to your father."

Bridie left so abruptly she collided with Mrs Burdich listening at the keyhole.

* * *

Hannah lifted her daughter and pressed her lips against the infant's skin, delighting in its puffball texture. "I had a visitor while you were out, Bridie. A clerk for a law firm called. He left his card on the table."

Bridie picked it up. "*Appleby, Parker and Mareuil.* Swanky address."

"At first I thought it might be the O'Briens again, but I don't think it has anything to do with them. The clerk said it was good news. He wouldn't tell me any more, except I'm to call to their offices at 3246 East 65th Street tomorrow morning and ask for a gentleman by the name of F Chester Parker. I'll get Ellen to mind Marion for an hour or two."

"Is it the *Titanic* compensation money coming through, do you think?"

"What else can it be?"

"It's just that Danny's been asking around and he's hearing it could be years yet before anything's paid out. Maybe they've speeded your case up because of the baby. Did he say anything at all, the clerk?"

"Just that it would be to my advantage."

* * *

Hannah hesitated at the door of the skyscraper on East 65th Street. A uniformed doorman stood to attention outside its imposing facade, while the people going through the revolving door looked well heeled. She felt shabby, even with one of Bridie's silk roses in her hat.

"No chickening out on me, Hannah O'Brien." Bridie caught her by the arm and frogmarched her in.

A receptionist cast a wintry eye over them.

Bridie refused to be cowed. "We're here to see Chester Parker."

"F Chester Parker," corrected the receptionist.

"He'll do just as well."

"State your business with him, please."

"He sent over a fellow to say he had business with us. Tell him it's Mrs Hannah O'Brien."

The receptionist lifted a shiny black telephone and dialled an internal number. She murmured down the line, before replacing the receiver. "You may go up. Second floor from the top. The elevator's over there to the right."

Hannah had never been in an elevator and clutched her friend's arm. Even Bridie was loathe to get into the cage with a metal grill at the front that slid open to admit passengers, but she was too proud to show fear in front of the lift attendant. They stepped in gingerly and the Buttons, white-gloved, fussed with a lever. The elevator pinged. "Going up."

A clerk met them on the nineteenth floor and brought them to an oval room where a man with the bearing of a bishop awaited them. "Mrs O'Brien." His pale eyes bored into Hannah. "During his lifetime I had the privilege of acting for Major Richmond Hudson and it's my sad duty to carry out his wishes after his death."

"We were at the funeral," interrupted Bridie.

"A moving occasion. Major Hudson was a prudent man and made his will some years previously, but several weeks before his death he paid me a visit with a number of codicils. Among them was a reference to you, Mrs O'Brien."

"Me? Sure I hardly knew the major. He was a lovely gentleman and all, but I only met him in April. We were on the same lifeboat after the *Titanic*."

"When dramatic events throw people together, a bond can develop. Major Hudson obviously took an, ah, avuncular interest in your progress, Mrs O'Brien, and your unfortunate situation must have touched him. It's my pleasant duty to inform you that you're the beneficiary of a bequest."

"What does he mean?" Hannah turned to Bridie.

"Are you saying the major's after going and leaving money to Hannah?"

"Indeed. A legacy in the sum of ten thousand dollars" – he

enunciated the figure slowly – "is bequeathed to Mrs Hannah O'Brien, formerly of County Limerick, Ireland, and now of New York City. He also left a letter for you, Mrs O'Brien, which I shall now hand over." An ivory envelope was passed to her. "I'll leave you for a few moments to absorb its contents."

Parker retreated to an adjoining office whose door fitted seamlessly into the panelling.

* * *

My Dear Hannah,

I hope I have earned the right to call you that.

Money solves many problems, although not all. It struck me it could alleviate some difficulties which may confront you after the birth of your child. I have not forgotten our conversation on the night of the moving pictures premiére, when you confided how you feared your financial situation might lead to the loss of your baby. Your plight brought it home to me how vulnerable a lack of funds can leave people.

Please believe me when I say I truly wish you well and have your very best interests at heart.

Yours sincerely

Richmond Hudson

Hannah thought how you could endure any amount of suffering, but be uravelled by an unexpected act of kindness. A tear trickled down her cheek as she passed the letter to Bridie, who had been attempting to read it over her shoulder.

"Hannah, you're an heiress!" She shot a wide-eyed stare at her friend. "I never knew you were such pals with the old boy."

"Neither did I." Hannah swung her simple, trusting gaze on Bridie and banished the suspicion that had stirred.

"So what are you going to do, Hannah?"

"I haven't a notion. $10,000 is a fortune."

"It'll go a long way, that's for sure."

It occurred to Bridie to wonder how Stuart felt about his patrimony being dispersed. Then she shrugged. He wouldn't go hungry. The connecting door re-opened.

"Everything in order, I trust?"

"Yes, thank you!" they chorused.

"Excellent." Parker's eyes drifted to the letter but he was too polite to ask outright to see it. "So there's nothing you need my advice on?"

"No, sir, not at present," said Hannah.

"In that case, it only remains for me to give you a cheque, Mrs O'Brien. We can arrange to pay it directly into your bank account, if you like. It's rather a large sum to carry about, even in the form of a cheque."

"I have no bank account."

"I see. Would you like me to arrange for one to be opened for you?"

"No, thank you, sir, a cheque made out in my name will be more suitable."

"Very well. In that case, may I suggest you take a cab home? It's safer – and you can certainly afford it."

* * *

They sat back as New York clopped past them.

"Imagine Major Hudson being so generous to you, Hannah. Aren't you the lucky one!"

"What's mine is yours, Bridie – we're both lucky."

"I'm just happy for you, *alanna*."

"But, Bridie, it goes without saying you're going to share this – I mean to do something for you. I know, I'll set you up in that milliner's shop you want. We can be partners."

Bridie's dark eyes were lambent. "No bosses – just us? You'd do that for me, Hannah?"

Hannah squeezed her hand.

Bridie sighed and settled back in her seat. "This is the life! You know what I'd love to do now, Hannah? I'd love this cab to drive along Fifth Avenue. That's where all the swells live. Wouldn't it be something to take a look at their mansions, and us sitting at our ease inside our own set of wheels?"

"Knock on the roof and tell the driver," Hannah invited. "We can afford it, F Chester Parker says so."

The cab turned up Fifth Avenue, slowing obligingly so they could gawk. Outside a particularly imposing mansion, with black railings and a tier of granite steps leading to the front door, they saw a woman with fluffy yellow hair.

"It's that Mrs Markova, Mrs Armstrong's mother." Bridie tugged at Hannah's sleeve.

"Do you think she'd mind if we asked whether Mrs Armstrong had her baby safely, Bridie?"

"I don't see why not. Driver, could you pull over here?" Bridie leaned out of the window. "Begging your pardon, Mrs Markova!"

Violet was inclined to ignore this common person, hailing her from a cab. She presented her back and addressed a remark to the footman.

"Not like that, Bridie, it's not proper." Hannah jumped out and approached Violet, dropping a curtsey. "Forgive my presuming on you, ma'am. I don't suppose you remember me but we met at Major Hudson's funeral."

Violet turned at the major's name, without recognizing Hannah. "Indeed?" She looked like a shop girl, and she had no interest in her. "Watts, did you remember to put extra rugs in the carriage?"

Just then Nancy emerged from the house, picking her steps as she held her infant son close.

"Mrs Armstrong, you've had your baby, same as me! Congratulations! Isn't it wonderful, after the *Titanic* sinking and us in that lifeboat not knowing if we'd ever see land again, and now we both have our babies, safe and sound!"

Hannah's round face was alight with pleasure and Nancy could not help smiling at her. She drew closer and moved a corner of the fleecy blanket away from her son's face. "Would you like to see him? His name is Samuel Frost Armstrong the Fourth, after his father."

"So you had a boy, Mrs Armstrong – I'm delighted for you, honest to God I am. I had a little girl myself. Marion. Marion Ethel O'Brien. You never saw such a darling child. But yours is a fine boy." She cooed into the face of the sleeping infant. "He's going to grow up handsome. Big and strong and handsome, just like his dada."

"You knew my husband?" Nancy frowned, some memory of having seen Hannah before plucking at her.

"Not exactly, ma'am. But he did me a good turn I'll remember 'til the day I die. My little Marion wouldn't be alive today if it weren't for your husband. He was a hero, Mr Armstrong, nothing more and nothing less than a hero."

Nancy blossomed, hearing her husband praised. "Samuel was the kindest of men. How did he help you, Mrs . . .?"

"O'Brien. Hannah. Why, don't you know? He jumped out of a lifeboat as it was leaving the *Titanic* and gave me his place. He saved my life."

Nancy gasped, winded.

"You're the woman my Samuel died for? I begged him not to do it, I pleaded with him. But he wouldn't listen."

Hannah faltered. "Yes, ma'am, he insisted I go in his place. I never asked for Mr Armstrong to do it, I wouldn't have dreamed of such a thing. But now I have my little Marion thanks to him."

Nancy clutched her baby so close that he awoke and cheeped. Above his bald head, her face radiated accusation at Hannah.

The Irishwoman tried to think of something to console her. "I saw him blow you a kiss, Mrs Armstrong, it was one of the last things he did. I thought he looked so distinguished there, with the ship sinking and your husband never letting on there was anything to worry about – just smiling away and blowing you a kiss."

Nancy glanced down at her baby squinting up at the cloudy sky. "My son lost his father so your daughter could be born."

"Why, ma'am, I'm desperate sorry that's how it worked out. All I wanted to do was thank you in your husband's name. I meant no offence. He did a fine thing, a noble thing. Your boy will grow up to be proud of him. And I'll teach my Marion to remember him in her prayers."

A range of emotions played across Nancy's features. Her mother bustled over and tried to take Samuel from her, but she held on tight. "I'm taking him to see his grandmother – his other grandmother," said Nancy. "She doesn't know we're coming, it's a surprise."

Hannah stretched out a finger and touched Samuel's cheek. "What grandmother wouldn't like the chance to cuddle this gorgeous fellow? I'm only sorry my mother's an ocean away and can't see Marion."

"You wouldn't know with this grandmother, but we'll give her a chance. She has a heart of ice but maybe my Sam can melt it."

"I'm sure he can."

"We must be going now, Nancy," said Violet. "It's not good for Baby, standing about in the cold." She shepherded her daughter and grandson towards their carriage, which stood importantly beside Hannah and Bridie's more humble hansom.

"Don't boss me so, Momma! You promised to quit treating me like a little girl. I'm a momma now myself." Nevertheless Nancy allowed herself to be led. But as she reached the open door of the vehicle she paused. "Would you bring your baby to see mine some time, Hannah? I'd like them to know each other. They both lost their fathers in the same way."

"Is that wise, Nancy?" intervened Violet.

"I believe so, Momma. I think Samuel would like it. I'd ask Mama Carmen only she seems to have disappeared. I can't understand why she'd just go off like that without saying anything to me."

"Yes, well, never mind about her."

Bridie, who had been craning her neck from the cab, could bear feeling peripheral no longer. She jumped out – ignoring the driver's cry of protest – and whirled up to peep at Baby Samuel. "He's twice the size of our Marion, Hannah – but sure that's boys for you." She threw a critical eye over Violet and Nancy's headgear. "I'm opening a milliner's premises. When I have some cards printed up I'll drop them off. I could do wonders for you, ladies. The right hat can take years off a woman." She looked meaningfully at Violet Markova.

Violet opened her mouth and closed it. You can't tell when a girl is a servant any more, she thought. All that finery, aping her betters – it shouldn't be allowed.

"Oh see, your little fellow is smiling!" exclaimed Hannah.

"Wind!" snapped Violet, recovering herself.

"I'll invite you and – is it Marion? – over some day," said Nancy. "Watts! Our card. Now wish us luck with Sam's grandmother."

Hannah waved reassuringly to the cabbie, who was looking anxious about his fare. She beamed at the baby boy. "Just pop him into her arms and watch that bonny lad win her over. No bother to him."

28

New York April 14th 1913

"It's our stop next, Hannah. You get ready and I'll ring the bell."
Bridie Ryan and Hannah O'Brien stepped from the omnibus, the conductor helping Hannah with her pram, and they cut through Central Park towards Fifth Avenue.

"I wish we'd taken a hansom cab," grumbled Bridie. "Imagine arriving on foot. It looks like we haven't a penny to bless ourselves."

Hannah smiled at the serious little face of her daughter peeking from the pram – a creature as fine-boned as her father but with her mother's copper hair. "Money's hard earned – we can't afford to go throwing it away. And sure the streetcar's handy."

Bridie swished her umbrella along the flower borders, accidentally decapitating a tulip. She knew her friend spoke sense, but it was fun to splurge from time to time. Hannah's trouble was she had no sense of occasion.

"I hope we have the right day," fretted Hannah.

"April 14th, there's no forgetting the date." Bridie counted house numbers. "It should be the next one. Imagine the view from these houses – they must be able to see clear into the park."

"This is the place, I remember those railings."

"Wonder how many servants it takes to run it. It's some humdinger."

"You and your Americanisms, Bridie Ryan. It's a grand house, though. Should we go in the front or . . .?"

Left hanging in the air was the suggestion they use the servants' entrance.

"'Course we go through the front door! Aren't we as good as anybody else? We were invited here fair and square, same as the others." Bridie tilted her chin in the air, marched up the steps and jammed her finger on the doorbell.

At the park gates behind them was Edmund Newton, limbs flapping in an invisible breeze as he walked at his usual breakneck speed. He was nervous, his Adam's apple working awkwardly above his collar, and he winced at the frayed end of his shoelaces as he pressed the doorbell a few minutes after the girls. He'd look as though he couldn't afford a new pair, instead of being too busy with work. A uniformed footman admitted him. As he stepped onto the red and cream chequerboard flooring of the hallway, he encountered a gangly fifteen-year-old with a baby in his arms.

"Have you met my brother Sam?" asked Adam Armstrong.

"A five-month-old Buddha in a sailor suit surveyed Edmund. Gingerly, he patted the fair head, at which the child emitted a howl and Edmund snatched away his hand. "Babies have never liked me."

The doorbell sounded again. Watts opened it and there was Stuart Hudson, natty in canary-yellow tie and gloves.

"Have you met my brother Sam?"

He's a baby." Stuart's tone implied nothing further need be said on the subject.

"You're dressed for a celebration." Edmund tried and failed to delete the critical undertone.

"I understood we were celebrating. Some people survived the sinking, after all."

"More people didn't."

"This is neither a celebration nor a wake. It's a commemoration." Nancy Armstrong materialised at Adam's side and held out her arms for her son. She wore black from tip to toe, but her mourning was alleviated by the smiles she lavished on the baby, who poked his fist into her hair and dislodged a waterfall of waves.

"That child is ready for a nap," announced Rebecca Armstrong, descending the stairs. "Why is everyone congregating in the hall? There is a perfectly serviceable salon in this house." With garish frescoes, she added mentally, but for once held her peace. Even she was not immune to the significance of the anniversary.

Nancy led the way upstairs.

Nancy's mother, Violet Markova, was already in situ: a little plumper, a little more discontented than before, even with a cruise to look forward to soon. Just a short one, however. Rebecca didn't want their grandson out of the country for long. Violet was restless with only Bridie, Hannah and baby Marion for company – Violet always felt time spent with women was time wasted. Besides, these Irish girls weren't their sort. She was completely in favour of being pleasant to the other classes: this was the United States of America, after all, not some feudal European statelet. But inviting them into a person's home was taking democracy to extremes. Violet sparkled into life, however, at the sight of Edmund and Stuart.

Left to their own devices, Bridie and Hannah were free to examine their surroundings. Overawed at the elegance of this formal, neo-classical room, Hannah made herself as unobtrusive as possible and looked around in cautious wonder, while little Marion chewed a fist on her lap. She wanted to commit every detail of this afternoon to memory, to tell Ellen and Kathleen. Bridie's glance darted brazenly everywhere. Her hand itched to stroke the damask of the seat coverings, assessing the material, and she longed to check the angle of her hat in a vast bronze mirror that reflected the tips of parlour palms in china pots. She even found time to watch Edmund and Stuart out of the corner of her eye.

Stuart ignored Bridie as roundly as she appeared to ignore him, but Edmund approached the girls and shook hands with first Hannah and then Bridie. Baby Marion he steered clear of, despite her flirtatious drooling in his direction – he knew the instant he paid her any attention she'd scream fit to shatter glass.

"I hear you're quite the businesswoman now, Miss Ryan."

"Ah Edmund, I liked it better when you called me Bridie." Her dark eyes danced.

"I didn't like to presume on our past, ah, acquaintance," stumbled

395

Edmund.

"Presume away," she said, "you have my permission."

Hell's bells, he was blushing like a schoolboy. To cover his confusion, Edmund decided to risk tickling Marion under the chin. The baby squawked in protest and the Englishman looked mortified.

Bridie smiled. "Let's be friends, Edmund. It's not everybody can say they met on a lifeboat in the middle of the Atlantic. We're shipmates, remember?"

"Are we all assembled?" Rebecca Armstrong could not conceal her impatience for the proceedings to start.

"One more to come." Nancy avoided her mother's gaze.

"Stubel?" Stuart Hudson spoke from behind a wreath of smoke.

"Yes, we're waiting for Mr Stubel," said Nancy. "He was in our lifeboat too, after all."

"Perhaps he can't make it," suggested Edmund. "I haven't heard a dickey bird about him in months. Could have done with his help on the major's book, as a matter of fact. Do you know anything about his movements, Hudson?"

"Why should I be in contact with one of my father's former employees?" Stuart blew a smoke ring in the direction of some empty champagne flutes on a sideboard, thinking it high time he was offered refreshment. He could use something – his head was pounding. Maybe he'd overdone it getting liquored up at his club last night. He needed a hair of the dog. If this crowd didn't shape up soon he'd slip outside and have a gargle from his hip flask.

"He may have gone back to France," said Edmund.

Nancy and Violet spoke in unison.

"He'll be here," said Nancy.

"We don't expect him," said Violet.

Flustered, mother and daughter glanced at one another, their eyes sliding away again.

"He'll be here," repeated Nancy.

Rebecca clicked her tongue against the roof of her mouth, checking her watch. "Punctuality is the politeness of kings. I do wish other races would remember that."

"Grandmother!" protested Adam, aware several other races were present in the drawing room. He made eye contact with Nancy, nodding towards the bell used for summoning Watts. His grandmother was apt to fly off the handle. Adam was eager for her to be sidetracked before she said anything too outrageous.

"I do think we ought to allow Mr Stubel some more time," said Nancy, but she took the hint and summoned the footman. "Watts, we're ready to proceed,"

Stuart disengaged himself from Violet Markova – he had no patience for over-primped women who committed the unpardonable sin of being twice his age – and propped an elbow on the mantelpiece. From this vantage point he studied Hannah: so this was the bit of skirt his pa made a fool of himself over. What had gotten into him? She wasn't even a looker. Not like her pal. He watched Bridie covertly. That purple velvet and net hat was ravishing on her. She should be on the stage – she'd hold an audience in the palm of her hand. What the heck, there was nothing to be gained by snubbing the little baggage. He threw his pride to the winds and sauntered over.

Edmund thought that Nancy had an edgy demeanour. She was listening for something – for someone, he corrected himself. It was impossible to miss the crackle between her and her mother, as though a tussle of wills was being played out. Then he was distracted by Bridie, dimpling at some remark Stuart Hudson whispered as he leaned in towards her in what Edmund considered an impertinent way. Really, the fellow should remember he was in a respectable woman's home – a widow at that – and not behave as though he was in a vaudeville theatre. Major Hudson had been an absolute brick; it was preposterous he should have produced such a son.

"A pity Captain Rostron had a prior engagement," said Rebecca. "He conveyed his regrets, of course, but his presence would have been the icing on the cake."

Surprise lent Hannah the courage to speak. "You invited the captain? It would have been wonderful to meet him here, so it would. He sent Marion a christening gift, a fine gold medal that was struck in his honour, on account of his rescuing us. But he still hasn't been introduced to my daughter. He was at sea when we had her christened." She stroked her child's hair at the front of her bonnet, and the baby fastened sombre olive eyes on her mother's face.

"He sent your daughter a christening gift? That was remarkably generous of him." Rebecca was mystified. This pair would have been consigned to the servants' hall by her, given half a chance, but she knew better than to suggest it to her daughter-in-law.

Hannah was unconscious of the condescension but Bridie pounced on it. "Of course he did – isn't he godfather to her."

"Captain Rostron is godfather to this child?" Rebecca was dumbfounded.

"Oh yes, he said he'd be honoured to stand for her." Bridie's earrings – bought from the Fat Man's Pawn Shop, although one day she planned to have some from Tiffany's – jiggled a jerky dance as she nodded. She was enjoying this.

"That was uncommonly charitable of him."

"In what way?" Bridie dared her to say it. They sized up one another. That one has a widow's mouth, thought Bridie.

Watts prevented Rebecca from saying what was in her mind by entering with a tray between white-gloved hands. She needed to supervise him. On the tray stood four bottles of chilled Perrier-Jouet in ice-buckets, a platter containing triangles of toast and a pot of caviar with a Lilliputian silver spoon protruding.

The champagne bottles had been popped and vapour trailed from their necks, reminding Bridie of the haze some claimed had hovered over the spot where the *Titanic* had sunk. She shuddered, remembering the black expanse of ocean they had bobbed around in all night.

"Poor Charlie Chadband," she said, suddenly remembering the steward.

"Poor Tom," sighed Hannah. "I can't believe a whole year has passed already. I feel terrible we were never able to give him a Christian burial. No pennies on his eyelids to show anyone cared enough to close his eyes." Hannah tightened her grip on Marion and the small girl whimpered, but seemed to sense she shouldn't cry out.

Adam stole a slice of toast from the platter and fed morsels to Sam, who crowed and clapped his hands. Watts set down the tray on a sideboard, wrapped a linen napkin around a bottle and began to pour its contents into polished crystal flutes. Stuart perked up. This was more like it.

"I wanted us all to be here." Unable to contain herself, Nancy drummed her fingers on her knees.

"Did Stubel definitely say he'd attend?" asked Edmund.

"He didn't reply at all," admitted Nancy. "But I was convinced . . ." Her voice faded.

Her guests studied her with curiosity. She seemed to be taking Louis Stubel's absence to heart.

Aware of their scrutiny, Violet cast around for a diversion. She overheard Rebecca decline a glass of champagne on behalf of her grandson, saying Adam was too young for intoxicating spirits and, greatly daring, Violet overruled her. "Come, now, it *is* the first anniversary. Let the young man toast his father's memory. It's what we're gathered here for today, after all. To remember those we loved and lost."

Rebecca harrumphed but agreed he might have half a glass.

When everyone held a flute in their hands, Violet turned to Nancy. "Didn't you want to make a toast or say a few words, darling?"

"I think Adam should do that."

Nancy's eyes, with that melting quality which made them so appealing, smiled into her stepson's. He was panicked for a moment, before taking a deep breath.

"None of us need rem-m-minding what day it is today. It's the first anniversary of the *Titanic* sinking. We're gathered here to remember those we lost on the *Titanic* – particularly my father, Samuel Armstrong the Third, and Mrs O'Brien's husband, Thomas O'Brien. We also remember Major Richmond Hudson, who survived the sinking only to be taken from us prematurely. But we give thanks for the lives which were spared and those who were saved to us – especially the next generation, Sam and Marion." Relieved he had only stuttered once, he dropped a kiss on the crown of Sam's head and grinned at baby Marion, who unleashed a gummy smile in return.

"Well said, young man." Edmund crossed the room and clinked flutes with him.

Stuart Hudson drained his glass at a gulp, moved by the reference to the major. It was useful having access to his father's money, no doubt about it, but he missed him. Major Hudson would never have allowed him to drop out of Yale, he would have insisted on him sitting his degree. Sometimes Stuart suspected there was an aimless quality to his days as a gentleman of leisure. There were plenty of fellows to clap him on the back at the club when he was ordering bottles of claret, but at times he doubted whether their friendship was genuine. He looked at Edmund Newton, remembering his loyalty to his father. Shame the Britisher was such a stuffed shirt or he might invite him to take a trip. Stuart fancied Berlin – the cabaret circuit there was supposed to be daring.

"Say, Newton, what'll you do now you're through knocking Pa's book into shape?"

"I've handed in my notice at Dulwich College. I've decided not to go back to London, at least not for a few years. I'm headed for a ridiculous-sounding place in California called Hollywood. There's a job waiting for me there. It's been held over for a few months while I sorted out *The Jinxed Ship*." Edmund pitched his voice loud enough for Bridie to hear. Let her see what she was missing. Everyone said Hollywood was the coming place.

Bridie, who regarded herself as an old hand at champagne-drinking but could never become blasé about it, was too busy enjoying the fizzing sensation on her tongue to pay attention. She was slightly disappointed it wasn't rosé champagne. She had imagined Nancy sipping it daily. Look at her – she wasn't even touching her glass. She seemed to be alert for someone's footstep. Bridie held out her flute for a refill as Watts padded around. "No, you must mean his younger brother, Freddie," she heard Rebecca contradict Violet. They were discussing a cousin of Samuel's, but the name acted as an earth tremor. Bridie's radiance evaporated. Freddie Bowe-Spencer sluiced over her. She twisted the crystal stem between her fingers. It's pathetic you are, Bridie Ryan, that a name should do this to you after more than a year. But she was ambushed by the memory of Freddie feeding her chocolates all the way from Harrods of London, and wiping her lips with his monogrammed handkerchief. I wonder does he ever think of me at all?

Edmund noticed Bridie's withdrawal, a remote expression stilling her mobile face. He could swear she winced. He was disgusted to find himself moved by this unexpectedly vulnerable image of her. Hang it all, I'm still keen as mustard on her. His acknowledgement left him torn between despair and euphoria. After all, there was nothing as life-affirming as being in love.

Stuart also spotted the change that overcame Bridie, but attributed it to the champagne. She must have gone at it too hard, he smiled, remembering how he liked this quality in Bridie: no half-measures for her. His glance wandered to Sam and Marion, poking at one another on a rug. They had been placed close together for company, lying on their backs. Already Sam was rolling onto his stomach, Marion content to watch his manoeuvrings. Funny to think those little guys were on the ship too, in a sort of a way. Wonder how they'll feel about it when they get older? He strolled over to the sideboard in search of another refill.

Edmund seized the vacancy on the couch to slide up beside Bridie. "How's your business doing, Bridie?"

"Well enough. Working for yourself is harder than I thought it would be, to tell you the truth. I'm kept going all the time, between the hops and the trots. There's no problem with the stock – I have an eye for what women will wear – but I pay a man to keep the books for me and I've no way of knowing if he's making an honest job of it or fleecing me. Everything seems to cost an arm and a leg and I have nobody to talk things over with."

"What about Hannah?"

"She thinks of nothing but her baba – she'd reach her the moon out of the sky if Marion wanted it. Not that she isn't a gorgeous wee thing, mind." Bridie rested her cheek on her palm. "Sometimes I think I was better off working for other people. At least I had no responsibility."

"Be careful what you wish for." He tried to strike a teasing note but it sounded more like a warning.

"Where did you learn to say that? My mother was always coming out with it."

"Don't you remember I told you once about the cook for the family next door to us, when I was a boy? The one who used to slip me food now and again? Her name was Biddy, she came from Monaghan. She used to say it sometimes." He ran a finger under his collar. "I was wrong to tell you I could never agree to my wife working. I was only worrying about what other people would think. Other people don't matter, Bridie."

Bridie looked at him and asked herself whether she had written off Edmund Newton precipitately. Her twin selves were reflected in his spectacles. She still preferred him without them, the way she remembered him from Lifeboat 16, but a year in America had improved Edmund Newton.

He might have been following the trajectory of her thoughts. "The Chinese say if you save a person's life you're responsible for them forever. There's always a bond between you."

"Are you making advances? And with that oul' battle-axe of a Mrs Armstrong just feet away? Lord, but you're a man who believes in living dangerously!"

Edmund laughed, although he shot a nervous glance in Rebecca's direction. "I handed in my notice at Dulwich College – I've decided to stay on. I'm hoping Minerva might join me for a month in the summer."

"Don't you miss home at all then?"

"You know, I don't. Apart from Minerva, of course. Perhaps something was slipped into my sandwich at my local lunch counter and I've became a lotus-eater." Bride looked bemused. "For forgetfulness?" He cleared his throat. "Never mind, I'm behaving like a pompous old classics master. I could take a look at your accounts if you like – if it would set your mind at rest."

Nearby, Adam spoke up. "Grandmother, see how strong Sam is, he's levered himself up on his arms to have a better look-see at everything."

"His father was curious about everything at his age, all the Armstrongs were." Rebecca Armstrong was complacent. No-one would have suspected how reluctant she'd once been to acknowledge the child.

Babies win people over, it's a knack they have, thought Hannah.

"How odd Louis still hasn't come." Nancy, unable to stop herself speaking his name aloud, attracted a scandalised glance from her mother. She had heard nothing from him since Watts had thrown him out on the street the previous November. Preoccupied with her baby though she was, Nancy sometimes puzzled over that. She hadn't expected the persistent Louis to vanish as though he had never existed. Her heart was hammering at the thought of seeing him again, and she watched the door while the others drank champagne.

Watts approached Rebecca Armstrong. "Excuse me, madam, there was a telephone call for you."

"Take a message – it's not convenient right now."

"The gentleman rang off, madam. It was an attorney, a Mr Bennington. Most insistent, he was. He says he must see you as a matter of urgency. He's on his way here with Mr Noah Armstrong. He says you're to stay here until they arrive."

"What on earth is Bennington doing giving me orders? And why is he with Noah?" Rebecca pursed her lips. "Still, it's unlike Bennington to make a nuisance of himself. I can't imagine what this is about." Her uneasiness communicated itself to the party, which began to peter out soon afterwards.

Hannah and Bridie were the first to stand to leave, Edmund bringing up the rear when he saw their preparations for departure. "It's not over between those two, whatever they think," Bridie murmured to Edmund, waiting in the hall for their coats.

"Which two?"

"Young Mrs Armstrong and the French fellow – sure a blind man could see he was on her mind all afternoon. She has an itch she'll never be able to scratch where he's concerned. He's her iceberg, waiting for her, just as sure as that iceberg glided into place and stood waiting for the *Titanic*."

"Do you mean he'll wreck her life?" Hannah goggled.

"No, just that their destinies are intertwined."

"Perhaps all our destinies are intertwined," suggested Edmund. "On account of sharing a lifeboat together." The tips of his ears turned scarlet as he said it, and it pleased Bridie for a reason she didn't care to examine.

Stuart, who had delayed to drain his glass of champagne, arrived behind them. "Old trout in there is working herself into a right state. Wouldn't like to fall foul of her, whatever those chaps on the telephone want with her. Bet she keeps a tight rein on business." He pulled on his canary-yellow gloves, flexing his fingers. "So long, Newton, ladies." Stuart stood aside to let Hannah through the open door, but delayed Bridie with a hand on her elbow. "Say, Bridie, I haven't forgotten how fond you are of a glass of bubbly. How about we go somewhere, just the two of us, and crack a bottle for old times' sake?"

Edmund's fists clenched as he listened for her reply.

Just then a carriage pulled up at the door, the horses lathered, and two men jumped out and dashed up the steps. They brushed past the group and were met by Watts, who tried to escort them upstairs, but they were in such a hurry they overtook him and raced ahead.

"What do you say, Bridie? Are you game? We could have fun, you and me."

Bridie wrinkled her nose, considering. "I don't have much time for gallivanting these days, Stuart – I'm a businesswoman, you know."

Edmund relaxed his fists, making up his mind to escort the ladies home. Perhaps they'd invite him to stay for tea. He might be a novice where women were concerned, but even a fool could see Bridie had been encouraging him earlier.

* * *

Noah Armstrong, Rebecca's cousin by marriage and the administrator of the Armstrong Hotel Group, cleared his throat. "I have bad news on the business front, Rebecca. It can't wait, I'm afraid."

Nancy gathered the baby in her arms. "We should leave these gentlemen to discuss business with Rebecca and Adam, Momma."

"Of course," Violet agreed reluctantly.

When the door was closed, Rebecca rounded on her cousin. "This is hardly the time or the place to discuss business, Noah. You should schedule a board meeting."

"I'm sorry but there's no time. It would be shutting the stable door after the horse has bolted."

"What on earth are you rambling on about? What have horses to do with my family business?"

"I'm afraid it's no longer your family business, Rebecca. There's been a hostile takeover."

"Impossible!"

"Unfortunately not impossible, Mrs Armstrong. You're listed on the New York Stock Exchange, after all." The attorney, Bennington spoke. "You're still a wealthy woman – the new owners have paid a handsome sum for the company."

"When I want your observations I'll ask for them."

"What Mr Bennington says is true, Rebecca." Noah's protruding eyes strained their sockets. "There was nothing we could do about it – the takeover bid caught us all on the hop. A consortium from Vienna has bought up the bulk of the company and we can't stop them taking us over lock, stock and barrel. Connected to the Viennese royal family, I believe."

"How can this have happened? Why didn't I know?"

"We have to accept it's no longer a family business, Rebecca. It's a dark day and no mistake. My great-great-grandfather founded the company."

"And my late husband forged it into what it is today. But nobody asked for my permission to sell. Is this legal?" She shot an icy glance in Bennington's direction but the lawyer was too cowed to answer.

"I'm afraid your permission wasn't necessary," said Noah. "Someone has been busy buying Armstrong stocks over the past three months. The new owner is due in my office tomorrow morning at nine o'clock." He swallowed. "I suppose it's not my office any more. I guess it must belong to the new fellow. An Austrian, I understand. Probably doesn't even speak English."

Ignored in a corner, Adam Armstrong felt the weight of ancestral expectation begin to disperse. If this was true, it meant he wouldn't have to work in the family business. He could do anything he liked with his life – in a few more years he could leave New York and his interfering grandmother behind. He could even become a lifeboat designer, if he wanted. The boy swallowed the beginnings of a smile.

* * *

It was early evening and Nancy and Violet sat in the salon discussing the day's events. Baby Sam, who was teething, chewed on a felt elephant on a rug at Nancy's feet, and from time to time she reached out to stroke him. She knew he should be in bed, but she didn't want to part with him just yet – not on his father's anniversary,

Violet had gleaned something about the hostile takeover from Adam, although Rebecca refused to discuss it. She was worried how it might affect her daughter's financial situation, not to mention her social standing.

Mercy, what an uncertain world it is, she thought. Just over a year ago she had imagined her daughter set for life, married to a wealthy hotelier. Now the business had been bought from under the Armstrongs' noses. Not that she had any objections to Rebecca being taken down a peg or two. She always condescended to her, despite their shared grandson. Violet was still obliged to call her Mrs Armstrong, for example – the intimacy of first names had never been offered.

Louis Stubel was on Nancy's mind. She had counted on him attending her gathering in honour of the *Titanic* dead. Was it possible she would never see him again now? Nancy tested the notion and almost immediately rejected it. She glanced up and, as though he had been conjured up by her thoughts, she saw him balanced on the saddle-board.

Violet followed her daughter's eye-line and saw the drawing room door had been pushed open. Louis Stubel stood there. "Mr Stubel, we'd given you up." It was a few moments before Violet collected herself to speak further. "Our little commemoration party is over – the others left hours ago."

"My apologies." He bowed. "I'm late, forgive me, but I suspect I had the furthest to travel. I come directly from Vienna. Unfortunately I had to stop off on Wall Street and conduct some business first, which delayed me longer than I expected."

Nancy rose and took a few steps in his direction. "You've moved to Vienna? You aren't in New York any more?" There was distress in her tone.

"I had business in Vienna – I still do. I'm not sure where I live any more."

Their eyes locked.

Violet came forward and placed a hand on Nancy's arm, urging discretion. "Do come in and join us, Mr Stubel. I'll ring for refreshments."

"Please don't trouble yourself. It is refreshment enough seeing you beautiful ladies." The habit of flattering women was engrained in the Frenchman.

Violet had to remind herself not to succumb. "A glass of champagne? In honour of the day?"

He hesitated. "Perhaps later. If there is something to celebrate . . ."

"We were marking the day, Mr Stubel, not celebrating it." Reproof narrowed Violet's eyes but Louis was intent only on Nancy.

He moved further into the room, and as he did Sam grizzled on a rug near his mother. Noticing him for the first time, Louis looked from the child to Nancy and back again.

She scooped up her baby, claiming him. "This is my son." She extended him at arms' length, Sam kicking his legs in furious choreography.

He nodded. "I haven't forgotten you're a mother now. So much has happened in the year since we met. Too much, perhaps." He sagged then, pressing the heels of his palms into each eye.

Violet sank onto a brocade sofa, trying to regain a sense of normality. "Do let's all sit down."

Nancy complied but Louis seemed not to hear. He took his hands away from his face and his travel-weary eyes lingered on Nancy in a way that made Violet shift in her seat. Why did he never look at her like that? The jealousy she believed was crushed spiked through her again.

Louis spoke to Nancy as though there was no-one else in the room but the two of them. "Can it really only be a year to the day since we met? Is it possible there was ever a time I didn't know you existed?"

Nancy nestled her son against the side of her neck. "Sam's five months old already."

"We were in the lifeboat together. You lent me a cloak to keep me warm."

"It was a velvet evening cloak, ashes of roses. The salt marks never did wash out." She laid her cheek on her baby's downy scalp and the ghost of a smile played across her features. "A night on the open seas will do that, I guess."

"Some marks never come out. Just as some connections can never be broken. I believe in the *coup de foudre*. Do you believe in it, Nancy? Do you believe in love at first sight?"

She lifted her head, searching his face, and nodded once.

It was enough. "Come away with me, my Nancy."

Violet gave a drawn-out gasp, like material ripped by a violent tug. Involuntarily Nancy glanced at her mother. Then she looked at her baby, wriggling in her arms, and propped him carefully in a corner of the armchair, wedging him in place with a cushion. She stood, trying to find the words to give Louis his answer, but there was a blockage in her throat.

He closed the gap between them, so close he could scent rosewater on her skin. And something else: the whiff of panic, perhaps. His voice was urgent. "The *Olympic* sails for England tomorrow night, *chérie*. From there we could travel on to Vienna. Don't worry about packing – we can buy whatever's needed. All you have to do to make it happen is say yes."

Nancy's eyes fastened on the man's, hypnotised by his conviction.

"Yes, Louis," he prompted.

Her lips were parched, making a rustling noise as they rubbed against one another.

He seized her hands between his own two, pulling her so close it was almost an embrace. "Did what happened a year ago teach you nothing? Don't you know happiness is fragile? That you have to reach for it, guard it, prize it, if you're to have any chance of keeping it?"

Her fingers curled around his, clinging to his hands, and her face betrayed the helter-skelter of her thoughts. But still she did not respond.

Exasperated, a harsh note entered his voice. "I've come into money, if that's what bothers you. I can keep you in comfort."

His change of tone fractured the spell which had paralysed Violet and she glided up, moving between the pair and forcing Louis to fall back.

"How dare you come into this house and seek to kidnap my daughter, Mr Stubel! And on the anniversary of her husband's death, too. Have you no shame?"

"Shame?" He tasted the word. "No, I have no shame where love is concerned."

"Do you dare to tell me you love my daughter?"

"Certainly I love Nancy. What else but love would bring me back to her?" His response had dignity and Violet was silenced.

Suddenly Nancy threw a hunted look at her baby. "I don't know what to do. What should I do? I wish somebody would tell me – I'm in torment!"

The appeal crackled around the room.

"If you go with this man, it'll all end in tears. Your husband's family will never forgive you. We rely on the Armstrongs for the roof over our heads. For our place in society. Think of everything you stand to lose, you silly creature!"

Louis stepped in front of Violet. "If you don't come with me you'll live to regret it. I love you, Nancy, and I know you love me. My heart tells me it's so."

Nancy's eyes on Louis's were scalded. "I do love you. I don't want to, but I do. The trouble is I love my son too."

"Bring the child. I'll care for him for your sake."

"I can't, it's all too uncertain. In Vienna he'll be nobody. With the Armstrongs behind him he *is* somebody – he has family, a name, a place in life. I can't steal that away from him."

A muscle clenched in Louis's cheek. "The future is always uncertain. Even love is uncertain. Please, put your trust in me. Let me spare you from this stifling death by slow degrees. You weren't made for widowhood – you were made for the world, Nancy. I can show it to you."

The air in the room seemed to thicken as Louis and Violet waited for her answer. Even Sam was saucer-eyed. Nancy's eyes fled from Louis's – from the insistence in them. He was doing it to her again, demanding more from her than she was able to give. Her heart had leapt, seeing him in the doorway, but everything was always so complicated with Louis. It was just as Mama Carmen had said – with him, life would be all highs and lows.

The suspense was broken by Watts with a message from the newspapers asking for permission to photograph Nancy and Sam on account of the anniversary.

"Tell them to stop pestering us!" snapped Violet, assuming they'd want to take her photograph too. "These people are leeches, Leeches!"

Sensing something momentous in the atmosphere, Sam burst into panicked howls. Nancy stooped to cuddle him, and the tension was diluted.

Violet was first to recover. "My daughter needs time to consider her position, Mr Stubel. It's been an exhausting day for all of us, in view of the anniversary. Why don't you call tomorrow morning? We'll expect you at eleven." She'd leave instructions that he wasn't to be admitted.

She made to usher him from the room before words best left unsaid were spoken, but Louis stood his ground.

"Tomorrow I have to complete my business on Wall Street. Today my business is with Nancy."

Violet sighed. He really was a handsome man. Look at him, he needed a shave and a good night's sleep, yet there was still something compelling about him. "Wall Street?" He'd mentioned something about that on arrival, but it hadn't registered.

"Yes, I've been negotiating a takeover on my family's behalf. We bought up the last of the shares we needed today. "

"It appears your circumstances have changed since our last meeting, Mr Stubel. I congratulate you."

"I've been fortunate. But not as fortunate as I hope to be." He looked at Nancy.

Her mother made a rapid calculation. If Violet Markova had one talent, it was the ability to smell money and she scented it now on Louis Stubel. "You've prospered, then, Mr Stubel?"

"I've spent the past four months making the acquaintance of my father's family in Vienna. They're not without means."

Violet snapped to decision. "What time will your business on Wall Street be concluded? If you're free we'd be pleased to have you join us for luncheon. Wouldn't we, Nancy?"

"Why yes, Momma."

"And you'll have an answer for me then, Nancy? You'll think about what I've said?" His tone was urgent.

She nodded, and he bowed and turned on his heel.

Violet caught up with him in a flurry of skirts outside the salon. "Mr Stubel, I can't help wondering – what   line of business are you getting into?"

"Hotels."

Violet was mute – hotels didn't come cheap. Louis watched her while she gathered her wits, wondering if she'd make the connection with the Armstrong takeover. But she was still grappling with his dramatically altered circumstances. "Forgive my being so direct: who are your family in Vienna? I was under the impression you were French, Mr Stubel."

"It's Salvator-Stubel, Madame Markova, as in a branch of the Viennese royal family. My people" – a flash of pride lightened the sombre planes of his face – "own Vienna."

Violet's mouth dropped open. She didn't want Louis Stubel as a son-in-law – but she didn't want to lose him as a son-in-law either. Not if he was connected to European royalty. Courteously, he inclined his head towards her and descended the stairs.

"Wait! Does this mean you're a count or something?"

"No, but my father was an archduke."

An archduke! "Don't you get a title too?"

He stopped on a half-landing and turned. "I'm not eligible for one, Madame Markova. I wasn't my father's heir. But my father's relatives have welcomed me for his sake. His sister recognized a christening mug she gave my parents, and paved the way for me to be accepted."

"Still, your family are aristocrats?"

"True. My aunt is a princess, and I believe there's a connection with the emperor. Distant, of course."

Violet felt short of breath. Archdukes and princesses and, Lordy, a connection with an emperor, however distant, were miles better than New York hoteliers! She had to lean her weight against the wall for support, but her brain continued racing. Better not leave matters overnight. You never know – Louis could get sidetracked on Wall Street and not make it to Fifth Avenue tomorrow after all. "Mr Salvator-Stubel – Louis – why don't I help Nurse put Sam to bed while you take a stroll in Central Park with my daughter? She's looking a little peaky. I believe it would do her good to take the air."

It was blatant, she knew, but Violet was past caring. She disappeared, spoke a few urgent words to her daughter, and reappeared with Sam, giving Louis a last, bright glance – of regret, yes, but of encouragement too.

"Nancy's waiting for you."

* * *

Nancy was at the far end of the room, staring through a floor-to-ceiling sash window with its curtains undrawn. She sensed his presence but did not turn around, watching him instead in the glass.

"Your mother thinks we should take a walk." Each word brought

Louis a pace nearer to her.

"It's dark outside," she said.

"I know. I don't suppose she'd mind if we stayed here instead."

She risked a glance over her shoulder and saw he was watching her, in that way of his which made her skin tingle. She turned back – it was less disconcerting to meet his eyes through glass.

He looked at her in silence for a little while, trying to find a way to reach her. "There is something I can do for your son, Nancy. I can give him what the Armstrongs can't, for all their social standing. Something that might make him happier than wealth or position."

Now she turned to face him and this time she managed to hold his gaze, even though the blood roared in her eardrums so riotously she wondered he didn't hear it.

"Another brother or sister," he said gently.

Her eyes widened as she absorbed the implications. Instead of feeling he was presumptuous, however, she found herself thinking how Louis had a knack for saying exactly the right thing: Adam was devoted to Sam, but he'd be going away to college soon. She'd like her little boy to have playmates of his own age.

Louis was as close as a shared breath now. He stood for a moment, allowing her an opportunity to draw back.

"Imagine if we hadn't found each other in our lifeboat, Nancy." His eyes were limpid, his voice little more than a whisper.

She shivered, not wanting to imagine it.

When she made no attempt to move away from him, he reached out to her. He drew her to him, slotting her frame against his, and they rested quietly against each other – his cheek on her hair, their heartbeats keeping time. The turmoil she had felt all day – all year, in truth – subsided. As for Louis, he had the sensation that he had been travelling through stormy waters and now at last, in his beloved's arms, safe haven was reached.

By and by, without loosening his hold on Nancy, for he never wanted to let her go again, he tilted her head to look into eyes with summer sky in them, for all it was night. "Do you still have that cloak you lent me? The one with the salt marks that wouldn't come out?"

"Of course. I'll never part with it."

"Will you wear it on our wedding day, *chérie*? Salt stains and all?"

With him, a woman would live in extremes. Joy and despair would be her bedfellows. Mama Carmen's prediction echoed through Nancy's mind. She made her choice.

"Yes. I will. Yes."

Louis knew this was not the finish, it was closer to a beginning, but still he had the feeling of journey's end.

THE END

Postscript

Shortly before *Ship of Dreams* was published I finally made contact with the descendants of Tom and Hannah in the US and received answers to some of the questions I had about them. I spoke to their granddaughter Catherine Hanlon Fisher, a lovely young-old lady of seventy and mother of seven, who lives in Manchester, Tennessee. Marion was her mother, and she told me about Hannah and Marion's lives in New York.

Hannah found work as a seamstress. Later she married a County Kilkenny man named Jim Quinn when Marion was two or three, and had a son. But she died just six years after the Titanic sank, in the flu epidemic of 1918. The orphaned Marion was raised by her stepfather, who burned all her mother's papers after the funeral – so she had no way of contacting her Irish relatives. She became the family breadwinner at fourteen. In time she became a telephone operator in Brooklyn and married an Irish emigrant, civil engineer Willie Hanlon, also from Kilkenny, who was related to Jim Quinn. They had three children and a happy life together in Albany, upstate New York. When she was widowed after forty years Marion moved to Tennessee to be near her daughter.

In her lifetime she avoided boats, was nervous of the ocean, rarely talked about the *Titanic* and resisted joining any *Titanic* societies.

Indeed, she only told Catherine about the family link when she was a young woman towards the end of the 1950s. Later she visited Ireland and met some of her maternal relatives, but never made contact with any of her father's people. She died in 1994 at the age of 81, on Independence Day.

It's uncanny how fiction can mimic life unwittingly. I gave little Marion red hair in my story – and her daughter told me she really was a redhead. Most poignant of all, however, was to learn that although Tom O'Brien never reached the US, he has nine great-grandchildren and fifteen great-great grandchildren scattered around the States. His descendants settled and prospered in the country he did not live to see. In that, he achieved a version of immortality – despite his premature death in a seafaring disaster that echoes through the generations.

Martina Devlin

Notes

(1) Captain Rostron received the *Titanic*'s SOS position as the famous, but incorrect, 41° 46' N, 50° 14' W. This was 58 nautical miles from his estimated position when he put about. The ship actually sank in 41° 43' N, 49° 56' W, some 46 nautical miles from the *Carpathia* when she turned. Rostron never reached the actual wreck site, but was heading for the false SOS position. The lifeboats moved south of west, and fortuitously met his vessel on her course line to the wrong position *Titanic* had transmitted.

(2) In 1912 it was believed there were 705 survivors, more recent figures suggest 712 survived. Two-sevenths of the survivors were crew. This ratio gave rise to complaints about fee-paying passengers being left to perish, but it was argued crewmen were put in boats to help row them – even though a number were stewards and cooks and had never handled an oar. Up to 2,229 people were on board the liner in total, more than 1,300 of them passengers.

(3) More than three-quarters of a century after the wreck, sonar imaging of the mud-buried bow section suggested the iceberg had sheared off rivet heads, popping some hull plating to allow the sea to flood in through narrow gaps. The great gash theory was wrong.

Published by poolbeg.com

Temptation

MARTINA DEVLIN

"Being single is the ideal state ... until it palls"

One lesson Kitty Kennedy has taken from her two marriages is that not all men and women are meant to live together ... forever.

Alone again on New Year's Day, Kitty is inspired with the ideal New Year's resolution – to become somebody's mistress. Except finding the right candidate proves trickier than she expects.

Sunny, Kitty's sister, always makes sure she never spends New Year alone. But men are only a diversion while the actress pursues her real goal, a Hollywood career.

Kitty's best friend Rose thought love was a foregone conclusion until her fiancé realised he couldn't devote his life to her. Or to any woman. Rose longs to risk loving once more when she meets a younger man ... but fear is holding her back.

For Kitty, Sunny and Rose, giving in to temptation may be their only chance of paradise.

978-1-84223-182-1

Published by poolbeg.com

VENUS REBORN

MARTINA DEVLIN

There's no shame in being adopted.
It means you were wanted. And chosen.

Venus Macken is back in Ireland after more than
a decade as a city girl in London, and she has mixed feelings about the
move. Except her return to the wilds of Roancarrick to care for her
elderly father offers the chance to search for answers. Answers to
questions that have haunted her all her life.

Venus is tired of feeling like an outsider. Who was her birth mother?
Why was she abandoned? Surely the people who love her and reared
her can help unlock the riddle of her identity.

Meanwhile there are distractions, among them
enigmatic artist Conor Landers who has bolted to Roancarrick to
escape the consequences of a life and death decision.

As the sketchy details of what happened on a stormy night thirty-two
years before take shape, Venus begins to realise that who she is matters
less than understanding who she wants to be.

978-1-84223-152-4

Direct to your home!

If you enjoyed this book why not
visit our website:

www.poolbeg.com

and get another book delivered straight to
your home or to a friend's home!

www.poolbeg.com

All orders are despatched within 24 hours.